REVIEWS

FIVE STARS by IndieReader: ". . . non-stop, action-packed adventure as Blake overcomes several attempts on his and his loved ones lives and becomes deeply entwined in investigating two murders, a litany of sexual assaults, lies, charges, counter-charges and outright hatred difficult to put down . . . a likeable and believable lead character and a cast of shadowy characters living in a world of wealth and privilege with deep, dark secrets. But those secrets may one day rip apart their lives and the lives of those around them." Under consideration for an IndieReader Discovery Award for best new writer mystery/suspense/thriller book of 2014.
— IndieReader

"Accomplished, ambitious crime fiction launching a sensitive, complex hero and a promising array of supporting characters . . . First-time novelist Babka weaves a multilayered tale that has shades of California noir à la Chinatown . . . there's rich material to mine in this strong start to a new series." Chosen as one of twenty independently published books in the country featured in the September 2014 issue of *Kirkus Reviews Magazine*.
— *Kirkus Reviews*

". . . A murder mystery in the style of Elmore Leonard . . . a compelling, well paced story, with some excellent characters — some we root for, and others we're happy to see in a body bag . . . a fun story, perfect for a day at the beach, or a long rainy weekend at home. Watch out for *Dirt Crappis*, the next iteration in the Detective Dylan Blake series."
— San Francisco Book Review

"Daniel Babka has created a protagonist caught in the duality of our time. Dylan Blake — a small town northern California cop — keeps his gun in a bread box, munches on raw almonds, and listens to NPR like a good liberal, but his anger at old injustices and a new rich-makes-right social order is as fundamental as a black eye. Checking on a businessman's suspicious suicide off the cliffs of Big Sur, Blake barely escapes an attempt on his own life. It won't be the only time Blake is nearly killed to stop his dogged pursuit.

At its heart is Kathryn Winslow, the outwardly devout business partner of the murder victim. Winslow is a worthy opponent to Blake, more than willing to use Blake's attraction to her to stop Blake from peeling back the layers of duplicity that surround not only Winslow but her treacherous ex-husband and her billionaire brother James Kilmer. The husband is one version of corruption and hypocrisy, a man so self-indulgent that he can't care if the daughter he molested becomes a whore. The brother is his flip side, a religious Puritan who thinks his superior position makes his judgment of others absolute while providing an excuse for his own greed, manipulation and lust for power."
— Lonon Smith, author of *Wise Men*

". . . Reminds me of Jonathan Kellerman, one of my long-time favorites, without the gory bits. Wonderfully complex, with lots of unexpected twists and turns; I could not recommend this highly enough . . . keeps you questioning "who dun it" up to the end . . . looks into the nature of white-collar, upper middle class vs blue collar — and lots of skeletons rattle in those expensive closets . . . have read detective mysteries since the 1950's beginning with all of the Hardy Boys. Since, perhaps hundreds of titles, authors and characters. I have to say this is the best detective mystery I have ever read. Love the character and supporting cast . . . simply put, totally engrossing, descriptive and scenes are imaged as if you are there . . . Have never read a detective mystery before. Usually do not choose this type of book, read in 3 sessions . . . I guess I am now a detective mystery fan, at least by this author . . . a love story as well as a murder mystery."
— Amazon Reader Excerpts

To Bruce & Chris ..

No More Illusions
...a Mystery

Enjoy the story. Tell people about it.

Daniel Babka

July, 2015

Blue Squirrel Press
Roseville, California

ISBN (paperback): 978-0-9910601-2-2
ISBN (eBook): 978-0-9910601-1-5

Library of Congress Control Number: 2014904140

First Edition: July 2014 by Blue Squirrel Press, Roseville, CA

Cover Photo by Ben Thompson Photography
flickr.com/photos/benft/

Interior Production by Williams Writing, Editing & Design
www.williamswriting.com

For my mother, Lois,
who has given so much to all her children.

ACKNOWLEDGMENTS

"No More Illusions"..........................special thanks to Cindy Riley-Burch for her creative input and support, to Sue Clark (suejclark@att.net) for her invaluable editorial advice, to the members of my writers critique group – Gini Grossenbacher, Robert Pacholik, Dennis Mahoney, and Paula Zaby, and also to Nick Overocker. The book is better because of all of you.

"Hard-core reality is, there are plenty of people, selfish people who want what they want and who pretend not to see the bodies in the street when they drive over them. It's just like what John Lewis, the Georgia congressman who marched with Dr. King and the Freedom Riders, said: 'You've got to put yourself in the way of what's wrong, find the courage to get in trouble, good trouble, necessary trouble.'"

"I don't much care what the consequences are," Blake said. "I like what I do, but I had a job before I became a detective and I'll have one afterwards."

BEFORE

Kathryn Winslow picked up Jack Hamilton's personal be-
longings, the easy-to-grab stuff, and dropped them in a
banker's box. She carried it through the middle of an office
full of employees sitting at their desks on both sides of the
room. Then, she put the box on the sidewalk out front, still
wet from a short summer rain, before walking back to the
desk where Hamilton stood. He didn't say a word.

"You've got thirty minutes to get the rest of your stuff and
get out," Kathryn said. Her lips trembled for a moment.

He could feel the color drain from his face. His stomach
knotted up. His hands began to shake. "You can't be serious.
This is crazy. I've invested twelve years of my life building
this business with you from the ground up. We're partners.
What the hell do you think you're doing, Kathryn?"

"I'm calling a locksmith," she said.

Hamilton was stunned.

"Thirty minutes, no more. You can sue me if you want. I
don't care. It's over."

• • •

He felt betrayed. Kathryn Winslow was his closest friend.
He'd played that day over and over in his mind for the last
six months, searching for an answer that made sense, that
would bring him closure. He didn't see the end coming. The
business was going to be the legacy he left to his children,
his retirement nest egg, and it was gone.

Kathryn Winslow had lied. She'd promised him half. He'd spent days staring at the ceiling, waiting for the phone to ring, expecting her to call and tell him she'd made a mistake. The lawsuit, the break-in, a real sense that someone had been watching him, the revolver in his glove box. All of it was out of sync with the way his life used to be.

His mind drifted with the fog across the highway. The vintage Jaguar picked up speed on the downhill side. The tires squealed when Hamilton rounded the first curve. The second turn came sooner than he expected. A line of three cars headed north on the other side of the double-yellow line facing him. He eased off the accelerator, and hit the brake. His palms began to sweat. He gripped the steering wheel harder. Then his knuckles turned white.

Hamilton's car crossed over the pavement, ran over the weeds, and ripped through the guard rail. The car sailed over the cliff along the coast highway like a baseball arcing over the center field fence, before it began to fall like a dead weight. He looked up at his rearview mirror for a long second and saw the mountains behind him before the rocks crashed through the windshield. The sea's foam swirled around him, and took his breath away.

CHAPTER ONE

Dylan Blake left the campground in Big Sur with no agenda in mind beyond letting the day unfold. He'd spent five days relaxing, swimming in the ocean, sleeping under the stars, and hiking. It centered him, the same way a Zen garden did other people. A condor, riding the wind currents along the coast near Garrapata, soared over his head the day before. And he'd seen another in the canyons below the Carmel Highlands near the cloud lines that stretched across the Pacific.

The sound of the Audi's turbo running through the gears and accelerating along Highway One, interrupted his thoughts. The car held the road and cornered with a surge of power that went straight to his head like a shot of good tequila. Blake turned his cell phone on and set it between the Audi's seats, then put in a CD.

Ten minutes later, the phone rang. Chief Cooper's name appeared on the blue dashboard display. The Rolling Stones went silent. Blake hesitated for a moment, knowing he'd be back on the clock as soon as he answered. He hadn't taken a real vacation for two years. Except for the chief's invitation to join the force, Cooper had never called him.

"I was hoping you'd check on something for me if you're still around the coast, Blake."

"Give me a minute to pull over, Chief."

Cooper's voice was as unmistakable as Spencer Tracy's. Blake had been on the police force close to four years. He wasn't naive, but when he heard guys like Cooper, he was inclined to believe what they said and do what they asked.

Blake's mother told him his dad could sell ice to the Eskimos. He figured Cooper had that same kind of James Garner, Rockford Files talent. Blake angled toward the dirt road off Highway One that ran down toward Partington Cove where mules pulled sleds loaded with tanbark oak down to the water's edge at the turn of the century, and liquor was smuggled during Prohibition. The black Audi sport coupe's tires crunched to a stop against the gravel. Blake left the engine running so the turbo could cool down, and reached for the black leather note pad on the seat beside him.

"I'll bet that water is cold as ever down there," Cooper said. "You probably thought you'd be surfing when you moved out here from the mid-west. Didn't know you'd need a wetsuit if you didn't want to freeze your nuts off."

"Yeah, you're right," Blake said. He rolled down the car's back windows, cut off the engine, got out to stretch his legs. "Go ahead, tell me what you need, Chief."

"I know somebody here in Sierra Springs, a friend of the department, whose business partner went missing a few days ago. She tells me he's turned up at the bottom of a cliff next to the coast highway. I'd like you to take a look, then check in with the local sheriff and see what he's thinking. The guy's apartment here in Sierra Springs was broken into last week and some business records are missing. His partner is suspicious."

"What's his name?" Blake said.

"Jack Hamilton. The car's somewhere south of Big Sur on the way to the sheriff's sub-station. I know the sheriff down there . . . Kowalski. I'll let him know you're coming. He and I go back a ways."

Kowalski, Blake scribbled. He underlined it twice and drew a circle around the name. "I'll have to check it out tomorrow morning. I'm too far away right now."

"Take a look at the accident scene. Whatever you see, keep it to yourself for now. Take an extra day or two. The department will cover your expenses and I'll clear your schedule. Have you caught any fish?"

"Didn't bring a pole," Blake said. "I don't do much fishing. I didn't plan on catching anything before your call, besides a suntan."

"That might change. You're on the clock now. I'll see you when you get back."

The last thing Blake wanted was to get caught in the middle of something between Cooper and a sheriff he didn't know in another jurisdiction. Blake pulled into a bait shop on his way to Big Sur, bought a Dr. Pepper and a chart that forecasted the tide levels.

He drove through town to the Henry Miller Memorial Library on the other side of Nepenthe where he could use an internet connection to email his girlfriend, Julianna.

He felt good about his life, close to certain he wouldn't find any other detectives reading D.H. Lawrence's poetry. He picked a copy of *The Tropic of Cancer* and flipped through the pages.

"I have no money, no resources, no hopes. I am the happiest man alive," Henry Miller wrote.

Blake had never pictured himself settling for everyday routine. He'd walked away from law school after his second year—too much paperwork, not enough action. He figured police work had to be more exciting than sitting behind a desk, reading case law and looking for legal precedents.

Twenty years earlier he'd stopped at that library with his ex-wife. Those were the days when he confused Henry Miller with Arthur Miller, an error he now attributed to his public school education and a fragmentary recollection obscured by smoking too much weed. Back then, he didn't know who Anais Nin, Henry Miller's lover, was. Now Blake's beat generation friend, Edison, at 24-Hour Fitness, was telling him stories about the week he and Nin spent together in Paris during the '60s.

The tall cross some artist had fashioned from computer monitors, was still standing guard in the museum's redwood grove. The ambiance, the books, live music under the stars —all of it was still happening. Henry Miller's library was a shrine more suited to intellectuals and free spirits than police detectives.

He'd been staying in a campground in Big Sur. The land kept him connected to the parts of himself he valued most, the ones that began to slip away when he got distanced from the mountains and the woods. He'd picked out a spot about thirty-feet from where the creek ran through the redwoods. He sacked out around ten and set his alarm for the ungodly hour of 2:45 a.m., so he could catch the low tide in the morning and escape attention from passers-by and the local authorities. It didn't take long before the sound of running water pulled him up like a magnet to pee in the middle of the night, just like it had the first five nights he'd been there. He looked up at the moon's midnight glow and a sky filled with stars that filtered through the tent's screen windows above his head.

The alarm clock broke into his dream. Blake grabbed some power bars and raw almonds, rolled up his sleeping bag, quietly pulled out of the campground, and headed south down Highway One toward San Louis Obispo. The road was close to deserted. He needed coffee but didn't have any. Sunrise was still a good two hours away. He turned up the car's CD player and listened to R&B and acid jazz to keep alert.

The mile marker on Highway One Chief Cooper had given him came into view. He slowed down and pulled to the side when he saw the yellow caution tape and sawhorses by the curve. The sun had begun to break. He got out and walked to the edge of the cliff where the coastal scrub trees and chaparral grew.

The car was silver gray, like Cooper said, an older vintage Jag, laying about three hundred feet below. There were no brake marks. The bumper arched upward, nested between the rocks, the kelp, and the water. A new day was rolling across the Pacific and the morning fog had begun to lift as the sun inched up the hills. The chill in the salt air wrapped itself around him.

"How the hell is anyone ever going to get that thing back up here?" Blake mumbled, when he saw the Jag. Search and rescue must have lowered somebody down in a sling to bring the body up. Either that or a helicopter.

The descent was obviously too dangerous from where he was, so Blake drove to the next turn-off. His hiking boots and poles, and the climbing rope he'd used in Utah when he ventured into some slot canyons, were in his trunk. He got his gear out, including a hydration pack and his binoculars, and scrambled over some rocks and scrub brush for a better look. He decided to rappel down. His legs were still fatigued from fourteen miles of hiking the day before.

He took his time to reach the water where Hamilton's body had lain motionless two days earlier, next to the tide pool full of hermit crabs, anemones, and starfish. The water was cold and crystal clear, with big jellyfish that looked like eggs over easy on steroids submerged in the water about twenty feet out. The long, tubular strands of kelp reached for the shore.

Blake set his backpack and gear on the rocks that were safe from the tide, and moved closer. He spotted a small shred of Hamilton's shirt mangled in with the metal and blood spattered on the car's steering wheel and dash. He dabbed his handkerchief where the blood was thickest, put it in a plastic zip-lock bag, and stuffed it in his shirt pocket. Then he forced open the glove compartment and found it empty. No doubt the local police had already bagged and emptied the contents. The sedan's back doors had been jammed shut by the impact. Blake climbed in through the front door window. He figured the car had been swept clean, that is, until he found a one-way airline ticket from L.A. to Playa del Carmen, the Mexican Riviera, stuffed inside a soggy newspaper behind the driver's seat.

The sun had begun to edge higher up the slopes of the Santa Lucia Mountains beyond the cliff's edge that towered above him. Blake climbed back out the driver's window, moved around to the back of the car, and pried open the trunk. Empty. He looked closely to make sure the car was steady and wouldn't shift, then crawled underneath to check the brakes and steering. Left front, right rear — the brake lines had clearly been loosened. Blake saw the markings and the fluid, and photographed them. He took a shot of the car's front end and another of the license plate. This is enough, he thought to himself. I need to get out of here.

Blake looked around with his binoculars. No one was in sight. Twenty minutes later, as he balanced his weight and climbed up the most difficult part of the trail open to view, he heard the rocks falling. Small ones slipped past him at first and then there was a thunderous downpour of dirt. He felt the earth shake. He swung back, grabbed the smooth hard root of a Madrone tree and pulled himself under a shallow overhang where the earth had fallen away. He kept his body as straight as he could, one foot jammed against a rock, the other dangling in the air. He stayed there for several minutes. The first rock tumbled down hard, a foot from his head, and smashed into Hamilton's car. "Holy shit!" he said.

Blake caught his breath, steadied himself, and waited before he began to inch his way out. He felt his heart pounding against his chest.

He reached for the binoculars on his belt as soon as he got to a ledge twenty-feet higher that felt safe. He dug his fingers into the grass and scrub for a grip, clawed, and pushed hard with his boot heels against the rock outcrops buried in the cliff's face. His head and chest were exposed and vulnerable, back and arms wet with sweat. Blake kept looking up. He didn't hear anything except the crash of the surf below. He saw a gradual slope to the right with a vein in the rock facing that looked safe. He moved across some lose patches of rock and the brush that was anchored in, zigzagging one step at a time. Blake skidded on a small avalanche of gravel, righted himself and continued to crawl up until he reached the vein. He followed it up to the rim and pressed his chest against the earth, relieved, when he got near the top.

Fifty minutes had gone by. The road was clear in both directions. He stood, walked to his car, stuffed his gear in the trunk and stashed the camera in the wheel-well next to the spare tire. Blake knelt down and looked at the Audi's underside before he headed south. He'd been a cop long enough to know the consequences attached to being careless or over-confident.

Blake braked a couple times before he picked up speed, with an eye on his rear view mirror. When he got back to the area the police had roped off, he got out to take a second look. He spotted some fresh boot prints in the mud near the berm and scratch marks near the bottom of two large rocks anchored near the edge of the cliff on the other side of the guard rail. Mother nature didn't make marks like that. Somebody with a pry bar had.

CHAPTER TWO

The smell of fresh salt air rushed through the coupe's windows and mixed with the California sun against his arm. Dylan Blake's hands gripped the wheel as he rounded the corner at sixty. He shifted his foot from the accelerator to the brake. He flew past the thirty-five mile per hour road sign, turned the black dial on the radio to where the bass vibrated and the sound surrounded his head and blocked out everything but the wind. "God, it's good to feel alive like this, to feel the energy I did in my twenties when I was on this road." He downshifted and pushed it hard to the curve ahead. The sheriff's office was an hour further south.

The ranch style, tract home in the middle of nowhere had been turned into a nondescript sub-station. Blake pulled in and walked up to the counter, behind which a middle-aged woman, wearing dark-framed glasses and a dress that looked like a sixties fashion statement from *Mad Men*, sat at a desk, fielding questions and answering the phones. He waited until she'd finished. "Good morning, ma'am. My name is Dylan Blake. I'm looking for Sheriff Kowalski."

"Have a seat. I'll let him know you're here. Is he expecting you?"

"Yes." Blake surveyed the reading material on the oak coffee table in what was once someone's living room — *Field & Stream*, a three-year old *National Geographic*, and *Reader's Digest*, the large print version. Helluva choice. He got some water from the cooler in the corner of the room and made small talk with the woman at the desk who looked more like a Playboy Vargas model, primed and ready for sex in the middle of the afternoon, than a civil servant. The name plate on her desk said "Maxine."

Her desk was a model of organization. The pencils and pens were all in a row next to a lime green stapler and her Diet Coke. "I expect it's pretty quiet here most of the time," Blake said.

"You're right about that, drug busts and DUI's. Once in a while, there's a scuffle or some vandalism, or a tourist doing something stupid. Beautiful country, though," she said.

Blake found it hard to focus on what she was saying when there was so much to stare at. He couldn't stop himself from thinking how good she'd be in bed and whether that's why she had the job.

"Stunning," Blake said. "Every time I come down here, it's like I discover how lucky I am to be alive."

She smiled.

She didn't have the slightest idea what his morning had been like.

Her boss' door opened and Kowalski walked toward the orange upholstered couch where Blake sat.

Blake stood and extended his hand. Kowalski gave him one of those quick looks that ran from Blake's head to his shoes, followed by a hand on his shoulder, a good strong grip, and a grin. Kowalski was built like a refrigerator with a belt around his middle. He wore black rimmed glasses, and had a gray flat-top. He looked like an NFL lineman or a guy who might go ballistic if he was pressed into a tight space. Either that, or he'd be comfortable drinking coffee, shuffling paperwork back and forth, and chain-smoking. Blake couldn't decide which.

"Come on in," Kowalski said, "have a seat. Coop said you'd be stopping by."

Blake followed him.

Kowalski reached for a smoke and tapped the pack on his desk. "'Bout that guy who went off the curve the other night." He pulled out a pack of matches from his desk and lit up. "You don't mind, do you?"

Blake shook it off. Kowalski didn't seem the sort who waited for an answer to a question like that.

"No skid marks. We figure he had to be doing at least fifty, maybe more. Had search and rescue pull the body up. The car's still down there. Might have to wait another day or two before they get to it, what with the budget constriction bullshit we have to deal with now days. We're in between the municipalities with money." Sheriff Kowalski took a couple long drags on his Marlboro, then set it to rest on a vintage glass ashtray full of cigarette butts that read Riviera, Las Vegas, in red.

"How's Coop doing these days? Haven't seen him since the last convention in San Jose."

"He's good," Blake said. "He's always been fair with me."

"That's good to hear," Kowalski said. "We went to the Academy together in L.A. I don't see him but every couple years. So what's his interest in this guy? What do you know that I don't?"

Like most cops, Kowalski appeared to be suspicious by nature, even though he didn't seem much interested in the case.

"Cooper didn't say, other than he knows somebody who knew Hamilton, and the guy's apartment was burglarized this past week," Blake said. "Do you have any idea how long Hamilton has been here? Where he stayed, anything like that? Anything out of the ordinary?"

"Let me check the file and see what we've got so far. We just bagged everything up the other day," Kowalski said. He hit some keys on his computer, then buzzed Maxine and asked her for the file. They both watched as she came into the office a few minutes later. Kowalski and Blake smiled at one another when Maxine left the room.

"Let's see, he had a thirty-eight in his glove box that hadn't been fired, and a carry permit. Interesting. And a credit card receipt for three nights. Not too expensive for these parts. I've got some bills for meals, one for two people, and a receipt for some art work he bought at a local gallery." Kowalski looked up and turned the manila file around toward Blake. "You're welcome to take a look."

Blake leafed through the file, making a mental note of the motel's name, the restaurant with two entrees showing, and the art gallery.

Kowalski watched him.

"No incidents, no car repairs, nothing like that?" Blake said.

"Nothing in the file, unless he paid with cash. Like I said, search and rescue bagged everything up."

"So what do you figure so far?"

"Looks like he was probably tired, going too fast, missed the turn. Either that or he wanted to park it in the ocean. People do that around here, sometimes. What can you tell me about the burglary?" Kowalski looked at Blake.

"Coop didn't tell me anything about it. He called me. I'm down here on vacation," Blake said. "I think one of his constituents back in Sierra Springs knew the guy and asked Coop for a favor. You'll check the steering and brake lines for us when you pull it up and give me a call?"

"Be happy to. Standard procedure," Kowalski said.

Blake gave him his card, shook his hand and headed toward the door.

"Enjoy yourself while you're here," Kowalski said. "Have a safe trip home."

"Thanks." Blake gave a nod to Maxine on his way out. Everything seemed cut and dried, except for the rocks and the hermit crabs he'd come close to swimming with. Maxine seemed as efficient to Blake, as Kowalski had been straightforward. He figured her for the glue that kept things together, and pulled Kowalski closer to the flow of today's technology.

Kowalski appeared to be protective of his turf and suspicious, like most cops.

Blake headed north, back along the coast. He wanted to update the chief, but couldn't pick up a signal on his cell. T-Mobile sucked, but then all the cell companies had places they couldn't reach. Cooper had never impressed him as someone who spent time texting or posting on Twitter. He and Kowalski were old school guys, straight-up bourbon on the rocks, beer chaser.

Blake found an old fashioned pay phone past Nepenthe, near the laundromat in Big Sur. His call to Cooper went through loud and clear.

"You think those rocks coming down were from Mother Nature?"

"I think somebody didn't want me nosing around," Blake said.

"Did you tell Kowalski about your climbing down the cliff and what you discovered?"

"No, just told him one of your constituents and supporters was suspicious, and to check out the car." Blake paused. "Chief, I need to ask you a question."

"Fire away," Cooper said.

Blake swallowed hard. "Why did you want me to check things out first and not discuss them with Kowalski?" He kept silent, waiting for Cooper's reply.

"It goes back a ways, between him and me. I'll explain later. Don't worry. I'm not going to put you in the middle of something. Run down the receipts and see where they lead you."

Blake pictured Hamilton's body lying in the water when the tide came in, the water rocking it back and forth. The sound of waves flapping against the Jaguar's metal coffin played in the back of Blake's mind.

● ● ●

Blake stopped at Anderson's Road House for a late lunch,

the restaurant Jack Hamilton had visited the day before he died. He was hungry. Blake spotted the white sign and red letters in front of the knotty pine log cabin building with a parking lot three-quarters full of California and out of state plates. He looked in the rearview mirror, raked his hands through his wind-blown hair as he left the car and walked toward the front door. He asked the hostess if Charlotte was working. Her name was printed on the dead man's bill. The hostess ushered him to the section near the front windows and gave Blake a menu.

"Wood-fired rainbow trout, green beans, mixed greens salad, thick-cut French fries. Sounds like Nirvana to me," Blake said when she came for his order.

"And what would you like to drink?"

"Ice water with a slice of lemon," he said, smiling. "How's your day going?"

"Just fine and yours?" She was tall, probably five-foot ten, had long blonde hair, and an astonishingly great pair of legs. She looked smart. Past experience told him people like her with Master's Degrees and PhD's could always be found waiting tables in places like Big Sur and Aspen.

"I wonder if I might ask you a question," Blake said.

"Sure."

Blake was attracted to her, the way she moved, how she stood with her hand on her hip, the way her eyes danced from one table to another, and those legs. "I had a friend who stopped in here about two days ago . . . six-foot, medium build, brown hair, about one seventy-five or so, in his early to mid-fifties. He was here with another fellow for a few hours, probably drinking beer. He told me the trout was really good. Do you remember him? Jack Hamilton? I'm trying to catch up with him."

"Maybe so. Let me get your order started. Sure you don't want a Margarita?"

"I'm good with the water." Blake loved camping, but fresh

broiled trout, air conditioning, white linens, and a waitress at your table trumped power bars and plastic camping bowls.

A couple minutes later, Charlotte returned with his water. "You sure he's a friend? You don't seem the same type."

"What do you mean?"

"Well, you have that kind of rugged, outdoorsy, laid-back hiker look about you. He seemed kind of tense and anxious looking. He kept looking around every few minutes, like he was expecting someone or was worried about something. I don't know, just an impression I got."

"And someone was with him?"

"Yeah," she said. "A guy about his same age, longer hair, more casual. They were here for quite a while. Looked like they knew each other. So you're camping?"

"Have been for a few days, up in the canyons around Garrapato. I headed south toward San Louis Obispo the day before yesterday and saw some police caution-tape along the highway. Someone went over the side."

"It happens around here once in awhile. Usually someone smoking too much weed and day dreaming while they're driving too fast. You don't do that, do you?"

"I did in the old days. Sometimes even I'm surprised by how much I've reformed," Blake said.

"Hey, I'll check back with you a little later. I've got to keep moving. You're going to like the trout."

She walked to another table, close by, where two children tested their parent's patience by kicking their feet against the wood base that wrapped around the booth. Crayons came with the food. She's got to be thankful for that, Blake thought.

The trout was his first hot meal in three days and the department was picking up the tab. Charlotte gave him her PhD smile and a view of her cleavage when she bent down to pick up the bill and his credit card. Blake was impressed with both and left her a generous tip. "Hope to see you again sometime."

"I'd like that," she said, as she turned toward the bar. A

woman like her could convince a man to cut short his time in the woods.

• • •

The art gallery Hamilton had visited a few days earlier was close by. Blake greeted the owner-artist with Phil Spector hair. The walls were covered with stunning photographs, oils, and watercolors. "Your work?"

"Yes," he answered, "most of what you see, anyway."

"Quite good," Blake said.

He picked up a photograph of the sunset off Point Lobos. "I had a friend in here a few days ago, Jack Hamilton. I'm looking for something for him, actually. I don't want to get what he's already picked out. I wonder if you could show me what he chose?"

The storekeeper pulled out a ledger book from below the counter identifying Hamilton's purchase. He walked over to the back wall and pointed with a beret in his hand. "Very close to this one. A landscape. He's got a good eye. At fifteen hundred, it was one of the more expensive pieces in the gallery."

"I've been worried about him," Blake said. "Did he seem like he was in good spirits?"

"He said the painting was going to be a getting-back-to-gether gift for someone special. He seemed okay."

If it was a gift, who was it for? Suicidal men don't buy paintings and plane tickets before they drive off a cliff. Blake glanced at his watch. He'd been up since three and didn't feel like a six hour drive home. Better to enjoy the sunset, stick around on the department's tab, and head back tomorrow. He'd catch the chief in the afternoon.

He stopped for coffee around 6:30. Blake spotted a big comfortable rock in the Big Sur River near the center of town. He closed his eyes, let his mind drift, and listened. Then, wondered why water running over rocks in a stream bed looked the same even though the water was always changing.

Blake looked up toward the road and the string of traffic heading into Big Sur. The explanation was right there in front of him — pry bars were long and heavy. They dented stuff and messed up car interiors. There was plenty of room for them however, in the back of a tow truck or a pick-up, even a jeep.

Maybe Hamilton had engine trouble or for some reason had stopped before the downhill grade. Or maybe someone popped the hood when he'd parked earlier, played around with the steering, or sabotaged the brakes. Hamilton was driving an older vintage Jaguar without the dual braking system common to newer models, so there wouldn't have been a warning light. The wheels turned in Blake's head. Hamilton might have paid for the repairs or a service call with cash. There didn't have to be a receipt. Kowalski knew that. The sheriff said as much when they talked.

Blake finished his coffee and went back to the pay phone next to the laundromat. He looked up towing services in the yellow pages, hanging from a shelf on a metal cord. He wrote down three names, and stuffed them in his shirt pocket. He bought himself a good bottle of wine and a dry, sharp cheddar, and then went back to the campground where he'd been staying. After he took a hot shower, he unzipped his sleeping bag, turned on a lantern, and listened to the frogs croaking.

● ● ●

A not so friendly raccoon walked straight into Blake's tent before he'd thought to zip up the flap. It eyed the open bag of potato chips on the tent's floor and hissed. The sudden intrusion sent a shiver up Blake's spine and brought him back, with an unsettling flash, to his climb up the face of the cliff. No way life ends like that for me. The reality that something could get that close to him without his noticing, bothered him. Blake took a book from his backpack and threw it.

He didn't set his alarm. The trip had started as a vacation and he wanted to keep it that way. The crows and the bluebirds woke him up the next morning when they came in looking for leftovers. Blake crawled out of his sleeping bag, grabbed a shirt, put on his pants, and made a good breakfast for himself, including fresh coffee with the camper's version of a French press Julianna had given him on his birthday.

"Have fun. Do what you love to do," she said. "Head for the coast. The girls and I have school so we can't get away and October is a beautiful time to be there. You need to take a break from police work."

He pictured her smile as she stood in the driveway, wearing the blue paisley shirt she had on the day he left. The tan lines on her shoulders were hidden from view. "You need some time to yourself," she told him. "I can tell. I'm that way, too."

CHAPTER THREE

Twenty years had gone by since he first crossed the Bixby Bridge that framed the Pacific and connected Big Sur to the rest of California. The place still drew him back at forty-six and inspired him. There was a lightness in his step, thanks to Julianna. She had drawn him out of a long, dull sleep like a piece of wood pulled from a ship wreck that shoots to the surface to find new life.

He was happy again. There were hours these past five days before his climb down the cliff's face, when his mind was empty, open only to his senses. His anxiety about Julianna, whether he'd blow it, whether their relationship would last, the frustration and confrontations that came with police work, had finally gone out of his head. Now, everything was creeping back in. "Balance," he said aloud. "I've got to keep balanced, keep myself positive."

Blake had struggled with depression on and off for years, never fully acknowledging it until he saw a therapist. Depression had washed over him, left him feeling empty inside and overwhelmed at times. The job, his mother, and his two younger sisters gave him purpose. But his life was stopped short of what he wanted it to be until he met Julianna. They'd been seeing each other for close to a year.

She was a second grade teacher with twenty-eight students, two ex-husbands, and two young daughters of her own. Before that, she'd been a high stakes baccarat dealer at Harrah's in Lake Tahoe. She had baggage, like most women her age — trust issues, disappointments, not enough spousal support. But hers was a better road than the one Blake had traveled. At least it seemed that way to him. And he was crazy in love with her.

Julianna's eyebrows were dark and full. Her eyes blue-green, thin lips, full, naturally formed breasts. The lines of her body were like an artist's sketch that kept revealing more of itself. He'd never met a woman he wanted so much to please.

After his divorce, the disappointment of dating airheads for a decade, and a relationship that didn't end well, Blake began to seriously doubt if he'd ever find another woman to share his nights and the simple things in life. "Not all of us get happy endings," he told his friend, Rob.

● ● ●

The ride home took him past Monterey Bay, through Steinbeck country, and Castroville, Monterey County's second oldest town where Marilyn Monroe was crowned the first Artichoke Queen in 1948. Blake turned northeast toward Watsonville and the strawberry fields that stretched on both sides of the road toward the horizon. He pulled his car over, bought three baskets of strawberries and ate half of one before he thought about washing them.

Blake hit Highway 101 North, connected to Route 152 and I-5. After a few hours, boredom inched in through the car's A/C vent along with the aroma from the dairy farms on the south side of Stockton. Blake closed the vent and thought again about Cooper and Kowalski. It goes back a long ways, Cooper had said.

By 2:00 p.m., he pulled into headquarters a little on the scruffy side in his hiking pants and a black t-shirt. He checked in with Sergeant Pierce at the front desk and asked for Chief Cooper.

"He's out to lunch. Due back any time. How was your vacation?"

"Peaceful," Blake said, "with the exception of one day."

"You going to be in for the afternoon?"

"Yep. I'm going to grab some coffee and I'll be back in a half-hour. Leave a message for the chief that I'm here and available. Thanks, Pierce."

"You don't want some of the rot-gut we've got on hand?" Pierce smiled.

"That stuff's toxic." Blake grimaced. "And I can't stand that non-dairy creamer. I won't be long."

Cooper buzzed Blake from his office at 2:35.

Blake walked down the hall past the break room.

"Go right in," Susan, Cooper's assistant, said.

Chief Cooper had held the job for twenty-six years as an independent in Sierra Springs, a politically conservative Northern California city. It was an appointed position, but he still had political obligations. Cooper had an untarnished reputation for honesty and keeping the crime rate low. Blake guessed Cooper was somewhere in his early sixties, rock solid with a little bit of a tire around his waist from too many dinners on the last campaign trail. He still had plenty of gray hair to accompany the thick Tom Selleck mustache he'd worn for years. The chief seemed to always know everything that was going on, good or bad, in Sierra Springs.

Cooper and Blake had never talked much, but Cooper had taken notice of him at the police academy and suggested Blake apply for one of the job openings he had. The Chief gave one of the welcoming speeches to all the recruits three years earlier when Blake was forty-one, on the old side for a rookie cop. The door was opened for him when the age restriction was lifted by the Civil Service Commission. His gray hair mixed in with the brown, and two days of stubble separated him from the crowd. Blake was deceptively strong, and looked like he was in his thirties. He'd walked away from two years of law school and a shot at serious money. But then, money had never been much of a motivator for Blake, despite his blue-collar background.

Blake shaved off the beard he'd worn for twenty years, two days before the academy's graduation ceremony, as a concession to the higher-ups and to surprise his mother. She'd been on him to do it for years. When he looked in the mirror, he hardly recognized himself. "The beard's part of who I am," he said. "The hell with it. I'm growing it back."

He'd proved himself with the paperwork and more importantly, in Cooper's eyes, on the street. He had good instincts and an eye for detail. He was soon promoted to Detective First Grade, eighteen months after joining the Sierra Springs Police Department. The Chief made a point to be there and personally congratulate him

● ● ●

"Good to see you, Detective," Cooper said, when Blake walked in the door that afternoon. "Have a seat. I'm glad you made it back okay." Blake felt Cooper studying him. The Chief adjusted his glasses. "I've been looking at your file," Cooper said. "You had two years of law school under your belt, switched careers and bounced around for awhile. Grandfather was a hell-raiser, owned a tavern . . . dad was killed by a drunk driver . . . first in the family to earn a college degree. I'm guessing you inhaled, too. Maybe a little bit of a new age hippie. You don't do that anymore, do you?" Cooper looked at Blake with some degree of anxiety.

"No, I'm done with that, Chief. I can't afford bad habits and I don't need any crutches." Blake ran his hand down both sides of his beard. This was the first one-on-one time he'd ever had with Cooper.

"Just so you know, Detective, I like the way you handled that last case. Not everybody around here did. Elder abusers going to jail, front page news, all helps shift support the department's way on the ballot measures." Cooper paused. "The guy was arrogant, mean-tempered. You know they were suing the department?"

"Bunch of creeps," Blake said.

"I know you talked to Bob Schmidt who lives at The Villas. I knew him when he worked on the bomb squad downtown. He told me a little about your conversation." Cooper leaned back in his chair and sat silent for a moment. "You know, when I asked you to check into this Hamilton thing for me, I figured I was giving you a couple more days of sunshine and fresh air. I didn't expect someone would try to crown you King of the Kelp Beds." Cooper rested his head against the back of the chair and swiveled back and forth. "Humph. Hard to figure. This woman I know, her name is Kathryn Winslow, she may be a little off-balance. She fired the dead guy, Hamilton, six months ago. Wrecks his life and now she's all upset and worried about him. Doesn't make much sense, does it?"

Blake nodded in agreement.

"She accused him of stealing office files that my officers recovered for her the day she fired him. I'll tell you about that in a minute. And now she's concerned when his apartment is broken into six months later. I'd say that's puzzling, wouldn't you, Detective?"

"Sounds like something more is going on," Blake said.

"What did Sheriff Kowalski say?"

"He seemed very agreeable and straight-forward."

"I'll be interested to see his report about the car," Cooper said. "And your tow-truck theory?"

"Maybe there was a receipt in the glove box or someplace else in the car," Blake said. "If there was, it should be reflected in the inventory of Hamilton's possessions. If not, I can check with Triple-A or Amoco, or see if he called for service from some place local, then take it from there. Nothing was in the preliminary report Kowalski showed me, Chief."

"So you want to stick with this?" Cooper said.

"Well, it's personal now. The rocks made it that way," Blake said, "and somebody interrupted my vacation."

Cooper grinned.

"You'll talk to Jameson about it?" Blake said.

"Not an issue." Cooper scribbled in his notebook. "You gotta understand him, Blake. He's the Captain of Detectives. He's good about keeping everybody in line, moving forward and wrapping up cases. He'd like to be chief someday, but his balls don't bounce."

Blake nodded.

"He's got a lead foot. He doesn't know when to ease off the gas or motivate people with anything other than warnings, quotas, and reprimands. It's all about the numbers for him." Cooper pushed a stack of paperwork to the side. "Take the rest of the afternoon off and wrap up any loose ends you have around here. Come see me tomorrow at eight, and we'll talk about Kathryn Winslow and the earlier incidents I mentioned to you."

Blake extended his hand. "I appreciate your confidence, Chief. You're the main reason I came to work here, you know. Besides the location."

"You got a wife or a girlfriend, Blake?"

"A girlfriend, Chief."

"I'm sure she's missed you if you've been gone a week. Unpack and go see her. We'll meet an hour later at nine instead. You can sleep late."

CHAPTER FOUR

"His balls don't bounce?" Blake said as he walked toward where his car was parked outside headquarters. "What the hell does that mean?"

Blake backed out and headed toward his friend, Rob Johnson's house. Rob and his wife, Samantha, lived in an older arts and crafts style house not far from Rob's criminal law practice in mid-town. He and Blake roomed together for two years back in the mid-west when they were both law students in Ohio. The school was near the Cuyahoga River that notoriously caught fire in 1969, and Shaker Heights, where Paul Newman's father ran a profitable sporting goods store.

"If you ever become a prosecutor, Rob," Blake said, "just remember, you can't blame the river fire on me. That was rusty brown oil sludge, and I was only three." Blake and Rob had become close friends, and made a point to get together at least every other week for lunch or coffee.

Blake had asked Rob to take care of his dog, Watson, while he was on the coast. He and Julianna had claimed the Gordon Setter from a neighbor who'd gotten ill and was unable to care for him. Watson seemed unusually smart for a dog but looked conflicted when he first spotted Blake at Rob's house — like he was happy to see him, but pissed that Blake had left him at the Johnson's for close to a week.

Watson barked a couple of times, ran around the backyard, and got a long drink of water from Rob's pool, after which he ignored Blake. Rob unlocked the backyard gate and the two of them set off for a walk in the neighborhood with Watson.

"How was your trip?" Rob said.

"Eventful. I saw two condors below the cloud line when I was hiking. Big Sur, Monterey, they're incredibly beautiful. Five days of nirvana and then I get a call from Chief Cooper asking me to check out an accident scene along the coast highway and before I knew it, somebody pushed some rocks off a cliff right above my head."

"Big rocks?"

"Does it make a difference? Even small ones do damage, and they weren't small."

"Are you serious?" Rob said. "Somebody tried to take you out? Who am I supposed to drink coffee with if you're gone? I deal with some real crap in the courtroom, but nothing like what you're describing. Politicians and criminals, sometimes it's a thin line."

"Yeah," Blake said, "I read about that politician in the paper today, the one you've been defending, the sexual misconduct case. Is the prosecutor going to drop the charges against him?"

"He's going to be back in public service. At least he votes right part of the time. He's no saint, but the prosecutor's case was really sloppy."

All of a sudden, Watson picked up the pace and they broke into an easy run under a canopy of Sycamore trees. "Samantha likes your dog, by the way. I'm surprised. She's been taking Watson with her on her morning jogs. He loves to run."

"Rob, did you ever hear of a woman named Kathryn Winslow?"

"I'm not sure. Her last name sounds vaguely familiar. There's a wealthy real estate investor in Utah named James Kilmer who's on the Forbe's 400 list. He holds a lot of medical patents, as well. I remember reading about him a few months ago when I picked up a copy of Forbes. I think Kathryn Winslow is his sister. She lives around here, somewhere."

"Thanks," Blake said.

"There was some controversy about one of Kilmer's companies evergreening patents. He caught some flack about that."

"Evergreening?"

"Yeah. That's what it's called when you make some slight changes in pharmaceutical compounds that allows a company to extend the patents so they don't go generic," Rob said.

They stopped for traffic before crossing over to the next block. Blake bent down to tighten his shoelaces. "Are you going to see Julianna tonight?" Rob said. "Samantha really likes her. Me, too."

"Yeah," Blake said. "In case you haven't noticed I have a tendency to romanticize women. You know, imagine them to be wiser, more caring and sensitive than in real life. I've got to watch out for that. It's gotten me in trouble before."

"She doesn't seem anything like your ex-wife and some of the other women you've dated. Not like the stories you've told me, anyway."

"You're right, she isn't."

"Dylan, old friend, there's a lot of guys with those same illusions. The knight on the white horse who comes to the rescue, the doctor with the magic pills who makes all the hurts go away. Our parents fed us that stuff. It's not real life."

Blake shook his head in agreement. "Brainwashed, I know."

"Julianna, she doesn't seem like those women. She's like the girl next door, only better. She's got some baggage. Most women her age do, but I think she's sweet. If I wasn't married, I'd be chasing after her. She's a catch."

Dylan looked at him. "You really think so?"

"Are you kidding?" Rob said. "Take my advice. Hold on to her."

"I didn't realize you were so smart."

"Hey, you're the one who was changing TV channels in the bathtub when we were in law school," Rob said. "You're lucky you weren't fried."

Blake feigned a dumb look.

"I still remember when you ordered something called Moo Goo Gai Pan in that Chinese Restaurant with no customers. No customers, that should have been a clue. Who the hell would do that?" Rob said. "And what is Moo Goo Gai Pan, anyway? I still don't know."

They crossed over to the other side of the street, switched directions, and picked up the pace.

"Let me get Watson's stuff from the house," Rob said. Blake popped the trunk and stretched. Rob loaded up his trunk.

"You remember what that blues singer said at the club outside Cleveland where we used to hang out? She was talking about breaking up with the man who cheated on her."

"Remind me," Blake said.

"She said, don't forget to take the dog's dish with you."

Blake laughed. "That's what I call permanent," he said.

"You and me, we're permanent friends. Take care, Dylan."

He rolled down the driver's window. Watson sat upright in the passenger's seat.

"Tell Samantha I said hello. I'll try and catch up with you next week. Be well."

Blake backed out the driveway and turned toward the expressway. He'd make a quick stop at home, unload his car, shower, grab something to eat, and head to Julianna's place. He grabbed Watson's leash from the trunk and took him for a short walk as soon as he pulled into the carport outside his apartment. "Let's go boy, quick. Time for one last pee," he told Watson. The two of them were back in ten. Blake poured some dog food and fresh water in Watson's bowls and made a bee-line for the shower. Thirty minutes later, he was out the door and merging back onto the freeway from the onramp. He turned on his blue tooth and kept an eye out for the Highway Patrol.

"Hello, sweet woman. I just got on the expressway from my place. I'm on my way. I can hardly wait to see you."

"You sound great, Dylan." Julianna's voice sounded confident and brimming with life. The time alone on the coast was good for Blake, but it had been four days since he'd talked with her.

"Did you miss me?"

"Yes, of course I did, detective. I want to wrap you up in my arms." He could hear her smiling.

"Are you on your Bluetooth?" Julianna said. "By yourself?"

"I am."

"The girls are at their dad's. I missed you. Save all your energy for me, you'll need it, Dylan. I just want you on top of me. That's all I want. Just you."

Blake moved to the outside lane and hit the accelerator. "How is it you always seem to know how to fire me up?"

"Female intuition, raging hormones, lust? I'm going to make love to you as soon as you get your overnight bag in the door. You're going to be the happiest traveling detective around."

"I think I need to hang up for now and concentrate on my driving before I run into something. I should be there in about thirty minutes."

Blake repeated in his mind what she had just told him. "Oh, my God." He shook his head in anticipation of his good fortune. Julianna had made his life so much brighter. He glanced in the rearview mirror and ruffled his hair.

He turned the radio on and drove past all the familiar landmarks on the way to her house — the rice fields, the water, the hay bales and corn maze, the causeway, past the neighborhood church they bicycled to with her daughters. He pulled in the driveway, waived at the neighbor across the way, and grabbed his overnight bag from the back seat. Julianna met him at the door. Blake dropped his bag in the hallway. She threw her arms around him and began to unbutton his shirt on the way to the couch.

"I want you in my bed, on top of me, anywhere you want

to be," Julianna said. She took his hand, turned off the front lights, and walked toward the bedroom.

They undressed each other and looked at themselves in the mirror above her bedroom vanity. He put his hands around her breasts and pressed against her from behind. She turned to face him. They walked over to her bed and laid their p.j.'s on opposite sides of the floor. He smiled and looked into her eyes and counted the freckles on her face. They climaxed together, then collapsed without moving, and made love again. The p.j.'s never moved.

Blake loved to see her without her clothes; the strawberry brown hair that stopped just above her shoulders; the lines and curves he saw when he was close to her. No one had ever been more satisfying. Julianna smiled and went to sleep. He nestled against her back when she moved to her side and stayed close to her, wanting their time together to always be this way.

Julianna made him a cup of double-bergamot tea and a home-made smoothie the next morning after they showered. Blake glanced at the sports pages before he jumped in his car. He'd spent too much time playing with Julianna and the soap in the shower for breakfast to be longer. It was like living a week in a single night that turned to morning, sweet and enchanting.

Blake sang in the car on the way to work and pulled into the parking lot at 8:50 a.m. He bumped into Jameson in the hallway.

The Captain of Detectives always looked like he was wound too tight — the black rimmed glasses, the efficiency expert demeanor, the white shirt and tie, the smile that seemed more staged than natural.

"The Chief tells me he's going to have you working on a special investigation he's started."

"I'm on my way to see him right now," Blake said. "We're going to go over the details."

"So, why does he want you on this?" A hint of envy and irritation appeared in his voice.

"I checked on something for him when I was on the coast," Blake said.

"The chief called you?" Jameson seemed surprised.

"I guess I was in the right place at the right time."

"Try not to fuck it up," Jameson said.

"You can be assured I won't do that, Captain."

They headed toward opposite ends of the corridor. He's such a charmer, Blake thought. He probably needs to get laid. He's always got a stick up his ass.

"I'll let him know you're here," Susan said as Blake walked into the Chief's waiting room.

Cooper came out and waved him in. "Detective, have a seat." He gestured toward the chair. "Good night last night?"

Blake plunked himself down in the brown leather chair on the right of Chief Cooper's large mahogany desk. "Couldn't have been better, Chief."

"You look happy. I like to see that. I wish more of these guys around here understood how important a good home life is." Cooper sat down and picked up a file on his desk. "You ready for this?"

Blake nodded.

"Kate Winslow, Kathryn's her full name. She's lived here for over twenty years, active in cultural affairs, fundraising, black tie events. Manages to get her picture on the society pages every so often. She's estranged from her husband who's done quite well for himself until recently, anyway. About twelve years ago she started her own business, probably to achieve some degree of economic independence from her husband who's been spiraling downward with his drinking and a string of legally questionable investment schemes. A few of our more well-off citizens have sued him for securities fraud. Nothing has been resolved at this point, so that's all still up in the air."

"Sounds interesting." Blake shifted his weight in the chair.

"You want a glass of water?" Cooper said. "Help yourself." He pointed to a table by the window.

Blake got up and filled a glass before returning to his chair.

"About six months ago, Kathryn Winslow called 911 to report that she'd fired Hamilton, the guy whose car you found at the bottom of that cliff. He'd taken a bunch of official company records when he walked out the door. She was concerned he was on his way back to her office to do something everyone would regret. That's how she put it. We dispatched a patrol car and they pulled Hamilton over about three blocks from his apartment. He had a clean sheet, was completely cooperative, and claimed he was on his way to the office to pick up his personal things. The officers told him Winslow was getting a protective order against him and to stay away from the office. They accompanied him back to his apartment and asked for the confidential records he had removed, at which point he handed them a box and a binder that appeared to be a customer list. The officers who stopped Hamilton returned the records to Kathryn Winslow later that afternoon. End of case."

Chief Cooper got up and poured himself a glass of water. "Pretty straight forward, right?" Cooper looked up at Blake.

"Seems easy to understand," Blake said.

Cooper continued. "A week ago, we got a call from Hamilton. His apartment had been broken into and ransacked. He says some business-related documents, including a partnership agreement with Kathryn Winslow, appeared to be missing. There was no evidence of forced entry. When the investigating officer asked him who else had a key, he said, Kathryn Winslow, his business partner. The officer knocked on Hamilton's neighbors' doors and checked with the on-site manager. Nobody had seen anything. Hamilton declined to file charges against Kathryn Winslow, so for all intents and purposes, the matter was dropped. We didn't question her about it. Several days after the alleged break-in, Hamilton, who is divorced and lives alone, pays his rent in advance for the next month and leaves town. Next thing we know, he's swimming without a life vest at the bottom of a cliff, the same cliff you climbed down."

Blake followed the Chief's narrative like a man with his ear to a keyhole. "So how is it you came to know about the accident which, as it turns out now, doesn't look like it was an accident?"

"When they air-lifted his body out of the car, Kathryn Winslow was listed as the emergency contact in Hamilton's wallet. Kowalski's office called her. They told her it looked like he'd lost control or simply drove off the edge. She called the following day and asked me to look into it."

"Why did she call you directly, if you don't mind my asking?"

"Good question. Kathryn Winslow is an influential woman in this town. She's always been a major supporter of the policy decisions I've made and the ballot initiatives we support. She wanted a favor and she didn't feel she was out of line asking for one."

"So what exactly did she say?"

"Now it gets more interesting," Cooper said. He leaned forward in his chair. "She told me about firing Hamilton, and then said she didn't think he was the type to commit suicide. She said he was a careful driver, and that she was shocked to hear about the accident. She wondered if something else, that's how she put it, was going on."

"And since then?" Blake felt puzzled, like someone had given him the wrong change and he was re-counting the coins in his hand.

"That's it. I told her I'd check into it. Haven't talked to her since."

"So pretty soon, Kowalski's report will be rolling in," Blake said. "Then the fact that it was a crime will become public knowledge."

"I think," Cooper said, "this would be a good time for you to visit Hamilton's place and then pay a courtesy visit to Kathryn Winslow. I want to keep this low-key. After all, it's not really our jurisdiction."

Blake nodded in agreement. He knew the Chief could see the wheels turning in his head.

"I'll get that address for you," Cooper said. "You can cruise by Hamilton's apartment this morning. There's a police seal on the door. You can get the key from the manager. Give me a call this afternoon and I'll set things up for you to see Kathryn Winslow."

Cooper walked Blake to the door.

Twenty minutes later, Blake turned the key to apartment forty-two at 1100 Winding Way Drive. He slipped on a pair of latex gloves after entering.

Hamilton had obviously straightened up after the place had been ransacked. It was an attractive, upscale apartment with lots of art on the walls, most of it reproductions. Blake looked in the file cabinet next to Hamilton's desk. A folder that said "K. Winslow" was empty. The rest of the files seemed inconsequential to his investigation. Blake looked under the couch cushions and the carpeting in the closets, in the freezer and the dishwasher, under the refrigerator and the mattress, behind the framed art, and found nothing. The desktop computer in Hamilton's office was password protected so that was a dead-end, at least until forensics examined it, if in fact they decided to go that way. There wasn't a laptop.

Blake sat down on the couch in the living room and studied the place. He did the same thing from the dining room table before walking down the narrow hallway to Hamilton's bedroom. He lifted the mini-blinds and surveyed the landscape, then walked to the other side, opened the bedroom closet door and leafed through the clothes — all of them were for men with the exception of a pair of women's blue silk pajamas. The label read size ten. Blake raised one eyebrow and filed the detail in his head. He walked back toward the window-side and leaned over the bed, inches above Hamilton's pillow. He wanted to capture each view in his mind. A hedge of rose bushes lined the property's boundary before three majestic Mission Oaks a few hundred feet away.

Blake walked into the kitchen and opened the refrigerator. Hamilton had soy milk, orange juice, and a bag of gourmet coffee beans on the top shelf, whole grain bread, fresh fruit and vegetables in the bin. The freezer had a few microwave dinners, three bags of frozen blueberries, and the same kind of vegetarian protein patties Blake liked to have for breakfast. He grinned. Hamilton's grocery list looked a lot like his.

● ● ●

On the way back to Sierra Springs, Blake stopped at one of his favorite neighborhood restaurants. He phoned Cooper from his car. "Hamilton must have left quick because he didn't empty the produce in his refrigerator. Either that, or he was only planning to be gone a few days. I'm going to grab some lunch."

"Cheeseburger and fries?" Cooper said.

"Not hardly. A falafel and tabouli salad, the best ones in town. If you reach Kathryn Winslow this afternoon and she's available, that'll work for me," Blake said.

"Let me see what I can do," Cooper said.

CHAPTER FIVE

Forty minutes later when Blake hit his car seat, his cell rang. "You've got an appointment at four this afternoon with Kathryn Winslow at her home." Cooper gave Blake her address in Sierra Springs. "I didn't say anything about our investigation or your preliminary findings," Cooper said, "only that you were handling this for me and wanted to touch base with her. She'll be expecting you."

Blake had two hours, so he stopped at the public library and did some reading about Kathryn Winslow and her husband, Phillip, in *The Business Journal's* past editions and the newspaper's microfiche archives. The older stories about Phillip were favorable. The more recent ones had a decided negative tone, mentioning his mounting legal problems and the allegations of securities fraud. The Securities & Exchange Commission was mentioned, as was the State Attorney General's Office.

Blake stopped at the dry cleaner on the way to Kathryn Winslow's home, went into the alterations room and changed into the freshly pressed navy blue blazer and grey pants he'd left at the cleaners before his trip to the coast. He wanted to look more the part of a rising, well-educated, Ivy League entrepreneur, like he supposed her late business partner, Jack Hamilton, had once looked.

He pulled up to the gatehouse. The uniformed attendant called the Winslow residence and the gated community's entrance doors swung open. Blake drove past the man-made lake and waterfall to her address. The drive was lined with cypress trees on each side, with a circular road that curved past a four-car garage and a beautifully landscaped yard. He rang the bell.

Kathryn Winslow answered moments later. She was in her late forties or thereabouts, and had an air of casual confidence about her. She wore a navy blue power suit with shoes to match and an expensive white silk top. She invited Blake in to her living room where they sat down, she on her couch, seeming very self-assured, and Blake in a stylish leather chair.

"Would you like tea?"

"That would be nice, thank you."

"Green, Earl Grey, or Darjeeling?"

"Darjeeling."

"I heated some water. I'll be right back. Make yourself comfortable."

"May I walk with you to the kitchen?"

"Of course." Blake got up and followed her. The tea kettle was whistling. She unwrapped two tea bags and let the tea infuse in a smaller pot made of fine china.

"You have a beautiful home," Blake said. He was standing by the granite counter top and custom, over-sized stainless steel sink.

She looked at him and smiled. "Would you like milk or honey?"

She had one of those large, double-door stainless steel refrigerators. He looked over her shoulder at the top shelf, two-percent milk, a quart of Silk brand soy milk, just the right size for company, fresh orange juice, yogurt, lots of fresh vegetables, and fruit.

"A touch of honey," Blake said.

Kathryn Winslow was attentive to her health and probably, he supposed, to her business as well. The dining room table was covered with an assortment of bills and files. She had three daughters—twenty, fourteen, and ten. Their pictures were displayed on the living room wall, their ages noted in the article he'd read at the library. There was a baby grand piano at one end of the living room and a white leather couch with two matching chairs at the other. An *Architectural Digest* magazine and an Ansel Adams book sat on the glass coffee table. He noticed she had an office off the hallway entrance as well. The view of the lake from the front rooms was serene and appealing. Blake couldn't help but wonder whether Jack Hamilton had ever been there, sat on the couch, or had breakfast at the counter in her kitchen. But that wasn't a question he would ask her today.

"You called Chief Cooper," Blake said, as they returned to the living room. "He asked me to stop by and bring you up to date on Mr. Hamilton. We don't really know much at all at this point, but we know it's important to you and that means it's important to us as well." Blake sat down.

Kathryn poured his tea.

Blake said, "I saw his car. He'd already been lifted from the wreckage the day before. It was a long way down. He couldn't have survived the impact so chances are he didn't suffer." Blake didn't know about the suffering, but he said it anyway to soften the stark reality of what he'd seen.

"Thank God for that." She looked upset. Her words seemed like a prayer of gratitude. "It's hard when something like this happens," Blake said, "to someone you know. I never quite know what to say." He lowered his head and took a sip of tea. "How long had you worked together?"

"About twelve years."

"So you knew him well?"

"Yes, we were close friends for a long time. He was a gentleman."

Kathryn Winslow's sincerity seemed heartfelt to Blake. They didn't impress him as toss-away words. "You told Chief Cooper you didn't think he was the type to take his own life."

"That's right. That's not a burden he would willingly place on his children and the people he left behind."

"And he was a careful driver, not the reckless kind? He didn't drink or text or get distracted talking on the phone?"

"He had a blue-tooth in his car. There's no cell phone service in Big Sur is there?"

"It's pretty sporadic, mostly unreliable or non-existent along parts of the coast," Blake said. "Have you've been there yourself?"

"A long time ago," she said, "with my parents."

"Before they opened the Henry Miller Library?"

"Way before then," she said.

Blake knew she was lying at that point. The library was a memorial to the famous and controversial writer and a local center for the arts. It opened to the public in 1981. Nobody had cell phones then. Even if her memory was only slightly off, she would still have been an adolescent or a teenager with conservative parents who wouldn't have intentionally introduced her to Henry Miller's erotic books. Kathryn Winslow had been there more recently. That's why she knew about the problems with the cell phone service. "So you called Chief Cooper when you heard about the accident because you suspected foul play?"

Kathryn Winslow turned to face Blake. "I don't know that I'd go so far as to say that. I was stunned when I heard about it and concerned."

"Is there anyone who might wish him harm?"

"Why do you ask? Did you find something?"

He could see anxiety in her eyes and in the way she fiddled with the cup and saucer. Her hand shook ever so slightly.

"Not yet. We're still waiting for the Sheriff's report."

"And when you get it, you'll know?"

"Probably."

"So, no one comes to mind. No enemies, no jealousies, no long standing resentments aimed at him?"

"Nothing," she said.

"How's your business doing these days in this down economy?"

"We're okay now. Jack's salary was a big number. Letting him and another employee go was a difficult decision. Sales were down. He was the Director of Marketing and the company's VP. Something had to give. We're back on track now."

Blake finished his tea. He had a clear sense that the conversation had gone about as far as he wanted it to, until he had more to engage her about.

"Your husband, Phillip . . ."

"My ex-husband, you mean." She was quick to correct him.

"Yes, well I was reading about him in *The Business Journal* a few months ago. I'm assuming you protected yourself from his reported financial troubles?"

"That's what the divorce was all about. That and his drinking and philandering. It's over now. The house is paid for. The business is supporting me, independent of him."

Blake stood up. "The chief is appreciative of your support. We'll keep you posted. Thank you for your hospitality." He reached into his coat pocket. "Let me give you my card. Please feel free to call if you think of anything else."

"Thank you for stopping by. You can call me Kate, by the way." She walked with him to the front door.

Blake followed the stone pathway to his car and drove toward the gate. She's a size ten, he thought.

CHAPTER SIX

Blake was nothing if not thorough. He believed in being well prepared even if time didn't always afford him that luxury. He exited from the upscale development and turned on to the street that wound through another wealthy part of Sierra Springs. He had some research to do before heading to the courthouse to take a look at the divorce records of Phillip and Kathryn Winslow.

The on-line stuff made it sound like Phillip Winslow was in deep shit trouble. At least three investors had filed suits against him, alleging securities fraud, mismanagement of funds, and embezzlement. If convicted, he'd lose his securities license and go to jail. He also had racked up two DUI's in the last six months. The last one in the drive-through lane at a fast food restaurant when he bounced off the wall and hit the car in front of him driven by an off-duty CHP Officer. Winslow had become an embarrassment.

Even so, he still had money. At least it looked that way. The real question was how much of it belonged to other people. There seemed to be an endless stream of investors ready to buy into the kinds of promises that Bernie Madoff types like Winslow made.

One of *The Business Journal* articles Blake read mentioned that Winslow skied competitively when he was in his twenties. After looking at the mug shots for the DUI's, Blake wondered how long it had been since his ex-wife, Kathryn, had seen sunshine reflected clearly in Phillip's bloodshot eyes. The divorce papers wouldn't tell him that. They would however, list the numbers, their property, custody percentages, debts, and who was liable for what. Blake poured through the pages of their irreconcilable differences.

Kathryn alleged that her husband had violated their marriage vows. She felt compelled to make note of his sleeping with prostitutes and call girls on business trips. She asked for full custody of the two daughters who were under eighteen and got it. The oldest girl was twenty now, and living someplace else. Phillip had very limited, supervised-only visitations. Her spousal and child support added up to about $4,000 a month, less than Blake had supposed. Phillip alleged Kathryn was having an affair, but didn't say with whom. For whatever reasons, the divorce papers hadn't been sealed. Blake shook his head as he sat on the bench in the courthouse reading them, speculating about why and whether it was an oversight.

The Winslow's had taken out a second mortgage with a balance of $750,000 showing on the house where Kathryn now lived. Phillip transferred title to the house and the debt that went with it to his wife. Kathryn, however, had told Blake the house was paid off. He called a friend at a title company who confirmed that both mortgages had indeed been paid in full eighteen months ago — six months after their divorce had been finalized. Kathryn Winslow now had clear unencumbered title and over a million dollars worth of equity. Blake was puzzled.

The older daughter's name was Allison. On a hunch, Blake ran a background search on her. She had been picked up on a prostitution charge in Stockton, and for possession of coke and weed. Blake figured that wasn't the pedigree her parents had expected for her at age twenty, and Stockton seemed like a strange choice for a young woman from her parent's neighborhood. Blake decided to pay Allison a visit.

The next day, he drove down I-5 to the address in her file.

It was a marginal part of town, the kind of apartment property that turns into a different place at night. He supposed a lot of people living there received welfare or social security disability checks, and slept late. The parking lot was quiet when Blake pulled up. He found Allison sitting on the top step of the second floor landing, smoking a joint in front of the red door of her apartment. Blake recognized her from the mug shot.

She was wearing a pair of provocative shorts and a top that showed enough skin to tempt anyone except an old Baptist minister on his way to church. Blake closed his car door, and walked toward the building. "You must be Allison?"

"Why must I be?" she said. "What do you want?"

He took off his sunglasses, propped his foot against a step, and leaned against the wrought iron railing twenty feet below where she was sitting. She looked him over with a sneer on her face.

"I guess I'm wondering why an intelligent, attractive young woman like you is sitting on these steps taking money for sex and doing coke."

"Who the fuck are you to lecture me?" She glared at him with contempt. "And what gives you the right to ask me a question like that? You have some hell of a nerve, mister."

Blake said nothing.

"Why don't you get back in that car of yours and go back where you came from?" She stood up, barefoot and defiant with her hands on her hips, and took a hit on a joint as she eyed him up another time.

Blake didn't move. He guessed she'd had a bad night. Either that or she was in a perennially pissed-off mood.

"Did it occur to you that maybe I'm doing exactly what I want to, that I like what I'm doing, and who I'm doing? Maybe you should find out how good I could make you feel before you climb back in that car and leave. That is, if you can afford me."

"That's not why I came here, Allison. I wanted to ask you about your mom and dad."

"So you're a probation officer? You want to save me?"

"No, I'm just a guy trying to figure out what happened to Jack Hamilton. You know him?"

"Yeah, he's my mother's business partner."

"You mind if I sit down here for a few minutes?" Blake moved up a couple of steps and sat down.

"It's a free country. Rich people would like us to think so, anyway." She took another long drag and sat back down on the concrete-slab step a few feet up from where Blake had stopped. "Jack Hamilton isn't hard to find. Call the office. Ask my mother. Does she know I'm here?"

"Not as far as I know," Blake said. "Do you want her to know?"

She crossed her legs and took a sip of whatever it was she was drinking. "I'm all grown up. I don't have to tell Mommy and Daddy what I'm doing. I'm a big girl, now."

"How long has it been since you've seen them?"

"This pair." She cupped her breasts in both hands. I'll bet you'd like to see them." She paused. "Oh, that's right, you meant my parents. Since before the divorce. I moved out. The drama and the hypocrisy were too much for me."

"And you're happy about where things are for you now?"

"At least I'm getting paid for it," she said, "and I'm good at it. I could show you how good."

Blake didn't expect her to be so blunt. Allison Winslow was growing up hard but she wasn't calling her own shots, not here in this neighborhood, not looking like she did. "What about your sisters? Do you miss them?"

"I'm taking care of myself. Hopefully mother dear will take better care of them than she did me." Allison put her finger in the glass she was holding and played with the ice cubes. There was a bruise on her thigh. Her cigarette had a circle of red lipstick around it and her denim shorts were unraveling.

Blake couldn't help but notice that she had a very round ass. His mind centered on what she meant about her mother not taking care of her and why the divorce papers only gave her father "supervised visitation" with Allison's two younger sisters.

"I'm going to give you my card. I don't think you need another lecture. You're better than this. Call me." He turned and walked back to his car.

"So what about Jack Hamilton?" she yelled.

"He's dead."

CHAPTER SEVEN

Blake drove back to the sign that said El Morro Apartments. He turned right the same time a gang-banger in a gold Impala pulled up with the window down and a big sound system. Stock fraud was one thing. This was worse. A young girl, twenty, her father, supervised only visitation. It wasn't right. Blake entered the freeway and headed home to Sierra Springs.

He hit the elliptical machine at the gym for an hour, then moved over to the gray and black medicine ball sitting on the floor. He lifted the ball over his head and slammed it down hard, fifteen times, three sets. Another messed-up, dysfunctional American family. What the hell is going on in this world? God help us if people accept this crap and don't speak up or do anything to stop it. He hit the sauna, then did a half-mile in the pool.

When he got home that night he didn't pay much attention to Watson. He didn't sleep well, either. Seeing young people like Allison, on a downhill slide, bothered him. He wasn't hardened to it like some cops. Sometimes, he couldn't check it at the door.

When Blake was thirteen, he and a friend staged their own imaginary bar room fight and trashed a cabin in the woods, knocked out the windows, busted up a table and some chairs. Afterwards, they felt bad about what they'd done. His dad sensed something was bothering him the next day after school, so he asked Blake about it. Blake confessed.

"You need to go see that man and tell him what you did."

Blake's dad drove him up to the house and waited in the car. Blake spent the rest of the summer paying off the debt, but he felt good when he made it right. That's what a dad was supposed to do. He sure as hell wasn't supposed to be like Philip Winslow and let his daughter fuck strangers for money in Stockton.

One-hundred percent supervised visitations? What exactly did Winslow do to his daughter to warrant that? Kathryn had to know. The questions reverberated in his mind like the sound of the medicine ball hitting the gym floor. Blake got out of bed and walked down the hall, poured himself a glass of water, and found himself thinking about what happened to his younger brother almost thirty years ago, and what he'd done to make it right.

Everything connected to it was a memory Blake had worked hard to erase. But Allison and her father brought it back. The hurt and the anger hit him like a tidal wave. He remembered the nightmares, the service revolver, and Felix Lewis. Blake kept it bottled up, in much the same way his twelve-year-old brother hid the story of how he'd been abused.

● ● ●

It was close to midnight when Blake picked up the phone and dialed his friend, Rob.

"Hey," Blake said, "I was thinking. Fifteen years since we met in law school. Long time. I wanted to call and mark the occasion."

"At midnight?"

"It's early. There's no curfew for guys like us," Blake said.

"Come on. I know you're thinking about that young girl you told me about, Allison. That's why you called," Rob said.

A moment of silence filled the space between them. "I don't like seeing people victimized. Inaction isn't what I'm good at. I think her father molested her. I'm not going to let him get away with it."

"Somehow, that doesn't surprise me. You're not the kind

of person who gets pushed aside. That's part of the reason were friends." Rob paused. "So what are you going to do with this woman, Dylan?"

"I'm not going to do anything at this point. She's not ready to leave it behind. She's not strong enough. I'm going to stop by her father's office tomorrow, though."

"I'm guessing you're going to mix some adrenalin with the confrontation."

"I feel like smashing something, Rob. My first inclination is to beat the hell out of him. I guess I'd be arrested for that, wouldn't I?"

"Yeah, you would, but I'd defend you," Rob said. "You know, you could go to battle against some of these same issues as an attorney."

"I'm not like you, Rob. I don't want to be neutral any more. I feel compelled to take sides and stop the hurt. If that means crossing the line sometimes, so be it. I'm not inclined to lull myself into thinking that it's okay to let it pass or wait for someone else to handle it."

"Don't admit to what you just said if you ever get questioned on the stand," Rob said. "For the record, I never heard it. We're friends first, before and above everything else."

"Hard-core reality is, there are plenty of people, selfish people who want what they want and who pretend not to see the bodies in the street when they drive over them. It's like what John Lewis said, the Georgia congressman and civil rights leader who marched with Dr. King and the Freedom Riders. 'You've got to put yourself in the way of what's wrong, find the courage to get in trouble, good trouble, necessary trouble.' I don't much care what the consequences are," Blake said. "I like what I do, but I had a job before I became a detective and I'll have one afterwards."

The line went silent for a moment.

"Where did you disappear to after your divorce and New York? You kind of dropped off the map."

"Oklahoma, the oil fields. Then I moved out of the country for a while. I needed some time to myself," Blake said.

"Six years is a long time between conversations. You can talk with me about it, you know. Friends do that."

"Yeah," Blake paused. "You've always been a good friend, Rob. How about the four of us go see the demolition derby at the county fair later this month, or do something else? I haven't been to one of those in years."

"Sounds good. In the meantime, keep your adrenalin in check. I'll talk to Samantha. We might have to sweeten our proposal with dinner or a cook-out."

"That's fine with me," Blake said. "Goodnight, Rob."

"Good night, John boy."

Blake turned off his cell and flipped the light switch in the living room before walking back down the hall to bed.

Watson curled up on the blanket next to Blake's feet at the foot of the bed. Blake rubbed his back for a few minutes before sacking out. Most days he slept like a rock, or as Julianna said, like an incredibly heavy, crinkled up pretzel.

He awoke to the beeping sound of his Ikea alarm clock that sounded like a New York city garbage truck had when it backed up to his brownstone when he lived in Brooklyn.

The clock said 6:30 a.m. "I need to get moving," he told Watson.

Blake stretched and yawned, the way men do when women aren't around. He put on his jeans, opened the door, picked up the newspaper, and headed for the bathroom with the sports pages in hand. He remembered reading how Earl Warren, the Supreme Court Justice, used to turn to the sports pages first because they recorded people's accomplishments, instead of the front page that always seemed to be about men's failures. "I don't get why more women don't understand that the sports pages aren't just about sports, Watson. I know you get it, fella. I think Julianna does, too."

After coffee and a good breakfast, he called Chief Cooper

and brought him up to speed. "I'm planning to visit Phillip Winslow today at his office. I'm going to rattle his cage."

"Don't make too many waves," Cooper said. "Remember, these are influential people with a lot to lose. You don't want to start swimming against the current before you have to. They're pretty impressed with themselves."

"More impressed than they should be," Blake said.

"They don't always take well to questions," Cooper added.

"I'll try to remember that. It's still early, but I need to kick start this thing."

Blake walked back to the second bedroom he used as an office, filled with lots of plants and art. The sunlight poured in. He logged in on his desktop and found Phillip Winslow's business address in Sierra Springs. The street ran toward the lake, mixed in with banks and brokerage houses. Blake leaned back and called the phone number.

"Good morning, may I speak to Phillip Winslow please?"

"And whom should I say is calling?"

"Richard Daugherty of Daugherty, Smith, and Jones."

"Just a moment please. He may be on another line."

Blake clicked off.

"Prime-time office space, Watson. Like I told you, who needs appointments? Better to simply show up."

● ● ●

An hour later he pulled into the parking lot, dressed in his most expensive suit, wearing a lavender Joseph Abboud Egyptian cotton shirt, and a pair of hand-sewn, Mephisto French shoes. He cleaned up pretty well.

The woman he faced got up from her desk. "Make yourself comfortable, Mr. Blake. I'll let him know you're here. May I get you a fresh cup of coffee or a glass of water?"

"Coffee would be good, with cream and a half-teaspoon of sugar." Blake watched her disappear around the corner.

The furniture was heavy and expensive — an oil on the wall

opposite him, an abstract to his left with a Paul Klee–William Kandinsky feel, and a chrome-plated oil drill bit sitting atop a credenza.

A few moments later, she was back. "Mr. Winslow will be with you in just a few minutes. He seems not to have had your name on his schedule."

Blake smiled. "Yes, this is a bit impromptu. We have a mutual friend who referred me."

"I'll get that coffee for you."

Blake noticed her name plate on the desk — Madeline Armstrong. Blake surmised she would convey his remarks to Phillip Winslow.

A few minutes later, Winslow emerged through a door marked private, and invited Blake to enter his office. Winslow looked excruciatingly dull and overweight. His short brown hair was thinning. He wore a white shirt and a boring tie with a gray pinstripe suit. Blake figured Winslow for the kind of guy who'd have turned him down for a job when he was in his twenties. Winslow's face was round, puffy, and hard to read. The divorce papers had indicated he made a solid, six-figure income selling securities when he wasn't drinking. Rumor was, he was good at spotting marks with money and pitching his own "can't miss" schemes, always looking for that next big score.

"I couldn't help noticing the drill bit in the reception area," Blake said. "You're involved with oil wells? That can be hazardous and profitable."

"I have some interests in Texas and Oklahoma," Winslow said. "It's a risky business. Does drilling make you nervous?"

"Sometimes . . . at the dentist's office." Blake smiled. "But not in the oil fields. I worked as a rigger when I was younger. Long hours, lots of dirt and sweat, but it gets in your blood. Green money, black gold, and sixteen-hour days."

Blake was having a little fun. He figured Winslow was gauging his risk tolerance, which went considerably beyond the thirty-two dollars and a coupon for free coffee in his wallet.

"So, Mr. Blake, to whom do I owe the pleasure of our meeting?"

"Actually, I met your ex a few days ago."

Winslow tilted his head to the side and adjusted his glasses. He looked surprised at Blake's pronouncement. "What was the occasion?"

"She called about Jack Hamilton."

"Jack Hamilton, her business partner?"

"One and the same."

"How was she?" Winslow said. "She's still a pretty tight package isn't she? . . . until you get to know her better, anyway."

"She was concerned," Blake said.

"Not about me, I'm sure."

"Concerned about Jack Hamilton."

"What about him?" Winslow said. "Why all the questions for me? I thought you came here to talk investments. She put cash in his bank account and he fucked her early and often."

"I didn't know that," Blake said.

"Well, you do now."

"And how does that make you feel?"

Winslow tapped his fountain pen on the desk. "What are you, my psychiatrist?"

"No, I'm a detective."

"In two words, detective . . . pissed off. How would you feel if your wife was fucking somebody else? I've got an appointment for lunch. I'm not making any money sitting here talking to you. This is over." Winslow stood and pushed his glasses further up on the bridge of his nose.

Just then, Madeline knocked and stuck her head around the door. "Your daughter is on the line for you, Mr. Winslow."

"Get her number. Tell her I'll call her back," he barked.

Madeline left.

Blake remained seated. "One more question . . . why so

little child support? A man of your means and stature you'd think would be a better provider, not a cheap-ass." Blake smiled the kind of smile that made people want to smack him. "You've got three daughters. Does it bother you that your visitation schedule is one-hundred percent supervised?"

Blake unrolled a Ricola throat lozenge as he spoke, slipped it in his mouth, and placed the distinctive yellow, green and white wrapper in the ashtray on Phillip Winslow's desk. He stood and walked toward the office door. Winslow followed him. Blake knew Winslow had no intention of answering his questions.

"Madeline, would you please open the door to the lobby for this gentleman. He's leaving. And he won't be back."

"Don't count on that," Blake said. He turned and walked out toward his car.

Blake reached for a Big Sur postcard from his glove box and placed it under the driver's side windshield wiper of Winslow's white Lexus. He unwrapped a second Ricola and stuck the wrapper next to the postcard.

"I believe I've accomplished something today, Watson," Blake said, as he climbed into his car. "Pissing off an arrogant rich guy. Maybe if we're lucky, he'll eat a poison blow-fish for lunch or choke on a chicken bone." Three girls. What must this asshole have done for his wife to insist on one-hundred percent supervised visitations? Blake turned the key. And a $750,000 mortgage pay-off? Winslow sure as hell didn't offer it up. He's too selfish. I get that her business is profitable now, but even with Hamilton off the payroll, it can't be that profitable. The money had to come from somewhere else.

He called Cooper at headquarters. "Have we gotten the Sheriff's report from down south, yet?"

"No word. Kowalski's probably waiting until the quarter ends and we roll into next month. My guess is we'll see it in a couple more days. I don't want to rush him. It's his jurisdiction and he's protective," Cooper said. "How did your meeting go with Phillip Winslow?"

"I'm not on his T-Mobile favorites list. My guess, either he ignores me or starts getting worried and makes some calls."

"Am I going to get one?"

"I don't think so," Blake said.

"So what next?" Cooper said. "Where do you go from here?"

"You mean, besides the fact that Phillip Winslow is a totally arrogant asshole? I'm gonna go back and see his ex-wife. You said you thought she was a little off-balance. What makes you think that?"

"She's rich isn't she?" Cooper said. "Rich people aren't like you and me, Blake. They have different fingerprints, a house on a hill, a yacht in the harbor, housekeepers to clean up after them. It's like they're thirsty and they keep wanting more and more to drink. They like to think they're different from us and when they're threatened and they have enough money, they use other people to push back. Remember that, Blake."

"Okay, Yoda."

"Now that's the kind of smart-assed shit that gets people like Jameson mad at you. You should watch that. It's a good thing I'm not like Jameson."

"I'm happy about that, Chief, real happy. You gotta see the lighter side of this job sometimes."

"Keep yourself busy, Blake. Don't take any wooden nickels."

"If I'd have stuck around longer in Phillip Winslow's office, he'd probably have tried to sell me some of those."

CHAPTER EIGHT

Blake drove to a close-by spot where he could park and walk down near the creek. He'd had enough of Winslow for a while. He needed time to think, and park benches had always agreed with him. They were uncomplicated. The solitude allowed his mind to go places and see things more clearly.

His mind flashed back to the hike he and Julianna had taken along the McCloud River near Mount Shasta when she asked him about the almonds he pulled out of his hiking pants.

"No plastic bag or anything?" Julianna said. "You can't just mix up nuts with change and dryer lint, that's gross."

"I don't. I keep the nuts separate, in my other pocket. I could live on fruits and nuts." He looked at the raw almonds in his hand.

"You're like a squirrel, always eating nuts," Julianna had said. "Me, I'll take a good tri-tip grilled to perfection. You're incorrigible. You know that, don't you?"

"Yeah, well," Blake said, "maybe charming, at least sometimes?"

Julianna gave him her girl-next-door smile. "Most of the time."

Blake watched two gray squirrels as they ran toward the bridge that crossed over the creek. She'll be busy in her classroom, doing lesson plans and grading papers until four. I'll call her then. Phillip Winslow doesn't think I'm charming, Blake thought. I can live with that just fine.

• • •

Blake walked back to where he'd parked and called Katherine Winslow from his car.

"You can call me Kate, by the way. Mrs. Winslow is much too formal "

"I had a question or two I thought perhaps you could help me with. Why don't we meet at the Starbucks near your house?"

"When?"

"This afternoon, sometime between two and five, if that works for you."

"Three is fine. I'll see you then."

The sun was shining like it always did in Sierra Springs during early fall. Blake liked being a cop most of the time, except when the paperwork started piling up. He felt good about life in the afterglow of the last case he'd handled that wound up on the front page. Blake knew that wouldn't last, but he was liking it while it did.

He was sitting at a table with an Americano when Kathryn walked in. She was a tight package, like her ex-husband said, with dark lipstick and an expensive handbag. He hadn't noticed that so much at their first meeting.

"Good afternoon. May I get you something?"

"I'll have what you're having." He held her chair and went to get a second Americano.

"Have you heard anything, yet, about Jack Hamilton?"

"We're still waiting for a report from the police on the coast."

"Is this typical? Does it usually take this long?" She took a sip of her coffee.

"It's not unusual. Reports take longer when you're outside a metropolitan area. We should hear something, soon."

"So what can I help you with, Detective Blake? You said you had some questions."

She seemed relaxed. Blake found himself liking her. He saw the attraction that pulled Jack Hamilton in. What he didn't see was how Kathryn Winslow had ever been drawn to Phillip Winslow.

"I met your ex-husband. If you don't mind my being so forward, he doesn't seem like he's in your league." Blake clinked his spoon on the rim of the cup.

"In my league? I'm not sure what you mean." She looked across the table at Blake.

"I know I'm not the first man to tell you you're attractive. You've built a successful business, raised a family. You've got a good reputation. Your ex-husband, on the other hand seems, well . . ."

"Sleazy," she said.

"I wasn't going to use that word but you probably have a better handle on that than anyone else. It's none of my business, but . . ."

"Go ahead," she said.

"What was the attraction?"

"When I was a young girl, detective, I lived in a small town in Idaho. My father was in the cattle business and my mother was a stay-at-home, take-care-of-the-children woman. She was also mentally ill."

"That had to be hard," Blake said.

"When my father was away, I'd hide for hours in the closets where my older sister, Jean, had put pillows and blankets to keep me warm. My brother, James, lived with us then, too. I wanted to be invisible. I wanted to be where I could feel safe."

Blake pictured Katherine as she drew her knees to her chest and wrapped the hem of her dress around her ankles, trembling.

"My sister and I took care of my mother for years. My father was too worn down when he came home after work. He ran the cattle auctions and we acted as her caregivers. Then Phillip came along. He skied and traveled. It seemed like my chance at a whole different life, so I married him. That was the biggest mistake I ever made."

"What makes you say that?"

"I raised three children while he was away. I wanted my marriage to work. I never cheated on him, not once during our first fifteen years."

"And then?"

"I began to hear the stories about how he flashed his money in bars and propositioned women when he wasn't being the good Christian going to church with us on Sundays like that Norman Rockwell illustration." She sipped her coffee and brought a napkin to her lips. "I started to feel like a woman whose oxygen line was being slowly pinched."

Blake eased back in his chair and tapped a pencil on the table between them.

"It went on like that for years. Phillip took me for granted. He became an abusive alcoholic. He was tearing our family apart."

Kathryn looked around the cafe and stirred her coffee. "Things kept spiraling downward. That's when I realized I had to break away and start my own business." Kathryn stopped and looked at Blake. "I can't believe I'm telling you all this. Do people usually confide in you this much?"

"Sometimes. I'm good at keeping secrets."

Kathryn pushed her hair back.

Blake was guessing she'd surprised herself with her sudden candor.

She uncrossed her legs and stirred her coffee a second time before moving her chair back from the table.

"I met your daughter." Blake said.

"How did she look?" Kathryn said, with what seemed more like curiosity than concern. So Blake ran with it. "Like she might have been high . . . harder than she should look at twenty, that's for sure."

"Phillip is a sick sonofabitch. He doesn't know where she is, does he?"

"I don't know. He didn't hear anything about her from me."

"You're a gentleman. I wish we were meeting under different circumstances."

"I'll take that as a compliment."

"I meant it that way. You're an attractive man." She paused. "You'll keep me posted won't you, about the case?"

"Sure." Blake was surprised Kathryn hadn't asked more about her daughter, even if it was limited to, was she okay? Or where did you see her? Or who was she with? Did Kathryn already know Allison was in Stockton? Had their relationship evolved to the point where the hurt between them had turned into some kind of self-preservation that demanded they keep their lives and feelings separate? Or had Kathryn written her off, emotionally? Being a parent wasn't always a walk in the park. Being the daughter of Phillip and Kathryn Winslow had to be even harder.

Kathryn left—to go back home, to her office, to the country club? Blake didn't know. He had his own work to do, but he couldn't stop thinking about the call from one of her daughters that came into Phillip Winslow's office earlier that day. The two youngest girls would have been in class at that hour. The oldest, Allison, didn't sound like she was on speaking terms with her father when Blake talked with her in Stockton. In all likelihood, that had probably been Allison on the phone, but why?

• • •

Blake pulled into a drug store on the way home to pick up some dental floss and Astroglide. He remembered Julianna's earlier embarrassment.

"Yes, I'm liberated, but that doesn't mean I'm going to ask some strange man in a drugstore where the Astroglide is. The Astroglide needs to be on your shopping list."

Blake approached the cashier to check out. He noticed the manager and a security guard arguing with a skinny black kid who looked to be about twelve or thirteen.

"You were shoplifting. You've got notebooks and pens, a calculator and some candy in your backpack," the manager said. "You're going to juvenile hall where you belong. I'm going to call the police."

Blake paid for his merchandise and followed the three of them to the back of the store. "Excuse me." He showed them his shield. "I heard you talking about calling the police. I'm on duty right now. Why don't we get this straightened out?"

The three of them sat down in the manager's office. Blake remained standing.

"What's your name, young man?"

"I don't got to tell you," the kid said.

"Let's see what's in that pack." Blake emptied it on the brown Formica folding table near the manager's desk.

"You know you can't do this." He looked at the kid. "You've got over twenty dollars worth of stuff here." Blake asked the manager to make a list and note the price. He turned back toward the kid. "How did you get here?"

"I took the bus."

"Nobody came with you?"

"No."

"Well, you're going to leave with me. What's your parent's phone number?"

"I don't know."

"You need to remember," Blake said, then turned away. "If you gentlemen would write down your names, the store's address and phone number, the date and time of this incident, I'll take that information with me. Do you want to prosecute?"

"That's our policy," the manager replied.

The security guard nodded.

Blake escorted the kid out the door and to his car.

"This isn't no police car," the kid said.

"Obviously. It's an Audi TT, my personal car. Get in. What's your address?"

"You're not going to take me to the police station?" The kid's eyes grew wider, his hands began to shake.

"Just give me your address. I'm going to take you home and you're going to tell your mom and dad about this."

The kid dropped his shoulders.

"You a real cop?"

"Duh. You saw the shield didn't you?"

"Why you helping me?"

"Why shouldn't I. We're in this life together. You're not exactly Bernie Madoff or Muammar Gaddafi, are you?"

"Muammar Gaddafi is that Libyan dude, right?"

"So you read the newspaper?" Blake headed his car toward the other end of town. He turned to the kid. "Which way am I going?"

"Turn left up here at the next light."

"You don't want a record do you? People will be stereotyping you for the next twenty years."

"I guess not."

"Who are we going to talk to?"

"My mom."

Blake could see the kid was dreading that. He looked out the car window and started scratching his hands.

"What's she going to say?"

"You're grounded. What were you thinking? I taught you better than that."

"Why did you steal those school supplies?"

"I ran out."

"We're going to stop someplace and I'll buy you some stuff. Next time, ask people to help you and if nobody will, then figure out a way to make some money to buy what you need."

"Okay."

"What's your name?"

"Freddie Roosevelt."

"Let's get those supplies and then we'll go talk to your mom."

"You got any kids?" Freddie said. He looked at Blake.

"A daughter. She lives with her mom in another state."

"Did she ever do stuff like this?"

"Not that I know about."

"I don't ever see my dad. He doesn't come around."

Blake looked sideways at the kid. "You better listen to your mom." He walked up the stairs and knocked on the door.

"Are you Ms. Roosevelt?

"Yes. What's this about?" She frowned at her son.

"My name's Dylan Blake. I'm a police detective. Your son's got something to talk with you about."

"Would you like to come in?"

"No ma'am, I'm fine. I'll let him talk with you about it." He recognized the look on her face as one he'd seen when he was a boy.

CHAPTER NINE

Blake drove to the gym. He sat in the parking lot for a few minutes and called Julianna to tell her how absolutely hot she was. "You knocked me out last night, you know."

"And I had fun doing it. There's nothing like having a policeman in your bed with a big stick and handcuffs."

Blake laughed. Julianna was bold and funny, brutally honest, at least she liked to think so, anyway.

"When am I going to see you again?" he said.

"What parts did you want to see?"

"All of you."

"Call me tomorrow after school. We'll figure it out. I love you."

Blake spent twenty minutes warming up on the elliptical, before he hit the circuit, lifted some weights, and worked on his abs. It felt good to help the kid.

When Blake got home he took Watson for a late night run. "We need to keep each other in shape. You and me, boy. Just the two of us."

The next morning, Blake made bacon and eggs, and dished out some home-made chicken soup with vegetables for Watson who'd long since gotten over being mad. Unlike people, dogs, at least smart ones like Watson, didn't hold grudges. Watson was back to being his normal, happy-go-lucky self who liked to chew on Blake's old bedroom slipper and sleep at the foot of his bed.

Once Blake was in full-work mode, he found himself still

fixated on the call, the one that came into Phillip Winslow's office from Allison. What had she said? Blake didn't have her cell number, which meant he had only one way to get the number and it wasn't going to be from her father.

Blake got in his car and drove back to Stockton, past the old bomber plane on the right side of Highway 99. After passing the parachute jump place and the cow piles with the tires on top, he took the exit to the seedier, central part of town where Allison lived. He followed a barbecue truck with a sign on the side, "Ribs so good, you don't need teeth." Two lefts and a right, then round the circle to the left side of a cinder-block apartment complex. He walked up the steps to the second floor and knocked on the door marked 23.

"Who's there?"

"Dylan Blake. We met the other day."

Allison opened the door, wearing a pair of pink pajama bottoms and a wrinkly, white shirt with no bra.

"Can I come in?"

"This is a surprise." She unfastened the chain and opened the door. "You can sit on the couch." She gestured in that direction. "I'm going to have some breakfast." Allison reached for a bowl and a box of Sugar Pops. She made herself a cup of instant coffee.

Blake looked at the ashtray full of cigarette butts on the coffee table in front of him and copies of People and Us Weekly. An empty shot glass sat on the counter. "So why is it you didn't think you'd see me again?" he said.

She ate a couple spoonsful of cereal. "It's not like we have anything in common."

"I think maybe we do. Did you call your father yesterday?"

"Why in God's name would I want to do that?" she said between bites of cereal.

"I was hoping you'd tell me."

"No, I didn't call him."

Blake figured Allison had not yet developed the art of lying when she looked someone in the eyes.

She drank coffee instead.

"Allison, I was sitting in his office when your call came in. The thing is, you've got to tell the truth to somebody, even if you don't want to tell yourself. That's how life works."

"You said Jack Hamilton was dead."

"That's right. His car went over a cliff in Big Sur."

"And you think my father had something to do with that, the guy who insisted that we all accompany him to church every Sunday when he was home?"

Blake heard the bitterness in her voice. He would have been deaf not to. "The guy you didn't want to be around when your mother wasn't home?" he said, in a calm voice.

"You know that?" She was still standing at the kitchen counter.

"I'm good at reading between the lines. I'm a detective, remember?" Blake spoke in a kind way. He didn't want to sound caustic.

"Did anyone see you come in here?"

"You shouldn't be doing this. Like I told you before, you deserve better."

"You didn't answer my question. Did anyone see you?"

"No."

"How do you know what I deserve?"

Blake looked at her from across the room. "I know about abuse and how it feels to be molested. What it can do to you."

She raised her voice. "Who said that happened to me?"

"It's written all over your face. That guy I saw in the pimp car the other day with the tattoos, is going to put some tracks on you and mark you as his property, the same way your father has tried to control you."

"Did you tell my father where I was?" Her cheeks turned red.

"I wouldn't ever do that."

"How is it you know about abuse? You read about it in a book or something?"

"I had a younger brother. It happened to him."

"He was molested when he was a boy?"

"Yes," Blake said.

"By your father?"

"No, by someone else . . . an older man."

"Did you know about it?"

"Not until twelve years later."

"I called my father to ask what happened to Jack Hamilton." Allison reached for a cigarette, then threw it down on the counter.

"What did he say?"

"He said he didn't know."

"Do you believe him?"

"No. He's a control freak. It's always only about him. And he's jealous. He wanted to control my mother. He probably still does. Fuck him. I wish he'd just go to hell and stay out of our lives."

"You can get past what you've been through. It breaks down to minutes when you add it up. It's not who you really are." He watched her to see if what he'd said was registering. Blake couldn't tell. "You've got the past, and then there's now and your future. You haven't been doing this that long. Believe me. It gets worse." Blake turned his head and stared into space, before looking back at her. "You don't have to be tied to the past. You can't be in two places at one time."

"So what are you going to do, detective?"

"I'm going to find out what happened to Jack Hamilton. You've still got my card, right?"

"Yes."

"Keep it between us this time. Don't call your father. I don't want him to know I was here." Blake got up and walked to the door.

"You're smarter than I thought," she said.

"Yeah, we've both got that going for us."

Blake took the stairs back down to his car. He circled through the property and headed for the freeway. A couple blocks later, he spotted a white, late model sedan in his rear view mirror. Blake made a couple of unnecessary turns and so did the sedan. He saw the driver talking on a cell phone before he hit the on-ramp.

CHAPTER TEN

"I must be getting paranoid," Blake said aloud. He leaned back and felt his body relax against the leather seat when the white Buick went straight. He didn't note the plate number.

Thirty minutes later, he was cruising down the freeway at seventy, listening to National Public Radio. Traffic was light, the windows were up, and the A/C was on. Blake began thinking about Freddie, the kid caught shoplifting. A few minutes later, his thoughts turned to Becky and Harper, Julianna's two girls, and the Sunday before last when they were flying kites.

Then everything changed. The kite was jerked out of his mind when the Freightliner rammed into the Audi's front wheel well and began pushing Blake toward the cement barrier on his right. He gunned the Audi, but the truck kept cutting closer to him, like a power saw that wouldn't stop. The sound of metal scraping filled his head. The Audi flipped over the barrier and twisted in the air like a gymnast high on drugs who'd forgotten what it was like to hit the floor without a mat. He felt a sharp blow to his side. The airbags exploded. The car hit the ground. His head bounced up against the headliner. Everything went black.

Blake had a sense of someone lifting him onto a stretcher. He caught an oily smell near him. He saw a red light flashing. He heard doors close behind him. He lost consciousness.

● ● ●

"What did I say about the dream?" Blake mumbled in the recovery room on his way to consciousness, when he saw Julianna — the same dream, twenty years earlier when he had surgery, and again, a third time when he was a boy and his appendix was removed. The dream that kept eluding him.

He was lying in bed. Something tight was wrapped around his ribs. Julianna was there, looking at him when he opened his eyes. She had her hand around his. "You've been in an accident. Try not to move . . . You're going to be okay. I love you, Dylan."

"Julianna . . . " He trailed back to sleep.

● ● ●

Blake's eyes opened. "Julianna," he said. "You're here."

She caressed his forehead. "I've been here since yesterday. You've been sleeping."

"My mouth is so dry."

She helped him with the straw. "Drink some apple juice."

"What happened?"

"You were in an accident."

"Was anybody hurt, besides me?"

"Just you."

"Do I have all my parts?"

"You have all your parts, Dylan. And the girls and I have you."

"I should call Chief Cooper."

"I already have. He knows," Julianna said.

Blake smiled "You're sweet. Thanks for being here." His head felt like a lead weight.

"How's my car?"

"It's totaled. Don't worry about your car. Just rest. You're going to be okay. The doctor said you're lucky."

"This is lucky?" He struggled with his thoughts. "When do I get out of here?"

"You've had a concussion. You've got some bruises on your

chest and shoulders. They want to keep an eye on you. So do I."

"Can I get something to eat?"

"I'll ask them to get something for you."

• • •

Two days later, Blake got his release. Julianna wheeled him out the hospital's front doors to her minivan.

"Freedom," Blake said. "It's a beautiful out here, the colors. When do I get to go back to work?"

"You're staying at my house for the rest of the week. I talked to one of your neighbors and the apartment manager where you live. They're taking care of Watson, making sure he gets to run. I picked up some clothes and personal stuff for you. You're going to rest."

"Yes, doctor." He pulled the seat belt across his chest and grimaced.

"I saw that," Julianna said.

"My chest hurts."

"Your ribs got bruised up pretty bad."

"I think everything else is still working. When do we have sex?" Blake smiled, reached over, and put his hand on her leg.

"We'll see what happens if you're good, and do what I say."

Julianna drove straight home to her house and carried Blake's hospital bag. "Promise me you'll lie down, or sit on the couch and watch TV. I've got to run some errands and pick up groceries. I'll be back in an hour or so."

"I promise."

"No stress and no lifting anything over ten pounds."

"You're kidding. Ten pounds?"

"Doctor's orders. You need to follow them if you want to be on my good side." She stood in front of him with her hand on her hip. "You've got to give it some time."

"Do you have my cell phone?"

"It's on the nightstand next to the bed. I charged it for you.

Chief Cooper called a couple times to see how you we're doing."

• • •

Blake was on the phone to headquarters ten minutes after Julianna left. "I met with Allison Winslow in Stockton. I think Winslow molested her."

"You okay, Blake? You're girlfriend called me."

"I'm all right. No permanent damage. My car got totaled."

"Don't even think about coming in to work until next week at the earliest. Everything can wait," Cooper said. "Nobody's leaving town. We'll talk about it when you get back."

• • •

The weekend at Julianna's was slow and lazy. The girls we're sweet. They brought him breakfast in bed, made tea, and baked cookies for him. He watched roadrunner cartoons with Harper, Julianna's ten-year-old, on Saturday morning. He woke up startled, in a cold sweat, that night. He'd been re-living the crash — the sensation of weightlessness and falling. The driver of the truck was wearing a hat and sunglasses, the wrap-around kind and glaring down at him.

Julianna woke up. She caressed his head and drew him close to her.

• • •

They went for a walk in the park near her house the next day. Except for the soreness in his ribs and one shoulder, Blake felt amazingly good. He held Julianna's hand. The girls were in front of them. Blake stopped, pulled Julianna next to him and kissed her with all the tenderness he could muster. She looked at him, put her hand on his forehead, and smiled.

Monday came and Julianna and the girls were off to school. Blake called his insurance agent and the rental car company. They brought out a cheap, four cylinder, red Chevy Aveo. The insurance rep told him the Audi TT sport coupe was headed for the scrap pile. Blake drove to his apartment and checked his phone messages and email, most of which fell in the junk mail category.

Watson had a kind of sad, forlorn look on his face. "You missed me, huh?" Blake said. "Just so you know, I've been thinking about what's important. I know food's at the top of the list for you. For me, it's about family and love. The material stuff doesn't matter much, but I do want a different car." Watson pawed at his pant leg.

Blake stretched out on the couch and stared out the front window, eyes wide open, not a thought in his head, as still as a marble statute. When he looked at his watch, an hour had passed. He fell into a deep sleep. He saw the truck again, bearing down on him. He got up from the couch and walked to the kitchen. "To everything there's a season, and a time to every purpose under heaven, Watson. That's somewhere in the Bible, Ecclesiastics I think. I should be thanking my stars for these hurt ribs." Blake poured some water in Watson's bowl.

You're not tied to your past. You can't be in two places at the same time. You've got to leave some of the rough spots behind to make the future you want. That's what he'd told Allison. Now if he could just convince himself.

He remembered how he'd pleaded with God when his brother, Jeff, died and cursed him when his father was killed. The "why God, tell me why?" questions had faded away for Blake. He didn't think about them so much anymore. But he still always found himself wanting to believe in something more, and this case, for whatever reasons, was bringing them back.

He'd come a long way from New York and Felix Lewis. Worked hard at forgiving himself, controlling the anger and depression that gripped him like an iron vice. He had a life of promise in front of him, now. His brother had lost all that, and his father's life was arbitrarily cut short when a drunk driver hit him head-on. "Yeah, Watson, I'm definitely lucky."

● ● ●

Blake packed up, drove to the auto mall in his rental car, walked straight into an Audi dealership, test drove a black, turbo-charged, fully loaded Audi A-6. "Divine sedan intervention," he told the Finance Manager. "I need you to fix it, so I can drive this thing right off the showroom floor this week. That's got to be part of the deal."

The salesman was standing next to the finance man. "We'll arrange the drive-off if you sign the papers today," the salesman said, as he smiled.

"I think you'll make those arrangements for me no matter when I plunk down the money," Blake said. "So don't get carried away, unless you want to knock off a couple grand. You're not that persuasive."

Blake signed the paperwork, then left to grab coffee at his favorite midtown café where he made a point of saying hello to Lauren, the manager, who'd helped him with an earlier case. "Best coffee in town. Best manager, too."

"I see you're driving that red Chevy Aveo? What's up? That's not you're style, Dylan Blake." She smiled, came around the counter, and gave him a hug.

"I know. It's temporary." Blake shrugged. "How've you been? Next time I come in, I'm going to surprise you."

"Seeing you is always a surprise. Coffee's on me. We've got some great estate beans from Panama just roasted a few days ago. I'll make a latte for you. So what are you doing today?" she said.

"I'm making the rounds and seeing some of my favorite people, the ones I'd have missed the most if I had bit the dust on the freeway the other day."

"An accident? That's not allowed. You're my favorite detective."

"I didn't know you knew any other detectives."

"Don't get technical. Are you going to get a falafel and some baklava at Lyla's restaurant?" she said.

"Yeah, one more stop."

Afterwards, he headed across the causeway to Julianna's with three roses and Thai food for her and the girls.

"When you've been in the hospital and leave with a good prognosis, all the colors in the world seem brighter," he told Julianna, "like a van Gogh painting."

● ● ●

At 4:00 a.m., Blake kicked violently at the blanket and bolted up in bed. He saw the truck again. The driver had a thick mustache. He looked tall.

CHAPTER ELEVEN

After breakfast at Julianna's, Blake called the Stockton P.D. from his car on the way to his apartment.

"What do you want us to do with it?"

"Email the accident report this morning. I'm going to go over it with Chief Cooper."

● ● ●

Blake pulled into his insurance agent's office to pick up the pictures showing the car's damages, before stopping at his place to check on Watson. He started berating himself for not writing down the plate number — somebody in that Buick had to have called the guy in the Freightliner to coordinate the timing.

Rich people have different fingerprints, Cooper had said. *A house on a hill, a yacht in the harbor, housekeepers to clean up after them. When they're threatened and they have enough money, they'll use other people to push back. That bastard Winslow tried to kill me.*

Blake didn't share his suspicions with Julianna. There wasn't any point in worrying her. After all, they were still just suspicions, and he wasn't the paranoid type. But he needed to tell Cooper.

He drove to headquarters and spread the pictures across his desk. "Look at these, Chief." Blake stood to his right, pointing. "Where the truck first hit me, look at the front quarter panel and the driver's side door. He rode me off the road, never swerved or straightened the truck out. There aren't any skid marks. He didn't brake. And there wasn't any traffic to speak of, or visibility issues. It wasn't late at night, the roads were dry." Blake settled back into the chair on the other side of Cooper's desk. "I know Winslow's got rights, but this shit has to stop."

"If we determine that Winslow was behind this, we'll find a better way to even the score. Your best bet right now, Blake, is to lay low, trim around the edges, and try to establish a connection between Phillip Winslow, Big Sur, and Jack Hamilton," Cooper said. "You're gonna need to go back down there. Find out who's working at those tow-truck road service companies you identified. You can snoop around town some more while you're there."

Blake leaned forward, agitated and impatient. "A lot of businesses outsource their payroll services. Maybe I can get hold of an employee list, or I can collect all the employee plate numbers and run them through the NCIC's database and check for priors."

"The last one's your best bet. It's less complicated, and you might get lucky and recognize somebody while you're down there," Cooper said, "like the guy who was driving the truck. Do what you need to do, but stay away from the Winslows for now. Let them think you're off the map. In the meantime, go home and get some more rest."

"Any word yet from Sheriff Kowalski's office?" Blake said.

"We got his report. They're calling it an accident. The report listed a gun among Hamilton's possessions, licensed a couple months ago. Hamilton had a permit. There's no mention of any mechanical problems with the brake lines or steering problems."

"What?" Blake said, with an air of incredulity. "He died with his foot on the brake, hard against the floorboard. Somebody killed him."

"Here it is." Cooper pushed the folder toward Blake. The

Chief looked puzzled, as well. "I don't want to jump to conclusions just yet. Maybe it was an oversight."

"It wasn't," Blake said. "I specifically asked Kowalski to check."

"I don't want you to make any contact with Kowalski. Let's keep this quiet for now, until we see what else we come up with." Cooper stood. "So you're going to get another car?"

"I'm not going to drive a red Chevy Aveo or some little tin box. I need some power and crash protection. I bought an Audi turbo."

"You don't have to sleep in a tent when you go down to the coast this time. Get yourself a good bed."

● ● ●

Blake was sitting at Julianna's kitchen table. She had just beaten him again at the match-up game in last Sunday's comics section.

"So, why is it you need to go back to Big Sur, Dylan? It's a long drive. Are you sure you're up to it?"

"I feel fine. My ribs are still a little sore, that's all." He cleared the table. "I've got to do the trip. It's part of an investigation the Chief and I are working on. We've got to identify some employees who work down there so we can run background checks. It's pretty cut and dried stuff."

"Promise me you'll be careful."

"I promise."

"Why don't we take a ride out to the Manas Ranch in Esparto? Sunset Magazine says they have the best peaches in the West. We can go this weekend when you get back from the coast. I'll pack a picnic lunch and the four of us can make a day of it."

"Sounds great."

"If you'd like, we can take your new car. I'll drive. We'll leave the mini-van at my place." Julianna winked.

"You want to test the turbo, don't you?"

"You surprised me, you know. A four-door sedan? That's not like you." She nudged him under the table with her leg.

"I wanted room for the girls. It's not that tame. I got the turbo."

"You drive too fast. You know that, right? You need to keep your eyes on the road, instead of me."

"Easy for you to say. It's hard for me to keep my eyes off you when you look so good."

●　●　●

Blake was on his way to the coast before the girls were up. Six hours later, he was sitting in the corner of the parking lot at A-1 Towing, writing down license plate numbers and making notes. His camera with the telephoto lens was on the seat next to him. A-1 shared a common lot with another business. Blake parked in the shade, sandwiched between cars, where he wouldn't attract attention. He left at 2:30 p.m. to hit the two other lots he had to cover, and grabbed a fish taco at a small, roadside taqueria a few blocks away. He timed his visit to catch the shift changes at all three locations. He didn't recognize anybody. It qualified as a long, dull day.

At 6:00 a.m. the following morning, Blake was back at A-1 with a power bar and a bag of raw almonds, determined to break the donut cop stereotype. The thought he might someday find himself with a gut and a bag of potato chips in front of a TV set was too bleak for him to accept. The idea of a good dinner and taking advantage of the department's budget, however, grew more and more appealing as the day dragged on.

Blake left A-1 at 10:00 a.m. for the other two locations where he picked up some additional plate numbers. By five, he was bored out of his mind. He changed into the dress shirt, hanging behind the driver's seat, before heading to the restaurant where Charlotte worked. Blake saw her and waved.

A few minutes after being seated, she walked over. "I didn't expect to be seeing you again. How are you?"

"I'm good."

"So you're back for seconds. Let me guess, the trout." She smiled.

"I accept your recommendation."

"We've got asparagus today, our official seasonal vegetable, and an excellent mixed greens salad. How's that sound to you?"

"Great. And life has been good since last I saw you?"

"Same old, same old, but hey, it's fall in Big Sur, that's the fun part. Would you like a beer?"

"Maybe a Beck's Dark, or a good micro-brew like Beck's Dark, or a good micro-brew like Gold Country Pilsner that comes out of Auburn."

"I'm sure we've got one of those. Tell me your name again?"

"It's Dylan, and you're Charlotte. Am I right?"

"You are." She turned and walked toward the kitchen.

If there wasn't a Julianna in Sierra Springs, I probably would make a play for her, Blake thought. A shape like that and smart.

Charlotte delivered a great looking plate of food.

"That's as good or better than it was when I was here a few weeks ago," Blake said, when he'd finished.

"I hoped you'd like it." She looked at him. "I'm off in a half-hour. Would you like to have coffee?"

Blake hesitated for a moment before he convinced himself that meeting her would further his investigation, and an innocent conversation with a beautiful woman could be just that and nothing more. "I have to be some place later tonight," he said. "I'll push it off. Why don't we meet at ?"

"Six-thirty?" she said

"Six-thirty it is." He left a generous gratuity, courtesy of the department, and headed down the road to admire the coastline. When Blake drove through Big Sur twenty years earlier, with hardly any money in his pockets, he pictured himself having drinks and intellectual conversations with literary giants like Kerouac, Ferlinghetti, Brautigan, Arthur Miller, and others. He imagined stopping at The Esalen Institute for a workshop and a massage, where he'd meet Alan Watts, or Buckminster Fuller, or Ram Dass. But he couldn't afford it. Back then it was Pemmican bars and an Igloo cooler. But there'd always been enough money for Nepenthe.

The name meant isle of no care. That's what Nepenthe gave him, a breathing spell away from routine and a view that never left his mind. Charlotte and Dylan watched the sunset at the long wooden bar that wrapped around the edge of the patio, with the Pacific on one side and the Santa Lucia mountains on the other.

"Thanks for the invitation. How long have you lived here?" Blake said.

"About three years, now. It's a hard place to leave."

"I can see why. I've always been drawn here. Big Sur is special."

"Did you find your friend, the one you we're looking for?" she said.

"I did. It's sad, actually. You remember that car that went over the cliff?"

"A few weeks ago, yes."

"He was driving it."

"You're kidding. I'm sorry." Her expression changed.

Blake could see she cared.

"Did he have a family?"

"He was divorced. He had a daughter in her twenties and a son."

"That's tragic. Did you know him well?"

"Just briefly. Life is unpredictable." Blake looked at the waves rolling in. "Hard to figure why stuff happens. There are things in life that go beyond coincidence and chance." The sadness he felt unexpectedly turned to contentment when he looked at her.

"I know what you mean. I kind of feel the same way. Here we are, spinning around on a globe in the middle of space with all this symmetry around us . . . and inside us. The human body is extraordinary, incredible really. To insist that everything, all of this, is some random shuffling of the deck seems short sighted," Charlotte said.

"You're right. I'm not much of a church goer, but I don't buy the notion that somehow it's hip when people dismiss religion as a fairy tale." Blake ran his hand through his hair. "I guess I stopped expecting to get answers to the big questions a long time ago."

"Has that worked for you?" Charlotte's eyes we're trained on his, waiting, or so it seemed.

"Not really. I don't think religion is an illusion. There's something there, an historical record," Blake said. "And there's something more beyond that, that can't be dismissed, and the questions keep coming."

Charlotte smiled at him in a soft and understanding way. "You don't filter things much before you say them, do you?"

"So I've been told. It's both a blessing and a curse."

"I think it's a good quality."

"I meet people on both ends of the spectrum who are convinced they have a monopoly on the truth. They're not honest enough to admit it, but that's what they think," Blake said.

"I've met some of those same people."

"I remember Stephen Wright, the comedian, saying, he could see way into the future, just off to the sides. I guess I'm kind of like that. Some people refuse to look anywhere other than straight ahead. If someone or something isn't right in front of them, they'll argue that it doesn't exist and that everyone else is mistaken or misinformed. I can't stand that kind of closed mindedness." Blake paused, drank more coffee and felt the warmness from the cup he cradled in both hands. "Maybe I'm talking too much."

"You're not. I think that's where a lot of religious hypocrisy comes from." Charlotte brushed her hair away and looked at him. "What do you do?"

"You mean for a living, besides hiking and eating trout?"

"Yes, that's kind of what I was asking."

"If I tell you, you're sworn to secrecy."

"I'm not that good with secrets." Charlotte laughed. "You're single, aren't you?"

"I am, but I'm involved. I'm in love with someone."

"That must be nice."

Blake was good at reading faces but he couldn't read hers when she said that. He thought he saw disappointment. Maybe he was flattering himself, instead. He knew he didn't want the conversation to end.

"Have you ever been in love?" Blake asked, as he savored the coffee.

"Once, a few years back. I discovered he wasn't right for me. Sometimes it's just timing, you know."

"I do know," Blake said, "and I know how much that can hurt. I probably shouldn't have asked you a question like that."

"Then why did you?"

"I'm not sure. I just wondered. You're the kind of woman who makes a man wonder."

Both of them fell silent. Blake watched her relax as the sun fell into the ocean.

"I didn't expect a conversation like this," Charlotte said. "I expected you'd wind up making a play for me and I wanted you to be successful."

"Timing is everything. If I wasn't involved, I'd be crazy not to chase after you." Blake ruffled up his hair.

"So are you going to tell me what you do?"

"Will you swear to secrecy?"

"I will, now."

"I'm a police detective up North."

"And you're working on something?"

"Most days I am."

"Tell me how I can help."

"I'm looking for a guy, probably in his thirties or forties. I don't know for sure. Tall, wears a baseball hat, wrap around sunglasses. He has one of those big, thick mustaches."

"That's like saying you're looking for a coastal redwood around here. You're going to have to be more specific than that."

"Chances are he drives a pick-up truck, has a license to operate a big rig. He's not someone who'd necessarily strike you as being a nice guy. And he probably wears work boots, maybe cowboy boots."

"Now you're giving me a little more to work with," she said. "Tattoos?"

"I don't know. He tried to run me off the road. I didn't get close enough to see any tattoos."

"I'll think about it and keep my eyes open. No one comes to mind, right now."

"Will you call me if someone does?"

"Absolutely, but I'll need your phone number."

Blake handed her his card.

"Charlotte, do you mind if I ask you another question?"

"Of course you can."

"Have you ever had occasion to meet Sheriff Kowalski. He works out of a small police sub-station down the road toward San Louis Obispo?"

"Kowalski?" she said. "No, not actually."

"Whatever you hear about him, if you do hear something, call me. But don't let anyone know we had this conversation about Kowalski. I'm serious."

"I'm sworn to secrecy. Officially, right?"

"Officially," Blake said, "and thank you, for everything."

Charlotte stood up to leave. "Thank you for the coffee." She looked at his business card. "Dylan Blake. Take care." She took a few steps and turned back. "What's your girlfriend's name?"

"Julianna."

"She's lucky, too. If it doesn't work out, you'll let me know?"

"Yes."

Blake stayed at Nepenthe for another half-hour or so before walking down the steps to his car. He drove back to A-1, and then to the other two garages to make sure he hadn't missed any plates. He added a couple to his list. After about three hours, he left for Deetjen's Big Sur Inn where he was staying. A hot shower, one of life's greatest luxuries, he mused, with or without your girlfriend. When he finished, he pulled out the book of poetry in his suitcase, and listened to the frogs before turning off the light.

CHAPTER TWELVE

Blake had breakfast the next day at Deetjen's — French toast, fresh fruit, and coffee. After some time spent daydreaming, he convinced himself he needed to get back to work, and stop thinking about Charlotte. He fought off the urge to drive to Sheriff Kowalski's office and ask how he could possibly have missed the fact that Hamilton's brake line had been sabotaged. Budgetary delays were one thing, sloppy-ass police work was something altogether different.

Blake walked across the road and stared out at the Pacific. All of North America ended a few hundred feet from where he was standing. No land for 2,500 miles and he still didn't have a connection between Phillip Winslow and the coast. There had to be one. Winslow was a taker. There had to be a trail.

The trip back to Sierra Springs felt like a bummer to Blake. He was coming home empty-handed, but then he hadn't run the plates, yet. There was still at least a possibility something would turn up. So what next, he asked himself?

After five hours on the road, Blake was two exits away from where he lived when he saw a hitch-hiker on the side of the freeway. "I'll be damned," he said aloud, "if that doesn't look like the skinny kid from the drugstore, Freddie Roosevelt." He slowed down and pulled over to the side about two hundred feet up the road. He rolled down the passenger window and waited. The kid ran up to the car.

"It's you," Roosevelt said. "I didn't recognize your car. This isn't the one you were driving before."

"Get in, already," Blake said. "Don't you know how danger-ous hitching is?" Blake was annoyed.

Freddie climbed in, put his backpack on the floor mat, and fastened his seat belt.

"So why are you doing this when you know it's stupid?"

"I didn't have money for the bus and my mom's at work."

"And she knows about this?" Blake looked at him as the Audi's turbo kicked in.

"Not really."

"What do you suppose she would say? Hey, wait a minute, before you answer that question, didn't we have a conversa-tion like this once before?"

"Yeah, but that was a while back and you know what they say about kids?"

"I'm not sure I do, but somehow I got a hunch you're going to tell me. That's not the point, but go ahead."

"They say we've got short memories." Roosevelt smiled.

"No," Blake said, "you've got it wrong. That's what kids say about old people who can't remember what happened a few minutes ago. Your problem is you don't want to listen hard enough."

"I haven't done any more shoplifting. I got all A's and B's at school." Freddie slapped his hands on his legs to accentuate the point, then he grinned.

"Your mom must be proud of you."

"She is. This's what she was hoping for when we moved from L.A."

Blake glanced at him. "So, did you figure out a way to make some money yet?"

"Well, I was thinking lemonade stand, but too many people in my neighborhood are drinking Colt Forty-Five Malt Li-quor." He threw his head back and laughed.

Blake did his best not to smile. "Freddie, you're twelve. Tell me you don't subscribe to all that lame-ass, bullshit stereotyping about cops."

"No, Detective Blake. I'm just kidding with you. Kids like me, we do that a lot."

"I got a business proposal for you," Blake said.

Freddie inched forward in his seat, seemingly a hundred percent focused on what Blake would say next.

"I live pretty close to that bus line that runs to your house. Suppose you come over to my place once a week and wash this car for me. I don't want to run it through a car wash. And sometimes my schedule gets pretty jammed up. I need somebody to take Watson to the park for a run. If your mom says it's okay, I could pay you, say, twenty dollars a week."

"That'd be cool. And you'll cover my bus fare?"

"Yeah."

"Who's Watson?"

"If you're taking him to the park, most likely he's my dog." Blake shook his head and started to laugh.

"If he's a pit bull, how come you didn't name him Spike?"

"Watson's a Gordon Setter. He's a cool dog. He's lanky, looks like he has a scraggly wet perm and just got out of the shower, and he can run all day long. You'll like him. He's plenty smart, way smarter than a pit bull."

"I'm up for it, D.B. You can count on me."

Blake stopped at the traffic light.

"You ask your mom if it's okay and have her call me. I'll give you a ride home. No more hitch-hiking. That's part of the deal."

"I'm good with that."

"Do you think your mom is home, yet?"

"Should be. Are you going to tell her I was hitching?" His eyes got bigger. He rubbed his hands together.

"Nervous?" Blake said.

"Yeah, so."

"I'm only gonna tell her if she asks me. But you've got to promise you won't anymore, if we make this deal."

"I'm square with that."

"Shake on it," Blake said. He reached over.

"This is one cool car, D.B. How fast does it go?"

"Faster than I'm allowed to drive it."

"How soon do I start?"

"You can start Monday. I'll be home by five-thirty. Just make sure your mom calls me before then."

"I'm going to need an advance." Freddie reached for his wallet and extended his hand.

"An advance?" Blake said.

"You don't want me to hitchhike. I don't have money for a bus ticket."

"All right, Mister Businessman." Blake pulled out a ten-spot. "I'll see you tomorrow."

"Thanks, D.B. You'll owe me another ten. I got to go help my mom with the dishes and stuff. Make sure you don't put any dents in this car before I come over." He closed the car door and took the steps to his apartment two at a time. Then waved.

Blake powered up the windows.

● ● ●

He called Julianna when he got home to let her know he was back. Blake told her about the trip and Freddie.

"I'd like to meet him, sometime. He sounds enterprising. Maybe you could invite him over for a cookout."

"I'd like that," Blake said. "He seems like a straight-arrow kid. I'm guessing his mom wants him to stay that way. Sounds like that's why they moved up here from L.A."

"Harper asked me if you could come to one of her soccer games, by the way," Julianna said. "She's warming up to you."

"Good. That makes me happy. I'm trying to connect more with her. It was special, seeing the three of you together over the weekend. You're a good mom, Julianna."

"I try. It's not always easy, especially when your ex is at odds with you."

• • •

Blake walked through the door at headquarters at 8:00 a.m., Monday. As soon as Captain Jameson saw him in the hallway, he approached Blake.

"Detective, glad to see you're still in one piece. We heard you were in an accident."

"I think it might have been on purpose."

"So you're back. When exactly are you going to be available for an assignment?"

"That's up to Chief Cooper." Blake had legwork to do, background checks, research, more interviews.

"So, what are you focusing on?"

"A dead guy named Jack Hamilton, here in Sierra Springs. I'm sure the chief can bring you up to date."

"You remember what I said?"

"About not messing it up? I've got no intention of doing that. I'm on track."

"Stay on track. Don't spend too much time philosophizing about good and evil. Leave that to the comic book heroes."

Blake kept quiet. Button it up, button it up, he kept telling himself. You can't tell your superior officer to fuck off. That just doesn't fly.

Blake ran forty-three plates through the NCIC's database. Except for a couple of old DUI's, and a misdemeanor for petty theft and public intoxication, everybody looked like a Boy Scout Troop Leader. The room was empty. Blake sat in front of the computer monitor and mumbled. "I still need a connection and I haven't got anything except a thousand extra miles on my car. I've got to shift gears." I need to learn more about Jack Hamilton, about the Winslows and Kate's company, and that woman who got fired the same day Hamilton did. I've got to talk to her.

He picked up the phone, leaned back in his chair, and dialed Strategic Business Reports. "Hi, Amanda. I'm trying to reach an old friend of mine. We went to college together at Chico State. I know she was working there several months ago until she changed jobs."

"Suzanne?"

"Yes. I wasn't sure whether she'd moved," Blake said. He gave Amanda his cell number, then told her his name was Charlie Parker.

"Suzanne hasn't gotten married or anything has she?"

"No, she's still Suzanne Leeds."

"Thanks, Amanda. We had a lot of fun together at Chico State. I'm looking forward to catching up with her."

Way too easy for me. I coulda' been a great con man like Steve McQueen was in *The Reivers*, and avoided a lot of this bullshit paperwork. Five minutes later, he was on the phone with Suzanne Leeds.

"I didn't know whether you'd heard about Jack Hamilton. I know the two of you worked together."

"I heard about the accident a few weeks ago."

"I was hoping we could talk in person."

"Sure," she said.

"This afternoon?"

"That works for me."

● ● ●

Suzanne Leeds was a good fifty pounds overweight, and strikingly attractive. Jack Hamilton hired her. They'd worked together for five years.

"So I'm confused about something," Blake said. "You were good at your job. From what I know, you should have been standing on solid ground, even in this economic climate. Yet you were fired. Did you know it was going to happen?"

"I didn't have a clue. I was completely in the dark. Kate Winslow asked to see me in her office. She sat there, all composed and pretty, told me that times were hard and she was going to have to let me go . . . that day, with no notice and no severance pay, after five years and stellar reviews. I was shocked."

"What did you do?"

"Besides sitting there stunned with my mouth open and fighting off tears? I gathered my personal things and called Jack on my cell phone."

"And how did he react?"

"I asked him if he was aware that Kate had planned to do this. He said he had no idea. He was dumbfounded by her actions. He said something like, let me see if I can make this right . . . talk some sense to her. I'll be there within the hour."

"And then what happened?"

"By the time he got there, I was already gone. From what I understand, the same thing happened to him in a much more dramatic fashion. Kate gathered all of his personal stuff and paraded through the office with a banker's box in front of all the employees. She put it on the sidewalk outside the door. Outrageous, wrong, all of it. Jack built the company. She tried to ruin him, and now he's dead."

Blake sensed that she needed a moment to herself. He looked away. "More coffee?"

"A latte if you don't mind."

The barista brought it to the table.

"So why do you think this really happened, the firing?"

She told Blake about the events leading up to that day. "Kate saw Jack talking with me about my daughters and he put his hand on my arm. Just a gesture. There was never anything between us. I think it made her jealous. She kept it to herself, but it was boiling below that moral, upright exterior of hers."

Blake leaned forward, still puzzled. "Any other reasons she fired you or Jack Hamilton?"

"No one in that office spoke more highly of Kate than Jack did. When Kate was gone and people bad-mouthed her, he defended her abilities. The plain truth was that he was the face and the substance of the company, not her. His sweat equity is what built Strategic Business Reports and made it a success. Every procedure, all the reporting formats, every system, the advertising and the marketing. It was all him. His name was on nearly all the contracts, Jack Hamilton pulled them in. Kate kept track of the money and did the books. She sat in and contributed to the staff meetings, but almost always in a secondary, supportive capacity."

"So why would she fire her most valuable asset?"

"I didn't know it then, but I think maybe she and Jack were involved at some point."

"When they were both still married?"

"There were rumors."

"And?"

"Jack got involved with somebody else, not anyone in the office. He was in love, and it ended all of a sudden. Jack told me about it . . . he was crushed, emotionally. He could hardly function for months. Kate seemed to comfort him. They were close. She wanted to re-kindle their romance, but Jack had no interest in doing that."

"Wow," Blake said. He shook his head and sat there, absorbing what Suzanne told him.

"Detective . . . in case you don't already know this, hell hath no fury like a woman scorned."

"That's what I've heard. Do you think her husband knew about their affair?"

"I don't know. He was hardly ever there. He didn't have anything to do with the business."

"Was there ever any kind of argument involving the three of them?"

"Not that I ever saw or heard." Suzanne arched her eyebrows and put her cup down on the table. "Wait a minute," she said. "I did see a rifle in the back of the office one day. When I asked Jack about it, he said it was Kate's. I guess she wanted it out of the house because of her husband's drunken rants and threats. It was gone the next day."

"How would Hamilton have known about the threats?"

"He never said. Kate probably told him."

"She says her decision to let you and Jack Hamilton go was all about the economy and having to make hard decisions. What do you say?"

"Two of my daughters still believe in Santa Claus and I'm fine with that, but this isn't make-believe. It was jealousy, pure and simple. She wanted to hurt him, but she didn't have to do what she did. The revenue picture had stabilized. Jack brought in nineteen new contracts the last month he was there."

"And you knew that?"

"We kept a new customer list posted on the wall in the break room."

"What about the 401-K and the pension funds?" Blake said.

"Kate hadn't funded them for nine months. Jack stepped in and got that straightened out when the employees complained. When the payroll checks bounced, he went down to the bank and withdrew money from his personal account to cover it."

"You thought highly of him."

"He was a great supervisor, kind and considerate, and Kate played him. She's like a black widow. She weaves a web, lures people in, and then turns on them and claims the high moral ground."

"Thank you, Suzanne. I appreciate you're being so candid." Blake shook his head and moved the notebook around he'd set on the table. "I guess you're the collateral damage, aren't you?"

"I guess so, but you know, I've got a better job, now. I'm supporting my family and working toward a teaching degree. I'm not cashing checks written by some hypocritical, unethical bitch. I feel sorry for the people who know what she's like and stayed for the money."

"I'd like to ask you a question, if I may, Detective."

"Go ahead."

"Do you think it was an accident? I can't imagine suicide."

"I'm going to find out." Blake handed her his card. "I want you to call me if you think of anything else. For right now, I'd appreciate it if you didn't discuss our meeting with anyone."

CHAPTER THIRTEEN

"Maybe I've been wrong, Chief." Blake sat in the brown leather armchair in front of Cooper's mahogany desk. "All this time I've been thinking Phillip Winslow was behind Jack Hamilton's death and what happened to me on the freeway."

Cooper looked up from the file on his desk. Blake filled the chief in on his meeting with Suzanne Leeds, the complaint Hamilton had filed against Kathryn Winslow with the Department of Labor, and Hamilton's lawsuit for wrongful termination.

"Kathryn Winslow told me she hadn't been to Big Sur for thirty years. She was lying. Hamilton had fallen in love with another woman. Then he embarrassed her by flirting with Suzanne Leeds. She was humiliated and angry when Hamilton wouldn't renew their relationship. If she couldn't have him, nobody would."

Blake got up and poured himself a glass of water, then turned toward the chief. "Maybe she wanted to show her brother she could be as strong and ruthless as he is."

"Kathryn Winslow's brother is a billionaire, Blake," Chief Cooper said, "Don't forget that. Not a millionaire, a billionaire. There probably isn't a whole lot that impresses him anymore."

"I know. James Kilmer. He's on the *Forbe's* 400 List. I haven't caught up with him, yet," Blake said. "All the men in my family were blue collar guys."

"Be careful when you do meet up with him. You don't get

that much money and power without stepping on people and grinding them up along the way. That's how some people play the game at her brother's level. Corporate greed. Isn't that what those Occupy Wall Street types are calling it?"

"I think she wanted to endear herself to her brother. Kilmer's in his mid-sixties. There's a big inheritance there. Wouldn't you want to be on his good side, Chief? Wouldn't you want your older brother to think you were the one who made the business work, not some guy that worked for you?" Blake paused. "And Kilmer couldn't have been happy with their affair. I hear he's a religious whack-job."

They both sat there, absorbed in thought.

"The theory makes sense," Cooper said. "She'd want to protect that inheritance. But it's all circumstantial. You haven't proved a damn thing." Cooper folded up some paperwork and pushed his chair back from the desk. "There's no reason to suppose Kilmer knows anything about this. He lives in Utah. She's in California. They may not even see each other or be that close."

"I need to connect Kathryn or her ex-husband with Big Sur. And I need to know where Kilmer fits in the puzzle. I'm going to talk to her again."

"That wasn't an accident you had on the freeway," Cooper said.

"Yeah, I know, but I don't like being threatened and pushed around. It bothers me."

"I don't want you to talk shop about this case with anybody else."

"I said something to Captain Jameson about looking into Hamilton's death earlier today when he asked me what I was doing. No details though, and nothing about Hamilton's car or mine."

"I'll talk with him," Cooper said. "That doesn't worry me. But I don't want to bring more people into this."

"Have there been any new developments relating to Sheriff Kowalski's report?" Blake asked.

"Nothing at all. Until we know something more, I'm leaving it alone. I hope what we're both thinking is wrong."

• • •

Blake walked back to his desk to call Allison. There was something between them now, maybe not a bond, but the beginnings of one. He wanted to know what her father, Phillip, had said when she talked to him before the truck ran him off the road.

"He said he didn't do it."

"And did you ask your mother about Hamilton?"

"She said Jack was dead. She sounded sad about it. I don't know how much of that was real and how much was for show. It's hard to tell with her," Allison said. "What did you find out?"

Blake had hoped for something more. There was a hint of disappointment in his voice. "How long do you think it's been since either one of your parents spent time around Monterey or Big Sur?"

"Most of the time I never knew where my parents went when they left the house. I couldn't stand being around either one of them. My mother had some customers in Nevada, and her brother lives in Utah. I know my father worked did some work in San Francisco and Santa Barbara, and he had friends someplace near L.A. He was gone a lot, thank God."

Allison sounded stone cold sober to Blake. "Do you think either one of them is capable of doing something violent?"

"They both are. It's more likely to come from my father, but my mother has changed. I've seen her slam doors and fly into rages when my father pisses her off. They're crazy dysfunctional, now."

"Do you remember any specific incidents?"

"I know my mother got bitchy and hella' mad at Jack once. They went to one of those Christmas parties for work. I heard part of their phone conversation when I was in her office one day and picked up the wrong line.

"What happened?"

"They were fighting about how crazy she was driving. He was yelling about her doing ninety, weaving in and out of traffic, tail-gating and screaming irrationally about some woman who was going to be at the party. She was jealous I guess. My mother used to be gutless. She watched my father molest me and pretended she didn't see what happened. I have this sick feeling he might try to do the same thing to my sisters. I don't know what my mother would do now."

Blake scribbled a note on the pad on his desk. "Have you talked to your father since that day I was sitting in his office?"

"No. I hate that sonofabitch."

"Do you think he knows where you live?"

"He has ways of finding out things. Sometimes I wonder if he has somebody following me around, spying on me. It's creepy. I don't want him anywhere near me."

"He's not going to hear anything from me," Blake said. "Just don't say anything about us talking. Somebody tried to run me off the road when I left your apartment a few weeks ago."

"For real?"

"I spent a couple of days in the hospital. My car was totaled."

"Holy shit. Are you okay?"

"Yeah, everything's intact, fortunately. So tell me how you're doing."

"I'm still screwing these losers here in Stockton. Thinking more about all this stuff, makes it harder to take. At least I'm drinking less, so I guess that's good."

"Try thinking of normal as a natural high." Blake clicked off, got up from his desk, and took a walk outside to clear his head and mull over what Allison had said. Her father was an arrogant, selfish control freak, a pedophile. And her mother? Blake shook his head. He'd grown up watching *Leave It To Beaver* and *Mayberry RFD* re-runs. What the hell had the Winslow kids been watching?"

He walked back inside and sat down at his desk in the

Detective's Room, oblivious to everyone around him. His forehead rested on his fingers above the keyboard, his elbows on the desk. Blake remained as still as a statue. He had to have looked more like some Indian guru's disciple entranced in meditation than a police detective. But he didn't care. He'd have walked into the woods if he could have. A long twenty minutes must have passed before Blake got up from the chair without warning. "I need to go back to Hamilton's apartment," he said.

Blake grabbed his bag and headed back to where he'd parked the Audi, under one of those big Mission Oaks the planning commission made sure the developers couldn't cut down when they built the new headquarters. He drove straight to Hamilton's place and got the keys from the on-site manager. Then snapped on a pair of latex gloves when he walked in the door and took a second look at Hamilton's bedroom. Nothing new struck him. Blake moved to the living room, sat on the couch, and stared at every article and piece of furniture as if he were gauging an invisible flow of energy. He looked at his watch — 2:15. His own energy level had started to drag. He walked over to the kitchen, opened the refrigerator, and saw the coffee. Gourmet stuff, Ethiopia Yirgacheffe. He'd had it before — a little acidic for his taste, but good. Blake stuck his nose in the bag and inhaled. He reached for the glass carafe and measured two cups of water. Then lifted the filter basket's lid, and gasped. A small, black flash drive was sitting inside like a frog waiting for a fly. Blake picked it up and held it in the palm of his hand, as if it were a twenty dollar gold piece. He started to make the coffee again before he thought the better of it. Hamilton after all, was dead.

CHAPTER FOURTEEN

The late afternoon light streamed through the windows and across Blake's dining room table. He sat up straight, poured himself a glass of water, and put Hamilton's flash drive into his laptop's USB port, opening one file and then another. What he read mirrored what Suzanne Leeds had told him. And there was more — the complaint to the Department of Labor, Hamilton's prep notes for his case against Kathryn, evidence of her diverting money from the employee's 401-k pension fund for her personal use, the personal journal Hamilton had deliberately mislabeled to hide it's contents.

Hamilton wrote about his three-year romantic involvement with Kathryn. How she'd decided to end their affair, and the straight and narrow, hands-off work arrangement that followed. How Kathryn labeled him an employee, instead of a partner, and fired him. She'd locked him out, refused to give him access to all of his personal papers and the independent, business consulting files he'd stored in the office, withheld payment of his salary and commissions. Blake read Hamilton's journal entry that quoted Kathryn.

"This is a conservative, predominantly Republican county. I'm a woman. That's a distinct advantage once we get to court and I've got a lot more money than you do. If you don't like it, you can litigate."

Damn, that's cold, Blake thought.

His friend, Rob Johnson, told him Hamilton's legal fees against her on the civil case would have been upwards of a quarter-million dollars with no more than a fifty-fifty chance of winning. Hamilton had been in love with Kathryn. She was his closest friend. She'd betrayed his trust, and decided to inflict as much hurt on him as she could. Hamilton's retirement nest egg went up in smoke. His head was slammed against the rocks on the coast.

"She's as sly as a fox," Suzanne Leeds had told him. "Like a black widow spider that turns on you when the moment is right. Kate Winslow is a lot more dangerous than you would suppose, Detective."

CHAPTER FIFTEEN

Blake picked up the phone to call Kathryn.

"Dylan Blake, I didn't expect to hear from you today. How have you been?"

"Recovering."

"Recovering? Recovering from what, may I ask?"

"My investigation of Jack Hamilton, your business partner."

"My former employee you mean."

"I think he was both. It worked out best that way, don't you think? No ex-wives or ex-husbands in the picture with claims to a share of the business." Blake paused.

"Yes, well . . . " she took a moment to compose herself. "That was a rather abrupt opening to our conversation. You sound a little irritated, detective."

"Sometimes police work has that effect on me. We need to talk. What's your schedule look like for tomorrow?"

"Not possible. I've got a meeting with my CPA in the morning about our quarterly tax report, and my computer tech is coming in for the afternoon."

"You can't juggle anything during the day?"

"I'm afraid not."

"For dinner then?" Blake said.

"There's a little restaurant called Tres Bien in Sierra Springs near the lake. You'll like it," Kathryn said. "I'll see you at seven."

● ● ●

Kathryn was waiting at a table in the corner when Blake walked in to Tres Bien the next day. She was wearing a silk top that draped across her shoulders and down the front to a V. The waiter brought a second menu after Blake sat down. Kathryn Winslow stood for a moment to welcome him and extend her hand.

"I'm sorry I had such a full schedule. I got the impression you were anxious to meet as soon as possible. You look dashing tonight."

"Thank you for the compliment."

She ordered galette au saumon fume, a smoked salmon crepe with cream, and Vichyssoise served hot.

Blake chose the Tilapia Meuniere and champagne custard.

"You're very skilled at what you do, aren't you, Detective?" She picked up her wine glass and looked at him.

It was nothing like the look Blake typically got from a suspect or a witness. Kathryn was an attractive woman and she knew it. Blake was noticing it more than he had before. "I'd like to think so," he said.

"There's a lot that a mature woman could teach you."

"I'm not sure I know what you mean." Kathryn was manipulating him. Blake wanted to see how far she'd go.

"I don't think you're that naïve, Detective. When a woman goes beyond forty-five, she tends to understand men better, their needs, what satisfies them. We have fewer inhibitions." She raised her wine glass, looked up at him, and wet her lips. "For example, I could give you whatever you wanted. We both know there are things you want." She pulled her chair closer to the table, reached forward, put her hand on his leg and moved it upward.

Blake cleared his throat and swallowed. "I didn't come here tonight to take you to bed. That's not going to happen, Kathryn. I'm involved." Blake moved her hand away, but not before she reached over, pushed her fingers together around him, and felt him warming to her touch.

"You can't blame a girl for trying. You're a handsome man. I'm sure you'll let me know if you change your mind." She looked at him like a Hollywood starlet who'd do anything for the part.

"That's not something you should count on. It's not how I work." He looked away from the V that revealed her breasts.

"I told you the truth when we met several weeks ago," she said.

"About some things, yes, but you didn't tell me you'd been to Monterey and Big Sur. That's an important detail, given what happened to Jack Hamilton and where it happened."

"I didn't want to cloud the waters."

"And you didn't say anything about the two of you being romantically involved."

"That was a long time ago." She paused, then looked at Blake. "How did you know?"

"You said it yourself. I'm good at what I do. It was in the complaint your partner filed with the Department of Labor. Your daughter, Allison, suspected it as well."

"That ungrateful little bitch. I'm out of her business. She should stay out of mine. Phillip and I provided for her. We got her into Stanford. We footed the bill. She's the one who decided to drop out."

"And the relationship she had with her father?" Blake's eyes focused on hers.

"What relationship?"

"The improper one."

Her face turned red.

He'd hit a sensitive spot.

"I don't know what Allison imagined. I didn't see anything. You can't think I wouldn't have stopped Phillip had I known."

"I'm not judging you," Blake said. In reality, he found it impossible not to, given his personal experience and what Allison had told him. Why didn't she stop him? Why not?, Blake kept thinking.

"Phillip is a pig. The drinking, the other women, the endless business trips, probably pornography, too. Who knows what the hell he was looking at on that computer of his. He wasn't always that way. He changed."

"It happens," Blake said.

"So maybe I did see something once. I told myself I was mistaken. I'm not perfect."

"Why didn't you talk with Allison? You could have done something more."

Katherine took a tissue from her purse and dabbed at her eyes.

Blake wasn't sure how much he was seeing was for real, and how much was for show. It was hard for him not to appear judgmental. Kathryn's ex-husband had damaged Allison like Blake's brother had been damaged, but it was worse, because Winslow was family. She could have stopped him.

"Phillip hasn't had one ounce of unsupervised visitation under the terms of our divorce. He hasn't been alone with those girls for the last two years. I've juggled my schedule to make sure of that. I've confided with the proper authorities in my church, had therapy and counseling. I've made a new life for myself and the two youngest girls, away from him."

"Good," Blake said.

"I'm not dependent on him, anymore. But when I see something I want, I go after it."

"So you went after Jack Hamilton? You were still married then."

"That was different. We both felt abandoned and lost when we met. After a while, the attraction became strong enough to pull a metal chair across the floor like a magnet. Gradually, my inhibitions fell away and, to be perfectly frank, I wanted to have sex with him every time I saw him."

The way she said it, seemed surprisingly matter of fact to Blake, like she was talking about the weather or putting together a piece of furniture from IKEA.

"So you spent time together in Big Sur, where I'm guessing you didn't have to be so discreet," Blake said.

"We went away for the weekend a few times. No one knew us there. I felt free, for the first time in years . . . liberated."

"You were in love."

"It was difficult for both of us to find time together and go back to what we had at home."

"Who broke it off?"

"I was preaching to my daughters about the sanctity of wedding vows and abstinence, at the same time I was having sex outside of marriage. I was torn with guilt so I finally ended it."

Blake filled her wine glass. "And then you continued working together. That must have been difficult."

"I focused on the church and tried to heal my relationship with the girls."

"You don't seem to have gotten very far with Allison."

"She's on her own." Kathryn paused. "I lost the only man I ever really loved."

"As soon as I walked in here, you came on to me." Blake waited, before continuing. "You put your hand on me and pressed."

"And you didn't mind, did you?"

"That's not the point . . . how do you square that with what you just told me?"

"Let me spell it out for you, Detective. Allison is gone. I'm not married anymore. The man I loved is dead and the girls are older. I'm not throwing my lifestyle in their face, parading around the house naked. I'm more philosophical about fucking men, now."

"What's that supposed to mean?"

"I know what I need and I don't expect a long-term commitment to come with it. I'm one of those women who needs a man in her life."

"So you're an easy lay. That's what you're saying?"

"I know what I want."

Blake felt himself blush, felt tempted. Feminism, breaking the glass ceiling, women and men simply being friends. He was fine with all that. He didn't see as how the repression his parents and some conservatives seemed to embrace had ever done much good. Kathryn Winslow had certainly gotten past it.

"You could come over to my place. You could come in to me. No one would ever know."

Blake rubbed his hand across his face. "It's not going to happen."

Kathryn paid the check. Blake stood and held her chair. She turned toward him, brushed her breast against his arm, and looked at him as if she was on the edge of the bed and he was in the doorway.

Blake thanked her for dinner and walked her out to her car.

"You never told me, Detective, what happened in Big Sur, whether it was an accident or not." She pulled her keys out of her purse and clicked the door locks open.

"We still don't know, not with absolute certainty. Maybe you were right to be suspicious." Blake paused for a moment. "What about Hamilton's ex-wife?" He opened her car door.

"Not a chance. She didn't have a clue we were involved and she's not the type. They hadn't had sex for years."

"Any enemies . . . people who'd benefit with him not around?"

"Are you saying it wasn't an accident, Detective?" She suddenly seemed agitated. She gripped the steering wheel like a man would around a dangerous curve. Then began to tap the wheel with her right hand.

"No, I'm not saying that. I'm just asking detective-type questions. It's force of habit more than anything else."

"But you'll let me know? And you'll let me know if you change your mind?" She sat behind the wheel, her skirt hiked up high on her thighs.

"I thought we already put that idea to bed."

"I was hoping you would take me to bed, Detective. Now all I get to do is say, good night."

"Thank you for dinner, Kate. Drive safely."

She backed up her Jaguar and drove down the road toward her home.

Blake headed back toward his place. He couldn't help talking to himself once the windows were rolled up. "Julianna asks me why I don't squeeze the air out of the cereal bags before I close them so when I spill granola all over the floor, it'll be fresher. Now I've got Kate Winslow inviting me to jump in her pants." He laughed at the thought of simultaneously being an idiot with his elbows on the counter and an irresistibly, attractive man.

Blake started thinking about undressing Kate. She didn't wear a bra. He thought about how the silk shirt she'd worn gathered close to her skin and outlined her nipples. He fantasized about her. He felt guilty, but he couldn't stop thinking about Kate.

CHAPTER SIXTEEN

Watson was waiting with one of those raggedy pull toys in his mouth, when Blake got home from work the next day. He changed clothes, grabbed the leash hanging in the hallway closet, and headed toward the park. Blake looked back at Watson as they started down the block. His mind bounced back and forth, fixated on an image of Kate Winslow naked one minute, and Julianna the next, smiling, as she undressed and walked toward his bed. He caught a glimpse of somebody sitting in a car on the opposite side of the street, about fifty feet up from where he lived, but the picture didn't register in his mind.

The fact that whoever tried to run him off the road might know where he lived should have made him more cautious, but it didn't. Blake left his gun in the bread box on top of the refrigerator. His friend, Rob, kept telling him he was too trusting in his personal life. "I'm surprised," Rob said, "you're a cop. You should be more suspicious."

Blake however, was dating women, and now he was involved with Julianna. He thought spontaneous was more appealing than suspicious. He grew up in a small town where people were friendly. And he was stubborn. He didn't want to change.

Blake stopped to tie his shoe lace. That's when he noticed — the man in the car was holding the newspaper upside down. "Not again. Tell me I'm wrong," he mumbled, before jogging to the end of the block and turning the corner. He tied

Watson's leash to the chair in front of the workbench in a friend's garage on the next street over. He saw the wasp spray on the shelf and left a note.

"Have them stop at the end of the block," Blake told the desk sergeant on the phone. "I'm going to walk back up the street toward where he's parked. You'll see him on the left in a gray sedan."

The car's engine started as Blake drew closer. He stepped off the sidewalk into the street, flashed his shield, and hand signaled the driver to lower his window. The guy behind the wheel had one of those faces that got lost in the crowd, and an expression that fell somewhere between surprised and annoyed. He lowered the window.

Blake saw the butt of the gun handle below the newspaper on the passenger's seat. He raised his arm and blasted the driver in the face with a constant stream of wasp spray, as he rushed toward him. The guy began coughing uncontrollably as he bent forward, eyes closed, skin burning, now swearing. Blake reached in and grabbed his arm.

The patrol car accelerated and stopped a foot short of the car's bumper.

"You're under arrest," Blake said.

"For what?"

"The gun, dumb shit."

Both patrolmen scrambled out of the cruiser with their weapons drawn and aimed at the driver who struggled to open his eyes.

"I have a permit to carry that."

They patted him down, cuffed him, and read him his rights. Then pushed him into the back seat behind the cage. His eyes were watering down both sides of his face.

"Give me fifteen minutes and I'll be down at the station to handle the paperwork. Don't let him make any phone calls until I get there."

Blake turned and jogged back to get Watson.

• • •

William Monroe was the name on his driver's license. Blake inventoried the contents of his wallet as he sat across the desk from him in the interrogation room. Stuffed in with bills and credit cards, was a small piece of paper with a phone number written on it. Blake pulled it out, dangled it in front of Monroe, and called the number as he sat across from him, using Monroe's cell with the speaker phone set on high. It rang four times before the greeting played for Phillip Winslow's office. Blake clicked off.

"I should have asked if you wanted to leave a message." Blake pushed the cell phone back across the table to Monroe.

"I'm not saying anything." Monroe folded his hands across his chest, his eyes still red and watering. "I want a lawyer. You shot me in the face with wasp spray. That's assault." Monroe leaned back on the gray metal chair with a smug, indignant look on his face.

"You were following me. You reached for the gun. Observable cause, resisting arrest, assaulting a police officer. That's serious. You sure you don't want to make a statement?"

"I want an attorney."

"You can go ahead and make that call, now." Blake stared. "Just remember, I know where you live. The playing field has been leveled. By the way, if the guy who paid you has an employee who drives an eighteen wheeler, tell him I said not to renew his license. I'm gonna find him and put him away."

Blake stopped at the front desk to see if Pierce was on duty. "I have a request, Sergeant."

"What can I help you with?"

"See if you can lose this guy for a while. Send him someplace uncomfortable for the rest of the night, and ask Chief Cooper to give me a call on my cell first thing tomorrow morning. I don't want to bother him tonight."

"I believe we can make those arrangements. We're busy and everybody knows the system's overloaded."

"Thank you, Sergeant Pierce."

Blake called Cooper the next morning from home. "The Chief has an emergency dental appointment," Susan said. "He should be in by ten. He's anxious to see you. Wanted me to ask if there was anything I could do for you in the interim."

"Thank you, Susan. I'm fine. I'll be in at ten."

● ● ●

Blake grabbed a plain white shirt box and some gift wrap from the shelf in his bedroom closet. He sorted through a cardboard container until he found the t-shirt he'd bought at the county fair, personalized with the motto, "I Know What You Did," that suddenly seemed so appropriate.

He leafed through his address book, until he came to "M" for Moriano. Tony, from The Villas. Blake had met him some time back in connection with an earlier case involving elder abuse and a sociopath who'd wound up dead.

Tony grew up in New York. He had a Miami Beach tan and was somewhere north of sixty, impossible to tell because of the glint in his eye and the spring in his step. He had an angular Italian immigrant face, always with a day or two of white stubble. He knew the ropes, and he and Blake had taken a liking to each other.

Tony seemed a lot like the salt of the earth working men Blake had grown up with, men who talked about FDR and unions, crooked politicians and corporations that didn't necessarily care so much about clean consciences or ordinary people. They weren't the compromising type who traded their principles for money.

"How've you been?" Blake said.

"I'm good as gold. No more Drappis' bullshit around The Villas. I'm walkin' every day. The ladies are still smilin' at me. Life is good."

"How's your son, Tony Jr., with the big panda eyes?"

"He's gettin' less shy. In his forties, for Christ's sake. He's got his self a girl. A peach." A grin crossed his face.

"And your dad, how old is he now?" Blake said.

"Eighty-seven," Tony said. "I spend Sundays with him, take him to Mass, make a good marinara and some gravy."

" I need a favor, Tony. You got a pen?"

"Hang on." Blake heard him set the phone down.

"Shoot."

"I got a package I'd like you to deliver for me to an office building at 5210 Willhaven. It's for a guy named Phillip Winslow. He's about fifty with a puffy white face and he drives a white Lexus. You should see it in the parking lot where he works."

"And the package?"

"A t-shirt."

"A t-shirt. What the hell's that? I thought it was goin' to be something excitin' like money or naked pictures."

"Winslow's going to find it plenty exciting. There's a message printed on the shirt. The guy's more dangerous than he looks."

"I'm a little dangerous, too, Detective. I did plenty of numbers and money drops in New York 'fore I retired."

"Make sure he's there before you deliver it, preferably when his secretary, Madeline Armstrong, is out to lunch. She looks like the redhead who runs the office in *Mad Men*."

"With the forty double D's?"

"You noticed," Blake said.

"Oh, yeah. I'm not that old."

"If Winslow asks you who it's from, and I'm hoping he does, just tell him a guy, who looked pissed off, gave you fifty bucks to put it in his hands, and tell him he shouldn't play games with other people's lives. Put on your gangster face. Remember, we don't know each other."

"Capish. This guy bothers you or your girlfriend, let me

know. I still know people." Tony paused. "So, do I get some jelly donuts besides the fifty?"

"If that's what you need, I'll get 'em for you. Call me tonight. Let me know how it went."

• • •

Tony Jr. borrowed his girlfriend's car. His father took the package that Blake dropped off at their house, and the two of them drove to 5210 Willhaven a little before noon. He called Winslow's office. A female voice answered and Tony clicked off. A few minutes later he saw a woman walking out of the building's lobby who fit Blake's description. "Definitely, forty double D's." He looked at his son and grinned.

Tony waited another five minutes and called again.

A man answered.

"Sorry, wrong number." Tony got out of the car and walked to the suite with Winslow's name on the unlocked door. The outer office stood empty. The white guy, with the puffy face Blake'd described, came into the reception area to greet him.

"You Phillip Winslow? I gotta package for ya." Tony had the usual two or three day stubble on his face and was wearing his navy-colored pea cap.

"What's this?" Winslow said as he took the package.

"How should I know? I ain't got x-ray vision."

"Who's it from? Who gave it to you?"

"Some guy, big, and mean lookin'."

"What kind of car was he driving?"

"I don't remember," Tony said.

"I've got twenty dollars more if you do, old man."

"A Hummer."

Winslow reached for his wallet.

Tony took the twenty.

"Was he white, black, Hispanic, Asian?"

Tony moved his mouth as if he was going to answer, glanced down at Winslow's wallet and then up at him."

Winslow pulled out another twenty.

"Black."

"Did he have a beard or was he clean-shaven?" Phillip Winslow spoke without hesitating.

"I wasn't gonna kiss him. I don't know. A shaved head. He said ya should stop what you were doin'." Tony stuffed the twenties in his shirt pocket.

Winslow turned away.

"Mister."

Winslow pivoted back toward him.

"He looked like a guy you don't want to mess with."

Tony walked toward the car with a spring in his step. No one followed him. He opened the door and sat next to his son, pulled out the two extra twenties, winked, and said, "Drive."

CHAPTER SEVENTEEN

Blake hit Chief Cooper's office five minutes early and smiled at Susan, his executive assistant. "Thank you for calling me earlier this morning. I appreciate it."

"Chief Cooper should be walking in any minute now. Make yourself comfortable." Blake sat down, having already decided that Tony's errand wouldn't make its way into the conversation he was about to have.

Cooper came through the door a few minutes later. He shook Blake's hand. "You want some coffee? Help yourself. It's fresh."

Blake reached for the thermos on the table near the window and filled his cup. The leaves had begun changing colors with the passage of autumn in the foothills.

"So you had a busy night. Had your night time visitor booked, I understand." Cooper paused. "Hand me a glass of that water over there if you would. Christ, I'm always drinking water . . . eight glasses a day, my wife keeps telling me. Pretty soon, I'll need a damn Porta-Potty in here."

Cooper belted down the water like it was bourbon.

"So what do you figure this guy was doing camped outside your apartment?"

"Keeping an eye on me. He had a handgun. I don't think he was planning to stop over and borrow a cup of sugar. I don't like it. Not after everything else that's happened."

"I hear you maced him."

"No, that was wasp spray. I saw one buzzing around and

I didn't want him to get stung before I had a chance to talk to him."

"I guess Jameson thinks you're some kind of an aloof, intellectual Ivy League lawyer. Jameson's got a pretty narrow focus. I don't see that at all. You seem pretty hard-ass when you're working." Cooper reached for another glass of water.

"Yeah, well, I'm getting pissed. But I do have a polite side. I read books and write poetry, too."

"So tell me, how long do you think this Monroe guy's been following you?"

"I'm not sure. I didn't notice him before last night, which means he's pretty good."

"You recall my warning you about being careful?" Cooper said. "You need to watch your rearview mirror."

"I'm getting an alarm system for my apartment."

"It can't hurt. What else happened yesterday before you ran into this guy?"

"I had dinner with Kathryn Winslow the night before. When I got home last night, I took my dog for a walk and noticed the guy sitting in his car up the street."

"And you found a reason to mace him? I don't want us getting sued."

"I'm not sure what he had in mind, but he had a gun and he wasn't inviting me to the prom."

"Did you complete all the paperwork?" Cooper said.

"I did after we booked him."

"That should make Jameson happy." Cooper squeezed the stress ball on his desk. "So what did you and Kathryn Winslow talk about?"

"She wanted an update on our investigation into Hamilton's death. I left her in the dark about what we'd discovered so far."

"Good."

"I also let her know that I was aware of her romantic relationship with Hamilton."

"And she acknowledged it?"

"She did."

"Do you think she killed him?" Cooper said.

Blake raised his eyebrows and exhaled. "She's complicated, but the fact is, even though she broke off their relationship and tried to ruin Hamilton, he was the love of her life. I can't see her killing him."

Cooper leaned back in his chair and kept squeezing the hand strengthener he kept in his desk. "So you're back to her ex, Phillip Winslow, the yet-to-be-convicted stock swindler. Interesting. And this guy, the one you booked last night . . . Monroe. He was working for Phillip Winslow?"

"He had Winslow's phone number in his wallet."

"Did he give us a statement?"

"He lawyered up right off the bat. He knows how to play the game."

"Did you threaten him?"

"Unfortunately, Chief, I'm not allowed to do that. It's one of those police rules."

"But he knows you're angry?"

"I didn't keep it a secret, not with the wasp spray."

"Good." Cooper opened the folder on his desk. "Monroe's from Salinas, not too far from Big Sur. He's got several priors for assault, a break-in, but no convictions. He's already out by the way. Posted bail this morning when they found him. I guess he got lost in the system for a while." Cooper looked at Blake and grinned. "I'm sure you know, the charges probably won't stick."

"Didn't figure they would. I just wanted to make a good first impression."

"I haven't gotten any calls yet complaining about you," Cooper said. "So you're pushing back?"

"It's occurred to me."

"Be careful with that."

"Believe me, Chief. I don't want anyone reading my name on some report that says injured or deceased. And God forbid the case would go to Jameson."

"Let me know if you need a search warrant or surveillance in place. Don't try and be some Lone Ranger hero." Cooper paused and scratched his head. "Do you even know who the Lone Ranger is, Blake?"

"I've seen the re-runs on cable. I think there's gonna be a movie."

"Think of me as Tonto. I want to make sure your back is covered," Cooper said.

Blake looked at him, pretending to be puzzled. "Aren't you supposed to be calling me, Kemo Sabe?"

Cooper looked up and smiled. "Get the hell out of here. Just be careful."

Cooper's comment didn't move Blake to re-examine his habits. Not taking his gun with him to the park was about leaving work at work and not being paranoid, Blake reasoned. Careful was about looking both ways when you crossed the street. It meant keeping an iron grip on the cables and three points of contact when he hiked up Half Dome in Yosemite. It came into play when he watched his footing on the way down the granite dome and grappled with his fear of heights as he faced an endless blue sky and what would have been a fatal fall. Careful was when he asked Tony Moriano to deliver the package to Winslow instead of doing it himself. Careful and sensible weren't always synonymous, not in his mind, anyway.

● ● ●

Tony called Blake that afternoon. "We got it done. We waited for the woman to leave for lunch. By the way, you're right . . . forty double D's."

"So I assume Winslow asked where you got the package."

"Yeah. Tried to bribe me, as a matter of fact."

"What happened?"

"I turned your fifty into ninety, same way Morgan Stanley tells ya they're goin' to. Guess what? You're a big, mean black guy with a shaved head, ya drive a Hummer, an' ya shouldn't be messed with."

"He bought it?"

"Hey, Blake, when I sell somethin', puffy white guys like Winslow are gonna buy it."

"How did you get to be so good at stuff like this?"

"Ya don't wanna' know. Let's say it's practice. Ya need more help, call me. Don't forget the jelly donuts. Me and Tony Junior, we both have a sweet tooth."

"How's everybody else doing over there at The Villas?"

"People I see, walk around smilin' now that that sociopath's dead. Nobody misses a maniac."

"I'll call you before I stop by." Tony reminded him of his dad and his grandfather. The men in Blake's family didn't make promises they didn't keep, no matter the consequences. Tony was like that, too.

Blake hung up the phone. Then began to wonder what kind of promises Sheriff Kowalski had made and to whom. Kowalski and Cooper had gone to the Academy together. They'd known one another a long time, but Cooper made a point of telling Blake they were acquaintances, not friends. Blake wondered about the distinction. Kowalski had spent most of his life working in law enforcement. His pension and reputation were on the line. He deserved the benefit of the doubt. And besides, Kowalski was the chief's call, not his.

● ● ●

Kathryn's daughter, Allison, phoned him again at home. He got the impression she was closer to taking a step away from Stockton and her pimp. Blake decided to talk with Julianna that night about Allison's problems.

"You reached out to her in a respectable way and let her know you were willing to help. That she had a choice," Julianna said. "I'm proud of you, Dylan."

He heard the TV in the background. "I wanted to do more."

"There are no magic words. If she wants to talk to another woman, I'll talk with her. I'm not a professional counselor, but they're safe houses and shelters out there where she can stay. There's a network of women who'll help her. She's probably not as tough as she pretends to be. She hasn't been prostituting that long, you said."

"What do I know about twenty-year-old women?" Blake said. "I thought I should ask you."

"You've dated some in your life, haven't you? I hope not recently."

"That's different."

"But it's relevant," Julianna said. "Help her keep the choice in focus. You're good at that."

Blake heard one of the girls in the background.

"Hold on a minute, I've got to help Becky find her homework assignment for tomorrow." Blake heard a door open and close. He assumed Becky had probably left her schoolwork in the car.

"So when am I going to see you? I need a policeman to protect me."

"How about Friday night?"

"The girls are with their dad this weekend. That means I'll be with you."

"Good. Rob and Samantha want to go with us to the Demolition Derby later this month," Blake said.

"And Samantha said yes to that?" Julianna sounded surprised.

"I think she will."

"Sounds like tom-girl fun to me."

"I'll talk to Rob and one of us will pick up the tickets."

"I always feel peaceful when I'm around you, Dylan. I like that you tell me how you feel without filtering it. That's everything to me. It's not just those blue eyes of yours and the shaggy brown hair you comb with your fingers. You know that, don't you?"

"I know it's sweet of you to say so. Tell the girls I said hi and let Harper know I'm going to her next soccer game. I love you, Julianna. See you Friday night."

• • •

Blake walked past his hallway mirror, stopped and stared. He noticed the gray hair by his temples. He hadn't given much thought to getting older. He was changing. It's good, he told himself, except for the hair in my ears. I can't stand this fucking hair growing in my ears.

He'd become more open with his feelings since he met Julianna. She kept showing him a picture of family life he thought had passed him by. He'd begun to want more.

She was guarded when they first started dating. Blake expected that. Julianna, an attractive woman, didn't expect to be divorced twice by the time she was thirty-four. She was confident enough to tell him what she needed, but the boundaries she drew weren't always visible to Blake and he'd inadvertently crossed them a few times. She hit back hard when he did, and it hurt. Women expect you to be able to read their minds. That wasn't always easy with Julianna.

She'd grown up surrounded by men who refused to surrender their youth. Her father was a Vermont downhill ski champion in the 1950s who strayed, and eventually remarried. Her two brothers were extreme sport athletes who appeared in Warren Miller's ski movies. One of them took a canoe down a snow covered mountain in a Chevy commercial, and the other drove a three-wheel ATV straight up the wooden steps in the hillside above the pond when Blake and Julianna were skinny-dipping.

Blake wasn't a womanizer like the three other men in her family. Julianna never would have put up with that, and it wasn't Blake's inclination, anyway. He was more old-fashioned. But he was a man, and she'd developed a distrust of men before they met. Blake had already realized he was more attracted to women like Julianna who listened to National Public Radio and had real opinions, rather than women in their twenties satisfied with *TMZ* and simple-minded sound bites on *Fox* and the network news. A quick wit and a great sense of humor had long since dethroned simple anatomy for Blake. Julianna had both, and that made for a double-edged sword. She made him want to be better than he was. Blake recognized he hadn't felt that way for a very long time.

• • •

Blake called Cooper the next morning. "I'd like to spend some time doing research here at my place. I need to follow the leads I'm extracting from Hamilton's flash drive and Phillip Winslow's business contacts. I wanted to make sure you're okay with me not being around."

"Do what you need to do, Detective. I don't care whether you do it at home or here, or while you're sitting in a tree house carving bears out of wood. How are you coming with your Big Sur connection?"

"Nothing, so far. I need to find something more before I go swim in the ocean again."

"If you do that, make sure it's on purpose, and let me know before you leave."

Blake sat down at his desk with Watson at his feet. "There's got to be more here," he said aloud. "Why did Jack Hamilton leave town, Watson? Why did he have a gun in his glove box?" He looked at the report from Kowalski's office.

The gun was purchased at the Sierra Springs Gun Shop within the last month and registered in Hamilton's name. There was no indication he'd ever owned a gun before, or even taken target practice. Hamilton claimed his apartment had been burglarized a week before he left town, but there were no signs of forced entry and, according to the police report, he told the investigating officer that Kathryn Winslow had a key. The file with Kathryn's name on it was empty when Blake searched Hamilton's apartment.

CHAPTER EIGHTEEN

Kathryn disputed Hamilton's ownership interest in the business. It hadn't been finalized in writing but the partnership agreement Hamilton referred to in his labor complaint and in the civil lawsuit, the one Kathryn had signed, was missing. It seemed probable that she'd taken the documents after Hamilton rejected her advances and brought suit against her.

His journal made their relationship clear. Hamilton was in love with her. He didn't see it coming when he was locked out, and he probably never expected Kathryn would break into his apartment. But why the gun? Hamilton was worried. Phillip Winslow was jealous and a control freak to boot. His divorce wouldn't have put an end to that.

Blake jumped into his car and drove to Hamilton's apartment with the password and contact list printed out and placed inside the manila folder on his passenger seat. He got Hamilton's key from the apartment manager, walked in, and logged on to his desktop. Blake started going through Hamilton's email. This time, he looked in the trash box where he found two threatening messages.

> Don't think I don't know you're sleeping with her. What's mine is mine. Don't get in the way unless you want to get hurt.

The second one said:

You'll pay. You fucked with her. Now I'm going to fuck with you.

"That sounds like gun-time to me," Blake said. "That's a good reason to leave town."

He made a mental note to talk with Cooper about sending over a computer forensics expert to track the email sender's ISP address. He supposed it would go back to Winslow.

• • •

On Monday, Blake found out the email came from a computer in one of the city's public library branches. The user wasn't identified, but Phillip Winslow had used his library card the day the emails were sent. Smart people who aren't practiced at crime make stupid mistakes. Blake learned that lesson years ago when he read about Watergate.

Blake told Rob about his discovery when he met him for lunch in midtown the next day. "You realize of course, we can't have these conversations, not about real people," Rob said.

"They're all fictional," Blake said.

"And I'll swear to never having heard them. Now, go on."

"Look at Winslow," Blake said. "He's unquestionably intelligent, but he's not adept at crime. The same was true for Nixon and his White House Staff . . . Haldeman, Ehrlichman, Dean, Mitchell. You read everything about them, especially their own words, and you'll usually find the clues to convict and unnerve them. Kate Winslow's brother, Kilmer, is involved in this mess, too. History is a great teacher."

"History and precedents," Rob said. "Just be careful about how proactive you get."

"I got a warning like that from somebody else, recently," Blake said. "Chief Cooper, actually."

"Yeah, well, maybe we're all trying to tell you something."

"I've got to run, Rob. I'm picking up Julianna in an hour or so."

• • •

The Big Sur connection he was looking for remained a blank until Blake played back his voice mail.

"Dylan, this is Charlotte. I have something to share with you. Call me."

"So Dylan, who's Charlotte?" Julianna said. "I haven't heard you talk about her." She moved her head back a certain way when she said it, as if she had some doubt about him that had just surfaced.

Blake noticed. "She works in Big Sur." He looked at Julianna. "You sound jealous."

"Should I be?"

He turned off the car's engine. They sat without speaking in the parking lot. Julianna's mood appeared to change. She straightened up in the passenger seat and turned to face him.

"My father cheated on my mother, both of my brothers play the field, and my first husband lost interest six months after we were married. It was all about the chase for my first husband."

"This doesn't have anything to do with that," Blake said.

"I worked in a casino as a high stakes Baccarat dealer for years before I became a second-grade teacher. I watched men hit on women all the time. They slipped their wedding rings in their front pockets and smiled. You know, I have issues. Should I pretend not to?" Her lips quivered.

Blake reached for her hand.

She pulled it back.

"Julianna, I'm not looking for anyone else. You should know that by now."

She stared out the windshield.

"I'm not going to bail on you. I can't remember when I've

ever been this happy. I mean it." Blake turned sideways, trying to read her expression.

Julianna looked at him.

"Charlotte is someone I met in connection with the investigation I'm working on. She's a waitress. I asked her to call
me if she learned something that might help me understand
what happened in Big Sur."

"So what did happen, Dylan?"

"A man's car went sailing off the cliff. It wasn't an accident.
When I was there on Highway One at the crash scene where
it happened, someone, I don't know who, pushed some rocks
over the edge. I was climbing back up the cliff from the wreck."

"Oh, my God! And you didn't tell me." Julianna's face
turned color. She clenched her teeth and slammed her hand
against the dash. "I'm not a child. I'm a grown woman. You
need to be honest with me about things like this. And the accident, what about your car accident on the way home from
Stockton? Was that related to this?"

"I'm not sure yet. Maybe. I didn't want to worry you."

"Maybe? Straight up from now on," Julianna said. "Don't
keep things like this from me ever again. I'm in love with you.
Our lives are linked together. I thought you wanted that, a
long-term relationship, that's what you said, anyway."

"I do."

"You can call her, what's her name, Charlotte, right now
if you'd like and talk with her privately. I'm okay with that.
But the truth, always the truth, Dylan. That's the only thing
that works if you want us to be together."

"I do, and I'm sorry."

"Worrying is part of loving somebody, Dylan."

He kept silent.

"I've got one brother who's a sexist pig. I wouldn't recommend anyone date him. And the other is just plain crazy.
He's an adrenalin junkie. I'm not so sure I'm even good at

long term relationships, and now this? I told you how I was a month or two after we met. Don't do this again."

"I'm new at this. I made a mistake," Blake said. "I've never claimed to be perfect." Blake was unnerved by her reaction. "Maybe I'm not as confident and worldly as you think. I've got my own insecurities, just like you."

"You don't talk very much about those, do you?"

"When I was nineteen, my dad was killed in a head-on crash with a drunk driver. Life changed for me when that happened." Blake felt vulnerable and uncertain about showing so much of himself to her. "I stopped believing in God and cursed him. It's taken me almost twenty years to recognize that I constructed a whole subconscious framework in my mind when he died. I convinced myself my father had abandoned me."

Julianna didn't interrupt.

"I used to have a recurring dream my father wasn't really dead and that at some point, he would walk back into my life. I'd be driving alone, cross country. All of a sudden I'd see him, unexpectedly, in some small town, and then my dad would find himself torn between going back with me, or staying where he was, like an episode from *The Twilight Zone*." Blake gripped the steering wheel. His eyes teared up. He turned away for a moment, embarrassed she'd seen him cry.

"I didn't have a clue. That fear of abandonment, a fear I didn't really understand, that I didn't even know was there, turns out to have impacted most of my relationships. I was afraid of losing you once I began to care more deeply about you. Afraid you'd abandon me like my father had. That I'd be distanced from you in some stupid, cold, arbitrary way that had nothing to do with who I was. And I didn't realize it was happening."

"I wouldn't do that, abandon you," Julianna said.

Blake paused, ruffled his fingers through his hair, and rubbed his eyes.

Julianna sat there in silence, watching him.

"I went to a therapist and got some counseling. She told me when you start thinking about this abandonment crap, you begin to subconsciously project it, and make it happen. You probably think of me as some guy who's got it all together. Well, I don't," Blake said.

Julianna adjusted her glasses.

"I talked to my two sisters about my father's death and how they reacted. Same family, same set of events. I learned that it was entirely different for them."

"How's that? What do you mean?" Julianna said.

"My youngest sister was living at home with my mother when my dad died. It was all about helping my mom and getting through high school for her. For my other sister, her life became about proving she was smarter and more capable than my father gave her credit for."

"So, how did you pull yourself out of it?"

"I was sitting in front of the fireplace by myself one night, about a year before you and I met, staring at the flames, thinking about my life. Suddenly, I realized the foundation I'd held on to so desperately in my mind, wasn't really true. It was a lie. That so much of how I was, had been shaped by a lie I'd constructed myself. I felt like I could see the devil in that fireplace, dragging me into the flames, deceiving me, taking my freedom away. The fire grabbed on to me. My whole body was electrified." Blake paused. "That was a watershed moment, an epiphany, a revelation."

"My father never abandoned me. No one did. I reclaimed my life that night."

Julianna leaned over and put her arms around Blake. They held each other. There were tears in Blake's eyes.

"I want you to stay here tonight, with me. You're never going to be that alone again." She wiped away the tears. "I was mad at you. I'm done with that, Dylan. I love you."

When they returned to Julianna's house, they put the groceries away and the girls to sleep.

She put her head on his shoulder and stayed close to him. They drifted off to sleep.

CHAPTER NINETEEN

When Blake opened his eyes, Julianna was standing in front of the sink in her baggy blue and white flannels with her electric toothbrush. She looked toward the bed and smiled at Blake. There was something about the moment, how ordinary and relaxed it was, that made him feel their relationship was more secure. Her smile, that girl-next-door quality, filled the room.

Julianna moved faster than Blake did in the morning. The girls blitzed through breakfast and were off to school with their mom like precision clockwork. He skipped a second cup of coffee so he could walk out the door with them. Ten minutes later, Blake was driving across the causeway with a view of the mountains sixty miles away, thinking about the case.

He returned Charlotte's call when he got to headquarters.

"You asked me to let you know if I bumped into that guy you're looking for, the driver, or heard anything about Sheriff Kowalski that seemed important. Maybe it's nothing, but anyway . . ."

"Go ahead. Everything helps." Blake opened a power bar with his teeth.

"I've got a friend in Big Sur who works as a hairdresser. Sheriff Kowalski's secretary, Maxine Jones, was in her shop the other day talking about her boss's gambling habits. I guess she found some markers in his sport coat, fifty dollar chips, Las Vegas leftovers, when she took his coat to the dry cleaners. Then Kowalski, I know it was him because I saw the name tag on his uniform, was in the restaurant a couple of days ago driving one of those brand new, expensive Lincoln SUV's."

"Any idea where he bought the truck?"

"The license plate frame said Rialto's Lincoln. That's in Monterey," Charlotte said.

"Did he eat alone?"

"Yes."

"The trout?"

"No, bacon and eggs, sunny side up. He cleaned his plate. I'm wondering if I'm going to see you again down here?"

"I expect so, at least for coffee and an existential conversation, anyway."

"How's that girlfriend you told me about?"

"She's good. So are you, by the way," Blake said. "If I wasn't already involved, I'd be asking you out."

"And I'd be saying, yes. Oh, well," Charlotte said.

"Yeah, timing . . . thanks for the tip about Kowalski."

● ● ●

Charlotte's call was the first hint of the connection Blake had been looking for. The news about Kowalski bummed him out, but then he reminded himself it was circumstantial. Nothing Charlotte said proved Kowalski was paid to look the other way on an accident report. People bought trucks and gambled in Vegas every day, including cops. So what if Kowalski was driving a fifty thousand dollar truck? Maybe he'd been putting twenty dollars in the cookie jar for years, or it was a lease, or perhaps he had a six-year loan. He's a cop, Blake told himself. He's earned the benefit of the doubt. He'll get that from me.

Blake sat at his desk, tapping his pencil. He figured Phillip Winslow paid somebody, somebody he knew and could trust, to sabotage Hamilton's car. It couldn't have been Kowalski. He wouldn't sink that low. Taking a bribe was one thing.

Tampering with a car was a whole other matter. But if he did take the money, then Kowalski had facilitated the crime. That'd make him an accessory and put an end to his career.

"Maybe he paid for the truck with cash." As soon as Blake said it out loud, he knew the dealership would have a record that included the form of payment. If Kowalski was as careless about financing the Lincoln, as Phillip Winslow had been with his library card, Kowalski's problems would shoot through the roof. Blake decided to investigate a little more before he talked to Cooper. Waiting made sense.

None of the drivers or mechanics he'd run background checks on had a serious record. And besides, they weren't the kind of people Winslow rubbed elbows with. His circle of contacts consisted of business owners, high-level managers, investors, and unsuspecting retirees who didn't know any better.

Winslow knew how to make money, and he was smart enough to pay whoever he'd hired to kill Hamilton with cash. The appeal of cash for somebody like Winslow, beyond booze, hookers, and impressing people, was to make more money. Not to leave it sitting around, collecting dust in a savings account earning next to nothing. Blake pegged Winslow for the kind of guy who'd pull money out of a brokerage account, a safe-deposit box, or an off-shore bank account. If he didn't have the money in one of those places or was short, then Winslow was the type, Blake supposed, who'd be tempted to borrow from a client's trust account. Winslow would also be pre-disposed to hire someone he knew for the job.

Blake got up and walked to the vending machine. He looked at the coffee, burned and brewing in the pot, and walked back to his desk.

He'd begun to understand how Winslow would have seen eliminating Jack Hamilton as a necessary first step to re-establishing his dominance over Kate — he wanted to eliminate the competition. Winslow was jealous. Once he'd re-established himself with Kate, he wouldn't have to pay alimony or child support any longer.

Blake knew he had gotten in the way, forcing Winslow to improvise. That meant Winslow would need more money for a second murder. And he was the intended victim. Blake needed a search warrant to get hold of Winslow's financial records, and track the money.

● ● ●

Blake called Cooper the following day. "I've got an idea."

"Go ahead," Cooper said.

"We did background searches on the driver-employees that work along the coast. We never did anything on the garage owners. I've got a hunch we're going to find something," Blake said. "I'm still looking for that missing connection between Sierra Springs and Big Sur."

"Do the research, get the names and we'll run them. Anything else?"

"I'm following up on Sheriff Kowalski's potential involvement in this mess."

"Do what you need to, Detective."

Blake didn't take long to uncover three owner's names attached to the road service companies that serviced the coast—Raymond Evans, Trent Williams, and Steven Hooks. The last one, Steven Hooks, had a criminal record from years back. He owned a small trucking company with an office in central California, and graduated from San Francisco State the same year Phillip Winslow did.

Blake drove down Highway 99 to Modesto the next day. The city of two-hundred thousand people, surrounded by rich farmland, had been the setting for the movie, *American Graffiti*, in 1973. Blake hadn't heard anything about Modesto since then, except for its high crime and unemployment rates. He pulled up to the building owned by Hooks in an industrial section of town, and parked next to the most expensive car in the lot. The one, he confirmed, with the plate registered to Hooks.

He entered the garage through an open, pull-down, thirty foot wide corrugated metal door. The place was empty, with the exception of a man at a work table on the far-end wall with his back to the door.

Blake moved toward the two Freightliner trucks parked inside. The new paint job on one truck's right front fender caught his eye. "Damn," Blake said. He turned and came back around to the second truck, next to the garage opening. He unfastened his jacket and took the safety off the service revolver strapped to his chest, before he stepped toward the work bench. "Hey," Blake shouted.

No reply.

"Hey. I'm looking for Mr. Hooks."

The workman gripped the valve to cut the welding torch off and removed his helmet, then turned to face Blake. The guy was at least six-two, built solid like a football player, with standard issue blue-striped coveralls and black cowboy boots.

His boots took Blake back to the edge of the cliff in Big Sur, where Hamilton's car had plunged into the Pacific, and the boot prints he'd seen by the rocks above where he was climbing. The thick mustache on the welder's face put him behind the wheel of the truck.

This was the guy who'd tried to kill me out there. "Police. Stay there. Don't move," Blake said.

The welder grabbed a bottle off the bench and threw it. Then took a pipe wrench and hurled it at Blake's head. Blake dodged left, hit an oil spot, and broke his fall before he hit the floor hard. The welder lunged toward the backpack on the bench and reached inside. Blake drew his weapon and shot him in the foot. The guy fell down on the warehouse floor.

"Keep your hands away from that pack," Blake said.

"Sonofabitch," he yelled. "Sonofabitch, that hurts."

The blood was coming through his boot.

"You remember me, I-5, that truck over there?" Blake nodded toward the Freightliner and kept his gun aimed at the man's chest.

"My foot, my foot. It's bleeding. You might have blown something off. Damn it."

"About the truck," Blake said.

"Damn it to hell," the welder continued. "Sonofabitch."

"You're under arrest." Blake read him his rights.

"I need a doctor."

"I'm a police officer. People tell me I'm supposed to call for help. But I keep thinking about how you tried to kill me and wrecked my car. I liked that car."

"Fuck you."

"You're lucky you didn't take one in the chest or I didn't shoot your pecker off. You'd be dead now. Maybe spend the next thirty years playing with a prosthetic."

The guy sat down on the cement and held his foot. He didn't say anything.

"What's your name?"

"I need something to stop this bleeding."

"I asked you what your name was."

"Red Flemming, goddamn it."

"Where's your employer, Steven Hooks?"

"Probably in his office in the building next door."

"How much did he pay you to run me off the road and sabotage Jack Hamilton's car, the Jaguar that sailed off the cliff?"

Flemming looked up at Blake without speaking. His face had gone white.

"I'm waiting," Blake said.

"I don't know what you're talking about," Flemming said. "I need a doctor."

Blake pushed the backpack to the side and moved closer to where Flemming was sitting. "Do you want the bleeding to stop or do you want it to start again?"

"Go to hell."

"You expect me to be nice?" Blake stomped on Flemming's toe, then put his foot down on Flemming's shoe, and crushed it with his weight.

Flemming screamed in pain. "All right, all right. Enough already." He grabbed his foot. "Twenty thousand dollars. I need a fucking ambulance."

"How did he pay you?"

"With a company check"

"Who else was involved?"

"I don't know. All I know is Steven Hooks," Flemming said.

"Walk in front of me toward that fence."

"I can't walk. You shot my foot. Sonofabitch, it hurts."

"Then pretend you're a one-legged frog and hop. I'm gonna cuff you to the fence. Sit here and keep your mouth shut."

Flemming nodded. "Call them. Just call them."

Blake dialed 911.

"When you're lying in that ambulance in a few minutes, I want you to think about making a very clear, emphatic statement about how you got paid by Hooks to rig the brakes on Hamilton's Jaguar and run me off the road with that Freightliner. I'll be reading your statement when I think about whether I want to add the attempted murder of a police detective on the coast and on Interstate 5 to the list of charges against you."

Four minutes later, the Modesto Police were there. No sirens, two cars, and the back-up Blake requested after Flemming went down.

After they'd arrived, Blake walked over to the building next door, flashed his shield at the receptionist, put his finger to his lips, and said "quiet." Then he knocked on Steven Hooks' office door and walked in.

"I'm Detective Blake from the Sierra Springs Police Department. This is Officer Morales from the Modesto Police Department. You're under arrest for the murder of Jack Hamilton and the attempted murder of a police detective, yours truly, as a matter of fact."

Hooks started to move.

"Keep your hands on the desk."

Morales read Hooks his rights.

Blake looked at Hooks. "You're in deep shit trouble, you know. You and your college buddy, Phillip Winslow. Maybe you'll want to give some consideration to spreading the blame here, instead of taking it all on yourself. You might actually be able to leave prison someday, as opposed to staying there forever."

Hooks kept silent with his hands on the desk.

"Turn your palms up, Hooks. I'm going to tell your fortune."

Hooks looked like he was grinding his teeth.

"Nice paint job on the truck in your warehouse, by the way. I met your employee on the way in, Flemming. He threw some of your tools at me. He had a gun in his backpack. He's already given you up. You got paid extra for me, didn't you? I don't much like that."

The three of them walked out of the office with Hooks in handcuffs. Blake looked at the receptionist. "I think you should go home early today. Your boss here, Mr. Hooks, isn't going to be back. I'd start looking for another job if I were you."

After a couple hours worth of Modesto Police paperwork, Blake and Morales went out for a corn beef on rye. Blake called Cooper from his car to share the news.

"I think we should schedule an appointment to see Phillip Winslow once we've had a chance to digest the confessions coming out of Modesto from Flemming and Hooks? They should tie it down pretty tight," Blake said.

"You know, I'm gonna give you some administrative time off because you discharged your weapon, pretty standard."

"I understand," Blake said.

"So you shot him in the foot," Chief Cooper said.

"Kemo Sabe's code of ethics, Chief. That, and not enough target practice."

"Seriously, Blake? I'm gonna give you the benefit of the

doubt this time. You're pressing your luck, you know. So let me see if I can remember the code."

"The code?" Blake said.

"That all things change but truth, and that truth alone lives on forever, and that when he had to use guns, The Lone Ranger never shot to kill, but rather only to disarm his opponent as painlessly as possible. Is that about right?"

"Yeah, you've got it. But according to Red Flemming, it hurt like hell," Blake said.

"Go see that girlfriend of yours. Sleep late. Watch what you say to the Internal Affairs people when they talk to you."

"Thanks, Chief." Blake clicked off, and stared at the street in front of him that looked like a thousand other city blocks.

• • •

Blake headed north on Highway 99 toward Sierra Springs. An hour later he found himself passing the spot where Flemming had run him off the road. "Jesus," he said to himself, "somebody could have put a cross next to the freeway over there with those cornball artificial flowers I hate. I could have wound up with some damn Walmart tombstone made in China, stuck in the ground over my head. Depressed for eternity, as well as dead."

Blake's mind flashed back to his childhood. His little sister used to hold her breath whenever their dad drove past a cemetery.

"Why do you do that?" he asked.

"So the life won't be sucked out of me," she'd say.

He cruised along at sixty, thinking about how his future could have turned on a dime, happy the life hadn't been sucked out of him.

He needed to get his mind off what'd almost happened. He could've killed Flemming.

CHAPTER TWENTY

Blake called Freddie Roosevelt on his phone.

"Hey, D.B. Your car's looking good, right?"

"You're doing a great job. I couldn't be happier."

"I like your dog. You're right about him. Watson's smart. You can just talk to him and it's like he knows what you're saying."

"You're being careful with my apartment key, right?"

"Nobody knows I have it and it doesn't have your name on it," Freddie said. "That's between you, me, and Watson."

"Hey, I was hoping you'd be able to get over to my place, feed him, and take him for a run today. I didn't expect to be out of town this late," Blake said.

"No problem. I got my bus pass, and my homework's done. Does your girlfriend like your wheels?"

"She likes them plenty."

"Maybe tomorrow you'll let me drive."

"You're twelve, man. You can't do that. I'll tell you what, though. Maybe you and I can shoot some hoops tomorrow."

"That'd be cool. You know white men can't jump, right D.B.?"

"Yeah, I saw that old movie, Freddie. We'll see about that tomorrow."

Blake torqued up the volume on his car stereo — *Listen Here*, Eddie Harris' wild, electrifying jazz piece from the sixties, was on. Blake's adrenalin started pumping. The music took his mind away from Modesto. He waited for the song to end, then called Julianna.

"This has been a heck of a day."

"Why don't you come over tonight and you can tell me about it? The girls are both at sleep-over's. I'll make you a late dinner."

"I may not make it until eight or nine. That's not too late?"

"Fine. Don't worry about it. Call me when you're a half-hour away. Don't eat before you get here."

• • •

Blake saw Julianna peek out the kitchen window when he pulled up. As soon as he stepped inside, Blake dropped his overnight bag on the floor and drew her close.

"I've got dinner almost ready to put on the table. Tri-tip, mashed potatoes, green beans, a mixed green salad with some tomatoes from the garden. What would you like to drink?"

"Do you have sun tea?"

"I do. Sit down and relax."

Blake suddenly felt ravenous. The tri-tip was on the grill in Julianna's backyard. He could smell the aroma drifting in.

"So tell me your exciting news about today."

"Well, I caught the two men who killed Jack Hamilton and tried to run me off the road."

"Dylan, that's wonderful. You've got to be relieved."

"Yeah, I'm happy. They're off the streets. They took a man's life for money."

"Sit down. Let's eat. Who paid them?"

"One of our local citizens here in Sierra Springs," Blake said. "A stockbroker, no less."

"And he'll be arrested?"

"Soon. Maybe as early as tomorrow." Blake filled her in on what had happened. "I shot him in the foot. I think I blew off one of his toes."

Julianna looked like she wanted to laugh. "His toe?"

"I'm a bad shot.

"On purpose, right?" Julianna started to giggle. "Sounds

like you had a Barney Fife moment. But really, you know, I'm happy you don't go around waiving your gun in the air like some kind of macho nut-case." She squeezed his hand.

"Most of the police work I do is research, listening, watching, boring stuff like that, trying to understand what motivates people to do things they shouldn't."

"I think you're understating the job. It's got to be more interesting or you wouldn't be doing it."

"This is so good," Blake said. "What's for desert?"

"Something non-fattening. Trust me, you'll be satisfied." Julianna winked.

Blake began imagining the small flowery print shirt she was wearing giving way to him as he undressed her.

"You can help me load the dishwasher," she said.

Blake got up.

"Then you can take me to bed."

"I'll shower first if you'll join me," Blake said.

"You get started. I'll be right there."

• • •

The alarm went off early. Julianna bounded out of bed to get ready for school.

"I've got the day off today," Blake said. "Thought I'd do some yard work for you before I leave."

"That'd be great, but you don't have to, you know. There's sun tea in the refrigerator." She grabbed her purse. "I've got to run. Love you."

Blake sat down to read the sports pages and have a second cup of coffee. A few hours later, he was spreading mulch, and planting shrubbery and flowers. He liked physical work, getting his hands in the earth. It was nearly four by the time he hit the freeway.

The black Audi sedan cruised across the causeway at seventy. Blake began thinking about Phillip Winslow and how good it would feel to know he was going to spend time at a real prison, instead of the minimum security places where white collar criminals who embezzle money are sent. He called headquarters.

"Sergeant Pierce. It's me, Blake. I'm wondering if those two statements came in from the Modesto Police Department."

"We've got them. They came in about a half-hour ago."

"Scan them and email it to me, or you can fax them to my home phone number?"

"No problem. Heard about what happened. Good work, Blake."

"Thanks. I'm trying to figure out what comes next."

"If you keep doing what you're doing, even Jameson is going to have to say something positive besides don't fuck it up."

Blake pulled in to one of his favorite coffee spots. When he got home, he called his mother in Georgia to say hello.

"We had a bear stand up on his hind legs yesterday and peek at us through the front door. He emptied all the sugar water from the hummingbird feeder, and was close enough to ring the doorbell."

"Did he try to get in the house?"

"No. I think he was just curious. The dog started barking and he ran up the driveway into the woods. I always keep my shotgun next to the fireplace, just in case."

"Have you got some wood stacked up for the winter? You shouldn't be lugging around all that heavy stuff," Blake said.

"Jim's already got it done for me. We got the best neighbors you could ever hope for up here on the mountain. They're planning to go skinny-dipping this winter. Eddy R. has started up a polar bear club. He's diverted some water from the creek that runs next to his cabin for a catfish pond. Dylan, you should come up this fall to see the leaves. They're really beautiful this year."

"Maybe I can take some time off."

"We can go antiquing and you can white water raft where

the gorge cuts through on the way to Chattanooga. That's only about forty minutes from here. That's where they had the kayak events when the Olympics were in Atlanta. If we can get your other sister up here, the four of us can take a trip to Savannah for a few days."

"That sounds great, Mom."

"You can bring your girlfriend, too. You'd have the downstairs all to yourself. You can make all kinds of noise at night and we won't hear a thing."

"Mom, you're going to make me blush."

"Do you like her, Dylan? I mean, are you in love with her?"

"Yes, very much."

"And she's a teacher, right?"

"Second grade, Mom. She's a great teacher."

"So you're having fun together? She likes the out-of-doors, like you do?"

"We go hiking in the Sierra and tide-pooling along the coast when we can get away."

"When you were little, you never used to want to come inside except to eat, and when it got dark. You always had mud on your hands. I'd love to meet her."

Blake pictured his mom smiling.

"Try and work it out. I'm sure your sister would like to see you. She's having a tough time."

"Maybe in the spring when the dogwoods are in bloom," Blake said.

"Sounds good, son. Do you bring her flowers?"

"Yes, Mom. You raised me right."

• • •

Blake microwaved dinner and poured a cold beer. Afterwards, he and Watson headed up to the park. He remembered to take his gun with him.

The Delta breeze blew and the temperature cooled to a

comfortable seventy degrees. He unfastened Watson's leash and threw the ball into the outfield several times for him to retrieve. Then he sat on the grass and played tug-of-war. The moon cut a sliver in a sky full of stars.

Blake showered when they got home and put on a comfortable pair of shorts and a clean t-shirt before calling Julianna. "So tell me, do you like the flowers and what I did in the backyard?"

"Sweet of you, Detective, thoughtful. The bougainvillea vines and scotch moss are really pretty. I'm not accustomed to someone being nice to me the way you are."

"I like doing things for you. You make me happy, Julianna. I do have one question for you, though."

"What?"

"Does this mean I get to have dessert again, the next time I come over?"

"Over and over again," Julianna said.

"Do you think we'll have sex this much when I'm sixty-four?" He was smiling.

"You're older than I am, but I know I'll want to," Julianna said.

"You know what my Mom told me today when I called her?"

"No."

"She invited us to Georgia and said we could have the whole downstairs to ourselves and make all kinds of noise at night."

"She sounds pretty spicy. I think I'd like her."

"I'm sure you would."

"So what's on your agenda for tomorrow?" Julianna said.

"I've got to complete the paperwork for some records we need to tie down the connection between what happened in Big Sur and the man with the money here in Sierra Springs. Then, I'm planning to spend some fun time with Freddie, the kid I've been telling you about, before I do some grocery shopping and the laundry."

"Are we on for the demolition derby with Rob and Samantha?"

"Later this month. We got the tickets. I'll talk to Rob tomorrow and give you a call after work. Have a great day at school tomorrow. I love you."

"I love you too, Detective. Keep thinking about dessert."

CHAPTER TWENTY-ONE

Blake stopped to fill out the paperwork for a search warrant so he could get the office phone and cell records he suspected would link Winslow and Hooks. He requested a second search warrant for Winslow's brokerage and bank accounts to confirm whether the withdrawal dates matched up with Winslow's payments to Hooks. Once the evidence was in hand, Blake and Cooper planned to stop by Winslow's office and personally invite him to the penal system.

Winslow had molested Allison, and he'd gotten away with it. He had two more daughters standing in the wings and Blake hadn't seen anything resembling remorse, just Winslow's steadfast determination to control people and get what he wanted. Winslow had paid Steven Hooks forty grand to kill Hamilton and agreed to add another fifty, according to Hooks' statement, as a premium "to eliminate some stupid, small town detective nobody would miss." He was batting five-hundred, a great number on a baseball diamond for a white guy with a pudgy face. But this wasn't baseball. With each passing day, Blake became more determined to throw high inside fastballs at Winslow's head and send him to the bench at San Quentin where he'd get a taste of his own medicine.

When Blake came in on Monday to see Cooper, Susan waived him right in. Cooper came around the front of his desk and shook his hand. "I'm glad to see you, Blake." Cooper looked him up and down. "You doing okay with the shooting?"

"I'm feeling good. Did they find Red Flemming's toe?"

"From what I've been given to understand, you blasted that into oblivion."

"Can't say as I'm sorry. I guess he'll have to cut a hole in his cowboy boot and limp around in the exercise yard at Pelican Bay or wherever he winds up."

Cooper looked uncomfortable. "Be careful what you say, Blake. Shooting off a guy's toe sounds sadistic, like you crossed the line."

"Chief, I didn't want to kill him. Besides, I slipped. There was oil on the garage floor."

"Yeah, okay," Cooper said. He walked behind his desk. "We should have Winslow's phone records, and the bank and brokerage stuff you got the search warrants for, in our hands within the next twenty-four hours. We've got enough to arrest him right now, but I'm figuring we'll make it even tighter before we turn the lights out for him."

"So, what are you thinking about Sheriff Kowalski?" Blake said.

"It's a shame, really. He threw it away, his whole career. Those records came in yesterday from the dealership where he bought the Lincoln Escalade," Cooper said.

"I haven't seen them, yet," Blake said.

"Ask Susan. She'll get them for you. They're like you supposed. Phillip Winslow funneled everything through Steven Hooks' company, A-1 Trucking. Hooks wrote the checks. Nine-thousand five hundred dollars to each of Kowalski's sisters and another one for the same amount directly to Kowalski. Both sisters endorsed the checks over to Kowalski and Kowalski tendered all three checks as his deposit on the truck."

"Incredibly stupid," Blake said.

Cooper shook his head. "All those years and the dumb ass never learned how to launder money. Winslow and Hooks kept the amounts under ten thousand so everybody could avoid filing those Cash Transaction Reports for the IRS," Cooper said.

"Wouldn't surprise me if Winslow was trying to figure out some way to write it off as a business expense." Blake sat there, shaking his head. "So what about the rest of the money? Kowalski would have demanded more cash."

"Oh, there was at least another forty-six thousand. That rounded it up to seventy-five grand for Kowalski, a pretty nice little pot of gold. He got paid more to look the other way than Hooks did for killing Hamilton. Cops are more expensive, I guess," Cooper said. He looked disgusted.

"So it looks like Kowalski used the rest of the money, after he bought the truck, to pay down the mortgage on his house and buy a fishing boat. Stephen Hooks has admitted to delivering the cash to him," Blake said. "And he and Flemming are being cooperative."

"Between the three of them, Hooks, Flemming, and Kowalski, this is shaping up like Monty Hall's *Let's Make A Deal* TV show, with concurrent sentences and time off for good behavior," Cooper said.

"Phillip Winslow won't have to worry about the Securities And Exchange Commission anymore," Blake said. "Not where he's going."

"We'll know exactly how the numbers and dates match-up when we get the rest of the records. Then you and I can mosey on over to Winslow's fancy-ass office, see how fast he lawyers up, and if he makes bail."

It was obvious to Blake that Cooper was looking forward to getting out from behind the desk. "That means Kate Winslow is cleared," Blake said.

"She's no longer a suspect. I'm planning to call her tomorrow to let her know we've arrested the men responsible for Hamilton's death." Cooper hesitated. "She's a complicated woman."

"Complicated, with a sexual complex that comes into play every time I see her," Blake said. He shook his head. "I'll catch you later, Chief. I'm going to grab some lunch."

"Magnetism," Cooper said, as he smiled. "She wants to grab you, Blake, but you don't look that irresistible to me."

• • •

A couple of uniformed cops stopped by Blake's desk before he had a chance to leave. "I used to think you were a little too full of yourself," one of them said. "Jameson still thinks you're an elitist asshole. Most of us know better. That was a good collar you made in Modesto, the guy who got paid to run you off the road." They shook his hand. "Some of the other guys are going to be at Donnegan's tonight. Why don't you stop by and have a drink with us."

"Thanks," Blake said. "I appreciate the invitation. Days like this when the traffic lights all turn green and nobody needs to pass out tickets to hit a quota, make me smile. What time are you guys gonna be there?"

"About seven."

"I'll try and make it," Blake said.

• • •

Cooper planned to call Kathryn Winslow the following day, but Blake had left for lunch and he was anxious. For years she'd been a good supporter of the ballot issues that mattered to Cooper's department. "Your instincts were right," Cooper told her. "Jack Hamilton was murdered, plain and simple. It wasn't a suicide or an accident. It was intentional. We've got the men who were responsible, some of them are already locked-up. The rest will be, shortly." He didn't mention names. That wouldn't have been appropriate, but Kathryn was an intelligent woman who'd learned how to connect the dots a long time ago.

"Was Detective Blake instrumental in solving the case?" she said.

"Absolutely," Cooper said.

"I had a clear sense of how capable he was when I met him.

I knew he wouldn't stop until he got to the bottom of things. Thank you. I appreciate the attention you gave this."

The Hamilton case was close to being wrapped. Phillip Winslow was a step away from being arrested and indicted. Blake ate his raw almonds for lunch down where the creek ran through the ravine. He wondered how many times Kathryn had looked down at the lake from the couch in her living room where she and Jack Hamilton made love while her two young daughters were in school. Soon, she'd at least have the satisfaction of knowing her ex-husband hadn't gotten away with murder.

● ● ●

The morning after drinks at Donnegan's began with a good solid breakfast for Blake — blueberries, his hockey-puck vegetable protein patties, expensive granola, and good coffee. He threw down a handful of vitamins, the same way Bob Schmidt threw down boilermakers. Schmidt was the retired bomb squad guy from The Villas who helped Blake in his earlier investigation of a sociopath.

He and Watson followed up breakfast with a run.

The road was clear so Blake took the turn onto the freeway at fifty without touching the brakes as he wheeled around the curve, then accelerated and blew out the Audi's turbo. He pulled into a spot in the shade. Blake walked in and waved at the woman working the counter behind the plexiglass, then went through the Authorized Personnel Only door. He walked down the hallway and sat behind his battleship gray desk in the Detective's Room, paid some personal bills, and addressed an envelope. He expected an easy day.

CHAPTER TWENTY-TWO

Kathryn Winslow set the phone on her kitchen counter and stared at it. A bitter, cold chill came over her like the fog that sometimes crossed over the lake in winter. She felt distanced and alone. At first, she couldn't think beyond the clouds outside her window. They enveloped her.

For a moment, she caught hold of the things that were right in her life. The business had a positive cash flow and nobody was suing her. The twice-monthly salary draws, spousal and child support, and her brother paying off her mortgage debt, meant she didn't have to worry as much about money. But what did it matter? The only man she'd ever really loved, the man she wanted to share her life with, was gone. Jack Hamilton was the father her children should have had, and she'd never feel his touch again.

Her mind drifted back to the day she drove to meet him in mid-town, wearing a full-length mink coat with nothing underneath. They'd made love in her back seat, on the top deck of the parking garage overlooking the river. She left her inhibitions behind when she was with him. Kathryn remembered the day Jack insisted she take the rifle from her house when Phillip threatened her in a drunken rant. They stuck it behind some boxes in the office.

Marrying Phillip was a tragic mistake. He took her dreams and her youth, brought shame to her family, and a sense of guilt no amount of therapy could cure. She was convinced — Phillip would never stop trying to control her.

She reached for the phone. Kathryn's stomach knotted up. She'd rehearsed the conversation a hundred times in her mind. Cooper's call that morning brought it to a boil.

"Phillip, I need to see you." She knew he'd agree to meet her. The invitation was too much for him to resist.

"Kate, you're calling me? Why?"

She heard a hint of surprise bordering on disbelief in his voice. She'd stopped calling him months ago, except when he was late with the checks.

"I need to talk with you about the girls."

"Is it about Allison? I know where she is and what she's doing. That's not my fault. We sent her to Stanford, for Christ's sake. She's had every advantage."

"It's about all three of the girls, not just Allison." She felt a force welling up inside her.

"What about them?"

"I'll tell you when I see you. Tonight after work. Do you remember our spot at the lake, by the point?"

"Of course I do."

"Bring a bottle and your little blue pills. I'll bring two glasses. I'll be there at seven."

She hung up.

"Twenty-four years, twenty-four years and he's still a pig," she said. "Still delusional." She opened the sliding glass door in her living room. The air was still.

Kathryn couldn't stop thinking how horrid it would be if Phillip got his hands on one of the other girls. How repulsive to lie in his bed and smell the alcohol sweating from his skin. He'd put their family's future on the line with call girls and prostitutes and other people's wives.

She picked out something revealing to wear that showed off her breasts, curled her eyelashes, and fixed her hair. She took two of Jack Hamilton's Viagra pills from her nightstand, and put them in the silver compact she kept in her purse. She uncorked a bottle of vintage Bordeaux from the wine cellar, emptied three inches from the top of the bottle, and poured some pure wood alcohol in with the rest of the Viagra she had ground with a mortar and pestle. After she'd re-corked the wine, she put it in the refrigerator to chill.

• • •

Kathryn walked down the lake trail. She spread the blanket before Phillip arrived, and looked around to make sure no one else was nearby. The spot she'd picked was hidden from view. She unbuttoned the light flannel jacket she'd worn on the way there and set it on the blanket. The white silk shirt underneath it clung to her skin.

The wine bottle chilled in an ice bucket. She filled her glass from the metal flask inside the picnic basket she'd carried.

"I was surprised by your call," Phillip said, when he saw her. He'd brought his own bottle of vintage Bordeaux and a corkscrew.

"I'm full of surprises. Come sit by me." She patted the blanket on her side, away from the picnic basket.

"Let's drink. Yours first. You do the honors. Pop it for me." She forced a pretend smile.

"I thought you were mad at me. You couldn't stand me," Phillip said. He looked surprised, and smug in a condescending kind of way.

"I've been thinking about us," she said. "Two incomes are better than one. Maybe we can make this work after all. The girls are older now. We're both more settled."

"You're right. I'm just surprised you're seeing it this way."

"I've been lonesome. I need you, Phillip. You know me. We don't have to play games anymore."

"I wouldn't," he said. "Not anymore."

"And it would have to be monogamous, just me. Can you handle that?"

"Yes, of course I can," Phillip said.

She didn't believe him. He was a serial liar. "Pour a glass for me," she said. "Did you bring your little blue pills?"

Phillip reached in his pocket.

"You should take one now."

He smiled and swallowed.

"Where did you have lunch today?"

"At Bennington's."

"Something rich in cholesterol, no doubt."

"A steak."

"And something to drink?"

"Two Jack Daniel's on the rocks."

"Sometimes drinking can be good for you." She took a sip of wine and laughed. She felt him staring at her breasts. She looked at them and then at Phillip. "I want you to try some of mine." She reached in the basket and filled his glass. No one was in sight. "A toast to us . . . to a new beginning," Kathryn said.

Phillip emptied his wine glass. Kathryn poured him another from her bottle.

"You know, this tastes almost bitter." Phillip had a sour look on his face for a moment or two, then shook his head.

"Must be your taste buds. It's a good vintage, Phillip. Let me get more for you." She reached in the picnic basket.

They looked out at the lake, where the fool's gold embedded in the sandstone layers around the water's edge sparkled before them in the autumn sunlight.

"Do you remember, Phillip, when we used to take walks around the lake and look for fool's gold? Are you still doing that . . . chasing business deals too good to be true?"

"Not as often."

"Drink some more. This is going to be a send-off party." She unbuttoned her shirt, and slipped it off. Then cupped her hands beneath her breasts. "These are for you." She could see his breathing quicken as he grew more excited. "Do you remember how good I am? It's been a while, hasn't it?"

"Too long," Phillip said.

She saw the sweat coming off his forehead.

"I'm suddenly not feeling too well, Kate. Kind of strange, actually."

"I don't want you to disappoint me, Phillip. I'm going to make you feel young again. "

Phillip stood and began to unfasten his belt. "Right here, right now?"

"I'm yours for the taking," Kathryn said. "You want to take me, don't you?"

Phillip took off his shirt. His pants fell down to his ankles. He sat on the blanket, took off his shoes, and folded his pants.

"Stand up, Phillip. I want to see how straight and tall you are. And what you're going to give me."

He did as she asked. "I, I just don't feel right, Kate. Something's wrong."

Phillip began to wobble. He looked confused.

"You want me, don't you? Those other women, they couldn't please you the way I can."

"It was different with them," Phillip said. His left leg buckled.

"You'll never do it again, you know that, don't you? Not to me, not to Allison, not to any of our daughters." She said it so calmly, it soothed her. "You sick bastard."

"Kate." He stumbled toward her and fell to the ground. His head struck a rock by the blanket. A small pool of blood and saliva mixed with the dirt.

She watched him lying there, twitching. "No more woodies, Phillip." She put her hands on his neck to check for a pulse. It was faint. She fastened her bra and put her shirt back on. She left the bottle Phillip had brought on the ground, and packed the rest of everything neatly into her picnic basket. She wiped her prints off his wine glass and Phillip's neck.

Kathryn looked around, then stepped through the brush, past the lupine and horsetail until the path connected with the lake trail. Phillip's car was parked in the lot where a ranger would ticket it the next morning. She walked the two miles to her home as the sun began to fall.

When Kathryn got home, she poured the rest of the wine down the kitchen sink, and washed all her clothes. Now, she thought, now finally, I can be clean.

CHAPTER TWENTY-THREE

Winslow's Lexus was towed to the police impound lot the next day. His secretary, Madeline Armstrong, called the Police to file a missing person's report when she didn't hear from him.

When Cooper saw Winslow's name on the daily log sheet that crossed his desk, he pounded his fist and bit his lip. Then reached for the phone. "Winslow's missing, Blake. Nobody's seen him for over twenty-four hours. Sonofabitch."

"Damn it," Blake said.

"Tell me about it," Cooper said. "I was looking forward to busting his ass. I should have told you to arrest him, and not waited. I've sent two officers, Reynolds and Smith, out to the lake to conduct a search. You should join them. They're going to cover the trail that leads out of the parking lot by the first boat ramp. Winslow's car's been towed."

"You don't think he's left the country, do you? He's got the money to fly someplace where he won't be extradited," Blake said.

"I've already checked. There haven't been any departures under his name from the Metro Airport or the two executive airports. Besides, he wouldn't have left the car at the lake. He could've dumped it in the long-term parking lot at the airport where nobody'd notice it." Cooper paused. "What did the search warrants for his phone records and his brokerage account show?"

"Everything matches up . . . his calls to Steven Hooks, the sale of some mutual funds transferred into his money market account at Merrill-Lynch, and the withdrawals. The time frames match up," Blake said.

"You know, Blake, I think I may have really fucked up. I called Kathryn Winslow yesterday after you and I talked, and told her we'd found the men responsible for Hamilton's death."

"But you didn't actually tell her that her ex was behind it?" Blake said. Cooper had fucked up. Blake knew. He just didn't want to say so.

"No," Cooper said. "I didn't tell her about her ex-husband's connection to the case, but I think she had a sense of it."

"What was her reaction?"

"I don't know. She didn't say much."

"Has anyone talked to her about his disappearance, yet?"

"No," Cooper said.

"I'm going to head out to the lake. I'll call you if anything materializes. Let me know if you hear anything more." Blake turned his car around and drove past office buildings and brokerage firms that lined both sides of the street leading to the lake. He caught up with the two uniformed officers about a quarter-mile from where Winslow's car had been parked. "Nothing yet, no signs?"

"Nothing," the officer said.

• • •

Another mile in and Blake saw the birds circling. His pace quickened and so did his pulse. He pushed the blackberry bushes to the side and went down a small incline, then back up to the overlook by the point. Phillip Winslow was spread out on the blanket with his face in the dirt. He looked like a beached whale with a forty-inch waistline and bloated pink skin.

Blake pulled out his cell and called Cooper. "He's dead. We just found him. His ass is pointing upwards to the heavens. Stark naked."

"He had his hands in a lot of people's pockets," Cooper said, "So what do you think?"

"Can't say. He's been here for a while. I'm going to wait for the coroner. Tell Phipps to look for our cars in the first lot off to the right. He'll need a couple of guys and a stretcher to lug Winslow out of here."

"Damn it to hell," Cooper said.

"After we wrap this up, I'll drop by her house."

"I'll talk with you tomorrow." Cooper hesitated, then said, "No pants?"

"No pants."

Blake shook his head and stood on the ground at the end of the blanket next to Winslow's feet. He looked at the scene in front of him, inch by inch. Then turned to the two uniformed officers. "Damn it to hell. Be careful not to scrape anything, or kick the dirt around."

The officers nodded. "Yeah, yeah," they said in unison. "We'll rope it off back there where the trail breaks off."

Blake shook his head. He didn't need to tell them what to do. They knew their jobs.

"I don't know whether to call this justice and be happy, or be disappointed as hell because we didn't catch him before this happened. My gut's telling me, this wasn't an accident," Blake said.

The officers began to look for footprints or other signs of activity.

Blake backed off the blanket and sat cross-legged on the ground, with his head in his hands, thinking.

Thirty minutes passed before Phipps, the coroner, arrived with an entourage of three attendants, a stretcher, some plastic evidence bags, two Diet Cokes, and an egg salad sandwich on ice. Officer Reynolds met them at the point where the path turned toward the crime scene. Blake and Smith remained with the body.

"I thought you were retiring," Blake said, when he saw Phipps. "Coming up close to thirty years, right?"

"You've never met my wife, have you, Detective Blake?" Phipps said. "Twenty-four-seven is tough to take. Besides, they're still trying to find an able-bodied replacement for me at the department. Cooper keeps telling me I'm indispensable."

Blake shook Phipps' hand. "I see you're still drinking Diet Coke."

"Aspartame and potassium benzoate. It's a great preservative," Phipps said. "Maybe that's why I've been here so long." Phipps eyed the crime scene. "So tell me, what have we here, Detective Blake?"

"We were hoping that's what you'd tell us. I'm thinking this wasn't just a picnic."

Blake watched Phipps pull his camera from his pack and take pictures from various angles. When he'd finished, without having touched the body, he stepped back toward Blake, the two other officers, and the three attendants. Phipps picked up his clipboard and made notes. "What time did his car pass through the park's entrance?" Phipps said.

"We don't know, yet," Blake said.

Phipps made eye contact with him. "Call me when you do. Where's his wallet?"

Blake pointed to the body. "We took it out of his back pocket and bagged it. Money, credit cards, it's all there."

"He could have picked a more convenient spot to expire," Phipps said.

"Yeah, this is going to be a trek all the way back with this stretcher," one of the attendants remarked. "He's not skinny."

Phipps glanced at all three of them. "Gentlemen, let's have some respect for the deceased, even if we don't feel especially akin to him."

"I haven't seen you since we closed out the elder abuse case," Blake said.

Phipps pulled a pair of latex gloves from his pack. "And

here we are again, next to another dead body. I've gotten accustomed to being around dead people after all these years.
They don't argue." He snapped on the gloves and glanced up
at Blake. "He's been here for awhile. A couple days, I'd say.
No pants, no shoes, skin's red from being out in the sun." He
gently rolled the body over. "Pasty white on his underside.
He wasn't a sunbather. Worked in an office, right, Blake?"

"Yes."

"Got his fingernails manicured not too long ago. Looks like
a drinker, too — the yellow skin color on his chest, the sores
on his legs, the finger clubbing. Oh, how we abuse our bodies," Phipps said. He looked down at Winslow and shook his
finger like a mother scolding a toddler. "You think anybody
was here with him?" Phipps looked up at Blake.

"I was going to ask you the same question."

"I'm guessing, yes. It's a secluded, romantic setting. He's
naked, probably was on his way to making whoopee."

"Whoopee?" Blake said.

"That's what my grandfather used to call it," Phipps said.
"Find any footprints to work with?"

"The main trail is a mess. Sand, weeds, limestone gravel
and tree roots mixed in. Too many people and it's too dry.
Maybe a few footprints."

"Any cloth fibers in the bushes on the way back here, detective?"

"Haven't found any, yet."

"Lets you and me look again before we pack it up," Phipps
said. "Reynolds and Smith, why don't the two of you go back
to where this dirt path forks off from the main trail and walk
back slowly this way. If you see something, don't touch it.
Call me. Then check the other direction, opposite from how
we walked in, for at least a quarter-mile down past where we
are now. Thoroughness is next to Godliness," Phipps said.

The three attendants remained behind with Blake and
Phipps.

"It's a vintage Bordeaux," Phipps said, as he picked up the bottle and placed it in a plastic bag. "A good year. Expensive. If this was a date, he wanted to impress her."

"He dealt in securities," Blake said.

"He's not going to be doing that anymore. He hit his head on that rock, maybe hard enough to kill him, maybe not. I'll find out when he's on the table."

"Give me a heads up on the time of death as soon as you can," Blake said. "We're back-tracking his movements. You'll be able to tell if he had sex?" Blake said.

"I'll know."

"It's going to be a workout getting him to the parking lot," Blake said.

"That's why I brought three guys, so they could spot each other. Two of these fellows look like they could use the exercise. I'm happy to be the guy who examines him, instead of the one who has to carry him back."

● ● ●

An hour later, Phipps snapped off his gloves.

He and Blake led the way as they headed down the trail.

"You doing okay, Detective?"

"I'm good Phipps, I'm good. What's your first name anyway?"

"Albert, but I don't advertise it."

They both kicked a little dirt around with their shoes, and tried to focus on enjoying the lake and the fresh air.

"I'll talk to you after you've done what you need to do. You really are going to retire, aren't you, Phipps?"

"Yeah, I was just kidding about my wife. She makes great egg salad."

"You want a ride back to headquarters?" Blake said.

"No, you go. I'll wait here and ride with the body. Chain of evidence you know. Got to make sure it's right."

CHAPTER TWENTY-FOUR

Kathryn watched as Blake parked next to her Jaguar. She'd been expecting him. He was a detective after all. He got paid to arrest people.

She walked with confidence to the front door, dressed in a pair of black pants and a lime green silk shirt. "Detective Blake. This is an unexpected surprise. Come in."

Kathryn took a moment to survey her visitor. She tried to read the blank expression on his face. She gestured toward the living room and took a seat across from him. "You're dressed casually. Is this your day off?"

"It was, but I got called in. I'm here on official business."

"That's disappointing. I was hoping you'd re-considered my offer. May I get you something to drink?" She inched forward to the front of the white leather couch.

"I'm fine," Blake said.

She sensed he wasn't good at delivering bad news, telling people he was sorry for their loss. That was one of the things about Blake that appealed to her most. He was nothing like Phillip, or her brother, for that matter.

"Are your daughters here?"

"They're upstairs in their rooms, watching videos."

"They won't interrupt us, then?" Blake said.

"It's fine. Don't worry about it." She wanted to make it easier for him.

"Your ex-husband, Phillip, when did you last see or talk with him?"

She'd been rehearsing a response that Blake would buy. "I called him at his office, yesterday, to discuss something about the girls. Why?" Katherine felt calm, in control.

"I'm sorry to have to tell you this . . . he's dead. We found him on a lake trail less than three hours ago."

Kathryn moved her hand over her mouth, looked down, and moaned for a long moment. This is the part I have to get right, she told herself. This is why I rehearsed in front of the mirror—to show sorrow and loss, surprise mixed with shock.

"Oh, my God," she said. Kathryn slumped. She noticed her hands shaking, unexpectedly.

Her eyes met Blake's. "What happened? Was it a heart attack?"

"We don't know, yet. "

"He didn't take care of himself, you know. He drank and drank. You can't abuse your body the way he did and expect to stay healthy." She shook her head and reached for a tissue, hoping tears would run down her cheeks. There weren't any.

"Do you know why he would have been on one of those trails?" Blake said.

"No, not really."

Blake seemed to be searching for the right words to say.

Kathryn waited, wanting it all to seem natural.

"He had his pants and shoes off."

"That's bizarre," Kathryn said. "Phillip was a bit of an exhibitionist. He was sick, mentally and morally. You and I, we talked about that."

"Well, I wanted to let you know in person. Someone at the Coroner's Office is going to contact you to identify his body."

Kathryn closed her eyes, then realized what else she'd have to do that she hadn't planned. She looked at Blake. "I'll have to tell the children," she said.

"It'll probably hit the papers tomorrow," Blake said.

Kathryn walked Blake to the door and watched through the glass as he made his way to the car. She hesitated, then went upstairs to talk with the girls.

CHAPTER TWENTY-FIVE

When Blake got home, he set off on a long run with Watson, and felt the cool night air moving through the trees. His mind jumped back and forth between a fast burn and thinking nothing at all, just running and listening to his heart pound. "What say we keep running, boy?" They did four miles at a fast pace.

Blake slumped back on his couch when he and Watson got home. He propped his feet on the coffee table, and looked out the front window and gulped down a Gatorade.

Phillip's death meant child and spousal support would end for Kate — that shifted suspicion away from her, as did the fact that she had no liability for her ex-husband's debts. All that had been spelled out in their divorce agreement. She was entitled to half the life insurance policy they'd put in place when they were married and that Phillip had subsequently agreed to maintain — five hundred thousand dollars.

Blake made a mental note to check and make sure there'd been no recent, suspicious policy changes. Kate had the equity in the house, and her business had a positive cash flow. Beyond her collecting the insurance money sooner, nothing seemed overtly wrong. On top of that, her ex didn't look like he was going to last long based on the way he'd been drinking.

Blake reached down to pet Watson.

Winslow was a control freak. I'm guessing he still thought he could win his ex-wife back. That and his own guilt, is why her name is going to be listed as a beneficiary on his will. I'd bet money on it.

He gave Watson a rawhide treat. "Enjoy it," he said. "Men like Winslow are way more delusional than dogs."

Death however, had a special appeal in its finality that Blake understood. Kate could be through with Phillip forever. She'd see his death as the final bit of closure that would make it possible for her to go forward with her life without a man she despised.

Revenge had pushed Blake to track down Felix Lewis, the man who molested his brother, twelve years earlier. It had pulled him like a fast moving current. Maybe Kate had gotten caught up in the same rush and needed to wash her hurts away. Blake remembered how he'd followed Lewis to the end of the block, and the sound of pigeons fluttering on an old, factory windowsill towering three floors above them. He thought back to the sweat and the fear he'd seen on Lewis' face, how Lewis had flailed on the street like a fish on the deck of a boat. Blake tried hard not to think about that day.

And then there was the money issue that so often was in play when someone got murdered — the time spent chasing it, concerned about whether there'd be enough, protecting it. Winslow was a taker. He ran a business built on relieving ordinary people and uneducated risk-takers of their savings with a callous disregard for their well being. He seemed to worship money. Like Kate told Blake, money was more addiction than ambition for Phillip.

Blake reminded himself that he had to consider those people as suspects before he excluded them and settled on Kate. Despite her performance earlier that night, Kate remained his prime suspect. A pissed-off investor, angry at the disappearance of his life savings, was reason enough to kill someone. He couldn't rule out everyone and assume she'd done it.

"I'll need to see Winslow's client list, Watson."

I'm going to need to get a search warrant for that and the complaints filed against Winslow with the Securities and

Exchange Commission and NASD, their regulatory organization. I need to know who shook their head and complained the loudest when they looked at their bank statement and saw what was left.

Watson looked up at Blake with his brown eyes, before he rolled over on the rug, stood up, and pretended to shake the water off—like he did when Blake took him for a swim. He tilted his head to the side and barked.

• • •

No matter how big an asshole Winslow was, or what he'd done to Allison, he was still her father. Kathryn didn't have her daughter's number, so it fell on Blake to make the call the following morning. The kid deserved better than reading about her father's death, or hearing about it from some stranger. Some of the money from his life insurance and the inheritance would probably flow her way. She'd have a real chance to get out of the cycle she was in.

"I hope I've caught you at a good time, Allison," Blake said.

"I'm just hanging out."

"You're by yourself?"

"Just me."

"How are you?"

"Okay. I been thinking about . . . maybe breaking away from . . . you know, what I'm doing here in Stockton."

"Good. I've got those phone numbers when you're ready." Blake paused. "I've got some news for you about your family."

"The good people, my little sisters, or my asshole, abusive parents?"

"About your father." There was a degree of discomfort in his voice.

"Okay, go ahead. You don't have to get all melodramatic about it. What?"

"Your father is dead."

"My father? How?"

"We found him on one of the lake trails yesterday, in the late afternoon."

"Jesus, that's a surprise. Not a shocker, but a surprise." Allison was silent for a moment. "I'm not going to cry. He doesn't deserve that. At least I know he won't spy on me anymore or molest my sisters. I'm happy about that part of it, to tell you the truth."

"He was behind the murder of Jack Hamilton," Blake said. "He paid someone to do it."

"That rotten bastard. He should go straight to hell for what he did. How did it happen?"

"We don't know yet. We found him stretched out on a picnic blanket with an empty bottle of Bordeaux. He hit his head on a rock. He'd been there for awhile."

"Are there photos?"

"Yes."

"You've talked to my mother?"

"She knows."

"And my sisters?"

"She was going to tell them last night or this morning. Is there anything you think I should be aware of?" Blake said.

"I suppose you know my father wasn't exactly the kind of guy to hit the trail on his own. He did most of his walking from his car to a bar or some sleazy motel."

"You've got my number," Blake said. "I'll call you in a few days and let you know about the services. In the meantime if you need anything, call me."

"Yeah. Okay."

Blake clicked off. Watson pulled at his pant leg. "I've got to go to work, Watson. See the chief. We've got stuff to talk about."

Blake dialed a second number. "Let Chief Cooper know I'll be there in a couple of hours, Susan. I've got one stop I need to make first."

Blake went back to Hamilton's apartment and took a second look at everything on Hamilton's computer. He drove faster than he should have when he left. Blake sat in the parking lot outside Cooper's office, weighing the possibilities in his mind before walking inside.

Cooper looked across the desk at Blake. "So tell me about it," he said.

"I've been re-thinking everything. I'm starting to feel like maybe I got ahead of myself. Hamilton, the truck that ran me off the road, the shooting in Modesto, and now Winslow's death. I went back to Hamilton's place before I came in here."

"What'd you find?" Cooper looked him straight in the eye.

Blake could see how anxious Cooper was. "Hamilton thought he was being followed the day Kathryn Winslow fired him. The records he took included stuff that dealt with how she juggled the company's pension fund. I don't think Hamilton gave those files back to your officers when they stopped him. He went to an all-night print store the night before and copied volumes of documents. There's a charge for seventy-four dollars on his Visa card. He also made a note in his computer about his suspicion that someone was watching him when he was there at the print shop. Later on, he seemed to chalk it up to his own paranoia and the shock of being fired."

"Someone was looking for those records and the copies he made," Cooper said, "when they broke into Hamilton's apartment and ransacked the place, weren't they?"

"Kathryn Winslow changed the office locks the morning she fired Hamilton and never let him back in. She refused to release his personal contact records, the independent work he'd done for his consulting business, and the rest of his stuff. He never got any of that back. She tried to ruin him."

"That's pretty damn cold," Cooper said. "As I remember, Hamilton's apartment was burglarized and the file with Kathryn Winslow's name on it was empty when you searched his place the first time."

"And he paid his rent a week in advance, and left town with a gun permit and a thirty-eight caliber in his glove compartment," Blake said.

"But we know Winslow paid Steven Hooks to kill him," Cooper said. "That's settled, so what are we talking about."

"Hear me out," Blake said. "What if someone else was following Hamilton and was watching Phillip Winslow as well? What if he, and by he I mean, James Kilmer, Kathryn's brother, planned to eliminate Hamilton. And Phillip Winslow simply beat him to the punch, and did the deed for him?"

Cooper hunched forward in his chair.

Blake knew he had his attention. "Go on."

"What if Kilmer was trying to protect his sister, Kathryn, from prosecution for her handling of the company's pension funds? She shares his name. What she does impacts the family's reputation, Kilmer's reputation." Blake paused. "Suppose Kilmer is still manipulating people behind the scenes, like a symphony conductor with a baton in his hand?"

Blake got up and paced around the room, waiting for Cooper's reaction. For a brief moment, he felt like Deep Throat talking about Watergate to Woodward and Bernstein in the underground parking garage.

"Interesting," Cooper said, "and disturbing."

Cooper rested his head in his hands with his elbows on the desk, immersed in thought. "We're getting ahead of ourselves. We need to wait and see what Phipps has to say. I hope to hell Kathryn Winslow wasn't involved. I hate to think I prompted her to kill her ex-husband when I called and implied that he was responsible for Hamilton's death. I shouldn't be making those kinds of mistakes."

"It's not your fault," Blake said. "You didn't kill anyone."

"Call Phipps tomorrow morning if you haven't heard from him," Cooper said. "So it looks like maybe we've got two murderers at work here. I'll be damned." Cooper lifted his right hand up from the desk. His forehead fell into it like a glove. He looked up at Blake. "Winslow had his pants off."

"He wouldn't have had them down around his ankles if he was just marking his territory. That's what zippers are for. My guess is he'd already had sex or was planning to, anyway," Blake said. "Why is the pants thing bothering you?" Blake said.

"I can't get it out of my head. I'm sure Phipps will check for Viagra. When you talk to him tomorrow, hear him out first, so he doesn't get irritated. I've never known Phipps to miss anything." Cooper closed the case file on his desk and moved it to one side. "Cialis or Levitra, besides the Viagra. See if Hamilton had a prescription. Ask Phipps exactly what he found."

"So you know about all this stuff, huh, Chief?"

"What, you think people over fifty don't have sex? Haven't you ever seen any of those *Desperate Housewives* shows? We need to get a handle on this."

Blake nodded in agreement.

"To hell with it. Just call Phipps now. See if he's working late," Cooper said. "And put the call on speaker."

● ● ●

Phipps picked up on the second ring. "For sure, something strange is going on here. Besides the alcohol, Winslow was packed full of Viagra. His erection could have lasted twelve hours if the fall hadn't broken his dick."

"He broke his dick?" Blake said.

"On impact, when he hit the ground," Phipps said.

Cooper's eyes widened.

"Things were looking up until then," Phipps said, "but there was something else there, too. I'm not sure what, but it was quite a concoction."

"The kind that could kill you?" Blake said. "And did you

have to use that particular word? What about the rock and his head?"

"Which head?" Phipps said.

"All right, already," Blake said. "No identifiable prints?"

"None, besides your victim's."

"Anything else?" Blake asked.

"A partial footprint or two, smaller size than his, a six or a seven, probably a woman. But the trail was dry, a mess, really. The footprint could have been there beforehand."

"So, all things considered, Phipps?"

"So far, every opinion I express is going to be subject to an effective rebuttal by a good defense attorney and an expert witness, unless I can identify the elements in his bloodstream. The tox screens will help me do that. Personally, I think he was intentionally over-dosed. Poisoned."

"Alcohol and erectile dysfunction drugs? They're going to make it sound like a party, instead of premeditated murder," Blake said.

"I'm not done yet, Detective. You got the short-form, preliminary report. Winslow had the long form."

Blake turned to Cooper after hanging up the phone.

"What the hell," Cooper said. "I had no idea Phipps had a sense of humor like that."

"Winslow was on his way to federal prison. Murder wasn't necessary. Kate Winslow could have continued to run her business and focus on being a better mother," Blake said.

"You said their twenty-year old, Allison, has been talking about changing her life. You don't figure her for killing her father?" Cooper said.

"No. She wouldn't do that. She was already out from under him. But somebody saved the two youngest daughters from their father's depravity."

"Nobody else is going to be swindled by him, that's for sure," Cooper said.

Blake got up to leave. He felt himself drift in a moral dilemma, like the one he had with Felix Lewis in New York before he became a cop. He couldn't allow himself to think about passing out a pardon to Kate Winslow or anyone else for that matter. People didn't get to play Macbeth.

CHAPTER TWENTY-SIX

"You want to see your sisters, don't you? Do you need a ride?" Blake wanted Allison's coming for the funeral to seem more inviting than simply asking if she planned to see her mother.

"No, I've got it covered," she said. "Are you planning to be at the funeral home?"

"Yes. There's a Starbucks a couple of blocks away. You can't miss it. Why don't we meet there around ten?"

"Fine. I'm coming for my sisters. I don't care if I see my father in a box. The idea of looking at some petrified mummy pumped full of formaldehyde has never appealed to me. It seems like a barbaric ritual, people standing around talking. My, doesn't he look good? . . . that's sick. He isn't going to look good. He'll look dead."

"To tell you the truth, Allison, I feel the same way you do. I don't see why anyone would want to hold on to a picture in their head of someone laid out in a casket. I can still close my eyes and see my dad that way, and it's been over twenty years."

"I don't care about him. I don't care that he's gone," Allison said. "But I want to see the pictures of where you found him."

"You may find that difficult," Blake said.

"I can handle it."

"I'll bring them, if you're sure."

"I'm sure."

• • •

Allison wore a modest black dress. Her eyes appeared strong

and clear, not like they had been the first time Blake met her in Stockton, hung over from the night before. She had styled her hair and scaled down the call-girl make-up look.

"It's good to see you," Blake said. "What can I get you?"

"Something sweet and hot. You choose."

He came back with a drink for her. She took a taste.

"I like it," she said. "Did you bring the photos?"

"Yes." He set the envelope on the table in front of her. Allison took a long sip of her soy latte and unfastened the clasp.

"Where were they taken?" She looked at Blake.

"On one of the lake trails, a secluded overlook a few miles from where your mother lives. Have you talked to her, Allison?"

"I will, either later today, or tomorrow."

She opened the envelope and slid each of the four pictures out that Blake had selected, one at a time. Her eyes were intent but not emotional, cold but not calloused. She studied each of them, as if she was storing them somewhere in her mind.

Blake sat, watching her. For a moment, he saw what he thought was a flicker in her eye. Allison was hard to read.

"Has my mother seen these?"

"Not yet. I haven't talked to her since the day we discovered your father's body."

"I'm going to stop at the park and smoke a joint," she said.

"Okay, as long as you don't hold up an AM/PM on the way or leave a child in the car."

"See you at the service."

"I'll be the guy in the back looking for suspects. Good luck with your sisters and your mother."

She smiled. "Yeah."

● ● ●

Blake stopped at a bookstore where he bought two poetry books, one by Bill Moyer, the other by Lawrence Ferlinghetti, before heading to the white brick funeral home sandwiched between the retail strip malls and a big box office supply store. He planned to begin reading one while he sat in the last row where he could make a quick escape. The idea of a eulogy for a child abuser disgusted him. The fact that his twelve-year old brother had been molested by one when Blake was in high school, made it worse.

After the service, he stopped off at headquarters where he ran into Chief Cooper in the hallway.

"Was anybody crying?" Cooper said.

"Just the two youngest girls. It looked like an obligation or a prolonged disappointment for everyone else. You know Chief, I just don't see Phillip Winslow as the kind of man who invites a woman to a picnic and has sex in the great outdoors. That's something I would do, but Winslow? I don't think so. He's more the hotel room, hooker type. This whole thing by the lake seems like nostalgia to me, the good old days that probably never were that good."

"You mean to tell me, Blake, you've had sex outdoors in broad daylight?"

"I enjoyed every minute of it, too." Blake grinned.

"Some of my constituents would call that indecent exposure."

"I call it fun. Most of your constituents are probably Republicans." Blake smiled.

"I've got plenty of support from the Democrats and we've got the Green Party here in California. I guess this means I don't need to ask if you're following my advice about balancing work and play." Cooper reached for the glass on his desk. "What did you learn at the funeral?"

"I got the names of two men from Los Angeles who signed the guest registry. One of them fit the description of the guy Hamilton had dinner with in Big Sur."

"You talked with him?"

"Outside, for a few minutes after the service. He and Hamilton were fraternity brothers. They kept in touch. He said

Hamilton was on edge, that he suspected someone was following him. Hamilton told him his apartment had been burglarized. That's why he left Sierra Springs. He was unnerved."

"I don't get it. So why was Hamilton's fraternity brother at the funeral?" Cooper said.

"I asked. He knew about Hamilton's affair with Kathryn, how much he cared for her. He wanted to tell her that, and be supportive."

"Did Hamilton say anything to him about who he felt was watching him?" Cooper said. He locked his hands together, stretched them, and cracked his knuckles.

"Suits, the kind who hurt people or steal their money during the day and go home to their families at night. He said Hamilton thought they worked for Kate Winslow's brother, the billionaire from Utah. There were Utah plates on one of the cars in the parking lot the night he copied the documents he removed from the business the day he got fired. Maybe, he wasn't so paranoid after all."

"I'll be damned," Cooper said. "I wonder if Kathryn did it, or if her brother lured Winslow over there with a hooker and finished him off. You've got to talk with her, Blake. See what she says. Check in with Phipps and see if the autopsy has been completed and what else you have to work with."

CHAPTER TWENTY-SEVEN

Thirty minutes later, Blake called the coroner's office.

"I was about to call you," Phipps said. "Winslow was poisoned. Besides a massive dose of Viagra and the wine, there was some wood alcohol in the mix. The guy probably never regained consciousness after he drank the stuff. If he did, his vision would have been badly blurred. He'd have been dizzy and disoriented. His pupils were dilated. His blood pH level was off the charts. The longer Winslow lay there without any kind of treatment, the worse his symptoms would have been."

"Sounds bleak," Blake said.

"You know, the federal government used wood alcohol back in the 1930s to try and scare people in to giving up drinking. The Feds got frustrated trying to enforce Prohibition, so they ordered the poisoning of some of the industrial alcohols that were regularly being stolen by bootleggers and resold to the public. Some recent estimates claim as many as ten thousand people were killed that way. Poisoned basically. Whoever killed your victim, used way more than they had to, which makes it more likely this was a novice poisoner," Phipps said.

"The past keeps happening over and over again," Blake said.

"If someone had found Winslow within a few hours and he'd gotten immediate treatment, he might have made it. But your victim got a big dose. This was made to look like an accident. He had another Viagra pill in his shirt pocket, so I guess somebody wanted us to think he had a heart attack when he combined the booze, the sex, and the Viagra."

"So he had sex?" Blake said.

"Actually, no," Phipps said. "but that was a smart catch, you're asking if he had."

"Thanks."

Blake closed the phone and sat in his car thinking about how black widow spiders kill their mates. I've got to talk with Kate tomorrow. She should have left him alone. Winslow'd have rotted away in jail.

• • •

Blake drove back home to his apartment. He didn't want to keep thinking about the case, but he kept playing it over and over in his mind like a forty-five record with a scratch. After three glasses of Port, he crashed. When he woke up at eleven, he picked up the phone and called Julianna.

"It's good to hear your voice. I'm sorry, I'm calling so late. I fell asleep," Blake said.

"I'm glad you called," Julianna said.

"I've watched you in your classroom a couple times. You're a talented teacher. I've been wanting to ask you something,"

"What?" she said.

"I just wondered what you like most about teaching?"

"I guess I just love helping kids learn and feel good about themselves. That's why I work so hard at it during the school year. Six days a week most of the time," Julianna said. "Dealing with the administration and the Board of Education is the irritating part. I feel bad when I can't give kids as much help as they need. Some of them don't get any support from their parents."

"That makes life harder," Blake said.

"Some of their parents are migrant farmworkers. They're here for all the open houses and teacher-parent conferences. They care. They sacrifice for them. Go figure — the American dream, a better life. Some parents take it for granted and others walk twenty miles through the desert hoping to find it."

"I talked with Chief Cooper this afternoon," Blake said. "We had a good conversation about the case I've been working on. He couldn't believe I'd ever had sex outdoors, in broad daylight."

"I'm not going to ask how the subject came up. I still can't believe we did what we did," Julianna said. "I may have to blush if I ever meet Chief Cooper. I'm a school teacher, after all."

"I didn't tell him it was you."

"Oh, so it was one of your other girlfriends?" Julianna said playfully. "You didn't go into any detail, I hope."

"I'm not the kiss and tell type. I prefer to think of myself as a gentleman, like Robin Hood."

"And I'm your Maid Marian, your woman in the woods? I suppose you're going to tell me your staff has found its true home?"

"I was about to say that," Blake said. "You know, I bought some poetry books today so I could serenade you with words from my heart."

"That should be exciting."

"There's an Open Mic this Friday night at a little café, near where I live. I'm thinking of reading some poetry and playing my guitar."

"Are you going to take your gun with you and shoot people if they don't like your poetry?"

"I promise not to, if you'll come."

"Pick me up at six-thirty?" Julianna said.

"You can stay over at my place. Pack your bikini or that black one-piece. You can leave your p.j.'s at home. We'll go swimming afterwards."

"Love you, Dylan."

"See you at six-thirty, Teach."

"No skinny-dipping this time," Julianna said.

"I'm happy we did," Blake said. "We should do it again."

CHAPTER TWENTY-EIGHT

Blake talked with Cooper the following afternoon. "Thought you'd want to know, Chief. I got a call from a friend who works as a realtor in a title office. The first and second mortgages on Kathryn Winslow's home were paid off by her brother, James Kilmer, the Utah billionaire, six months after her divorce was finalized. He tendered a cashier's check for seven hundred-fifty thousand dollars.

"Really," Cooper said.

"Makes me wonder if Kilmer paid her off for divorcing her husband, whether he offered up the money as an extra incentive for her to divorce him once and for all. Phillip had to be an embarrassment to his brother-in-law. Kilmer's got a big Initial Public Offering in the works. I've been reading about it in *The Wall Street Journal*."

"The local paper doesn't cover much in the way of financial news," Cooper said.

"I'm sure Kathryn's brother doesn't want anything to disturb his IPO, or the image he's cultivated. There's also been a rumor floating around the internet that Winslow was planning to change his last name and make it Phillip Kilmer-Winslow. James Kilmer couldn't have been happy about that," Blake said.

"Maybe he heard about the abuse, what Winslow did to his niece, Allison. Either way," Cooper said, "it's beginning to look like you're right about Kilmer being the other player in the game. He's got more money and markers to move around the Monopoly board than anyone else. I've got a hunch you're going to have an interesting conversation with Kathryn Winslow. Have you called her?"

"I was minutes away from doing that."

"I saw Phipps' report. We don't have any fingerprints or tie-down evidence yet about who else was at the lake," Cooper said.

"Be nice if we did, wouldn't it? How come life gets so complicated?"

"I been trying to figure that out for years, now. When you're dealing with women," Cooper said, "things usually do get more complicated." He rolled his eyes. "I've been married over thirty years. Can't begin to tell you how many times I put my foot in my mouth. Good luck with Mrs. Winslow."

● ● ●

Two hours later, Blake drove past the gatehouse on his way to Kate's front door. He looked at his watch — 1:25 p.m. The kids were in school. Blake followed her inside and through the house to the patio overlooking her backyard.

"I'll be right with you. I just got home from the office." She walked back into the kitchen and brought out a pitcher of iced tea with two glasses, then filled them both. She looked stunning. "Why did you want to see me?"

"Your ex-husband's death wasn't accidental."

"I thought it was a heart attack."

"He was packed full of Viagra. He'd been drinking quite a bit, too."

"I heard you weren't supposed to do that. It's a dangerous combination isn't it, pills and booze? Do you suppose he was planning to have sex with some bimbo he picked up?"

"Perhaps he was, or it could have been with somebody he already knew," Blake said.

"His taste in women has been going downhill for years now.

Did you find the woman who was there? Maybe you could ask her about it."

"No such luck, not yet anyway. Where were you when this happened?"

"When did it happen, Detective?"

"Sometime between four and eight p.m. last Monday."

She paused for a minute or two. "Let me think . . . Monday, I was probably home that night, working on the books."

"Did you make any calls? Was anyone here with you?"

"No, I don't believe so. The girls were here, doing their homework, of course. Is that problematical?"

"It is what it is."

"You're not suggesting . . . "

"That you had something to do with it? I didn't say that."

"Detective, I didn't kill my ex-husband. He was paying me alimony and child support. I like getting those checks every month. I have two young girls to take care of, and a business to run. That costs money. I don't make that much. Our gross sales are less than two-million dollars annually." She touched her mouth with a napkin.

Blake watched her carefully. The theory was that when people moved their head to the left, they were trying to remember something. When they moved to the right, they were making stuff up. Hers moved right.

"Does it pain me that he's dead? I won't lie about that. I didn't cry at his funeral."

"What did your brother, James, think about him?"

"James lives in Utah. He's a busy man. He has his own life and concerns. We didn't talk about Phillip."

"You didn't discuss Phillip's death with him?"

"No, not really. He sent a card. He asked if he could help. I told him I was fine."

"And that's it?"

"Not much to tell."

"And Phillip's will?"

"That was settled years ago. The inheritance was spelled out and agreed to in our divorce settlement. Nothing's been changed. I'm leading my life. Phillip led his."

She reached for the iced tea and filled Blake's glass, extending her leg toward his. "I'm unattached, Detective, available."

He could almost feel the heat coming off her. "I told you I'm involved." He moved his chair to establish more distance between them. "We can't go there."

"You could have any position you wanted with me. Just so you know, in case anything ever changes."

Blake paused to get back on track. "Did you speak with your daughter, Allison?"

"After the service, for a few minutes. She talked with her sisters. They seemed happy to see her."

"What else can you can tell me about your ex?"

"Nothing that I can think of right now, anyway. I'll call you if something occurs to me. He shouldn't have been mixing his medicine and liquor."

Blake got up and Kate Winslow walked him past her bedroom, where she stopped for a moment and looked back at him, before continuing to the front door. "Tell Chief Cooper he has my full support."

Blake walked down the stone path to his car. The sun had made the black leather seats heat up. Kate Winslow had done the same thing to him. He shook his head and exhaled. "She must have some seriously strong customer loyalty if she's this friendly with her business clients."

● ● ●

Blake started questioning himself on the way to the gatehouse. Was I too easy on her? I can't seriously expect she's going to confess, or hand over evidence her brother murdered Phillip. Allison's eyes had stopped and moved again a certain way when I showed her the photos of her father on the lake trail. I need to ask her if her mother said anything at the funeral.

There was a good six hundred milligrams of Viagra in Winslow's system, six times high-end normal, and he had another blue pill in his shirt pocket. Except for the wood alcohol, it wouldn't have been a bad way to go — making love to a woman. Not from a man's perspective anyway. Winslow wouldn't, have taken more than two pills of his own volition. The more Blake thought about it, the more everything pointed to Kate.

When her ex-husband's doctor faxed over the prescription records to headquarters, it read Cialis. The toxicology report said Viagra. Made Blake wonder where a woman like Kate Winslow would turn to get Viagra without a prescription? Not from an internet site with all the scams and ED drug-counterfeiting going on, and she wouldn't have wanted a paper or a phone trail. The more likely scenario was from a source she could trust. Maybe, someone she knew, someone a little older she was intimate with — like Jack Hamilton.

● ● ●

Blake drove to Hamilton's place to look for a prescription bottle or a medical record file. If that didn't work, he'd call Hamilton's HMO provider or his doctor and try to con them and avoid the HIPPA privacy rules. He remembered Cooper's insistence they check for all three ED drugs in Winslow's system, not just Viagra. Cooper was smart. His reputation as an investigator was established long before he became an administrator.

Once Blake got Hamilton's apartment key and started looking, it was easy to find the little empty, orange prescription bottle. Blake went out to his car, got a pair of latex gloves, and removed the bottle from Hamilton's top dresser drawer. He congratulated himself when Kathryn's prints were lifted off the bottle later that day.

● ● ●

"I need to talk with you again," Blake said, when he called Kate the next morning.

"About what?"

"In person, alone, when your daughters aren't around."

"Late this afternoon is good for me. Are you re-considering my offer?" Kathryn said.

"I'll talk with you about it when I see you."

Blake parked next to the silver Jaguar at her house. She answered the door, wearing black pants and a sheer white silk top that left little to his imagination. They sat at the table off the kitchen in front of the sliding door. He looked at her eyes and then at the full roundness of her breasts. It was all he could do not to stare. She glanced down, then back at him. The sun was streaming in. Her eyes and the way she moved her lips made it clear she wanted him to stream in, too. He was tempted.

"I don't think you've been honest with me."

"What do you mean?"

"You acted surprised when I gave you the news about your ex-husband's death that first night. It turns out, he didn't have a prescription for Viagra. Phillip used Cialis. You probably didn't know that. You got the Viagra from Jack Hamilton. You picked up his prescription refill. Your fingerprints were on the bottle at his place. I think you emptied that bottle the same day you entered Hamilton's apartment to look for the partnership agreement he had. You took most of the pills back to your place, crushed them, and poured them into a wine bottle."

"What are you talking about?"

She had what Blake thought was a pretend-to-be-puzzled expression. Blake stood, walked over to the kitchen and opened first one, and then a second cupboard door.

"What exactly are you doing, Detective?"

"Is there a mortar and pestle in here?"

Kathryn was still sitting at the table. "And what if there were? What would that prove? Are kitchen appliances against the law?"

Blake looked across the room. "I think you invited your ex for an early evening meeting and packed a special picnic basket for him."

"I think you should close my cupboard doors and cool down your misconceptions. I'm a mother, not a madwoman. I told you, I get an alimony and a child support check every month. Why would I risk that? If someone did in fact kill Phillip, it wasn't me. I'm certainly not a murderer and if I were, I would be considerably more clever than you give me credit for."

She looked across the table at him, seeming, Blake thought, to look for a sign that her explanation was prevailing. He didn't give her one.

She took a sip of the sun tea on the table. "I admit to having had some problems with the company's pension fund," Kathryn said. "Jack was right to be concerned about that. But that's all been corrected and made right. I fell behind. That happens with a lot of businesses these days. Temporary cash flow problems, nothing more than that. I didn't kill anyone."

"It's going to come apart. You know that, don't you?" Blake stared at her before opening another cabinet door.

"You're way off-base with your accusations. You need to re-think this and we can start over. What you're suggesting doesn't make sense. I wasn't at the lake."

"You called your ex-husband earlier that afternoon and invited him to meet you."

"I called him to talk about the children's schedules and school."

"He was going to jail, Kate. It was unnecessary. Don't you understand that? We tied Phillip to Hamilton's murder. He paid someone to do it. Your ex-husband was about to be arrested."

"So why then would I bother to kill him?"

"I thought perhaps you'd want to tell me."

"I didn't do anything."

"I'm going to wind up coming back here to arrest you at some point."

"You don't have to do that. If you want to put the cuffs on me and tie me to the bed, we can do that right now."

"Would you please stop it with the offers of enticement."

"You're wrong, Detective. So I twisted the cap on Jack's prescription bottle, so what? We were lovers. I think you and I should call it a day before my children get home, unless you really think you have enough to charge me. And next time, you might want to Mirandize me. Isn't that what they call it?"

"You signed for the Viagra when you picked up Jack Hamilton's prescription refill."

"We were going to get back together."

"You're sure about that," Blake said, "after you fired him?"

"We needed each other," Kathryn said.

Blake thought about the painting Hamilton had purchased in Big Sur. He remembered the studio's owner telling him how Hamilton had said it was a getting-back-together-gift for someone special.

• • •

The case against Kate was circumstantial. There wasn't enough hard evidence to convict her. Blake knew it, Cooper knew it, and so did she. He didn't Mirandize her because he assumed she'd be unnerved when he confronted her, that she might just confess and he could gloss over the legal technicalities. But she seemed emboldened, and that surprised him. He'd thrown his suppositions out there like a fly fisherman, hoping she'd take the bait. She darted away instead.

He'd been on the force almost four years, a detective for close to three. Long enough to know investigations ebbed and flowed. Something important gets revealed, suspects and witnesses clam up, frustration sets in. Most of the time, the silence had to do with people not wanting to get involved or incriminate themselves. It was more like a habit ingrained in their cellular DNA than a real decision. Confessions seldom came easy. If some pissed-off investor didn't do it, Blake reasoned, then either Kate or Kilmer had. Either way, Kilmer could be involved in the cover-up.

● ● ●

Blake called Allison's number in Stockton from the cell phone in his car. He wanted her to confront the truth about her mother. He guessed she wouldn't expect to hear from him so soon. "How did things go with your sisters?"

Blake heard the stereo in the background.

"I miss my sisters," she said.

"And you got to talk with your mother?"

"We were speaking, anyway," Allison said.

"Did she say anything about how she thought it happened? Who was responsible?" Blake heard a male voice on the building's intercom speaker. Allison had a visitor, which meant she'd only have a minute or two for him.

"Detective, there's only so much I can say. Who's going to take care of my sisters? I can't. A twenty-year old college drop-out doing drugs?"

Blake heard a knock on her door.

"Hold on. I'm coming."

Blake guessed Allison was standing in her kitchen where she'd made him coffee.

"I've got to go. I'm still trading money for sex."

"There's probably an inheritance out there," Blake said.

"In the meantime, I've got bills to pay."

The line went dead.

The dial tone was all Blake could hear.

CHAPTER TWENTY-NINE

Blake wondered how much of what he'd said to Kate reverberated in her mind. He pictured her standing on the balcony off her living room, looking down toward the lake where the trail wound through the scrub brush turned yellow with autumn. Did she relive how it felt when she watched her ex-husband fall to the ground? Did she re-trace her movements and ask whether anyone had seen her that night? Could she be that confident she hadn't made a mistake?

He'd blocked Frederick Lewis and New York out of his head years ago. The nightmare drove him to begin with, the one that kept coming back where he descended through a trapdoor in the floor going from room to room in a high rise apartment building, down the fire escape on the outside of the building, through the windows, intruding into stranger's lives looking for Lewis, moving one step closer to hell. After the nightmares, guilt set in from time to time.

Blake figured Kate had done the same with her memories of Phillip—shoved them in a room and closed the door to remembering, like soldiers did during war. He guessed she was better at compartmentalizing than he was. He'd never been able to turn them on and off like a water faucet, the way she seemed to.

"It was pre-meditated." Blake looked out the window at the street from his dining room table. "She's an amateur, Watson, and amateurs make mistakes." Kate probably never thought there'd be an autopsy.

• • •

Blake picked up the hardback copy of Kilmer's autobiography he'd been reading. Kilmer had become a fixture on the *Forbes'* 400 List. He'd made a fortune in pharmaceuticals and real estate. Kilmer had a dozen patents for medical devices in his name, and a fifteen-thousand square foot cabin near Park City, Utah. He and his sister had grown up in the Idaho Panhandle where the wind blew hard and the snow blocked the roads in winter. They didn't come from old money.

Forbes Magazine called him inventive, intensely competitive, secretive, and resourceful. So did the book's dust jacket.

Allison said he was a religious whack job, judgmental, suspicious, and an even worse control freak than her father.

• • •

Kilmer wrote about being smarter and more resourceful than the other children in his family. And how he'd learned to do things for himself when he was a young boy. He admitted to never putting much trust in other people. And while he loved his sister, Kathryn, which was evident in his book, Blake suspected he didn't really trust her judgement. Kilmer's mantra was self reliance.

Kathryn told Blake the story, when they first met, about how she hid in the closets when their mother was in her dark moods. Her brother wrote about how he'd read science and chemistry books, and the biographies of famous people. He wrote about how he felt destined to be a powerful man others would come to for favors. And now he was.

She told Blake she hadn't heard from her brother in months, except for the card he sent when Phillip died and a call asking if she was okay. The phone records he examined however, showed that Kilmer had called Kate three times, after each of Blake's last three visits to her home.

Had Kilmer asked her if she'd killed Phillip and applauded

her initiative? Did Kilmer wonder, like Blake did, if his sister had made any mistakes? Why had she lied about talking to her brother?

Blake's mind kept coming back to Kilmer. Blake's grandfathers never trusted rich men, neither did his dad, and Blake had the same kind of bias he didn't always disguise. He needed proof of Kilmer's involvement. Blake's instincts told him the evidence had to be out there, somewhere. One way to find the proof was to put himself in Kilmer's head, so he could feel the power a man like Kilmer commanded and understand the dilemmas he faced.

The white knight, romantic illusion Blake and his friend, Rob Johnson, had grown up with came into full view. For him, being rich meant you could live anywhere, travel any place, surround yourself with fine art, and eat like a king. You could drive an Aston Martin DB9, buy the best technology and your own computer guru. Hire your own personal trainer He could create opportunities for the people who mattered most to him, and for anyone he wanted to whose life intersected with his.

He guessed that illusion didn't match up with Kilmer's billionaire reality, the one that might just as easily have been about greed and gold faucets, and looking at the people around him, including his own family, with distrust and doubt. Are they after my money? Is their affection genuine? Maybe those were the questions Kilmer kept asking himself. That left Blake not knowing, but reasoning, that being wealthy could be all those things.

Blake was a scrapper as a grade-school kid, who'd duke it out with anyone regardless of how big they were. So Kilmer was a billionaire, so what? His parents would have told him that didn't mean Kilmer was better or smarter than he was. Money couldn't make all of someone's problems go away. Sometimes, money brought new ones.

There was a permanence to death. Blake found his younger

brother at the bottom of a stone quarry. He'd shot himself in the head with his father's service revolver. That ended the myth for him, that people didn't bleed when someone pulled the trigger. Later, when his father was killed in a car accident during Blake's sophomore year of college, he got reminded a second time that nothing brought back the dead.

Now, he and Allison, and Kate Winslow, had to deal with the consequences of events that weren't of their making. "So will James Kilmer if he's involved," Blake said aloud. "If there's a free pass to hand out, it goes to a commoner, not a rich prick who uses people."

CHAPTER THIRTY

Blake sat across the desk from Cooper. The chief was wearing a freshly pressed white shirt and tie, drinking coffee. He looked well rested, in command of everything.

"What did Kathryn Winslow say when you laid your chips on the table about the Viagra and her ex-husband's last rites at the lake?" Cooper asked.

"She claimed complete innocence, said there was no reason for her to do it. That she wasn't a murderer. She was composed. She knows we don't have enough to charge her."

"She's right, you know, and smart." Cooper's expression was somewhere between a smile and a frown.

"She invited me into her bed," Blake said.

Cooper looked up. His eyebrows danced up and down, Groucho Marx style. "She's quite a temptress, isn't she?" Cooper got up from his desk. "You better be careful with her. I don't have to tell you what kind of trouble you'd get into if you strayed. Imagine your admirer, Captain Jameson, pacing back and forth, pointing his index finger like Richard Nixon did when he gave his Checkers speech.

"I told Blake not to fuck it up and that's exactly what Mister Ivy League, ass-bite did. I was right all along and Blake was wrong, wrong, and wrong again."

Cooper slapped his hand on his leg and laughed. "I guess you know, I'm not just kidding."

"Yeah, Chief, I get it. Don't worry. My girlfriend is plenty for me. Life is complicated enough with one woman. Kate Winslow is tempting, but I'm not going to make that mistake. I appreciate you're channeling Nixon and Jameson, though. With a little more practice, you could do stand-up on Conan's show."

"You've got to get Kathryn Winslow to crack, shake that foundation of hers. Get more from her oldest daughter and her brother. Kilmer must suspect his sister had something to do with the murder. Either that, or maybe he was behind the whole thing. But he's smart. If he was keeping an eye on things, like you think he was, he probably knew we were about to put the cuffs on his brother-in-law. And if that's true, he would have left Winslow alone. He wouldn't have killed him," Cooper said.

"So if it wasn't some pissed-off investor that Phillip Winslow ruined, and neither one of us thinks that right now, then we agree . . . Kate Winslow is still our most likely suspect."

"I think you're right," Cooper said. "Make sure you've covered the investor angle and keep pressing on the other fronts. Keep me posted and keep your zipper up. Check out her phone records, and see if anybody saw her on the lake trails that night, and whether her two youngest daughters were home."

"I'm gonna need to go to Utah at some point," Blake said.

"Let's cross that bridge when we come to it."

"Chief."

"What, Blake?"

"There's no bridge. It's dry land all the way there once you get over the mountains."

"Get out of here, Blake. And think about taking a little time to yourself with that girlfriend of yours. You look tired."

The parallels with his own life—Allison and his brother, Jeff's, abuse and death. Abandonment, lives cut short were wearing down hard on him. Cooper seemed to pick up on that.

• • •

At 4:30 Monday afternoon, Blake dialed Allison's Stockton number. "We didn't get to finish our conversation the other day. I need to talk with you for a few minutes?"

"So?"

"Did you find out anything about your father's will?"

"Maybe this week. We're supposed to have a meeting in some attorney's office."

"It may be risky. If I stop turning tricks, my pimp's not the understanding type."

"I told you, I'd help. Call me when you're ready to make a move."

"You'd do that for me?"

"I don't say things I don't mean."

"By the way, why did you call me?"

"You called your Uncle James the Godfather of Morality. Where did that come from?"

"Life. He was around a lot when we were little. Mother took us to his place in the mountains and to Lake Powell. Children should always be obedient, Allison, he'd say, just like wives should be. I heard that a hundred times."

Blake heard a crinkly potato chip bag and a reality TV show in the background. Sometimes Allison seemed sixteen to Blake, other times she was a tired thirty.

"Good old Uncle James. Would you like to hear another one of his speeches, Detective? I've got to warn you though. He was long-winded. He didn't have to come up for air and we weren't allowed to interrupt."

"You've memorized it?" Blake said.

"It's like he stamped the words in my head with a branding iron, the way they did the livestock at the cattle auctions we went to when I was a kid."

"So, what did he say?"

"He'd start off telling us how women have more professions open to them now, than our mothers did. Then he'd go on about how we'd need to heed our husband's counsel. Just like when your father tells you to do something, you do it. No questions. Women should stay silent and listen, he said."

"How did you feel when you're uncle told you that?" Blake said.

"I went shopping and smoked weed. I couldn't stand his platitudes. He told us the same things over and over, like we were deaf mutes."

"Sounds like one of the kind of broken record nagging my ex-wife used to engage in," Blake said.

"I guess maybe that's why my mother didn't say anything when she saw my father molest me. All that misplaced piety and blind obedience is pure bullshit."

"I agree. It is bullshit," Blake said.

"He ruined people's businesses, too. I remember hearing him rip people out on the phone when we stayed at his house in Utah. One time I saw a woman run out of his office in tears when I was little, and we were waiting to visit with him. A minute later, he was all smiley with us and talking about how we needed to be nice. Uncle James wasn't who he pretended to be. Neither was my father."

"*Forbes Magazine* described your Uncle James as generous," Blake said.

"Oh, he's generous, all right, when it suits him. He makes people feel indebted so he can control them."

"What did he think of your father?"

"Not much, like my father was too puffed up about himself. That stock market investment stuff my father was involved with bothered Uncle James, especially the booze and the SEC investigation."

"Did he know what your father did to you?"

"Are you kidding? My mother never told anyone."

"What do you suppose he would have done had he known?"

"He would have paid someone to kill him . . . oh, my God, did I just say that?"

They both went silent. Her words hung in the air like a single piece of worn, wet clothing left outside to dry in the wind.

CHAPTER THIRTY-ONE

"What now, Detective. What are you going to do?" Allison said.

"I'm going to think about how to get from Point A to Point B. Call me when you need me."

Blake felt frustrated and fenced in, like a butterfly in a glass jar banging his wings against the walls. He needed some fresh air and solitude, some time to himself in the woods. He stopped off at his place to pick up Watson and change clothes before heading toward a stretch of the American River Canyon near where he lived. He parked in the wide-out along the road and cut through to the path with his climbing poles and a water bottle in hand. The start of hunting season was a few weeks away, not that it mattered to him. He never enjoyed the sport. The odds weren't in the animal's favor. A bow and arrow okay, a thirty-aught-six with a telescopic sight, not fair. An AR-15 — seriously?

The woods were a sanctuary for Blake, a place for quiet, communing with nature, and meditation. Five minutes in and the sound of traffic was absent. Just him and his dog, Watson. He hadn't called Julianna for several days. He missed being next to her and seeing her smile. She was out of town on a women's retreat. The girls were at their dad's, who reportedly, had stopped drinking.

Watson tugged at his leash. Gordon Setters were originally bred in Scotland and the north of England to hunt game birds. Watson was an excellent tracker. He liked to get his nose down in the bushes and point at anything that moved.

The path was mostly level. Blake and Watson had it to themselves, so they ran. It was a good mile before they stopped. He poured some water for Watson in one of those collapsible canvas bowls. Watson lapped it up before barking at a squirrel and readying himself to bolt again. Blake tugged on his leash, and the gray squirrel scrambled under the brush. Blake stretched out atop an old cement piling abandoned decades ago, staring at the sky. "You and me, Watson. So tell me, how's Freddie been treating you?"

Watson barked and flapped his ears around.

"You got some advantages being a dog. No deadlines, no assholes to deal with, no criminals, just good grub, lawns and grass to roll around on. I bet you never think about getting from Point A to Point B. Just hit the trail, go where it leads you."

Watson pawed at the ground and stretched, before barking at Blake's toes.

The two of them got to a place where there was a waterfall, smaller than it had been in the spring when the snow melt was running. They went beyond it, to where the crows circled and rode the wind currents. No phones, just the river, the wind, and the trees.

The confluence had become a familiar spot for Blake, close to where he lived. He went there when he was pressed for time, but wanted a taste of nature away from people. Four years earlier, he had sat near the bank where the north and middle forks of the river met, depressed, drinking too much. He'd spent days staring out the windows of his old apartment, and lying on the floor staring at the ceiling. He felt like he'd wasted too much of his life, didn't see the point of it. A year passed. He went to a therapist, tried Prozac, then came back to the same spot at the water's edge where he decided he was strong enough to change.

"Do something more with your life," his mother had told him on the phone. "Get the lead out of your ass and stop feeling sorry for yourself." Her voice and the memories of his dad and two grandfathers, all strong men who so far as Blake knew had never given up on anything, pulled him out of what he thought of now, as a long sleep.

That day by the river marked the start of a gradual, steady climb back from his personal abyss. The police job was about making a difference, doing something that mattered. Blake stuck to himself when he started. He had a lot to sort through. That's probably why some of the other people in the department thought he was stand-offish, or assumed he had a superior attitude.

● ● ●

After a couple of hours, Blake and Watson hiked back at a leisurely pace, past a place overlooking the river where he'd picnicked once with a woman he dated a few months before Julianna. Blake smiled. The location had seemed secluded back then, until two nude gay guys drifted by on inner-tubes with their flagpoles raised. His date was good natured, but the relationship was short-lived.

She was a hiker and a scientist for the state. They diagnosed each other and decided they weren't a good match, but neither one of them had been with anyone for a while. The sex was like finding out you could still ride a bike after a stay in the hospital. Later, when he told his friend Rob about what happened, Rob told him there was a nude beach downstream from where he'd been, where people had been going for years.

When Julianna came along, everything crystallized for Blake. There was color in the world again, and a sense of newness. She wasn't easy, but then he didn't care so much about easy. He had that when he was out of the country, before California. After a while, Julianna began to seem like everything he ever wanted in a woman. His life became better, and he was happy again. His mood, however, began to darken whenever he went for a month or so without time in the woods.

• • •

He called Julianna when he got home and told her how much he loved her. Blake got in his car and decided to bring her and the girls a decadent dessert of chocolate mousse accentuated by fresh raspberries, and a bouquet of fresh flowers. She invited him to stay the night. Once the girls had gone to sleep, they made long, passionate love. She fell asleep with her head on his shoulder.

After breakfast the next day, Julianna and the girls were off to school. Blake moved a bit slower. He locked up with the key Julianna had given him. The drive across the causeway gave him time to think. He had some decisions to make about the investigation and needed to stop at his office to review his messages.

• • •

Silver Springs had a lower than average crime rate. Murders and muggings were few and far between. Bank robberies and business break-ins were infrequent. Car thefts and small-time burglaries were more the norm, with an assortment of domestic disturbances, vandalism, and a growing number of identity theft cases. This was a slow day, and morale within the department was high.

He picked up a copy of the local paper and read through it. The story about Jack Hamilton's death and the arrests in the case were on the front page. There was a local crime section in the middle of the paper before the sports pages — three car break-ins, two DUI's, and a notice about an office burglary. Blake recognized the address of the office — the therapist he'd seen was in the same building. No suspects were noted or details provided, beyond the date and time.

He checked to see who was handling the case. He saw Sandusky's name and went down the hall to see if he was in.

The therapist's office was in an older Victorian house, close to the center of Sierra Springs that had been zoned commercial. There wasn't an alarm. Sometime after 11:00 p.m., the back door lock had been drilled. The cash box in the building's administrative office was looted of several hundred dollars. Sandusky figured the perpetrator had walked up the back steps from the parking lot, through the community kitchen to the reception area, and down the hall, where he punched out the passage locks in two offices — the medical secretary's and Myra Sebring's office. Sebring's file cabinet was in plain view once the door was opened. All of her client files for people whose last names started with "W" were missing.

"Keep me posted, will you, Sandusky? I'm curious about this. I'm wondering if it might tie into my case, somehow. You know, Phillip Winslow's death. Chief Cooper and I are working on this together. Has the therapist notified her clients?"

"I don't believe so. She said she didn't want to upset anyone and cause them undue anxiety. Evidently, she has duplicate records or notes of some sort that she can rely on."

"Don't publicize the details yet and don't alert or approach Kathryn Winslow or her daughter, Allison, about this. Kathryn is a suspect in her ex-husband's death. She might have had a file in there."

"I'll let you know what develops. I've got no clues at this point and no witnesses. It looks professional. No prints. Nothing was missing from the secretary's office besides the cash box," Sandusky said. "They didn't go into any other offices, just Sebring's."

"Small pickings for a pro, unless he was looking for blackmail material or hoping for a lot more cash." Blake walked down the hall to what he fondly called his General Eisenhower desk. He stopped at the vending machines and then thought better about drinking rot-gut coffee with powdered coffee-mate additive and eating a cellophane-wrapped sweet roll. "No wonder we've got an obesity epidemic in this country." He pulled some raw almonds out of his pocket and a pack of pro-endorphin energy powder he occasionally mixed with water or soy milk.

"W" for Winslow, he thought. I wonder if Myra Sebring was Kate's therapist, and Allison's?

Blake climbed in his car and drove to the Winslow house. He stopped to talk with the security guard who manned the small, stone structure twenty feet in front of the gate. Blake lowered the window and held up his shield. "I need to ask you a question?"

"Sure," the guard said.

"Have you ever had the feeling in the last month or two that somebody's been watching the comings and goings of your residents?"

"Yes, once in a while, anyway. We've got some wealthy people here . . . NBA players, a couple newscasters, CEO's at stock brokerage firms, real estate developers. We get some paparazzi every now and then. Maybe a divorce lawyer who puts a P.I. to work to get some dirt on one of his clients."

Blake sucked it up. He didn't want to interrupt.

"They usually park right across the street, or down the road a few hundred feet with their cameras and legal pads. I know they're writing stuff down. Sometimes they wave or even bring us coffee. It makes the day go faster for me. It's pretty boring in here."

"Anybody ever watching Mrs. Winslow on Lauren Way?"

"Hard to say. Maybe."

"Next time, write down some plate numbers for me."

"Sure."

"Anything come to mind now that we're talking about this?"

"Maybe. I've seen one car here, a rental from Enterprise. Two guys, suit and ties, straight-arrow types. They look almost like Mormon missionaries or Baptist preachers. You get the feeling they'd like to come over and convert you."

"How often?"

"Quite a bit. Especially lately. Stop by, you might see for yourself."

Blake reached into the Audi's side door pocket. "Here's my card. I'd appreciate if you'd keep your eyes open and give me a call when you see them again. It doesn't make any difference what time it is."

"She seems like a nice lady."

"I think she is. Thanks."

Blake pulled up next to the Jag. The gardener trimmed a hedge of Photinia and spread mulch. Blake rang twice and smiled when Kate answered the door.

He started shuffling his feet on the door mat, the same way he was schooled to do as a teenager when the guy he was working for dropped him off in a strange neighborhood to sell magazine subscriptions. "May I come in?"

"You keep coming back. Call next time. I run a business. I'm not always here."

"I thought I'd take a chance and see if you were available," Blake said.

"We can go outside on the patio. The fresh air will feel good."

Blake followed her.

"Would you like something to drink?"

"Iced tea, if you have it."

He watched her walk to the kitchen. She opened the cupboard door by the kitchen sink.

"Do you want to look through my cabinets again?" She was back in a minute with two glasses and a lemon wedge.

"I'm fine with where we left it."

"Do you want to stare at my tits? I couldn't help but notice you were doing that the last time you were here."

"I'm a man. We're made that way, and you're blessed in that department."

"I'm pleased you noticed."

"You're ex-husband was abusive, uncaring, and selfish. I'm

sorry for what he took away from you, but he's dead now and I'm supposed to find out who did it, how and why. You understand that, don't you?" He locked his hands together.

"Yes, of course. I just wish we could get past that."

"We can't. You're in trouble."

"Why? Because I felt the need to protect my daughters? Because I was done dealing with Phillip's sick sense of morality?"

"Your brother has been watching you. That shouldn't come as a surprise to you after all this. Allison thinks he might have had something to do with Phillip's death."

"Really? That's interesting."

"What do you think?" Blake said.

"What do you want me to think, that the world is flat? Or maybe the world is round like my breasts and you should just put your head between them and make love to me over and over?"

"You need to talk to a therapist. Myra Sebring, is she the therapist you've been seeing?"

"She is."

"Did you know her office was burglarized earlier this week? The W files are missing. Your files. Do you think your brother had something to do with that?"

"That sonofabitch control freak."

"Is that a yes or a maybe?"

"I'm tired of this, tired of pretending to care about Phillip. He got what he deserved. He brought it on himself with his cheating and lying, swindling his investors. He used me. I don't know what my brother did. I'm raising two daughters. I don't always like what I've become. I need to feel desired for who I am. I'm not some piece of furniture a husband can move around."

Kathryn squirmed in her chair, seeming to look for some comfort that wasn't there.

"Do you think your brother burglarized Myra Sebring's

office?" Blake said. "You didn't, that's for sure. Maybe he made the arrangements for Phillip's last day at the lake, too."

"Whoever did should be applauded," Kathryn said.

"That's not the way the system works."

"Sometimes the system doesn't work. That's the point, isn't it?" Kathryn said.

"This isn't the Wild West."

"It's California, the edge of the continent. It all falls into the water here," she said.

"So about your brother?"

"The hell with my brother."

"How did James do it, and why?" Blake said.

"You'll have to ask James that question."

"I'm asking you." Blake's patience was wearing thin.

"I don't know. Why don't you just drink your goddamn tea."

Blake sat there, looking at her — an imperfect woman, probably a murderer, who deserved better, who should have had better. "I'm leaving." He stood and opened the slider.

"You always say that and then you come back. Why? Why don't you just leave me alone? Go find whoever it is that did this . . . one of Phillip's investors, a woman from some bar he picked up, a billionaire. Who cares, really. All Phillip ever did was fuck up people's lives."

CHAPTER THIRTY-TWO

Blake got home around six. He climbed the stairs to his apartment, and found a wreath of dead roses hanging from the doorknob. An envelope was pinned to the greenery. He looked around to see if anyone was watching him, then sat down with his feet resting on the steps and opened the envelope. "What the hell." The words on the paper were cut and pasted like a kidnapping note.

No good will come of your pursuing this.
Only harm.

Kilmer. Blake's stomach knotted. His jaw tensed when he ground his teeth. Kilmer can take this warning and shove it up his ass. Blake took a deep breath, like a dragon would before unleashing fire. At least he had the decency to aim his threat at me and not tack it on Julianna's door. I'll give him that, but nothing more.

He turned the key and walked in. Watson's greeting brought a sense of relief for a moment or two. Blake went over to the refrigerator and grabbed a beer. Then looked at the note on the counter from Freddie.

*D.B. I was here after school at 3:30. Took Watson for
a run. How about a raise?*
Freddie

That made for a tight time frame — the roses were placed there sometime after 3:30 p.m. He speed-dialed Freddie, figuring he might have seen who delivered the flowers.

The kid answered on the first ring. "Yeah, I thought it was weird . . . dead roses. I stopped off at the manager's office and washed his car before I walked back by your place on my way to the bus. I saw two guys by your door. They looked like the people at my Sunday School, except they were white. I took their picture with my cell phone. I got their license plate number, too.

"What made you think to do all that?" Blake said.

"You're a detective, right? I watch TV. I study people. I'm learning stuff. You want me to email the pictures to you?"

"Heck, yeah!"

"No problem. Give me five minutes."

"This is big, Freddie. Smart thinking."

"So why'd those guys do that? The flowers were ugly."

"I don't know for sure. They didn't see you, did they?"

"No way. I've got eight megapixels in this phone and an optical zoom."

"I owe you one."

"I like helping you. Maybe we can meet at the park, or you can pick me up and we can do something."

"Basketball or soccer, your choice. Say hello to your mom for me."

• • •

Blake called Susan, Cooper's assistant, the following morning.

"He's in all day. Stop by this morning before twelve and you can sit down with him."

The flowers weighed on Blake's mind. "I need to tell you about some stuff, Chief . . . I've talked with Kate Winslow a couple times since you and I last met."

"And . . . " Cooper said.

"She's still our prime suspect. I keep coming back to her and her brother."

"Nothing there with her ex-husband's investors?"

"Not really. I've spent the last two days running them down. None of them seem probable, and most of them have a witness for their whereabouts." Blake edged forward in his chair. The brown leather squeaked. "I got a wreath of dead flowers on my door last night and a note."

Cooper reeled forward all of a sudden and arched his eyebrows. "What did the note say?"

Blake slid it across Cooper's desk.

Cooper shifted his eyes at Blake before opening the envelope . . . "That's a hell of a warning. Got any idea who put this on your door?"

"Better than that. I've got pictures and a plate number straight from Salt Lake City."

"Her brother's behind this, isn't he? These rich people piss me off. Who the hell does he think he is? Interfering with a police investigation, threatening one of my men?"

"I figure on driving to Utah, but I've got to do some groundwork first."

"One percent of the people, forty percent of the wealth. Pretty soon they'll be outsourcing crime," Cooper said. "We need to get this done."

"Sounds like you're getting radical on me."

"It's a good thing nobody in China can do our jobs. We missed our chance with Phillip Winslow. I want to put this guy behind bars. Maybe we'll get that chance with his brother-in-law. . . You going to run that plate number?"

"I already have. The guy's on Kilmer's payroll. His name is Jensen. He works for a wholly owned subsidiary of the mother ship, Kilmer Enterprises."

"Sometimes people like Kilmer think they're invincible, like teenage boys but more arrogant. You have to show them they're not. That's when they start making mistakes. In the meantime, you need to be extra careful. I mean it, Blake. Let me know about Utah."

"I'm not going to climb into the ring with Kilmer until I'm ready."

"Make sure about that. I like having you around here. You might even be a good influence on Jameson." Cooper shook his head. "I hope to hell he never becomes chief."

Blake checked out an old copy of *Business Week* from the library with Kilmer on the cover. He was in his late sixties, solid build, steel-gray eyes, hard creases, angular cheek bones like Vladimir Putin, the Russian President. Kilmer was "ahead of the curve," the writer said, "always cautious in his personal relationships, and suspicious about business alliances . . . a shrewd negotiator who usually winds up getting exactly what he wants."

Blake waved the magazine cover in front of Cooper, then set it on the desk. "I've been reading Kilmer's autobiography. He goes on for a couple of chapters about expanding his reach, growing his brand via mergers and acquisitions. Blake picked up the hardback of Kilmer's autobiography he'd put on the floor next to him by Cooper's desk, and opened it. "Listen to this . . . 'It's better to dominate than cooperate with lesser players who don't understand the marketplace and what it takes to be a leader. That's why God wanted me to be where I am and who I am. He picked me for this purpose.' Kilmer is a real piece of work." Blake stared at the cover. "I can't help but think God could have made a better choice than this s.o.b."

Cooper stared at the magazine for a moment before pushing his chair back from the desk. He shook his head, and got up to get some water.

"Thousands of people work for this guy, the companies he owns and manages, including his two sons who don't seem nearly as accomplished or driven. There's never been a hint of personal scandal associated with his name. He's been married to the same woman for forty-one years. He has three daughters, all of whom live near him in Utah, and fourteen grandchildren. His wife, Barbara, collects Barbie dolls and Happy Meal Prizes."

"How the hell did you find that out?" Cooper said.

"Research. His daughter's Facebook page."

"What else?" Cooper said.

"He doesn't drive a flashy car, or own a yacht or a plane. He's at work by seven, six days a week, never on Sundays. Kilmer endorses conservative candidates who extoll the virtues of God and the free-market system. He lunches with the Coker Brothers on a semi-regular basis."

"No liberals or hippies in the family?"

"Not hardly. No gay or lesbian members either, at least not that anybody's talking about. He seldom drinks, and if we believe what Kilmer says, he's never smoked or used drugs. Weaknesses, he calls them. Deficiencies."

"That's not all bad, you know," Cooper said.

"Kilmer talks about how important it is to take the initiative in his autobiography. The pre-emptive strike, he calls it. Maybe that's what the break-in at Myra Sebring's office was about—a precautionary measure aimed at protecting the family's name. An easy burglary. The kind of move that reflects Kilmer's distrust of other people and his concern about how his sister, Kate, might have handled killing her ex. The guy has been secretive, even as a kid."

"No doubt, he likes to keep his personal life private," Cooper said. "But I'll bet he makes a big splash when he wants you to know he's in the game, and sees something he wants."

CHAPTER THIRTY-THREE

The climb up Half Dome, the ledge on Angel's Landing in Zion, the point on Cloud's Rest in Yosemite — Blake liked getting closer to the edge than most people. The adrenalin rush that came with facing off against Flemming, who'd run him off the road, and Kilmer was pushing him. He found himself almost wanting the confrontation, like what he felt when he was standing over Felix Lewis on the sidewalk in New York, an addictive sort of revenge that he found repulsive and satisfying at the same time. The covenant Blake felt with his father and his grandfathers, all of whom were gone, didn't always help because it pushed him to take risks, and never give in. Blake had inherited their stubbornness.

He walked to his car and looked up at Cooper's office window. What if Kilmer had chosen to deliver his message to Julianna's door? She seemed to accept his job, but revenge and threats weren't part of her life. Blake wanted to shelter her from that. He gritted his teeth. Then opened the car door, slammed it and walked around in a circle. He opened the door a second time, tossed his briefcase on the seat, and stared over the car's roof at a row of office buildings. "Kilmer," he mumbled.

Blake turned the key. The car idled, waiting. Sometimes it was timing and nothing more. Jack Hamilton died alone on the edge of the continent with his foot on the brake, hard against the floorboard. Blake hit the accelerator when he tried to outmaneuver Flemming on the freeway outside of Stockton. Hamilton didn't see death coming, and neither had he. Blake threw the Audi in reverse, dropped it in first, and wheeled out of the lot.

He needed to clear his head. Julianna had plans to be out of town, and the weekend was in front of him. In another month, the snow would hit the Sierra's higher elevations and linger until April or May. The temperatures were already dipping down to the mid-forties in the foothills at night.

"I'm planning to go hiking his weekend when you're out of town. The cell phone reception isn't very good where I'm heading, so I'll just call you Sunday after you get home from Chico, probably sometime in the late afternoon."

"Are you going to take your GPS?"

"I haven't had time to play with it yet. I always stick to well-marked trails. I don't want to spend time in the woods with the bears, believe me."

"Have fun," Julianna said. "So are you going swimming like you and I did in the McCloud River near Mount Shasta?"

"That was glacier melt. You know that, don't you? I almost had cardiac arrest when I dove in after you. You're way braver than I am. If it's warm enough, I'll probably just stretch out on the rocks and catch some sun. If I get too cold, you can warm me up when I get back."

"Sunday night? The girls are supposed to do their home-work at their dad's house. Be careful, okay?"

"Don't worry. I'll see you Sunday. You're the best." Blake was sensitive to giving her the space she wanted. He sensed she needed time with her friends, away from the kids and from him. Julianna was straight-forward and direct, except when it came to talking about her own needs. Sometimes, he felt like she expected him to be able to read her mind, and that didn't seem altogether fair.

"Just be who you are, not what you think I want," she told him.

Blake got his hiking stuff together that night, loaded up the car, and was on the road at seven the next morning.

CHAPTER THIRTY-FOUR

Every woman Blake had been involved with for any length of time, took issue with his driving — how he watched them instead of the road, drove too fast, accelerated when he went into the curves. He'd begun to admit they were right, that it was a dangerous habit he needed to rein in. He didn't however, feel obligated to give weight to any of those concerns that morning. He'd bought a turbo. He wanted to drive it fast with the radio volume torqued up louder than any of the women he knew would tolerate.

By the time he got out of his car two hours later, he was relaxed but stiff. The trailhead was nearly empty, the sky more grey than blue. A green Ford pick-up with a gun rack and a Bush-Cheney bumper sticker was parked at the edge of the clearing, alongside a Subaru Outback and a Jeep. He pulled his car's trunk release, got out, and lifted his gear from the trunk. Blake stretched his arms toward the sky, leaned against the bumper, laced up his hiking boots, adjusted the height on his climbing poles, and set his camelback on the trunk's lid. He stuffed the shirt he wore in his pack before heading up the dirt trail with seventy ounces of water on his back. The weather was cool, but he figured he'd warm up once he started moving.

After hiking a couple of hours, the wind seemed to pick up as it rustled through the leaves and whistled against his ears. He stopped and pulled the shirt out of his pack. A lizard ran across the trail with a small snake dangling from his mouth.

Minutes later, Blake's boot slid sideways over some stones. He heard a bird fluttering in the bushes and turned his head left. In the millisecond before the sound of a whip cracking rang through the woods, a bullet moved through the air at a speed he couldn't calculate, tore through the trees, and struck a rock inches away from where he was standing. Blake dove to the ground. His heart raced as he lay completely still. A second shot landed within inches of his head. His hand trembled. His mouth was bone dry. He could feel the dirt in the back of his throat.

Blake pushed himself back off the trail into the brush that cut away at his skin. He kept his face rubbed flat against the dirt. His hands were on his head, as if that would stop anything. Blake reached for the binoculars fastened to his belt. Nothing around him was moving.

He scrambled to his right through the brush that ripped his shirt and scraped against his chest, then inched forward, and panned the area where he thought the shot had come from. He caught sight of an eyeglass reflection and focused on a man, a quarter to a half-mile away, moving toward him. Blake scrambled sideways in a frantic crouch. He stood half-way up, and a third shot rang out. He leaped over a rock ledge and tumbled down fifteen or twenty feet. His knee was bloodied by the fall. His shoulder landed hard against a rock. He looked down at his hand covered with blood where he broke his fall. A piece of flesh was missing. Nothing felt broken, only hurt like hell. He was afraid to move for a minute, unsure about his footing, whether his legs and arms would still carry him and work the way they always had. Blake gulped some water and started scrambling again, looking for a place to hide.

Where was the shooter? How close was he? Blake hadn't taken his gun. His thoughts swirled around in turmoil. Oh, God, he said. His shoulder ached. A bruise the size of a golf ball throbbed below his knee. He didn't want to leave a trail of blood or torn clothing behind, or broken branches. He tied a bandana around his hand and wiped away the blood with a handkerchief. Blake headed toward a cluster of trees and a granite ledge that looked like good cover, hard to reach. Three or four miles, might not be that far. He kept moving. His heart was pounding. The cat and mouse game went on for at least an hour.

He stopped and crouched down to look for the first aid kit he carried in his backpack to clean up his cuts. This was bear and mountain lion country. He dug frantically with his hands and a rock, then jabbed at the ground with his hiking pole to bury the blood soaked gauze and handkerchief he'd used. He thought he heard somebody twice, maybe three times, branches breaking, before he reached the granite, but he couldn't be sure. The sky turned more gray as the sun began to fall. The wind had picked up, steady at around thirty or forty miles an hour. The rain came and the mountain got colder.

He reached the granite, stumbled on a crevice behind some scrub trees, and inched his way down. He dug his heels into the side of the ledge to keep his balance. He found a crawl space that jagged in and dropped down where he could spend the night and wait for dawn. He sure as hell wasn't going to go back where he'd come from, or down the trail with a cheap ass target on his chest. He poked his climbing pole inside the crevice and aimed his LED light at the ground to look for snakes.

The rain came down hard. His bones ached but there was room in the crevice to stand straight, lean back and rest. The granite shielded him from the wind. The rain fell, running down the rocks and pooling at his feet for two hours before stopping. Blake thought about the gun he kept in a locked file cabinet next to his desk in a pendeflex file labeled "G." I should have brought it. How fucking stupid am I? How could I not notice someone following me for three hours on the road and two hours on foot?

His knee felt like someone had hit him with a baseball bat. He'd caught a glimpse of the shooter, not enough for a positive I.D. — aviator reflective sunglasses, a brown leather jacket, jeans. Blake cupped his hands together and blew hot air over them, then stuffed them in his pockets. He pulled his shirt collar as high as he could.

Be careful, Cooper told him. I should have listened harder. I should have just listened harder, he told himself. He couldn't see his hand in front of his face.

Blake hunched over and pushed the leaves together to absorb the puddle of water at his feet. The shot wasn't a warning. The shooter wanted to take everything away from him. Blake clenched his teeth, angry, determined to even the score. Kilmer wanted him dead and wanted his death to look like a hunting accident.

• • •

Felix Lewis crept into Blake's mind as the darkness surrounded him. How many children would a man like Lewis have molested, if he hadn't been stopped? Kilmer was like that, too. Waiting, for the legal system to run its course, wasn't going to work. The stark reality of what was happening slapped Blake in the face.

CHAPTER THIRTY-FIVE

When the light came, Blake emerged from the crevice. He set his poles on the ledge. The raw, bloodied part of his hand scraped against the rock as he dug his fingers into the edge and twisted his left leg up to where he could get a foothold. He scanned the landscape with his binoculars before he came out from the shadows and headed through the thick of the woods to where it looked like it intersected with the trail, about two miles away. He watched for anything that moved. He guessed the shooter wouldn't have stayed in the woods overnight, not if he wasn't an experienced outdoorsman, not with the rain and the wind and the cold, and not if his attempt on Blake's life had drawn the attention of any passers-by. He'd have gone back home, determined to try again. No more mistakes, Blake told himself. Not any more.

Once he hit the trail, he hiked for close to two hours, before he spotted a man in the distance. His stomach tightened up. Blake kept hidden, studied him carefully before he stepped through the trees — how he moved, how he breathed, the backpack he carried, the hiking boots, his hands, what he was wearing. He looked to be in his twenties, dreadlocks, a steady gait like a regular hiker.

"You're out early," Blake said. He watched the hiker's hands and the woods behind him. "Where are you headed?"

"Up to Shadow Lake, then on to where it connects with the Pacific Crest Trail."

"Did you see anyone further down?"

"Nope. I think we're the only two people out here today so far." He looked at Blake. "What happened to you?"

"What do you mean?"

"You look a little ragged. Are you okay?"

"I spent the night in the woods."

"Where's your gear?"

"I didn't bring anything besides this. I'm a police detective. Somebody down there at the trailhead followed me yesterday."

"Why?"

"Some guy with a brown leather jacket took a shot at me."

"You're kidding, right?" The young hiker's demeanor changed. His eyes shifted to the blood stains on Blake's clothes and the dried blood caked on the bandana around his hand. He looked behind him.

"I wouldn't look like this if I was kidding," Blake said.

"You sure it wasn't a hunter? It's hunting season, you know."

"Not for hikers."

"Holy shit. You're not joking, are you?" His smile went stiff.

"Tell me about it," Blake said. He took some deep breaths, closed his eyes for a few seconds, and let normal settle in. He leaned back against a granite boulder dropped thousands of years before among the fir and pines. "Did you see anyone down there? Any cars at the trailhead or down the access road, anyone hanging around?"

"No, not a soul. You want some water? Do you need anything to eat?"

"No, I'm okay. Thanks for the offer."

"You sure you're okay?"

"I'm happy to be alive," Blake said. He wiped his forehead with his shirt tail. The sleeve was torn and caked with dried blood. His pants were ripped. The cloth above his knee hung down. Blake drank some water from the blue tube hanging from the hydration pack strapped to his back.

"Can I ask you what may be a stupid question?"

"Sure," Blake said. "Hikers don't usually ask stupid questions."

"Why did you ever decide to become a detective? You don't exactly look the part."

Blake took off his hat and scuffed up the dirt with his boot. "Right now, I'm thinking, maybe it wasn't such a good idea. I don't especially like guns. I used to inhale, and I been thinking about going to The Burning Man Festival in Nevada next year." Blake pulled out some jerky. "I guess I like catching bad guys and not being cooped up in an office. And there's always the adrenalin rush. I got tired of seeing people get pushed around or taken advantage of. Sometimes I can stop that."

The young hiker nodded, like he understood. "If you want, I'll go back down to the trailhead and check it out, before you come down. You know, make sure nobody's around."

"You'd do that?" Blake said.

"It's not that far. I've got time. You seem like a stand-up guy to me."

"What's your name?" Blake said.

"Josh."

"I'll take you up on that offer, Josh. Keep your hat on if you see somebody. If you do, drive down the road a mile or so until you're out of sight. Then call 911. Tell them my name is Dylan Blake and that I'm a detective with the Sierra Springs Police Department. Then get in your car and leave. If you see a plate number, write it down for me, but don't be obvious about it . . . You sure you're okay with this?"

"I'm good."

"Thanks." Blake extended his hand. "I'll be up on the right, closer to the tree line. I'm not going to come down the service road. If you take your hat off, it means it's safe. Otherwise, I'll stay in the woods." Blake paused. "Ready?"

"Let's go," Josh said.

Blake gravitated to the right, before crossing into the trees and disappearing. Josh headed down the old dirt service road toward the trailhead. The sun's rays illuminated the creek bed and the leaves that crossed over the path, opposite from where Blake was moving. The route Blake chose afforded him a better vantage point, and about thirty feet of elevation gain above where the forest road had been carved out of hard-pan, red clay.

So what exactly am I going to do if they're there, Blake asked himself? Throw rocks? I could have been bear meat back there, covered over with flies before somebody discovered me. Three hours. The bastard probably had a rifle with a scope stashed in the trunk, and drank hot coffee in the front seat before he hit the trail behind me.

Blake kept Josh in sight. Thirty minutes passed. "Good of the guy to do this," he mumbled. Blake had food and water. He could last another day or longer, easy enough. A 911 call from Josh would bring help within an hour. Blake watched as Josh walked down the road, past an open meadow where a big, burly guy was pouring coffee by a campfire. A battered-up, gray pickup patched up with gray primer was parked nearby. The picture looked right to Blake.

Another quarter-mile and the clearing came into view. Blake saw two cars — his Audi and a second he guessed belonged to Josh. The gravel parking lot looked safe.

After five minutes, Josh took off his hat and swept it across his body. Blake closed his eyes for a few seconds and breathed a sigh of relief. He stayed in the woods for several minutes before he made his way down the embankment and into the open.

"Can I ask if you'd do one more thing for me, Josh?"

"Sure."

"Keep your eyes open while I look under my car. Let me know if you see anyone." Blake knelt down before Josh had time to answer, rolled over on his back and pushed across the dirt under the driver's door."

"Wait a minute. Are you saying you think there's a bomb down there?"

Blake saw Josh's feet back-pedaling away from him. "No. I'm thinking there's a tracking device on the frame. Don't worry. Nothing is going to blow up. But hey, good thinking." Blake dug his heels in the ground, as he kept inching backward.

"It's here. I've got it," Blake called out.

Josh watched as Blake came back into view with the black box in his hand.

The young, long-haired hiker stared at it and shook his head.

"This is how he followed me without getting too close," Blake said. "It's a transmitter."

"So what now?"

Blake looked around the clearing. "I'm going to check the brake lines, look under the hood and the dash. Make sure everything is okay before I stick my key in the ignition and get out of here. This has been one helluva of a miserable experience. I don't want it to get any worse."

"Yeah," Josh said, "this seems way beyond bad."

"This isn't my normal, either," Blake said. "Some of my days are actually dull. Blake fished his car keys out of his backpack. "Keep your eyes open while I'm doing this."

"This detective stuff makes graduate school look better," Josh said.

When he'd finished, Blake pulled a notepad and pen out of his pocket. "I'd like to write down your name and phone number in case I need to get in touch with you at some point down the line, Josh. Write down your email, too."

"No problem."

Josh scribbled it down and handed it back to Blake.

"I'm going to write down the serial number and manufacturer's information off this GPS transmitter. I want you to take a close look when I'm done and make sure I've got all the numbers right. I'm not taking this GPS thing with me. I'm going to leave it here, so they'll think this is where I am, that I never left. Later I may need you to corroborate all of this."

"Corroborate what?"

"That I found the GPS, that these are the right numbers." Blake handed the paper back to him. "Look at it carefully, make sure. Then sign it and write down the time and date." Blake dug a hole with the garden tool in his trunk next to a boulder where the car was parked. "Don't tell anybody where I put this thing. I might need to come back for it."

"So that's it?" Josh said, when Blake had finished. "We're done?"

"Now I try and find out who's responsible for this," Blake said.

"Pretty spooky, Detective. Good luck. You'll call me if you need me?"

"I really appreciate what you did," Blake said.

Josh turned and headed back up the trail toward the mountains looming beyond where they'd met. He turned back toward Blake after seven or eight steps. "So if I light up a dooby, you won't bust me?"

"You've got a free pass from me for life." Blake walked back to the car. Nobody else involved in this case, besides Josh Friedman, was gonna get a free pass. Not Sheriff Kowalski or Kate Winslow, and for damn sure not her brother, James Kilmer. Or, Blake thought, the guy who'd shot at him.

He'd have to tell Chief Cooper what happened, minus the part about leaving his gun at home, which prompted him to think back to something Cooper had said. "Young men and old men with money, think the rules and averages don't apply to them. But they make mistakes and miscalculate. They forget they can't control everything, especially when they delegate."

Blake resented the price Kilmer had extracted from him. He felt like he'd left some part of himself lying on the ground in the dark. He didn't know exactly what it was, but life seemed more fleeting and uncertain than it had been before he was thrown against his own mortality a second time.

The idea that a small, inanimate, GPS transmitter had allowed a killer to pierce the wilderness, shatter his serenity, and track his movements to Kate Winslow's address, to Allison's, and to Julianna's home, made him bristle with anger. He'd make Kilmer answer for what he'd done, once he knew for sure. Part of it would be by the book. Not all of it.

He started to move around the pieces in his head as he drove down the access road toward the freeway. He jammed the gears hard, felt the turbo's power under his foot, and gunned it. He began to plan a trip to the firing range when he went back to work. This time it wouldn't be about qualifying.

CHAPTER THIRTY- SIX

Blake took the freeway exit to a small town in the foothills where he could sit down and enjoy a cup of coffee without having to look over his shoulder. He parked his car out front by the antique store, walked inside the cafe, and took a seat facing the plate glass window that offered a view of Main Street and the old train depot.

He found himself thinking more about what to tell Julianna than concerned about someone having tried to kill him. I can't blow this relationship. I've got to do this right. The abandonment issue connected to his dad's death was charging back into his life, like a black cloak covered in anxiety and doubt. I can control it now, Blake told himself. Julianna said she wanted the unvarnished truth. But did she really? There were times when reading a woman's mind seemed like trying to see a wood floor under the carpet.

Blake called her when he got closer to home. She'd gotten back later than she'd expected from Chico, and the girls hadn't finished their homework. All of which struck him as good news. Two days worth of dirt was caked on his clothes, his body ached all over, and he hadn't gotten any sleep. He felt relieved, like he'd dodged another bullet, and been given more time to figure out what to tell her.

• • •

He circled the parking lot's perimeter before driving through the entrance leading to the second floor apartment where he lived. He drove past his door twice before he pulled under the carport out front. Clicked off the radio and his ignition, and stared at his front door with apprehension. Kilmer knew where he lived. The rules were no longer relevant.

Watson barked when Blake hit the top of the landing. He entered the alarm code he'd shared with Freddie, gave his dog the attention he demanded, and grabbed a cold beer. Freddie's sticky note about basketball and Watson was tacked on the fridge. Blake unlocked the file cabinet and pulled out his gun, handling it like an everyday implement, a dangerous dinner plate.

He grabbed a frozen entree from the freezer to microwave, put some cheese and wheat thins out, and fixed himself a salad. He sat quietly at the table. No music, no distractions. When he'd finished, he walked down the hall and drew the hottest bath he could stand, kept adding more hot water every ten or fifteen minutes to keep it that way. He stayed under, with his shoulders, bruised, scraped, and red, submerged, and his weapon within reach.

He dressed his wounds and bandaged himself, set the alarm, put on some boxers, and laid the gun on the nightstand. Watson stretched out on the floor by the bed. Blake said a prayer of thanks when he crawled under the covers. He conked out as soon as his head hit the pillow.

● ● ●

After breakfast on Monday, Blake headed straight to the firing range. He spotted Frank Thomas, the guy he was looking for, and gestured to get his attention. BullsEye Thomas was old school, tough as nails, built like a college linebacker, the kind that made your head rattle when he threw you to the ground. "I need some pointers, Frank, if you've got time."

BullsEye nodded. "Strange words coming from you, Blake,"

he said, as he cleaned his weapon. "What's up? You've already qualified, haven't you?"

"I have, but people seem inclined to shoot at me these days. I need your help, Frank. I'm serious."

"I can tell. You look like shit, by the way."

"I spent last night freezing my ass off in the mountains. Somebody was hunting me."

"That's not a good thing. How 'bout you shoot? I'll watch you," BullsEye said. He walked around to Blake's right.

Blake stuffed the plugs in his ears and fired, reloaded, fired again, and reloaded. Then reeled the target in. "Passable, but not much beyond that." He looked over at Bullseye.

"Yeah, you got some problems going on," Thomas said. "First thing, when you pull that weapon, you've got to be ready to put somebody down for good. You want to hit the bad guy's body mass, not his toe." BullsEye let out a smile. "Anything less than that can get you killed. And remember, your aim is going to be worse when you're shooting back at somebody real and he's moving."

"I know," Blake said. "I've done that once. I'll probably have to do it again."

"Hesitating, too much thinking, will get you or your partner or some civilian killed," BullsEye said.

"How about I watch you for a while. You can show me what I need to work on."

BullsEye looked down range at the target. "Watch my breathing." He fired off a dozen rounds.

Blake examined the target. "You're better than good. I want to work with you some more."

"Friday, nine a.m. I'll see you here. You've got to put in the time. You'll shoot better if you keep your elbows in tight. Remember, concentration. Breath through the shot."

• • •

Blake gathered up his stuff and walked to the Detective's Room. He pulled the note from his shirt pocket, with the GPS unit's model and serial number, and began the process of tracking it down. Later that afternoon, he buzzed Cooper on the intercom.

"I've got to talk with you about something important, Chief."

"Thirty minutes," Cooper said.

• • •

Cooper looked at Blake as he limped to a chair, the scratches on his face, the bandage on his hand. "What happened?"

Blake told him how he'd spent Saturday night in the woods on the side of a mountain and what he knew so far. The tracking device had come from a spy shop in Salt Lake City and had been purchased by someone named Jensen, employed by Logic, LLC, a subsidiary of Kilmer Enterprises. Blake had stared at the computer screen and clenched his teeth when he saw the results earlier that afternoon. He froze the frame, printed two copies, put one in his desk drawer along with the paper with Josh's name, and the other copy in his back pocket. Blake pulled the paper out and showed it to Cooper.

"Goddamn it," Cooper said. "This pisses me off. When someone on this force becomes a target and their life is threatened, that's the last straw for me." The veins were popped up and down on Cooper's neck. He brushed his right hand, turned into a fist, against his mustache. "I'll do everything in my power to protect you, but understand this. Nobody's gonna compensate for over-confidence or carelessness on your part. It doesn't work that way."

"I get it. I've been thinking about what you said earlier."

"If Kilmer is behind this, and it looks like he is, we'll pull out all the stops and nail him. I'm not going to treat this like some kind of big bank, Wall Street financial scandal where the CEO gets a free pass and a golden parachute, and some subordinate, like this Jensen guy, is offered up. That may be the way it plays out in some quarters, or with somebody like Kowalski, but it's not going to happen here. I've had this job for twenty-six years. I don't lose men."

Blake hadn't ever seen Cooper mad before. "I'm going to get him," Blake said.

"This isn't going be some one-man, lone wolf pursuit, either. You're the lead here, but you're not going it alone. A smart man bent on revenge, gets stupid. Whatever resources you need are gonna be there," Cooper said.

"I'm planning to see Kate Winslow, again. Afterwards, I'll need to go to Utah to do some legwork on Kilmer and his hunter friend, Jensen."

"In the meantime," Cooper said, "I'm going to assign a cruiser and an unmarked car to keep an eye on your apartment. I don't want you making any moves unless we've discussed them in advance. Understood?"

"Don't worry about it. I'm planning to be one of those old codgers with a baseball hat and a bottle of Viagra." Blake paused. "I want someone to keep an eye on my girlfriend's place for the next week, a couple of times a night while I'm in Utah. Can you do that for me, Chief?"

"It's done. Write down her address and some details for me. Get me a picture, too." Cooper slid a legal pad across his desk.

Blake breathed a sigh of relief. "Thanks."

"No unnecessary chances. I mean it." Cooper stood up from behind his desk. "The wiretaps for Kate Winslow's phone, the shooter's, and Kilmer's will be in place by noon tomorrow. When you meet with Kathryn Winslow, see if you can push her to confront Kilmer about his involvement."

Blake nodded in agreement. Cooper felt like family. He couldn't involve him in what he was planning.

When he left headquarters, Blake called Tony Moriano. "I need to see you. I need your help, Tony. How bout we go for a walk in that green belt near where you live?" Tony was tight-lipped, an old stallion. Just what he needed

"What time?"

"An hour or so."

• • •

Tony tipped his cap. They shook hands and walked.

"You got to be careful," Blake said. "I don't want you sticking your neck out too far."

"Don't worry, Detective. I'm gonna bring somebody with me who doesn't have a neck. He's visitin' from New York. He knows all about this stuff. It'll be like old times for him and me." Tony rubbed his hand against the stubble on his face.

"Just remember, I'm a detective. You can't bust his knee caps."

"So does this guy owe you money or what?"

"I wish it was that simple. He paid somebody to try and kill me."

"Sonofabitch," Tony said. His eyes widened. He shook his head, like it was something he'd heard too many times before.

"I want him to know I'm going to push back," Blake said.

"We'll make sure he gets the point. Ya got his picture?"

"It's in the envelope. Nobody can know about this. I'd lose my job or get hit with a suspension."

"Nobody's gonna find out nothin'. This is old school."

"What about your friend?"

"He don't talk. He takes orders," Tony said. His arms shot forward in front of him, crossed over like an "x." His lips curled up and he dropped his arms.

Blake took the envelope from his jacket pocket. "There's five hundred bucks in here to cover your expenses. If you need more, let me know. You sure you're okay with this?"

"Ya helped us. I told ya I'd help you anytime and re-pay the favor. This keeps my blood circulatin'. Ya got the dates and addresses?"

"It's all there. I'll call you later this week once I get to Utah."

"The picture's inside?" Tony said.

"You got it."

"Me and Georgie'd like two days. We'll hit the road and meet ya. Got time for an espresso? I know a good place."

"I got time," Blake said.

"Your girlfriend know somebody tried to shoot ya?"

"I haven't told her, yet."

Tony frowned.

"You got any suggestions how I should handle it?"

"That's a hard call. If ya don't, she'd be pissed 'cause she'd think ya don't trust her. If ya do, she's wonderin' how she got herself into this mess, and what to do if the same business happens again. Ma used to tell me, always err on the side of truth 'cause lyin' gets too complicated. Sooner or later ya forget what ya said, and ya wind up swallowin' a mouth full a marbles."

"A mouth full of marbles?"

"Yeah, like Demosthenes, that old Greek guy who practiced talkin' with pebbles in his mouth. Lyin' doesn't go over so good, 'specially with girlfriends and wives."

"So you think I should tell her, then?"

Tony looked back at Blake with a puzzled expression of disbelief.

"Ain't that what I just said? Ya swallow marbles, you're gonna choke." He grabbed his throat and stuck his tongue out to the side.

Blake laughed. "I'm going to take your advice. I'll call you from Utah when I see how things line-up."

"Me and Georgie, we'll take care of it for you. Kilmer'll get the message. We'll put the fear of God in him."

"Say hello to Tony Junior for me."

"Watch your back, Detective."

"I will."

Tony headed for his car, a gold-colored Olds Cutlass, early to mid-nineties with wire rims.

"How's it run?" Blake called out.

"The same way I do, smooth and dependable."

CHAPTER THIRTY-SEVEN

Fall was in the air and the leaves were turning brighter every day. A group of noisy Canadian honkers flew overhead in wing formation toward the fields in the distance. At 9:00 a.m., Blake called Cooper to make sure the phone taps were in place.

At 10:00, Blake called Kathryn Winslow. "I need to talk with you."

"You changed your mind about us?"

"Not about us. About the investigation, your brother, what happened over the weekend."

"I'll take a late lunch. I've got to pick up some records from my house. I'll meet you there at one," Kathryn said.

Blake drove to Lauren Way. He stopped at the gatehouse and flashed his shield. "Call me if you see anyone parked across the way and get the plate number."

"No problem," the security guard said.

"Here's my card with my cell number. Make sure you get the plate number right."

He parked next to Kate's Jaguar. She answered the door, true to form, in a shirt that showed her nipples in all their grand glory. Why does she keep putting herself out there, offering herself up this way? Why doesn't she just wear a bra and pretend this is the day she goes to church with her daughters, or does a show and tell at school?

"Detective Blake, how good to see you." She gestured toward

the couch in the living room. "Can I get you something?" She was wearing sheer, form-fitting pants.

Time at the gym and genetics, Blake thought. "I'm fine for now."

Kathryn sat down across from him, bent forward toward the coffee table and reached for a mint, giving Blake an opportunity for a second look down the white silk shirt she was wearing. Her eyes met his as she straightened up. She moistened her lips, crossed her legs and leaned back in the couch. "Now tell me, what can I help you with?"

"I talked to Allison. She was puzzled, troubled is a better word, by something she saw in the pictures of your ex-husband at the lake."

"Of course, she saw her father dead."

"It wasn't just that."

"What then?"

"I'm not at liberty to disclose that with you, right now."

"Then why did you come here? My guess is that it wasn't to sleep with me. You've already made that clear on a number of occasions." She tugged at the ends of her shirt.

"I came here to tell you you're putting me at risk. Your ex-husband paid someone to run me off the road when I was on my way back from visiting your daughter a few weeks ago. I spent a couple days in the hospital.

"He did what?" Kathryn said. She looked surprised.

"We were going to arrest your ex before he turned up dead. This last weekend, when I was hiking up in the Sierra, one of your brother's men tried to kill me. I spent the night in the woods . . . cold, soaking wet, shoved between two rocks. They put a tracking device on my car and followed me . . . to my friends' homes, here to your place. Now your brother is paying somebody to sit in a car down by the gate and watch you and me. He probably knows exactly how many times I've been here."

"That meddling bastard. He can't ever leave it alone."

She looked mad as hell. "Tell me something, Kate. When does this brother of yours stop trying to control everything and everyone in your life?"

"You don't understand, Detective. It doesn't stop. He's always been this way."

"I was under the impression you actually cared about your family, maybe even about me, that you meant at least part of what you said. I even thought there might be some truth attached to the innocence you claimed."

"I do care. I didn't mean for you or anyone else to get hurt. All I've ever wanted is to protect my daughters and be free of Phillip and my brother."

"You need to tell him to back off." Blake leaned forward and looked for some sign or acknowledgement beneath the surface of her polite smile that she understood. "Did he kill Phillip, Kate, or did you?"

Kathryn looked away without answering, and stared through the patio glass at the trees on the way to the lake.

"There's no point in protecting him, Kate, allowing him to continue. You told me you wanted to set an example for your daughters. What they're seeing now is you being an enabler again, like you were when your ex-husband abused Allison. I thought you wanted to be done with that."

Blake watched as she recoiled in pain. His remark hit her like a drill on an exposed nerve at the dentist's office.

"That's not fair."

"You could go away for this . . . to prison. Or he could. Someone's going to," Blake said. "You need to protect yourself, and your daughters."

"He got an attorney for me."

"An attorney . . . he's not appointing a jury to acquit you. And the attempted murder of a police officer, guess what? That's a capital offense."

"I didn't tell him to do anything like that. I wouldn't."

"Maybe you should ask him about it. Tell him you found

out, and he needs to stop. Tell him to stay in Utah, that you don't need his help."

"Why do you care what happens to me, Detective?"

"Just because I don't want to sleep with you, doesn't mean I don't have feelings for what you've been through, and for your family." Blake looked at her. The expression on her face made it seem like she understood.

"I don't want this to get worse for you or me. I can't go on like this. He needs to pay for what he's done."

"Remember," Blake said, "your brother hired the lawyer. The guy's on his payroll, not yours. Who do you think that lawyer's going to protect?"

"What's that supposed to mean?"

"You need to take care of yourself. You're not that naïve. You should know your brother is going to put himself first. You're not some dumb blond from the Idaho Panhandle, anymore."

"So what's next for you?" Kathryn said.

"Getting to the bottom of all this. I won't give it up until I do, Kate. You know that."

"I've said too much already. I think you're right about my getting a different lawyer. That bastard. I'm sorry for what you've been through." Kathryn stood up and began to walk toward the door. "Did you notice?" she said, when they reached the front door.

"Notice what?"

"I didn't make any last minute invitations for you to stay. I'm trying to behave myself."

"It's easier on me," Blake said. "You're an intelligent woman. Find somebody else."

She closed the screen door behind him.

CHAPTER THIRTY-EIGHT

Harper and Becky, Julianna's kids, were at their dad's. Blake hadn't settled on how much of what really happened he'd share with Julianna. His first thought was to tell her everything, but how could he? What if she decided the risk that came with his job was a risk she didn't want in her life? What if he lost her? What if it all blew up in his face? What if Kilmer went after her and the girls? He'd have to tell her something. His mind raced. Sierra Springs wasn't L.A. People didn't run around shooting at cops. He convinced himself he could make his story sound believable.

"I lost track of the time, slipped on some stones on the trail, took a fall, and got banged up. Night came sooner than I'd expected," Blake said. "Since it was the first day of hunting season, I thought it best to hunker down and eliminate the possibility of some hunter mistaking me for a trophy."

Julianna applauded his last minute decision to be careful. "Men. Sometimes you guys aren't too bright. That's why people wear watches," she said. "You're lucky nothing worse happened to you."

● ● ●

The next day, Blake stopped by headquarters to clear his travel schedule with Cooper and get a travel allowance to cover his expenses.

"By the book. Nothing stupid, Detective. Check in with me on Friday. I want an update."

"Not a problem, Chief. I'm giving Freddie Roosevelt, the kid who watches my dog for me, your number in case he sees anything strange happening around my place. He has a key, and the code for the alarm system I'm installing. Nobody else, except my girlfriend, will have the code. The kid's smart. He's the one who got the Utah plate number for me."

"Have a safe trip. I want to put Kilmer away," Cooper said.

Blake left work early, grabbed Watson's leash and went jogging. He kicked off his clothes, and climbed in the shower when they got home. The alarm people finished up the job, while Blake made himself a cup of tea. He telephoned Rob, and arranged to meet him later that afternoon. He told him about the attempts on his life and the tracking device on his car. "Don't say anything about this to Samantha. I don't want your wife mentioning it to Julianna. I think there's a way for me to wrap this up and protect everyone. This rich guy, Kilmer, is over the edge."

"And he runs a Fortune Five-Hundred company," Rob said. "I guess he didn't get where he is playing by the rules."

"What do you mean?"

"If he did this to you, what else might he have done? There's probably more out there."

"Maybe not. It could be limited to his family, protecting his sister, being in control," Blake said.

"Or he could be the kind of guy who always has to win, no matter what the cost."

"I'm going to Utah to dig around and see what I can come up with. I'm not going to roll over and play dead. Kilmer's got to have some weak spots, some vulnerabilities."

"And let me guess. You're going to find out what they are. You're going to play Sherlock Holmes, the Securities and Exchange Commission, and Superman all rolled into one."

"I think I'll bring a more personal, innovative commitment to the process, if that's what you mean."

"Just make sure he doesn't bury you. This guy has a lot of money and power and he's going to use it against you."

"I've had first-hand experience with that already. He hasn't had any experience with me. I'm just a name, an irritation he wants to brush aside." Blake paused. "Do me a favor, Rob. Be in the neighborhood and invent some reason to stop by Julianna's place or invite her for a cup of coffee. Check on her while I'm away."

"You're worried?"

"I think Kilmer knows where she lives. I don't know what he'll do next. I asked Cooper to keep an eye on her house." Blake finished his coffee. "I'll catch up with you when I get back."

● ● ●

Blake called Tony Moriano on his way to Julianna's house. "You're still with me on this?"

"I already told ya. I'm in.'"

"I'm leaving for Utah tomorrow," Blake said. I'll plan on seeing you on Wednesday. Call me when you get there and we'll talk about where to meet. Kilmer's business headquarters are downtown."

"You sure, Dylan?" Tony said.

"I'm sure about this."

"We'll take care of it, me and Georgie. Watch your back, Detective."

CHAPTER THIRTY-NINE

Ten hours drive time across the mountains on I-80, over Donner Pass to Salt Lake City, the land of salt flats, Mormons, and no Sunday sales. Too bad he wasn't going to hike the Zion Narrows or Bryce Canyon.

Blake knew Kilmer's workout routine. The information was easy enough for Blake to get when he asked the club manager, where he was a member, for a favor — 24-Hour Fitness, four days every week. Kilmer preferred the club closest to his office because he could be anonymous there, come and go largely unnoticed, with no one hitting him up for stock tips, pitching investment schemes, or angling for insider trading information like they would at an exclusive club. Kilmer would enter his work phone number on the mobile keypad and press his right index finger against the fingerprint reader, just like Blake did at the Sierra Springs Club. The check-in system would appeal to Kilmer, because he didn't have to make small talk or interact with the hourly people at the front desk.

When Blake got there, he used his own card and walked to the back of the gym where the free weights were. He spotted Kilmer and watched him move to the black bench, find his weights, lie down on his back, and begin his bench presses. He waited until Kilmer was several reps into his third set, then walked over and stared down at him.

Kilmer adjusted his position on the bench, inching back slightly.

Blake reached into his shirt pocket and pulled out a handful of black rose petals and dropped them on Kilmer. "Accidents happen . . . You just never know."

"Excuse me, what did you say?"

The way Kilmer said it, sounded like a dare to Blake, not a question. Blake glared back. "I was talking about accidents."

"I don't think you know who you're talking to," Kilmer said with contempt, as if he were talking to someone too stupid to know any better.

That irritated Blake. "I know exactly who I'm talking to. You're James Kilmer. I'm investigating your brother-in-law's death, and your sister and you." Blake began to roll the dead rose, he'd taken from the wreath on his door, between his fingers. My name is Dylan Blake, but I'm supposing you already figured that out. I hear you're smart enough to at least know that much."

Kilmer took his hands off the bar and rested them on his chest. "You're out of your jurisdiction, aren't you?"

"It's a free country. They don't check Californians at the border. I know where you live, where you work, where you go to relax. I wanted to introduce myself in person." Blake smiled in an unnerving way that didn't seem to bother Kilmer as much as Blake supposed it would.

"You could have called my office to make an appointment, but you wouldn't have gotten one." Kilmer snarled.

"I figured as much," Blake said. "That's why I'm here. I met up with one of your employees, by the way. He wasn't as good as he should have been, not with a rifle in the mountains, anyway. Did he tell you how he botched that up?"

"I have no idea what you're talking about. You're stepping over the line." Kilmer began another lift.

Blake placed his hand firmly on top of the barbell and pushed it back down against Kilmer's chest.

Kilmer's face began to turn red. His mouth tightened and

he clenched his teeth. His rage bubbled to the surface like hot water in a pan. He began another lift.

Blake stared down at him, poker-faced, cold. "You know, Kilmer, lifting weights in a health club won't make you as strong as you might think. You're in serious trouble, and it's not gonna go away."

"You've got some hell of a nerve. You can't just come in here and threaten me." Kilmer said, with what looked to Blake like equal parts of defiance and indignation. "You can't intimidate me, Detective."

Blake's anger welled up. "I can do whatever I damn well please. I'm not some fucking store you can close up." There was an air of explosive control around Blake that was erupting and he wanted Kilmer to see it. "I could give you a list of assholes like you that have under-estimated me, but they're behind bars now. Their grandkids don't get to visit them."

"Did you look around here before you came in? There are streets named after me. There's even a recreation center for underprivileged kids with my name on it."

"I don't give a shit," Blake said.

"I've got a room full of lawyers and accountants on my payroll. I can bury you. You're nothing more than a small-time, police detective from one of those liberal, Podunk, California towns."

"You tried to bury me, already," Blake said. "It didn't work, did it? The idiot you paid to go hunting didn't get the job done. Now you're assuming I'll feel compelled to play the way you expect me to. I'm not that predictable." Blake stared at Kilmer with as much contempt as Kilmer had shown him moments before.

Kilmer looked up from the bench.

"I know people on both sides of the line. It's easy for me to call in favors. When you walk into that locker room to shower, you'll be just as vulnerable as I am. There won't be anyone there to cover your ass when you bend down for a bar of soap. You're a smart man, but you don't have any idea what I'm capable of. You're gonna get hit with an iceberg if you don't stop." Blake took his hands off the barbell and opened his jacket.

Kilmer saw Blake's gun.

Blake dropped his hands to his side.

Kilmer finished his set and stood up. "Get out of my face, while you can."

"I'll come back if I need to," Blake said, "if we don't leave this here. And when I do, you're going down. It may take a while, but you can bet on it. You won't be walking out the door the same way you came in today." Blake turned and headed to the front desk.

CHAPTER FORTY

Thirty minutes later, Kilmer came out the gym's entrance carrying his brown leather bag and feeling for the keys in his front coat pocket. A trace of snow had fallen in the parking lot and mixed with the leaves still clinging to the trees.

Blake was sitting in his black Audi sedan watching. He wanted to make sure he put a taste in Kilmer's mouth he wouldn't like. He wanted Kilmer to feel the same apprehension he'd felt when he laid in the brush on the side of the mountain and waited for nightfall. He knew how fear could make you forget about the assets available to you. How it compressed your thoughts and anxieties and shook your confidence.

Tony Junior moved to Kilmer's left as he approached the club's front door, ten feet away — just enough to catch Kilmer's eye and distract him. Strangers usually did a double-take when they saw his big panda eyes with the dark circles.

Kilmer followed Tony Junior's movements.

Papa Tony was waiting on Kilmer's blind side with his friend, Georgie, for the right moment. He quick-stepped in front of Kilmer who unintentionally bumped into him. "Heh, Mister," Tony called out, "watch it."

Tony Junior stood still.

Kilmer's eyes shifted. He righted himself, annoyed and still preoccupied. "Watch it old man."

Papa Tony glanced back at Georgie who followed a few steps behind him. "Ya hear what this guy said?"

"Disrespectful," Georgie grunted.

"He's a smart ass. One of those rich pricks."

"Get out of my way," Kilmer said, "and watch where you're going. I don't have time for this." Kilmer seemed accustomed to dismissing people who bothered him.

"Kilmer's smart mouth, Tony later told Blake, "rubbed me like salt on a flesh wound." The one thing Tony disliked most about being older was how some people looked past him, as if he was invisible.

"Ya hear that?" Tony said again as he looked at Georgie before his eyes moved to his son. Tony Junior' s role shifted from distracter to observer in the triangle Kilmer suddenly found himself in. "Maybe this guy's got less time than he thinks." Tony grabbed Kilmer's coat below the neck line and twisted it, then released it as if it were trash. His jaw bone, with two days of gray stubble, angled toward Kilmer as Tony turned his head to the side.

"Accidents, Mister, in California and Utah. I'd watch my step if I was you. Somethin' might get broken real bad, like both of those legs."

Georgie stood next to Kilmer, towering a good foot above, in an expensive, size forty-six suit. His hair was darker than it should have been for his age, slicked back and thick. He looked like an NFL lineman on steroids, minus the tattoos. "Let it go, Tony." He paused. "I know what ta do ta him."

Kilmer's face went white. He stepped around them and hurried toward his car. He got in and locked the doors. Kilmer looked in his rear view mirror, backed out, then turned away from the gym and pulled the seat belt across his chest.

Blake followed Kilmer out of the parking lot on the side street toward the freeway that ran to Kilmer's house.

• • •

The next day, Blake met Tony and Georgie for breakfast at the motel. "Anything else ya'd like us to handle for ya while we're here?" Tony said. He was smiling and stone cold, New York serious. There was a glint in his eye underneath the hat.

"As a matter of fact, there is one other thing," Blake said. "The guy that shot at me. His name is Jensen. He works for Kilmer. He's got an office in one of Kilmer's warehouses. It's about thirty minutes from here."

"What did ya have in mind?" Tony said.

"A business envelope on his dash."

"What's it say?"

"The words are cut out. Now you're in my sights. Find another employer."

"I like it," Tony said. "Got an old school ring."

"Knock the window out on the driver's side and put it on the dash. You've got gloves, right?"

"Detective, ya talkin' to professionals."

"Then I'll catch up with you back home," Blake said.

"At the Villas, the steak at the casino."

"I'll look forward to it," Blake said. He looked at Georgie and tipped his hat.

"Like I said, Detective, he don't talk."

The two of them walked over to the gold Olds Cutlass.

Tony kicked the tires and climbed behind the wheel.

Georgie rode shotgun.

CHAPTER FORTY-ONE

When Jensen called Kilmer, he told him about the windshield. "I've been identified. I think it best I bow out."

"Admit to nothing," Kilmer said and hung-up.

Cooper had it on tape.

Blake had anticipated the call and secured the wiretaps before he left California. They had another link. The pieces were falling into place.

Kilmer still had resources — a room full of lawyers, money to burn, mounds of paperwork he could throw in front of any prosecutor. "They're not like us," Cooper had told Blake, "rich people."

Maybe so, maybe not. Blake kept looking for the right edge, what made Kilmer tick, and what he valued. When Blake found it, he'd know what to take away.

He spent the next three days in Utah doing things he figured would unnerve Kilmer — following him in his car, taking pictures of his house from outside the front gate, talking to suppliers and associates, having lunch at one of Kilmer's favorite spots, even visiting the church Kilmer attended. Blake circled the quote in his notebook.

We live in a celebrity-obsessed world. Most wealthy people want to protect their privacy and the time they spend with their family. I think that's what James values . . . his private time with his family, the normal

*stuff like you and me. That's what's hardest for him
to have.*

This thing between them had become a dangerous, in-
toxicating game. Blake knew he'd crossed over the line, but
he felt himself liking it, wanting to go deeper, like a scuba
diver at a hundred feet drawn by the rapture of the deep. He
was smack in the center of Kilmer's radar, but now Kilmer
was in the cross hairs. Blake felt certain the CEO whose wife
liked Barbie dolls, had stopped thinking of him as a Podunk
detective. He called Kilmer's office on the way out of Salt
Lake City and left a message thanking him for his hospitality.

• • •

Blake looked out the car window at the mountains covered
with a light dusting of snow, as he drove back to California.
The fact that Jensen knew he'd been identified meant he'd
likely have to step back and Kilmer would have to reconsider
his options. Losing wouldn't be acceptable. And his little
sister going to jail? Blake couldn't see Kilmer letting that
happen. But the match-up didn't seem as much like a David
and Goliath battle as it had before. Arrogance begets over-
confidence, Blake kept telling himself.

Tony, Georgie, and he had pushed Kilmer hard, to the
point where Blake hoped Kilmer would feel vulnerable and
make a mistake. But Blake began to wonder whether he'd
gone too far, whether his over-confidence had put Julianna
or somebody else in danger.

He called Cooper to let him know he was on his way home.
As soon as the call ended, he started thinking about the relationship between Kilmer and his sister, Kate. They'd grown
up in the Idaho Panhandle together. They didn't start out
rich. Were they close? Did they confide in one another? Or
was this one of those dysfunctional American families where
the siblings never talked to each other? If Kilmer pushed the

panic button, maybe he'd call Kate and Cooper could capture their conversation on the wiretaps.

Blake clicked on the Audi's Bluetooth a second time and called his friend, Rob, to ask if he had visited Julianna.

"I did. I've got to tell you, Dylan, she's very appealing. Intelligent, charming. You should hold on to her. Don't let her get away."

"You didn't say anything to Samantha about someone shooting at me, did you?" The fact that he hadn't been straightforward with Julianna kept playing in Blake's mind.

"Not a word. How did it go in Utah?"

"I think I made a strong first impression on Kilmer. We're definitely not going to be roommates like you and I once were."

"He's got the resources to fight you forever on this."

"That doesn't mean he'll win," Blake said.

"He can make your life a living hell. You can't make any mistakes with him. He'll make you pay for them."

"I might need your help down the road," Blake said.

"Legal advice, or shouldn't I ask?"

"You're like a brother to me, Rob. Where else would I turn for legal advice?"

"I'll see you when you get back. Call me," Rob said.

What came next, besides waiting to see if Kilmer's revenge would only be aimed at him, wasn't nearly as clear as the blue sky towering above the fir trees in the Sierra. Blake lowered the car window, hoping a blast of fresh air would help him think more clearly.

Allison had already wondered out loud if her uncle had been involved in her father's death. Blake was confident there was enough animosity there for him to build on. Persuading her to help bring Kilmer down was critical, but he'd have to meet her face-to-face.

A hundred miles later, he telephoned Julianna to assure her nothing terrible had happened. "Utah was very routine.

I talked to some people, did some research connecting the dots. I was hoping you'd let me take you out to dinner and a movie tomorrow. I've missed you."

Blake stared out the window, worried about Kilmer, whose whole life had been a winning streak.

CHAPTER FORTY-TWO

He was old enough to be Allison's father, but that wasn't a reality Blake could relate to. It hadn't been that many years since he'd dated women in their twenties. The fact however, that he now found her mother more attractive than Allison wasn't lost on him.

He called her before taking the on-ramp to Stockton. "It's important," he told her, "I need to talk with you."

• • •

Her place was neatened up. The ashtrays were empty. She had a bouquet of flowers in a vase on the kitchen counter. The sun filtered in through the window blinds. Allison's eyes were clear, brown. He hadn't noticed the color before.

"How've you been?"

"Better, I guess." Allison clicked her lighter and drew on a cigarette. "Have a seat."

"You got some coffee?" Blake said.

"I'll make some. I could use a cup myself."

"Real coffee? Not that instant crap with powdered creamer chemicals?"

"You'll get the real deal, don't worry."

"I met your uncle," Blake said. "I drove to Utah."

"And?" Allison walked to the kitchen.

"He's plenty arrogant, that's for sure."

"I could have told you that. And he talked to you?"

"I didn't make an appointment."

"Yeah, that seems to be your style," Allison said. "So, what did he say?" Allison appeared to be a little curious.

"I asked him about your father's death, and Jack Hamilton. And the wreath of dead roses he paid somebody to put on my front door."

"He did what?" Allison suddenly looked apprehensive. Her eyes narrowed.

"Before I left for Utah, last week."

"Why?"

"To get his message across . . . leave it alone, you'll get hurt."

"Now, that sounds just like my uncle. Wanting everything his way, calling all the shots."

"All that power and wealth. You could use it to your advantage, Allison."

"How's that?" She stopped what she was doing in the kitchen and turned around.

"I think you're getting closer to breaking away from this place. Your uncle could play at being your savior. He'd probably like that. He could give you a place to stay in Utah and some family-motivated protection from the guy who drives the pimpmobile around here."

"I hadn't thought about that, Detective. But Utah? They probably still don't serve beer on Sundays."

"Buy it on Saturdays. Besides, Utah would just be temporary. Once your dad's estate is settled, you'll probably be able to go anywhere you want."

"I don't want my father's dirty money."

"You're entitled to it. You've already paid for it. If he's in hell, he won't need it there."

She blew smoke and set her cigarette down, before running her hands through her hair. She tossed her head back and closed her eyes for a moment or two. "You've got a point."

"You can help me," Blake said. He leaned forward toward the coffee table in front of the couch. She was standing next to the kitchen counter while the coffee brewed.

"How's that?" she said. Her eyes locked on his.

"Your uncle's messed up, crazy. He hired somebody to shoot me when I was hiking in the mountains. And now the wreath on my door? I think he's going to try again."

"And you went to Utah, anyway?"

"Yeah. I don't like being threatened," Blake said. "The people in my family fight. They don't take flight."

"And now you're telling me you think my uncle had something to do with my father's death and Jack Hamilton's, aren't you?"

"We've got the two men your father hired to kill Hamilton in a holding cell right now. Your father beat your uncle to the draw. I think your uncle's men were following Hamilton. They didn't have to kill him. Your uncle watched, while your father made it happen."

Allison stared at Blake. Her hands were trembling. She ground her cigarette into the ashtray.

Blake could see her thinking. "As for your father's death, that's still up in the air. Your mother and your uncle are at the top of the list."

"So, what do you want me to do?"

"For starters, go to Utah. Keep your wits about you and listen. My guess is, you'll hear something that will put all this in perspective. What I don't want you to do, is discuss our conversation today with anyone."

"Duh," Allison said. "So how do I get out of this mess I'm in?"

"Pack up quick. I'll find a place for you to stay temporarily in Sacramento. Then call your uncle and ask for his help. Tell him you want to stay there for awhile, where it's safe."

"When do I do this?"

"Look at your schedule. When you do that last piece of business for the idiot you're working for and think he's going to be out of sight for a while, we'll throw your stuff in a car and you can leave everything else behind. No calls, not to anyone before you split."

"Sunday. Sunday would be best. Guys are either in church, watching football games or hanging out with their wives and families, not fucking call girls and prostitutes."

"Remember," Blake said, "no calls about this to anyone. I'll take care of the place in Sacramento. Seven a.m., Sunday. We're out of here. Be ready. Call me, Saturday night, sometime after seven."

"You got it," she said.

CHAPTER FORTY-THREE

Blake met Cooper at Elaine's for lunch, at Cooper's suggestion. Elaine's was a popular local eatery with an eclectic clientele ranging from businessmen and politicians, to retail and financial managers, to women like Kathryn Winslow who dressed well and filled out their clothes even better.

"Sit down," Chief Cooper said. "Lunch is on me. Tell me about Utah."

"I found Jensen, Kilmer's employee, who bought the GPS unit strapped to my car. He's the guy who's cell and office phone numbers we've got a wiretap on. I don't think he's going to admit anything other than being an employee. As for Kilmer, I went to see him outside his office. We had a talk. He knows I suspect he tried to kill me."

"Did you threaten him?"

"Can't do that according to the rules, Chief. I think he knows I wanted to."

"What else?" Cooper said. He looked hungry for more details.

"I made a point of talking to a lot of people he knows, suppliers who do work for him, people at his church, the guy whose handling his IPO later this month."

"So, you're trying to piss him off, make him pick-up the phone, make a mistake." Cooper cracked a smile. "You kind of remind me of myself when I was younger, Blake."

"I appreciate the compliment."

"What makes you so sure it was a compliment?" Cooper inched up higher in the booth.

"Because you've been doing this for the last twenty-six years and you're damn good at what you do."

"You really know how to butter the toast when you want to, don't you, Blake?"

"Yeah, well." Blake and Cooper both smiled.

"Order something good. We're below budget. Campsite rentals in Big Sur are less expensive than bed and breakfasts, or decent motels. You've earned it."

Blake drank some water. "What happened with Kowalski, Chief?"

"He's resigning next week. He knows he's going to be indicted. There was no other way. It was all too black and white. It's a shame, really. All those years on the force. He walks away with nothing and goes to a minimum security prison, instead of his boat off the coast." Cooper shook his head.

"So what was it between you and Kowalski earlier?"

"It had to do with some evidence that disappeared on his watch. I was never sure about it," Cooper said.

"Did we get anything new on tape, yet?" Blake said.

"You got my voice mail about the call between Jensen and Kilmer."

"Yeah, I loved it," Blake said.

"But it's not enough. It's not an admission per se. Some lawyer will dance around and make it sound like less than what it is. The bastards." Cooper planted his fork in a medium rare New York Strip. "You were in law school, weren't you, Blake?"

"None of us are perfect. We all make mistakes."

Cooper laughed.

"Any calls between Kilmer and his sister?"

"Not yet, I'm still waiting for that one."

"You and me both," Blake said. "I suspect there's a lot they could talk about."

"I'll let you know when that happens. What else is going on?" Cooper said.

"I'm trying to help Kate Winslow's oldest daughter get out of Stockton and spend some time with her uncle in Utah. That should happen in the next week or so. I think she'll be amenable to helping us. She doesn't like Kilmer, never has." Blake cut into his steak. "I'm going to see her mother again, too."

"Just make sure you don't see too much of her, the parts that are normally covered up," Cooper said.

"You know, Chief, I never supposed you had sex on your mind this much." Blake scratched his head.

"I guess you haven't heard or read the studies about how much the average man thinks about sex? Thirteen times a day. We're surrounded by it, for Christ's sake. It's flashed in front of us everywhere. Look at that woman over there." Cooper moved his eyebrows and nodded toward the blond in her thirties, four tables away, wearing a dress that looked like it had been sewn on. "You tell me, Blake, are those natural or man-made? And her backside? She's got a bigger one than Kim Kardashian."

"You've got a point, Chief."

"Yeah, and she's got two of them. You know what I'm getting at. Watch yourself."

"Thanks for keeping an eye on my place and my girlfriend's house while I was in Utah."

"Not a problem. Everything was quiet."

"You didn't get any calls from Freddie Roosevelt, did you?"

"Who?"

"The kid who takes care of my dog and runs a few errands for me?"

"No, not a word." Cooper cut into his steak. "Where are you off to this afternoon?"

"I've got an appointment with a stock market guy who's going to tell me about the IPO Kilmer's about to launch. Then I'm off to the library to do some more research."

"Don't tell all the other guys you've got a library card," Cooper said. "It's bad enough some of them know you listen to National Public Radio. I'm waiting for Jameson to ask me if you carry around a tote bag."

"That sounds about right for Jameson. He probably thinks I take ballet lessons, too."

"Good luck with the research," Cooper said. "Keep me posted. I like some of those programs on NPR, by the way."

"Thanks for lunch, Chief.

● ● ●

Blake was a mile away from the investment firm where David Gibbs worked.

"I'll let him know you're here. Help yourself to some coffee or tea over there, if you'd like," the receptionist said.

"Thank you." Blake picked up a copy of *The New York Times* and a bottle of water. Gibbs appeared a few minutes later, mid-thirties, in a pin-stripe suit and power tie. "Rob said you had some special interest in Kilmer Enterprises and their upcoming IPO. It's launching next month."

"He told you I'm a detective?"

"Yes, he said you were very good at what you do. I handle most of Rob's investments. We've been working together about seven years, now."

"My interest isn't entirely from an investment point of view. I need to understand the kinds of things that would affect the stock's valuation and the timing of an IPO. I'm also interested in anything you know about James Kilmer," Blake said.

"The man is practically legendary. Everything he's touched has turned to gold. Kilmer has a squeaky clean image. No scandals, no financial improprieties, no problems with his balance sheet, lots of financial reserves to draw from. He did take some heat a few years back for refusing to allow generic drugs to be distributed in third-world countries on some of the patents he holds. The drug companies made slight changes in the compounds, evergreening they call it. They do it to extend the patents and protect their profits."

"His brother-in-law, Phillip Winslow, has an office not far from here. You've heard of him?" Blake said.

Gibbs' expression changed. "You mean the guy found dead on the lake trails a few weeks ago? I saw the story in the paper."

"Yes."

"He was a charlatan, unscrupulous as hell. The SEC was about to come down on him. It should have happened a long time ago. You know there's also been a rumor floating around on the internet that your victim wanted to legally change his name to Phillip Kilmer-Winslow so he could capitalize on his relationship to James. Name recognition, branding, pulls in clients and money."

"And how do you suppose Mr. Kilmer felt about that?" Blake said.

"Well, I don't know either one of them, but I can tell you that's not an association that James Kilmer would want to publicize. The investigation, it's ongoing right? *The Sacramento Bee* and *The Chronicle* both said his death was suspicious."

"It is," Blake said.

"You don't really think this has anything to do with James Kilmer, do you?"

"Not at this point, but theoretically, if it did, what would the consequences be?" Blake said.

"Believe me. You don't want any distractions or unfounded rumors when you're setting up and timing an IPO. You sure as hell don't want any news that calls into question someone's good name, physical health, emotional or financial stability. Not when he's the head of the company. Investors and syndicators want dull, successful predictability and the sparkle of something new that spells long-term profitability. Criminal liability is off the charts."

"So what kinds of events immediately precede an IPO?"

"We can look online right now." Gibbs swiveled left and keyed in the stock ticker for Kilmer's parent company. "The quarterly financial report for Kilmer Enterprises is due out at the end of this month. Says here Goldman Sachs is handling the IPO and there's a meeting with them and Morgan Stanley scheduled in three weeks, along with a second meeting with some hedge and mutual fund managers."

"So what's the word on the street about Kilmer's new venture?" Blake said.

"People are excited. Kilmer has always had a Midas touch. It looks like an excellent opportunity. Is there any reason for the investment community to be concerned?"

"How 'bout if I let you know?" Blake said. "I may need some more help. At this point, the answer is no."

"I would appreciate that, Detective. I really would."

I'm sure, Blake thought to himself, especially if it impacted the stock price and you could make a lot of money. "Thanks."

"I can set up a retirement account for you," Gibbs said. "Outline some options, discuss your goals and an investment strategy that you'd be comfortable with."

"I'll keep that it mind," Blake said. "I'm pretty jammed up for time, right now. Maybe later this month."

CHAPTER FORTY-FOUR

Blake walked to his car and called Freddie Roosevelt to thank him for taking such good care of Watson.

"Sure. I like that dog. I think he's getting even smarter since he's been hanging out with me."

"You would say that, wouldn't you? Seriously, you've been a big help to me. I appreciate it."

"You helped me, D.B. I like hanging out with you."

"You didn't notice anyone, anything strange going on around my place when I was gone?"

"Everything was quiet and peaceful. Me and Watson got a lot of exercise. I took him on some good runs. He's fast, and he got to chase Frisbees in the park."

"If you notice anyone suspicious by my apartment, I want you to call me right away and if I don't answer, you call that number for Chief Cooper that I gave you. Okay?"

"I got his number in my wallet. Why are you so worried?"

"I just had a run in with some people. I need to be careful."

"That's why you got the alarm system?"

"Yeah, I thought it would be a good idea," Blake said. "You always turn it on when you leave, right?"

"Always. I grew up in Compton. I lock up everything."

"How'd you like to meet my girlfriend, Julianna? She wants you to come over for a cook-out. She has two girls. Your mom can come, too."

"Cool. Your girlfriend's a good cook?"

"A really good cook. I was thinking maybe sometime during

the next week or two you and me could go to this gym I know where some NBA and college players work-out."

"I'm definitely in for that."

"You think that'd be okay with your mother?"

"I'm sure she'd let me," Freddie said.

"Make sure you ask. I'll get it set up."

"That'll be so cool."

"Take care of yourself, young Roosevelt."

● ● ●

Blake set his alarm for 4:00 a.m., Sunday. Stockton wasn't his favorite place at any time, but Allison needed help, and Blake wanted to take Kilmer down. Julianna had made the necessary arrangements with a women's center for sexual assault and domestic violence victims. Allison would be safe there. The center didn't publicize the addresses where battered women stayed, for obvious reasons. Blake took his service revolver. The days when he left it locked in the file cabinet were gone.

CHAPTER FORTY-FIVE

He filled up his thermos with coffee, and hit the freeway. Three hours later he was driving toward number twenty-three in the back of the El Morro Apartments where Allison lived. Most of the windows were still dark. The people receiving general assistance and government checks who lived there and didn't work, weren't inclined to get up early. Neither were people in Allison's line of work.

Blake planned to back up the rental van to the stairs that led to the second floor until he saw the low-rider pimpmobile. "What the hell," he mumbled. He looked around before he parked in the row facing the steps. The shades in her front windows were drawn, but he could see a man's shadow, hand raised above his head, and a woman's figure move across the floor. Blake grabbed the tire iron in the back of the van and took the safety off his revolver. He remembered telling her, no calls, not to anyone, and now this? "Goddamn it." He ran up the stairs, and stopped at the door. His heart pounded when he heard a man yelling and what sounded like a chair slammed against a wall.

"Bitch. You were going to run out on me, weren't you. Nobody does that."

Blake gripped the doorknob to test it.

"Who the fuck do you think you are? Huh? You want me to cut up that pretty face of yours, you stupid whore?"

The deadbolt hadn't been set, but the chain lock was in place. Blake's body tensed up.

"Diego, you don't understand. I wasn't. I was going to see my mother." Allison was crying.

"You work for me, bitch. You do what I say. The manager told me you gave notice. I'm no fool. Who the fuck do you think you're messing with?"

Blake kicked the door open with the heal of his foot like a bad nightmare and rushed across the room. He saw the knife in Diego's right hand inches away from Allison's face, smashed the tire iron against the back of his legs like a baseball bat and upended him. Blake pointed his gun in the pimp's face. "Give me a reason. Please."

Diego strained to reach for his leg. His face twisted in pain.

Allison looked one step away from full panic mode. She had bruises on her face where she'd been hit. Her shirt was ripped.

The knife Diego'd been holding slid across the floor, a body length away.

He lunged toward it.

Allison jumped back.

Blake stomped on Diego's hand and kneed him in the back. Then picked up the knife.

"Motherfucker," Diego yelled. He rolled over on his side but Blake pinned him to the floor.

"Shut-up," Blake said, "before I bust your head." He looked at her. "Get me some belts or extension cords. We need to tie him up."

Allison ran down the hall.

Blake called after her. "Get the rest of your stuff together. I've got a van out front. We're going." Blake's eyes remained fixed on Diego. "Don't move."

Diego was silent.

"You come after her, you'll find this tire iron wrapped around your head."

"You're a cop?" Diego said.

"She's not going to testify against you. You get a pass for

now on assault with a deadly weapon, but you won't get one from me." Blake stuck the gun in Diego's chest before he stepped across the room. Blake wiped his prints off the tire iron in his left hand. "We're going to keep this simple, so you can understand it."

Allison emerged from the bedroom a minute or two later with the cords and some rope.

"Roll over," Blake said. He holstered his gun. "I'm going to tie your hands behind your back. Then I'm going to wrap this cord around your legs and tie it to that refrigerator handle. And while I'm doing it, you're going to keep your mouth shut or I'll stuff a sock in it."

Fifteen minutes later, he and Allison had loaded the van. She sat in the passenger seat. "You made sure you didn't leave any paperwork in the apartment with your mother's address or phone number on it, nothing like that?"

"I got everything," she said.

"Let me have your keys. I'm going back upstairs to lock up."

Diego was next to the refrigerator on the floor.

"You pull too hard on that extension cord after I leave, and that refrigerator just might land on you. Then you'll be knocked out cold." Blake smiled. "Where's your wallet?"

"My back pocket."

Blake bent down and pulled it out. He copied Diego Morales driver's license number, address, and credit card information. He emptied the money and counted it. "Five hundred and twenty-eight dollars. This is going to the management company for damages. I don't want to ever see you again. And don't think about making a complaint."

"You're just going to leave me here like this?"

"I'm sure as hell not going to take you with us."

"I need to go to the hospital."

"That's not my problem. I don't want to hear your voice when I close the door. Your cell phone is in the toilet. I've got somebody listening outside who's gonna stick around here for a while. You'll give me two hours of silence if you know what's good for you. No pounding, no loud noises. Quiet."

Blake tossed the tire iron and the knife in the back of the van, and climbed in. The apartment below Allison's was vacant. The lights were still off at her neighbors. He handed her the ice he'd wrapped in one of her kitchen towels. "Put this on your face. It'll keep the swelling down."

She looked at him and kept silent. They were half way to Sacramento before she spoke.

"Thanks for helping me. I hate to think about what would've happened if you hadn't come when you did."

"No calls, Allison. No notices. Diego is not the forgiving type. This is a new start."

• • •

Blake pulled into the driveway of a two-story suburban tract house in a nondescript neighborhood. Two women came out to meet them and unload her bags. "We'll take it from here, Detective. It's better you not come in. She'll be safe."

Allison ran over to where Blake stood in the driveway and hugged him.

"I'll call you later this week and we'll talk about Utah," Blake said.

He climbed back into the van and called the number for the Stockton Police Department. Diego had been lying on the floor for three hours.

CHAPTER FORTY-SIX

"Uncle James, it's Allison. I know this is out of the blue. I didn't know who else to call. I'm hoping you'll help me. I got involved in something in Stockton that I shouldn't have."

"Go ahead. I'm listening."

"I did some drugs. There was a man. I stopped. Now he wants to hurt me."

"Where are you, now?"

"I'm in Sacramento. I've got a place to stay for the rest of the week, a women's shelter."

"Have you talked to your mother?"

"I don't want to do that. We're not on good terms."

"Can't you stay at her place?" Kilmer said.

"Diego, the man I'm afraid of, he could find me there."

"What is it you need, Allison?"

"I need help, Uncle James, a place to stay where I'll be safe until I can get back on my feet."

"If you come here, there'll be rules. No drugs, no hanging out with low-lifes or guys with pants half way down their ass, and no job. That's not acceptable here."

"You've got to help me, Uncle James."

"Can you commit to what I'm saying?"

"I'll try."

"Trying isn't good enough, Allison. You're a Kilmer. We don't just try."

"I can do it, Uncle James. I promise, I will."

"I'll make your plane reservations for Saturday morning.

Your Aunt Barbara and I will meet you at the baggage claim area in Salt Lake City. You can stay with us at the house for awhile. We've got twelve bedrooms, so there's plenty of room. I expect you to find a job, and then you can get your own place. Let me have your phone number so I can get back to you with the details. Eventually, your mother will have to know."

"Thank you, Uncle James."

"The promise you made to me starts now, Allison. Don't disappoint me."

• • •

Allison spent the rest of the week with three women who had escaped from abusive relationships, under the guidance of Mitzi, her counselor, who told her she'd gone through the same thing herself seven years earlier.

"It's not easy, but you can leave it behind. The key is to take it one step at a time and have a goal. Don't let somebody talk you into making the same mistakes all over again."

"The same mistakes . . . that's what makes it a habit isn't it?" Allison said.

"Bad habits can get you killed. Good ones can change your life," the therapist said.

"That guy you came with, Dylan Blake. He's got a good heart. I've heard about him."

Allison said, "He put himself out there for me."

"You pay him back by making it work," Mitzi said. "We're making dinner tonight, all of us. How are you at cooking?" Mitzi began to walk toward the kitchen.

"It's not a good habit at this point," Allison said.

"Well, we'll have to change that." Mitzi handed Allison a saucepan and a colander from the cupboard.

The next day, she drove Allison to the appointment she'd set up for her with a gynecologist. "You've got to be tested."

"Yeah, I know."

"One step at a time, Allison. Whatever it is, we'll deal with it. You'll have help."

● ● ●

The night before she was scheduled to leave for Utah, Allison met with Blake. She told him she was still waiting for her test results.

"That's been the hardest part . . . except for Diego and the knife," she said.

"Hope for the best. Maybe you'll be lucky," Blake said. His mind was focused on how she could help him gain the upper hand in dealing with her uncle. He only half-heard everything else. Allison was strong. He expected her to heal. "All I want you to do is let me know what you hear. Your father didn't die of natural causes. He was lured to the lake, and he was poisoned. It was deliberate. Your father was a liability for your uncle. He offended him."

"My father is the one who molested me. That's what's offensive. Uncle James didn't know. It wouldn't have happened under his roof."

"My guess is, you're right about that," Blake said. "But your uncle paid somebody to kill me. I'm in his way."

"Maybe, he's the one who killed my father at the lake. You can't expect me to help you send my mother to prison. She's allowed people to control her all her life . . . Uncle James, my father, her own mother. Maybe she is actually trying to change."

"That's all well and good, but I'm not going to let somebody keep shooting at me," Blake said. "I'm not a cat with nine lives. I don't get to pick and choose which cases to solve. Just listen and watch when you get there. That's all I'm asking you to do. You need to take hold of your own life. You're not responsible for everyone else."

The wheels turned in Blake's head . . . having to think what someone else would do . . . how someone would orchestrate it . . . what would trigger a violent, criminal reaction? There were plenty of people like Kate Winslow and James Kilmer who were able to lock things away in their heads and keep them there. Blake had never been one of those people. Blending morality with self-interest the way the two of them did, never seemed admirable to him. Allison's mother and her uncle, seemed to have an easy way with bending the truth.

"You'll call me from Utah when there's something I should know?" Blake said.

"I'm not going to stand around and watch my uncle destroy you. I have no fond memories of him. I'll let you know."

Blake couldn't ask for more than that. At least she'd be safe, away from Diego Morales.

CHAPTER FORTY-SEVEN

Blake was relentless with his research. He read everything about Kilmer he could get his hands on — newspaper articles, blogs, social media stuff. Her uncle was an immaculately groomed, confident man. Every button was buttoned, his shoes were always shined, even his belts looked brand new. Kilmer was intelligent, always on message, and in control of everything around him. Those attributes made people feel safer in a volatile, complicated world. Kilmer's measured intensity attracted investors, and kept his family in lock-step with him. They knew what he required and that he'd accept nothing less.

Blake, Tony, and Georgie had penetrated the veneer of Kilmer's life. Blake needed to rattle him and he was confident they had. He wanted Kilmer to pick up the phone and dial his sister once the wiretaps were in place. When Cooper called Blake and told him they had something, Blake made a U-turn and headed straight for police headquarters.

• • •

Cooper and Blake sat next to one another in the surveillance technician's audio room late that afternoon in Sierra Springs. "Go ahead, play it," Cooper said. "I'm anxious to hear this, again." He watched as Blake pulled a yellow note pad out of the backpack he'd set on the chair and clicked the pen.

Kilmer: Kathryn, it's James. How are you?

Kathryn: I'm okay. We're getting back to our new normal
           here, the girls and I.

Kilmer: And Allison? Have you talked with her?

Kathryn: I think she's living in Stockton. She was here for
           the service.

Kilmer: I've been concerned. When I told you it was time
           to end it with Phillip, I meant your marriage. You
           understood that, didn't you?

Kathryn: Yes, of course.

Kilmer: My paying off your mortgage was a private arrange-
           ment, an incentive for you to do what you had to
           do to secure a stable future for you and my nieces.
           Your marriage was a horrible mistake.

Kathryn: Yes, it was. But at least I got three daughters out
           of the deal.

Silence.

Kilmer: Your daughters needed to be protected. Sometimes
           God needs our help.

Kathryn: I'm glad you understand that, James.

Kilmer: Family always comes first for me. You know that,
           too, don't you, Kathryn?

Kathryn: I thought it was more about secrets, and your repu-
           tation, James.

Kilmer: Material things don't cloud my judgment. They shouldn't cloud yours.

Kathryn: What you mean is that I should be just like you, isn't it?

Kilmer: I go to church every Sunday and pay my ten percent in tithing. You should be doing the same thing. I don't routinely give out cost-of-living allowances. That money is for the church. I pay people to further my interests, to protect me and my name. Not to buy backyard spas and more toys for their children.

Kathryn: Yes, James, I'm aware of that. I've heard you say it many times.

Kilmer: Your ex-husband was a pretender, a fraud. His word meant nothing. He didn't even take his own family to church most of the time. He cheated his investors. He cheated on you.

Kathryn: It must be nice to see everything so clearly all the time.

Kilmer: He didn't provide for your future. He abused your trust.

Kathryn: All that and more.

Kilmer: We need to take care of ourselves. The have-nots aren't my concern. The fact that they hold their hands out asking for more, doesn't mean I'm obligated to reach for my wallet. Phillip can't pull you down to his level anymore.

Kathryn: You're right about that, James.

Kilmer: This young detective, Blake, he's visited you at least three times, now. He came here to Utah to see me. He's a threat, isn't he?

Silence.

Kilmer: Tell me what he's going to find.

Kathryn: There isn't anything to find.

Kilmer: Are you still seeing a therapist?

Kathryn: Yes. She's been helpful.

Kilmer: Sebring. Didn't you tell me that was her name?

Kathryn: Yes, Myra Sebring.

Kilmer: She's Jewish?

Kathryn: I guess. I never asked her.

Kilmer: Did you tell her what you did?

Kathryn: Not exactly.

Kilmer: Does she have a file on you?

Kathryn: I suppose so.

Kilmer: You know, Kathryn, you can't trust therapists. They're paid to help people rationalize their failings. I pay people to get stronger. It works better. You shouldn't be seeing her any longer.

Kathryn: James, I need to go. The children will be home soon. How did you know the detective had been to my home three times?

Silence.

Kathryn: I don't want you spying on me. You don't run my life. You can't control everyone.

Kilmer: I wouldn't be so sure of that. I've done quite well controlling people.

● ● ●

The phone clicked off, audibly.

Blake looked at Cooper. "It's good, but it's not an admission of guilt."

"I think she killed her ex-husband," Cooper said, "and it sounds like Kilmer was behind the break-in at her therapist's office. But you're right, there's not enough. That rich, arrogant, bastard will buy his way out of this."

"We link him to the break-in. That's a felony." Blake paused. "He paid somebody to kill me. He's not going to get away with this."

"I think you can move Kathryn Winslow to help you get him," Cooper said. "There's some real resentment building up there. She's reaching the end of her rope with him."

"I think you're right," Blake said. He shook his head. "This family's been messed up for a long time. There's no Disney movie here."

"More like a polite Quentin Tarantino without all the blood," Cooper said.

CHAPTER FORTY-EIGHT

"Are you doing okay?" Blake asked when Allison called.

"Clean and sober, Utah dull," she said. "How's life in Sierra Springs?"

"Demolition derbies, soccer games, life goes on. Your mother's therapist's office was burglarized, by the way."

"What?" Allison sounded startled. "Damn, that's why my Uncle James was talking with my mother about her therapist."

"You heard them on the phone?"

"That's why I called . . . to tell you. Uncle James thought I wasn't in the house. He had my mother on the speaker phone in his office. How did you know?" Allison said.

"We've got a wiretap on your uncle's phone. I listened to the tape, yesterday," Blake said.

"So he did it. He actually had somebody break in and steal my mother's therapy records? My records, too, I bet."

"I'll let you draw your own conclusions," Blake said.

"He's a two-faced manipulative liar, isn't he?"

"When it suits his purpose. Your uncle is a man who decides what he wants and takes it. He doesn't understand anyone telling him he can't have it."

"That's sick."

"I'm glad you understand that," Blake said.

"He really did try and kill you, didn't he?" Allison said.

"He paid someone to do it for him."

"You think he'll try again?"

"I'm more concerned about what he might do to the people who matter to me."

"You're kidding. He'd go that far?"

"Look at what he's already done. Your uncle isn't someone to be underestimated."

"Who's going to stop him?" Allison said.

"I think you know the answer to that question," Blake said. "We are."

CHAPTER FORTY-NINE

Allison walked down the hall outside her uncle's office. "Oh, my God," she muttered to herself, "what the hell is wrong with this family?"

She appreciated her uncle's offer to let her stay with them. It seemed kind and unencumbered. He hadn't asked a hundred questions or insisted on any cures. She was welcomed. Her Aunt Barbara was sweet, like she'd always been, and not at all judgmental. Barbara smiled when Allison entered the kitchen. "Come sit over here and talk with me. I've missed you. I'm mixing up a salad for tonight and some pasta. You can join your uncle and me for dinner. You should eat something."

Allison pulled up a chair and nibbled. "It's great you're letting me stay here, Aunt Barbara."

"It's nice to have you here, Allison. Your uncle is away a lot, always pre-occupied. Seems like he spends all his time working on his IPO. I think he's looking forward to finishing that up, and getting back to running his other businesses."

Barbara reached across the table and touched Allison's hand. "Forgive me for asking. But how did you get that nasty bruise on your cheek?"

"A man."

Barbara seemed startled. "A man hit you?"

"Yeah."

"Well, you won't have to worry about that here. Your uncle would never let that happen. He's got one of those AR-15 assault rifles in his gun cabinet.

"I noticed."

"Hopefully, the two of us can dissuade him from talking about the Second Amendment and taxes tonight."

"It's beautiful here, Aunt Barbara. How long have you and Uncle James owned this house?"

"Close to twenty years, now. It's a comforting place to be." Barbara smiled.

It seemed to Allison her aunt always smiled. There were cottonwoods outside the window stretching toward the forest service land in back of the house, and the aspens and evergreens at the base of the mountain range. Her uncle called their home a cabin. To Allison, the house was like a castle for the super rich.

She'd gotten away from Diego and now she felt torn between the safety of living under her uncle's roof, and what Blake had done for her. "Has my mother ever been here?"

"Once or twice. She and James don't see one another very often. Your mother has never seemed comfortable when she's been here."

"Why?" Allison said.

"Maybe because of the tension between your father and my husband. They never got along. I think your mother sensed James disapproved of Phillip. I guess those days are over, now." Her aunt seemed genuinely sad.

Allison shuddered. She pictured Blake on the side of the mountain, being hunted by her uncle's men who tried to kill him. Jack Hamilton was killed. So was her father. Diego had put a knife to her face.

"Allison, you seem distracted. Did I say something to upset you?"

"No. I got a lot on my mind." She took a sip of the tea her aunt had handed her. "Did you ever think, Aunt Barbara, how families have secrets?"

"That's a rather strange question."

"Just thinking," Allison said. She continued to stare out the window at the cottonwoods. "It's so pretty outside. I think I'll take a walk before dinner."

"We're going to eat at seven, once your uncle is home."

Allison pulled her jacket from the closet and headed down the road about two miles to the neighborhood corner store. She felt alone, like she was adrift at sea. She opened the wooden screen door and looked at everyone inside the store to see if she could score. She wanted a hit. Just a taste, one taste. She bought a pack of cigarettes and walked around the side of the building by the propane tank where she could lean back and watch the people going in. I'd do somebody for coke right now, if I had the chance. When she'd finished her second cigarette and an energy drink, she mumbled, "Utah clean. I hate this stupid state."

Her cell phone was set to vibrate. She reached for her front pocket.

"Your test results were negative," Mitzi said.

Allison took a deep breath and exhaled. "Thanks."

"How are you doing today?" Mitzi said.

"I don't know. I was trying to score just now. But I didn't."

"Get out of wherever you are and go home to where you're staying," Mitzi said. "It's a one-step, one day at a time commitment. You can do it, Allison. Call me when you get home and don't stop until you do. You lucked out on the test results. You can't count on that happening again."

Allison threw the cigarette pack in the dumpster before turning back to the house. She didn't know what to think. She had disappointed people, disappointed herself, and was an inch away from slipping back to where she'd been. "I know better, and I still wanted to. Stupid, so fucking stupid," she told herself.

She liked feeling safe. She wanted someone to be interested in her for more than money or sex. Her uncle made Utah look like an ocean of calmness, but she'd begun to feel the rip current beneath the surface. She recognized the danger when she heard him on the phone, berating her mother.

Blake had told her she was headed down a dead-end road. She didn't want to hear that. But nobody else she knew had shared a story about their younger brother's sexual abuse, and they wouldn't have risked what Blake had done for her. Somehow, Blake had seen through her hard ass, I-don't-care-attitude to the fragile place she was coming from. Her parents had never been that honest with her. She'd gone past listening to anything they had to say.

She couldn't help but wonder, as she walked back to the house, how her uncle could be so kind and generous on one hand, and try to kill someone with the other. How he could make such a beautiful home for his wife, his family and grandchildren, talk with them about tithing and church, then turn around and vilify his competitors and anyone who questioned his judgment the same day? She remembered the stories she'd heard and the glimpses into her uncle's life she'd seen as a teenager. How her mother seemed almost afraid of him, yet appeared to always be looking for his approval, like she was under a spell.

• • •

Later that night, Allison, her Aunt Barbara and Uncle James sat around the dinner table talking about Kilmer's favorite conservative causes and the local community theatre production Aunt Barbara was sponsoring.

Being rich didn't seem as fulfilling as Allison supposed it might be when she watched her aunt, whose life appeared to revolve around bridge parties, occasional social events, and her Barbie Doll collection. She hadn't seen much in the way of physical affection coming from the patriarchal head of the family.

Barbara excused herself around ten to nurse a migraine. After she left, Allison stared across the dining room table at her uncle. "What is it about money that interests you so much?" she said, with equal parts of curiosity and antagonism.

"Besides just having it, you mean?"

"Yeah."

"Well," he said, as a frown formed on his face, "if you must know, what it can do for you." Kilmer gestured with his hands. "Look around, Allison. Tell me you wouldn't like to have all this, and the servants that come with it."

"Working twelve, fourteen, sixteen hours a day. That's not appealing to my generation, Uncle James."

"You have to work hard if you want to get ahead. I've earned every penny I have. Your mother and I, we didn't come from money. I didn't get all this the easy way."

"Did you get all your money honestly?" Allison said.

"I didn't wait for people to hand it to me, if that's what you mean. I had to take it when the opportunity presented itself. I didn't have someone like your father dragging me down. You think he didn't take people for whatever he could get, including your mother?"

"He cheated on her. He was a pig," Allison said. "So what are you saying, Uncle James, that it's okay to take what you want and push people out of the way when you need to?"

"Excuse me?" Kilmer said. "Do you have any idea who you're talking to?"

"Don't get me wrong. I appreciate your help. I was in a bad situation."

"I know, the El Morro Apartments are a far cry from Utah."

Allison caught her breath. "How did you know where I lived?" Allison's voice jumped an octave higher.

"You'd be surprised what I know, my dear." He wiped his mouth with a linen napkin and threw it down on his plate. "What matters is that you're here, not hanging around with a bunch of lowlife, inferior people." His stare turned cold. She felt the chill in her bones.

"By inferior, I take it you mean people who haven't achieved your exalted status."

"What I mean are the millions who are put on this earth to

serve the rest of us. This country was once a nation of slave owners and slaves. Our founding fathers wanted it that way. Now we have white niggers to do our bidding."

Allison's skin began to crawl. "I'd expect to hear that from a neo-Nazi skinhead, not somebody like you."

"Watch your tongue, young lady. You're living under my roof now. You don't know much about this country's real history. They don't teach that in school."

She could see him getting angrier by the minute, grinding his teeth, clenching his jaw. "I know your brand of history means keeping quiet about racism and abuse," Allison said. She could feel herself growing more defiant. "Money, it's like a drug, isn't it?"

"I've had about enough of your smart mouth. You don't understand how real commerce works or what it means. There'll always be worker bees."

"And people to control, who'll do your bidding . . . that you can just do with as you please? White niggers . . . that's what you call them?"

"Enough already, I said," Kilmer yelled.

Allison leaned back in her chair and felt the emotion drain out of her. Her hands were shaking.

"Tell me. How long has it been since you talked with your mother?"

"We talked the day of my father's funeral."

"So she doesn't know you're here?"

"I'd like to keep it that way . . . for now."

"Its obvious the two of you have issues. Too bad your mother has never been able to elevate herself to the level of the other Kilmers.

"Issues," Allison said. "That's what you're calling them?"

"Some people, people like your mother, are too weak to act. When they make mistakes, they don't have the strength or moral character to make amends."

"And you do, Uncle James? You've made amends? Is that

why you built the recreation center and had them put your name on it?"

The anger swept over her uncle's face like a rattler unwinding, ready to strike. The vein in his forehead bulked out like the hull of a boat. His face turned red. He slammed his fist, hard against the table. The china cup and saucer jumped, then shattered on the floor when he swept them aside with the back of his hand. Kilmer's eyes flashed with rage.

Allison took a deep breath. Her ears were ringing, her palms wet with sweat. She stared back at her uncle. "You're not used to somebody who talks back. Attacking your competitors and enemies like a corporate drone you control from a bunker, that's probably more to your liking." Allison got up from the table and stepped toward the broken china.

"Leave it," Kilmer commanded. "Sit back down here. You'll get up when I tell you to." Kilmer's voice had an edge to it that had begun to unnerve her.

"I didn't realize you were so different from your mother. You're more assertive." Kilmer eyes moved from her feet to her head.

"Leave my mother out of this. My father was killed. You know it wasn't an accident, don't you?"

"I've had just about enough from you, young lady."

"The detective who's investigating the case told me. I saw the pictures."

"What pictures?" Kilmer voice got louder.

She saw the hate in his eyes. His shoulders tensed up.

"The ones the police took at the lake."

"What about them?"

Allison decided to plow on, no matter what. "The picnic blanket was there. Mom's blanket, the one with the bears on it. She's had it since we were little kids. She would never have given it away. Not when they divorced, not ever."

Her uncle's face turned a shade whiter. He was silent for the first time that evening. "Does that detective know this?"

"I haven't told him, yet." Allison saw the surprise in her uncle's eyes turn to contempt. Then she realized the blanket was the mistake her mother was thinking about when she assured Uncle James she hadn't made any mistakes. That's what the two of them had been talking about on the phone.

Kilmer folded his hands as if he were about to pray.

Silence lay between them.

"So tell me, Allison," Kilmer said in a sugary-sweet voice, "how do you feel about what happened to your father?"

"The bastard raped me. How do you think I feel? At least now he can't do it to my sisters."

"Your father got what he deserved." Kilmer paused for a moment. "You know, he planned to legally change his name to Phillip Kilmer-Winslow so he could capitalize on my success. The gall of that man."

"Oh, my God, did you hear what I said? He raped me. And you're comparing that to his wanting to change his name?" Allison yelled. Her stomach churned. She threw her hands toward her uncle, as if to say get away from me.

"We're all better off without him."

"That's the first thing we've agreed on, even if it isn't very Christian," Allison said.

"If you actually knew anything about history, you'd know The Church embraced The Crusades. The knights were pardoned for their excesses by Popes and Kings."

"I guess you can justify almost anything if you want it bad enough, can't you, Uncle James?"

"That's called business, Allison." Kilmer smirked.

"I'm sick of talking about all this crap. The whole goddamn bunch of you and your religious hypocrisy."

Kilmer snarled. "Rape is a fact of life. Get over it."

"You're sick," she screamed.

Kilmer threw his wine glass against the wall.

Allison rose from the table and stomped the glass into the floor with the heel of her boot. As she turned to leave the room, the Exceptional Achievement Award given to her uncle for his philanthropic contributions caught her eye. Allison grabbed it off the dark walnut sideboard, her hands shook with anger, raised it above her head and threw it down the way she remembered Charlton Heston had when he shattered The Ten Commandments. "You disgust me."

She stepped around the glass. "I'm going to bed. I suppose you'll have the help clean this up in the morning." Allison slammed the dining room door, with all her strength, leaving her uncle sitting alone under the crystal chandelier, bristling with anger.

CHAPTER FIFTY

Kilmer was up at 5:15 and enroute to his office by 6:30. He'd completed the filing with the Securities and Exchange Commission, secondary trading among his employees, former employees, and private investors had already been halted. The traditional, fundamental analysis of revenues, profits, gross margins, cash flow, and growth rates had been done and re-done. He'd settled on Goldman Sachs as the lead underwriter with Morgan Stanley as a secondary. Their final preparatory meeting was scheduled for next week. Initial Public Offerings like this one were time consuming and expensive.

Kilmer called his secretary from the car. "Set up an appointment for me with Richard Jensen. You can reach him at the Logic offices. Tell him to meet me downtown at the fountain in front of the Marriott, this afternoon at five."

Jensen was six feet plus a few inches, big-boned, strong, with cold, brown eyes and hair that had begun to thin. He looked to be in his late forties, ex-military. He'd been on Kilmer's payroll for over a decade, spent most of his time in Salt Lake City, when he wasn't traveling on special assignments. No one in the suburban offices, where he worked, seemed to know what he did or what his job title was. He was married, well-paid, with a house in the suburbs, and a fourteen-year-old daughter.

Kilmer circled the fountain in his Lincoln Town Car.

Jensen was sitting on a circular bench, dressed in a dark green overcoat, dress slacks, and black wingtips.

The passenger door swung open. "Get in," Kilmer said.

Jensen fastened his seat belt and looked straight ahead.

Kilmer drove down the boulevard toward a green belt area. Five minutes passed. "You didn't get it right the first time. That's what you get paid for . . . getting it right."

Jensen showed no emotion.

"You called to alert me when someone damaged your car. You didn't see who did it?"

"No, but judging from the note on the dash, it must've been Blake. I understand he was in town, asking questions, bothering people," Jensen said.

"He was bothering me," Kilmer said. "You calling me on the office phone was stupid. The name of the company you work for is Logic, LLC. That should be a clue."

"Yes, sir. I'm sorry. It won't happen again."

"You told me you were going to bow out. That's not going to happen. You're going to finish the job I assigned you. I want Blake out of the way."

"But sir, he knows who I am. He knows I work for you."

"Maybe you didn't understand. Figure out how to get it done. He's a cop. He's got enemies, people he's sent to prison. It doesn't have to point back here. Make sure it doesn't."

"Somebody's going to look in this direction," Jensen said.

"You work for a subsidiary of Kilmer Enterprises. So do thousands of other people. Don't pretend to tell me what I already know. Either you kill him or I'll kill that daughter of yours." Kilmer pulled to the curb at Fourth and Elm. "Time for you to go hunting, Mr. Jensen. I warned Blake."

CHAPTER FIFTY-ONE

Blake felt compelled to go out on a limb for Allison. It wasn't just about closing the case. She was abused, like his brother had been. He didn't want her to end up an anonymous casualty. She was the canary he'd placed in the mine, and that worried him.

Kilmer's connection to Jensen, the rifleman on his payroll, had been laid bare. Blake and Cooper both smiled when they'd heard the wiretap.

Blake sympathized with Kate, but if getting Kilmer meant he had to kick the chair out from under her, he was willing. He wanted to destroy Kilmer. Nothing in this case, besides Allison, mattered more.

The rest of the day panned out well for Blake. He worked out at the gym, talked to Rob and Julianna, and got home at a decent hour. When he saw the red light flashing on his answering machine, he hit the play button. He didn't recognize the voice on the other end of the line.

"Your mother lives in Georgia at the end of a country road. They have hunting seasons there. It's not just about you any longer."

Blake stared at the phone, half-expecting it to jump off the table. Blood rushed to his head. His hands turned white. He reached for the phone and called his mother. There was a moment before she answered. The weight of the silence settled in his gut.

"Mom, are you there?"

He waited. Blake felt his body relax when he heard the sound of his mother's voice. He poured a glass of water from the refrigerator and sat down at the counter between the kitchen and living room. All he wanted was to know everything in Georgia was okay.

"Your sister and I went to a Cuban restaurant in Blairsville, yesterday, with Natalie and June. We stopped to get some fabric and batting for the quilt I've been working on."

"Has anything unusual or out of the ordinary happened around there in the last week, Mom?"

"We've had all kinds of deer, young ones, running around lately. I don't know why we've had so many. It's fun to see them. Everything's been good except for Tuesday when we got up and found that somebody had slashed your sister's tires. We've never had that kind of problem before." She sounded more surprised, than alarmed.

"I know. You've got great neighbors," Blake said.

"The best. I guess it must have been teenagers. Stupid kids."

"Let me ask you a question, Mom. What would you have done if you'd caught somebody slashing those tires or threatening you?"

"I'd call the police or fire a warning shot if I had to. If they did something really bad, like assaulting me or your sister, I'd shoot 'em. But then, I'd have to drag him into the house so I wouldn't get charged." She paused. "Why are you asking?"

"I'm investigating a case and this guy is threatening to hurt someone close to me."

"And you think he's serious?"

"I have to assume he is, based on what I know."

"Don't worry about me, son. Georgia is a long way from California. I can take care of myself. I keep my shotgun propped up next to the fireplace, just like always. And I've got my thirty-two caliber Walther. I used to have a forty-five, but the Walther isn't so heavy. I don't need two hands to hold it up."

"I just want you to be a little more careful, Mom."

"I'll keep my eyes open. You don't need to worry about me. And just so you know, the last time I went on a cruise and did skeet shooting off the stern of the ship, I beat all the men."

"You're not quite as young as you used to be."

"I'm not as old as you think I am, either."

"I want you to make sure you tell my little sister about our conversation. Will you do that for me?"

"Of course."

"And you'll ask Eddie R and your neighbors to keep an eye out for strangers?"

"Sure. It's a one lane road to the house. I told you, I can take care of myself. Nail him. . . What's he done, anyway?"

"He paid somebody to shoot an adversary. They missed, but this guy's mega-rich and he has a dark side."

"Do you think he could have had something to do with the tires?" she said.

"It's a real possibility."

"Well, he owes your sister close to five hundred dollars then. Get a check before you throw him in jail."

"I love you, Mom."

"I love you too, son. Thanks for calling."

Blake set down his cell and walked over to his desk to look for Eddie R's number and Walt Davis', who lived close by. "This is unacceptable," Blake said out loud. "Unacceptable."

He didn't sleep well. He woke before the alarm sounded, made breakfast, and phoned Cooper's assistant, at eight.

"Let me check his appointment book while I put you on hold."

"Juggle it, Susan. This can't wait," Blake said.

"Just come in this morning. I'll clear his schedule for you."

● ● ●

Blake told Cooper about the call and the tires.

"You know what the difference is between a Porsche and a porcupine, Detective?" Cooper paused. "The pricks like Kilmer are inside the Porsche."

Blake felt himself wanting to smile, but he couldn't. He wanted to grind Kilmer's face in the dirt.

"Nobody, no matter how much money or power they have, is going to threaten the people who work for me and get away with it. I'm going to get the County Sheriff in Georgia on the line, and let him know what's going on. Ask him to pay as much attention as he can to your mother's neighborhood. Then I'll check with airport security in Chattanooga and Atlanta for any quick round-trip turnarounds from Salt Lake City, during the days before and after those tires got slashed. I can label it a Homeland Security matter. Maybe we'll get lucky."

"Thanks, Chief."

"I'm going to increase the surveillance and keep an eye on your girlfriend's house as well for the next week while we sort this out. I figure you can take care of yourself, so we'll aim our resources in her direction instead."

Blake wanted to feel relieved, but he wasn't. He leaned back in the chair across from Cooper.

"I'd be mad as hell if I was in your shoes, Blake, but you've got to hold that in check."

"I'd like to stick a fork in his ass and grill him over an open pit," Blake said. "He should be swinging from a tree in the middle of the prairie like one of those horse thieves in *Lonesome Dove*."

"That was before Miranda and the golden age of enlightenment we're in now," Cooper said.

"It's not easy when trouble hits this close to home," Blake said.

"You've got to keep hold of your temper," Cooper said. "Remember, you went to law school. Two years, right?"

"Did we get anything new on the phone taps?"

"You heard the call Jensen made to Kilmer. He's behind it, all right. But we need more."

"Jensen isn't going to roll over," Blake said. "He's going to get a pile of money and legal assistance aimed at keeping his mouth shut. Kilmer will bankroll his defense."

"Aggravating, isn't it?" Cooper said. "You need to press that young girl, Allison, or her mother, to shake up Kilmer."

"That's exactly what I had in mind," Blake said. "You'll call me if anything else breaks on the phone taps?"

"Right away. You'll know as soon as I do."

Blake headed down the hall toward the Detective's Room. He grabbed his jacket off the chair and walked out to his car, drove to a neighborhood cafe, and sat alone at a table out front. First he'd call Allison, then her mother. Or should it be the other way around? Boulders were about to fall. He wasn't sure where they'd land.

CHAPTER FIFTY-TWO

Kathryn received a message from Blake on her voice mail. An hour later, she called him back.

"You wanted to talk with me?"

"In person," he said. "It's important. I met with your brother."

"And so?"

"And so we need to talk. Are you home?"

"I'm at the office. I can be home after three. Official business?"

"Yes."

She greeted him at the door dressed in black capris and an electric-green chiffon shirt. "Come in. We'll sit in the back."

Everything was in bloom—the bougainvillea, the crepe myrtle, the roses. Blake smelled jasmine in the air. His eyes were drawn to Kate's and then to what she was wearing. It was the first time he'd seen her wear a bra.

"Would you like me to take it off?" she said.

"Was it really that obvious?"

"I can read men pretty well these days."

"I heard you took my advice about finding someone else," Blake said.

"What do you mean?"

"Your accountant told a friend of mine at the Midtown Business Association meeting last week how good you were in bed."

Kathryn smiled. "He spoke the truth. I used to think he was only good with numbers."

Blake pointed to the edge of the lawn. "That's the path that leads to the lake trails, isn't it?"

She nodded.

"It's two point three miles to where your ex was found."

"We used to stop at that spot," she said, "a long time ago."

"Why did you do it, Kate? I know I asked you before, but he was going to be arrested." Blake pretended to look puzzled.

"Who said I did?" Her lips trembled.

"We've been down this road before," Blake said. "The prescription you re-filled, the mortar and pestle, the wine, the invitation, the woman who saw you on the lake trails."

"What woman?"

"It doesn't matter. We both know you were there."

There was no woman. Blake was bluffing. "You called his office the day he died."

"Is this why you wanted to come over this afternoon, to gently float your theory again, hoping that I would crumble and confess?"

"Partially," Blake said.

"And the other part?"

"Your brother is putting people close to me in harm's way. He paid someone to shoot at me. He's threatened my mother, for Christ's sake."

"When he's not in church, he's dangerous, Detective. I warned you about him. He has his own set of rules."

"When we first met," Blake said, "you told me a story about your mother and how you'd hide from her in the closet when she was in her moods." Blake hesitated for a moment. "Did you ever have to hide from your brother?"

"I'm not sure I understand what you're asking." She shifted from one side to another in her chair.

"I can ask it again. Did you ever have to hide from your brother? Was he part of the reason why you wanted to leave the Idaho Panhandle so badly?"

"That was a long time ago . . . a lifetime ago. I don't want to think about that now."

"How would you feel if your daughter, Allison, was under his roof?"

"She's not. She never will be."

Blake watched as Kate's hands began to shake. Her breathing accelerated.

"Sometimes the people who claim the high road carry around the most guilt. They push the blame off and their guilt turns into someone else's shame. Nothing about that is right," Blake said. He paused, hoping what he'd said would sink in. "Family always comes first. That's what your brother said to you on the phone, isn't it? I think it's more about secrets for him, protecting his reputation like you said."

"How do you know that?"

"Allison was listening on the line in your brother's house. You don't have anything to be ashamed of. You don't need to keep carrying around that secret."

"Allison's at his house?" She struggled to stay silent.

Blake felt like he could almost see the blood rush to Kate's head.

"Oh, my God." Kathryn glanced up from the table between them, then averted Blake's eyes. "All my life . . . controlling, manipulative men. My father wanted the best for me, but he didn't know how to deal with my mother. And Phillip was more like my brother James, than James will ever admit."

"I know, Kate."

"I don't know why I turned my back on Jack. . .religious doctrine, some misguided desire to please my brother. Maybe my wanting to take singular credit for what Jack and I had accomplished together. It was a mistake. Jack was kind and loving. He didn't have an agenda. There's a regret in my heart that never goes away, now. You've made me do this again, Dylan Blake . . . cry and wonder why I've told you so much." She reached for a tissue and dabbed her eyes.

Blake leaned forward and touched her hand. He didn't expect Kate to show him that much pain and anxiety. "People need to see this side of your brother. They need to know what he's taken along the way from people like you. Sooner or later someone's going to demand you tell the whole truth, Kate. So help you God, that's what they're going to say. Then you'll have to choose between burying more secrets, or being the kind of woman your father hoped you'd become, and that Jack Hamilton saw."

A long silence followed.

"All those compartments in your head, most of us have them. You probably talked with Myra Sebring, your therapist, about them. That's why your brother had her office burglarized and the files stolen. He's never going to accept you as an equal or trust your judgment. Sometimes you have to let the walls come tumbling down before you can re-build them. You've been doing that with two of your daughters. Now it's time for you to do it with Allison." Blake kept his hand on hers. She began to regain her composure.

"I can call Allison right now. I have her cell number. You can warn her about your brother, and the three of us together can put a stop to this madness." Blake stood up from the garden table where they were sitting. "I'm going to talk to her first before I put you on the line. Will you do this . . . for me and for Allison?"

Kathryn looked at Blake and brushed away a tear. "It's the right thing to do, isn't it?"

Blake spoke with a quiet assurance. "It's what I would do. It's what your father would want . . . honesty."

Blake walked to where the jasmine grew. He supposed Allison didn't know her mother hid in closets when she was a girl, or why.

● ● ●

"Hello," Allison said.

"Can you talk?" Blake said.

"I'm alone, outside."

"I need your help. You remember my telling you your uncle tried to have me killed?"

"That's not something I'd forget."

"He's threatened my family, now. He had somebody stick a knife in my mother's tires. The car was parked in front of her house in Georgia."

"Oh, my God. And you know it was him?"

"Yeah," Blake said. "Your uncle has a long reach."

"Clear to Georgia?"

"You need to understand something, Allison. Love, compassion, kindness . . . when your uncle shows you those qualities, mostly it's an act. He's going to manipulate you to get what he wants . . . to control you, the same way he's controlled your mother. She's here with me, now. She knows where you're staying. She knows something about your uncle that you don't. Your mother is going to help me stop him before it gets worse."

Allison remained silent.

"Your uncle can't play God. He's got to be held accountable. We need your help, Allison. We've got to do this together."

"What do you want?"

"I'm going to put your mother on the phone." Blake walked over to where Kate sat and handed her his cell.

"Allison . . ."

Blake sat across from her and watched Kate as she waited for Allison to answer. She looked nervous.

"Are you okay?" Kathryn said.

Blake didn't hear a voice on the other end of the line.

Kathryn began. "Everything Detective Blake said is true. Your uncle had somebody following Jack Hamilton. He's had somebody watching me. He was probably watching you in

Stockton." Kathryn paused. "He broke into my therapist's office, Allison. James has tried to hide all this. And your father, you know how he felt about your uncle."

The cell phone's volume was low, but Blake could hear most of what Allison was saying when she raised her voice.

"Stop it, Mother. Uncle James didn't try to run detective Blake off the road. I know Dad paid somebody to do that, and I saw the pictures by the lake." Allison's voice fell silent. Kathryn turned her back away from Blake. Allison continued. "I saw Dad lying on our favorite picnic blanket. I know you didn't let him take that blanket when he moved out. You had to have been there."

Blake watched Kathryn slump in her chair, like an air mattress someone was deflating. Her head dropped to her chest. She closed her eyes to shield herself from the pain.

"But, Allison," Kathryn said.

"Don't lie to me, Mother. Why can't you be honest? Why can't you just say you messed up, that you're sorry? Why didn't you stop my father when you saw him molesting me?"

"I couldn't believe my eyes. I convinced myself I was mistaken. I was afraid, Allison. There wasn't anyone else to provide for us financially."

Blake watched Kate's every move and breath.

"Financially, mother. Financially!" Allison yelled. "What the hell is wrong with you?"

Kathryn began to cry. "That's why I started the business. That's why I never gave him unsupervised visitation with your sisters. It happened to me, Allison. Your uncle James molested me when I was a young girl about your age. I didn't ever face up to my own fears and the shame I felt. Somehow, I think your father sensed that."

Blake presumed Kate had never told anyone about her brother, except her therapist. Now he and Allison both knew, and Blake had a second reason why Kilmer had broken into

Myra Sebring's office. Kilmer had always been the driver, never the passenger.

"Why didn't you tell me, Mother? I would have understood. We could have helped each other." Allison's voice rang with sadness.

"I should have talked to you," Kathryn said. "I know it's not enough to say I'm sorry, but I want this to end. I'm tired of it all, Allison."

"I'm sick of these secrets, too, Mom. What does detective Blake want us to do?"

The look on Kathryn's face, her eyes, the way she moved, were awash with the relief that came from letting go of her darkest secret. Blake could see the weight lifted from her shoulders.

Kathryn handed the cell phone back to Blake.

"Your uncle is a strategist, Allison. It's a game he plays," Blake said.

Kathryn moved her chair closer to where Blake was sitting.

"He needs to feel that he's always in control, that he's a step ahead of whomever he plays against. We're going to use that to our advantage. We want him to convict himself." Blake looked at Kate, smiled and pointed to the phone. The color came back to her face.

"I want you to tell him you think your mother is about to confess, and that you're worried she'll go to prison."

"Are you serious?" Allison said.

"Yes. My guess is, your conversation will inspire him to call your mother."

"Then what?"

"Let me handle that," Blake said. "I'll talk to your mother. You need to set this in motion, and focus on keeping yourself clean. No drugs."

"Uncle James is helping me. He's been supportive. We talked again the other day," Allison said.

"Good. Just remember, he doesn't pass out free lunches. There's always a catch. That's how life works for him. We'll talk more tomorrow. Call me when you're off by yourself. I don't want your uncle to get suspicious." Blake set his cell on the table in front of Kate.

She looked at him. Tears filled the corners of her eyes. "You must think I'm a horrible person," she said.

"I don't think that at all. What matters more is how you think of yourself." Blake unfolded his hands. "You've got to keep letting go. This thing with your brother. It's like an addiction you have. He abused you, and yet you keep seeking his approval. You don't need that any more than you need alcohol or pills or crack cocaine."

"So what's your plan?"

Blake recognized Kathryn's need for reassurance. "You and your daughters are going to be okay. He's going to fight back against me. I'm the one who's in his sights."

"But that's dangerous," Kathryn said.

"It's how he plays the game."

"You said he threatened your mother. You're worried about your girlfriend, too, aren't you?"

"I've got somebody watching after them. Right now, he hopes I'll back off. He's accustomed to winning. Allison's conversation will disturb him."

"Why?" Kathryn said.

"Your brother doesn't want you to confess. That would make your ex-husband's death, what came before it and what followed, about the Kilmer name and the Kilmer brand. The timing is all wrong for him. He's got this IPO happening, lots of money at stake. A hint of scandal involving him would be like a land mine on the highway."

"So what do I say?" Kathryn said.

"You tell him you're thinking about turning yourself in. Then we'll see what he says, and whether he decides to obstruct justice and engage in a cover-up, or something worse."

Blake paused. "I'll need your permission to put a tap on your phone." In truth, Blake and Cooper already had one in place.

"Do you have to do that . . . to record our conversations?"

"It's for the best. Then the record will speak for itself and when this plays out, you'll be seen in a more favorable light."

"I haven't admitted anything," Kathryn said.

"Then be careful what you say. If he calls you, let it sit for a day," Blake said. "Don't talk to him. He'll call back."

CHAPTER FIFTY-THREE

Blake was worried about what Kilmer might do. He figured his sense of justice was closer to North Korea's where revenge washed over from one generation to the next. Guilt beyond a reasonable doubt was a tough standard when it boiled down to circumstantial evidence, especially when the perpetrator had an unlimited amount of money to defend himself, and cops were saddled with things like probable cause and rules of evidence.

He couldn't kick back and wait for justice to take its course, not with somebody like Kilmer, and not with the uncertainty about his mother's well-being. She was a tough, old broad, but she was vulnerable. Things were moving fast. There was a lot to tie down. He jumped in his car and drove to head-quarters. He wanted Kate Winslow's signed authorization for the phone tap on file before Kilmer called. He also needed to touch base with Cooper.

Blake was in and out of the police station in ninety minutes. He wanted to talk with Freddie Roosevelt before he left for Utah, and more importantly, he needed to see Tony.

• • •

"Sure ya can stop by. Me and Tony Junior are goin to stop by and visit my father. I know he'd like to see ya, too. Georgie's back in Jersey."

Blake hadn't been to The Villas for months. The buildings

looked better and the vibe was altogether different, pleasant actually. Blake went through the front door and up to the third floor where Tony's father lived. He tapped on the door.

Tony extended his hand and put his arm around Blake when he entered. "Good to see ya." He gestured toward the couch. "Ya wanna drink or coffee? I can make ya an espresso."

"No, I'm good. Just water," Blake said.

"We got somethin' better for ya." Tony pulled a cold Limonata out of the refrigerator. He twisted the top off and walked over to the couch where Blake sat. "Try this."

Tony Junior leaned forward from his chair and offered Blake a smoke.

"No thanks," Blake said. "Your father tells me you have a girlfriend now. Congratulations."

Tony Junior smiled. The panda circles under his eyes looked even bigger than the last time Blake had seen him.

"She's got a Cadillac with big fins on the back. She takes Pop and me to the casino once every couple of weeks. Did he tell you I won a thousand dollars on the slots?"

Tony waved off his son's comment from across the room. He poured himself a shot of Grappa, and sipped it. "So ya liked what me and Georgie did for ya in Utah? It was good, right?"

"You couldn't have done it better," Blake said.

"The guy, what's his name, Kilmer? He's backed off?"

Blake leaned forward. "For awhile. Now he's coming back. He threatened my mother. That's why I'm here."

"Ya don't ever threaten a man's mother. That's not acceptable," Tony said. He arched his eyebrows with a thickness that rivaled Andy Rooney's. Tony took another taste of the Grappa. He'd grown up on the Lower East Side of Manhattan in a cold-water flat with a bathtub in the kitchen. His parents were immigrants from Sicily who met and married in New York, and his first language was Italian.

"That's the first word that came to my mind when Kilmer threatened my mother—unacceptable," Blake said. "I had the Chief of Police here contact the County Sheriff in Blue Ridge, Georgia, where my mother and sister live. It's a small town up in the mountains near where Tennessee, Georgia, and North Carolina come together. He's running a man up the road once in a while toward where they live. They have to cover a lot of territory. My mother's neighbors are great, but they're busy. Everybody's got their own lives."

Tony raised his glass. "Salud. In the old days, Genovese, Gambino, ya wised off to somebody's mother on Mulberry Street, maybe ya didn't wake up."

Blake looked across the room. "How does the idea of an all expense paid trip to Georgia for a week or two sound to you?"

Tony twisted his mouth around like he was feeling his gums, moved his jaw back and forth, then put his hand over his mouth and around his chin and felt the grey stubble. He looked at Blake. "They got a good deli there?"

"I can't speak to that, but my mom and sister are both gourmet cooks and you can get some fried apple fritters at an orchard stand nearby," Blake said.

"I'm not goin' for the fried apple fritters, whatever that is. I'd be goin' for you."

"You'll have the whole lower floor of their house to yourself, with a shower and bath. It's a beautiful setting on top of a mountain, about thirty-five hundred feet, with woods in the back. There's a private deck, with a hammock and a fire pit."

"I don't want nothin' to do with bears. How old's your mother?" Tony said.

"Women don't like to tell their age."

"Your dad, he's dead?"

Blake nodded.

"I remember you sayin' your younger sister lives there. The one's got lupus."

"It's a nasty disease. No cure for it. My Mom takes care of her. They live together."

"Why ya askin' me to do this?" Tony said.

Blake filled him in. "Things are going to take another turn for the worse. Kilmer knows I'm after him. I made that clear when I was in Utah. There's a lot at stake."

"I'm not gonna fuck around. If I need to, I'll shoot somebody," Tony said.

His son nodded his head. "Pops'll do it, Blake."

"Have you ever had to do that before?" Blake said.

"Do us both a favor. Don't ask me that no more. I told ya before," Tony said.

"But not unless you have to. You have a gun?" Blake said.

Tony laughed. "More than one. I'll be takin' the forty-five. It's registered and I got a carry permit. Does your mother have guns?"

"She's got a twenty-two propped against the fireplace, and a thirty-two Walther."

"Good. She knows how to use em?"

"She's a pretty tough old broad."

"Ya talk to her about this?" Tony said.

"Yeah, about Kilmer's threat and being more careful. She's not the paranoid type."

"I mean 'bout my coming?"

"I will tonight if you say you can do it. They'll pick you up at the airport in Chattanooga, then drive back to their place. It's two or three hours. What do you think?"

"Ya got any pictures of what these guys look like?"

"Not yet. I'll see if I can come up with something, but I'm probably going to draw a blank," Blake said.

"Ya know I don't use blanks, right?"

"Yeah, I know that, Tony."

"How soon ya want this to happen?"

"The sooner the better. You tell me what you can do," Blake said.

"Day after tomorrow. Ya pick me up and drive me to the airport. Get me some coffee and a good glazed donut. Ya still owe me and Tony Junior a steak."

"I'll talk to my Mom tonight and make your reservations."

"I'm takin' my own piece. Check-in luggage."

CHAPTER FIFTY-FOUR

Blake called Freddie on his cell from the parking lot outside The Villas. "I'm going to be out of town for awhile. I want you to be extra careful. Take a good look around my place every time before you go in to take care of Watson. If you see anything out of the ordinary, anything at all, back off. Then call me. If you can't reach me, call Chief Cooper. Understood?"

"Yeah, D.B. I've got you on my speed dial. I'll put the chief in there, too. You worried about somebody breaking in?"

"Or maybe worse," Blake said. "Keep your eyes open for anybody hanging around."

"Why would somebody want to mess with you?"

"There's all kinds of people in this world. Way more good ones than bad ones. Sometimes I run into the bad ones."

"So what would these guys do to you?"

"They'd like to take me apart so I couldn't be put back together again. Kind of like taking a hammer to one of your transformers," Blake said.

"I get what you're saying. I'll watch out."

"I'm gonna get some tickets for that basketball game I told you about. You still want to go?"

"Heck, yeah. I'm lookin' forward to it."

"Ask your mom. I'll catch up with you when I get back next week."

"Where you headed?" Freddie said.

"Utah."

"I hear there's lots of people who go to church in that state."

"Some people just stand in the back or sit in the pews and jiggle the change in their pockets. They don't really hear what's being said."

"Be careful, man. I don't want anything bad to happen to you. I wanna see that basketball game."

• • •

Blake pulled out of the parking lot and headed toward the freeway. It was a beautiful, blue-sky day full of white clouds, like he used to see in the Midwest when he was growing up. The kind of day that made you think more about baseball and fishing than murder, but Blake's timeline was getting shorter. He reached for the phone when he got home and dialed his mother in Georgia to talk with her about Tony. "Please tell me everything is quiet and peaceful there."

"Your sister and I are doing fine."

"No more vandalism or anything strange?"

"Not an inkling of anything," she said.

"I've got somebody coming out to visit you."

"Oh, really, who's that?"

"A friend of mine, a guy named Tony Moriano. He's Italian, probably somewhere in his sixties. He's from New York, originally."

"Why's he coming out here?"

"As a precaution. I want him to stay with you for a week or two, until the dust settles on this case I'm working on."

"And you really think that's necessary?"

"Yeah, I do, Mom. He's a gentleman and he knows his way around. I'll feel a lot better, you're letting me do this. Can you pick him up at the airport in Chattanooga or Atlanta?"

"When?"

"In a day or two. I'll call you with the flight information."

"Send him on if you think you really need to."

• • •

Blake was relieved. Tony'd look like a harmless old man sitting on his mother's front porch to a passerby, but he had instincts embedded in his DNA that other people didn't.

Watson's tail was wagging back and forth like a flexible flyswatter on steroids when Blake walked past him on his way to the kitchen. Watson stood up and pawed Blake's pant legs before he started pulling them. It was a take me out or I'll pee on your shoe dog request. Blake changed into his jeans and running shoes, strapped his ankle holster on, grabbed Watson's leash, set the alarm, and headed for the park. Calling Julianna would have to wait until he got back home, either that or a wet shoe.

Blake headed up the block and around the corner, past the baseball diamond to the soccer fields and a meadow with a Montana sized view of a blue sky. He unfastened Watson's leash and watched him tear across the field while he stood at the edge of the tree line.

Something silver shined, half-hidden in the grass. He reached down, picked up a Saint Christopher medal, and saw a shadow moving behind him. The hair on his back stood up. A rush of adrenalin shot through his body. Blake stayed low, pivoted right, and drove back hard against his attacker's chest, knocking him to the ground. The man stumbled backward, righted himself, moved forward, and pulled the bat back to deliver a blow aimed at Blake's head. Blake scrambled to his feet, grabbed the bat as it began to move forward, and slammed his elbow into the side of his attacker's head. He heard a sick, crackling sound. He grabbed the bat off the ground, then put it under the man's neck to make sure he couldn't move. His attacker laid on his back like a rag doll, out cold. Blood and spit spilled out of the corner of his mouth onto the turf where children had played earlier that day.

He opened the man's green jacket and took the gun out of the shoulder holster. He reached for his assailant's back pocket and pulled out his wallet — Jensen, Salt Lake City.

"Damn it to hell," Blake said. "The crazy bastard doesn't know when to quit. It's gone beyond reason to thugs, now." Watson walked over near Jensen's head and growled. Blake called 911 and followed the ambulance in his car. There was nothing to do, but wait.

• • •

"How is he?" Blake said, when he saw the doctor come into the waiting room.

"We've induced a coma. He's got a severe concussion. That was a helluva blow to his head. He's still out. We're going to try to bring him back slowly. It's touch and go."

"Is he likely to have some memory loss?" Blake said, concerned for the sake of the case, not caring nearly as much about Jensen.

"It's too early to say. He may not come out of the coma."

Blake handed the attending physician his card with Chief Cooper's number scribbled on the back as well. "Call me or the Chief if there's a change in his condition." Blake walked down the hall, past the gurneys and empty wheelchairs. He climbed in his car and headed home. He'd forgotten about phoning Julianna. Tomorrow, he told himself, when she gets out of school. I don't want to talk with anybody right now.

Blake took a long, hot shower, poured himself a glass of port, and sat out on the balcony watching the moon and the trees sway in the delta breeze. Watson plunked himself down next to Blake's feet.

What difference does morning make to a dog, Blake wondered. What difference?

CHAPTER FIFTY-FIVE

"He came up behind me. I almost didn't see him. If I hadn't bent down to pick up that Saint Christopher's medal . . . " Blake's voice trailed off.

"Saint Christopher offers protection to travelers and against sudden death," Cooper said. "You're not Catholic are you, Blake?"

Blake looked up. "No."

"But you're Irish, right?"

"Some, and a quarter Welsh, Canadian, and Midwest American. I grew up in Ohio, in the days when there were more auto plants and steel mills there."

"Ever spend much time in church?"

"Growing up. I was a Sunday morning Methodist," Blake said.

"Maybe you should think about converting to Catholicism. If I were you, I'd at least think about taking that medal with me when I went back to Utah. It might do you some good."

"Are you superstitious, Chief?"

"It doesn't have anything to do with being superstitious. I'm always open to the Lord's help. When I was in the 101st Airborne Division, I saw a lot of atheists and agnostics convert. Sometimes it's a matter of acknowledging what you see."

Blake took the silver medal out of his pocket and smoothed it with his fingers. Cooper watched him.

"Yeah, I'd definitely hold on to that." His eyes locked on Blake's. "Has that fellow come out of the coma, yet?"

"Not yet. The doc has your number as well as mine. Kilmer hired him. He's the same guy who shot at me in the mountains. Kilmer's worried about me. He should be. Have we gotten anything more on the phone taps?"

"No, and that's kind of surprising," Cooper said.

"I guess I'm going to need to talk to Kate Winslow again and shake the tree harder," Blake said.

"I want to see Kilmer locked up," Cooper said.

"That's where he belongs, not in some board room." Blake got up to leave.

Cooper came around the desk and gripped Blake's upper arm. "You're gonna be all right, whether Jensen comes out of it or not. You had to protect yourself. It was self-defense."

"I can still hear the crack when I hit him."

"You did what you had to do. You didn't have a choice. You wouldn't have been here for that girlfriend of yours with the two kids if you hadn't."

"Thanks," Blake said. "I guess you're right."

"I heard you finally made it down to Donnegan's the other night. Heard you did an Irish jig and read some poetry. Nobody shot at you, either. You must have been pretty good." Cooper managed a laugh.

"I had fun," Blake said. "Made me feel accepted."

"Jameson wasn't there?"

"I think he was out of town or something. He still thinks I've got a stick up my ass."

"Jameson's the one with the stick up his ass."

● ● ●

Blake stopped for coffee at the place on Scrippshollow Drive. He thought about what he should say to a woman with a dead husband and a seriously disturbed billionaire brother bent on killing him. It was a good cup of coffee, not like the slag at headquarters, and no one was behind his back or following him. He drove to Kate's house.

The area across from the gatehouse was empty when he got there. Blake showed his shield to the guard who waved him past. He'd called her, so she knew he was on his way.

Kate had a worried look on her face when she opened the door.

The morning light was illuminating the wall behind the couch. A swatch of color refracted through the six foot glass sculpture framed with polished steel. "The sculpture, it's from Big Sur isn't it, the gallery just down the road from Nepenthe?"

"You have a good eye, Detective."

"I recognize the artist. Was it a gift?"

"From Jack," Kate said.

"Did you know he bought an oil when he was in Big Sur, the day before his death?"

"No."

"It was in his car. I'm thinking it was probably for you. The local police inventoried it. The painting's being stored down there, along with his other possessions that have not yet been claimed. I can probably get it assigned to you, if you'd like," Blake said.

"That's very sweet of you. I'll treasure it."

"Despite everything, I guess he still loved you," Blake said.

"If I had it to do over again, I'd never have fired him. What was I thinking? Looking more to please my brother than him?" She shook her head and stared vacantly at the sculpture. A long moment passed. "I could have the painting he bought restored, if it's damaged," she said.

"Some things can be repaired. Your relationship with Allison, for example. You've got a chance to do that now, a chance you didn't think you'd ever have again," Blake said.

"Do you honestly think she'll forgive me?" Kathryn's eyes glossed over like a sheet of water hit by the bright, noonday sun.

"She's a strong, young woman. What the three of us do now will be the foundation for what follows. The control your brother has exercised over you, you're forever being the victim. That has to end."

"Tell me what you want me to do and I'll do it," she said. Kathryn's eyes were focused on him.

"Your brother has tried to kill me twice."

"Oh, my God," she said, "again?"

"In the mountains, when he paid one of his henchmen to shoot me, and again yesterday, when the same man attacked me in the park with a baseball bat. At this moment, your brother's probably thinking I'm dead, laid to rest at the side of the road. Well, as you can see, it didn't work out that way. The guy he hired is in a coma in a hospital bed."

"There will always be an again, Kate, unless we stop him. I want you to call your brother. I want you to tell him the detective who's been investigating you was attacked and beaten by an unidentified man, and that he may not live. When he asks, and I'm sure he will, you tell him the police are saying his attacker was shot and killed. Then, we're going to listen very carefully to what your brother says, whether he admits to orchestrating the attack. When you tell him the news, keep quiet and don't say anything until he does. Do you understand?" Blake said. "It's important." He stared at her. "Pull it out of him, Kate."

"I understand."

"Then, I want you to let him know I told you someone shot at me when I was hiking in the mountains. Ask him if he knows anything about that, whether he was behind it. We want him on tape," Blake said. "Once he stops talking, you can rant about how he's always trying to control you, and the break-in at your therapist's office. He's not going to suspect you'll have the courage to stand up to him. He'll be thrown off balance and won't weigh his words so carefully."

"So we have a plan," Kathryn said.

"And it's gonna work." Blake leaned back in his chair.

Kathryn inched forward in her seat. "Would you like any-thing?"

"I'm fine."

When Kathryn returned from making herself something in the kitchen, Blake turned to her and asked if she was ready.

"Ready? You mean now?"

"It's time," Blake said. "Allison's already told your brother about you're wanting to confess. He's got to be worried."

CHAPTER FIFTY-SIX

The anonymous brown, four-door sedan turned right off Cashes Valley Drive onto the one lane dirt road a hundred feet past Mrs. Baker's wood barn.

Tony Moriano sat at the kitchen table. Blake's younger sister had gone to bed early and his mother was reading in her bedroom on the opposite side of the living room. Tony had just come up the twenty steps from his downstairs room for a glass of juice and to check on Bocci, the dog. Tony looked out the kitchen window as the car's lights came up the rise in the road. He watched the black shadow creep forward to the turnaround, a hundred feet up from the driveway that led to the house. The red brake lights flickered when the driver backed up, through the trees and the blackberry bushes the bears feasted on. Tony walked to the fireplace and took hold of the .22. He propped it against the wall and tapped on Blake's mother's door to alert her. "Shhh. Stay in your room. Get your thirty-two. Give me ten minutes, then call 911."

He pulled the door closed, took the rifle in hand, walked down the stairs, got his .45 and the extra clip he'd laid on top of the clothes in the suitcase he'd yet to unpack. Tony reached over, turned the table lamp off in the bedroom where he slept, and walked across the downstairs living room to the door that opened to the rear deck. His chest was wet with sweat. He hadn't fired a weapon for years, but he knew what it was like and how it felt to aim a gun at someone and pull the trigger.

Tony had scouted two paths the first day he was there,

each from a separate direction. He knew where the high ground was, and how to move through the woods to where he'd have cover and a clear vantage point before an intruder could enter the house.

There was just one man. Tony watched him open the car's trunk and lift a red gas can with his left hand, while he kept his right free. The stranger, an easy six-foot and a little on the heavy side, wore dark clothes and gloves. He moved like a professional.

Tony moved up the hill to the place he'd picked, five-feet in from the tree line at the edge of the lawn. He moved the safety levers off both guns. The .45 rested in the shoulder holster strapped to his chest. He knelt down in a firing position, set his footing, and drew a bead on the shadowy figure walking toward Blake's mother's car.

Tony had talked to her enough to know she'd shoot anybody who stepped in the door. He watched, as the stranger in the ski mask poured gasoline in a circle around the Jeep. When he came back around to Tony's side of the car, with the gas can in his hand, Tony shouted, "Hey, Mister," and squeezed the trigger the moment the stranger turned his bulk toward him.

The bullet hit the guy square in the chest just down from the shoulder. The gun shot shattered the stillness and set the coon dogs howling. "Move again, I'll blow that kneecap off. Keep ya hands stretched in front of ya."

Tony came out from the woods, holding his pistol in his left hand and the rifle in his right. "Get up. If I'd wanted to kill ya, you'd be dead already. Keep ya hands where they are, palms up, away from that jacket ya got on. If ya don't run your mouth, the woman inside will bandage ya up. She's an R.N."

Blake's mother turned on the kitchen porch lights and came to the door.

"Keep your gun aimed at this guy. He's probably carryin' a piece under his coat. If he moves, shoot him."

"Are you okay, Tony?" Blake's mother held the gun steady.

"I'm fine."

"He was plannin' to torch your new car."

Tony moved forward. "Put ya hands behind your head, mister. Lock those fingers together up in the air where I can see 'em . . . nice and easy. I'm keepin' this gun aimed at your chest."

Tony called for Blake's mother. "Leave your gun back there, and come over here for a minute. I want ya to reach under this guy's jacket. He's probably carryin' somethin' besides a lunch pail."

She pulled the nine millimeter out.

"Take it back to the house," Tony said. "Now turn around, Mister." Tony took the wallet from his pocket, and stepped back toward the house, before he flipped it open — "Salt Lake City, huh? John Stevens . . . Lay down on the gravel in front of ya and stretch out," Tony said.

"I called 911. It'll be awhile," Blake's mother said.

"Ya got some bandages? He's losing blood," Tony called out. He sat down on a plastic lawn chair by the front steps with the nine millimeter on his lap, pulled out his handkerchief, and blew his nose.

"Yes, we've got some," Blake's mother said. "But maybe some duct tape will do."

Tony grinned. His back was turned to Blake's mother.

A few minutes later, Blake's mother walked over to where Stevens was sitting in the driveway, and dressed the wound.

"I got family in New York. We know what to do with punks like you. Ya come near these people or me again, you're history. There'll be a contract on your head. Who put ya up to this, anyway?" Tony waived his .45 around like a kid with a neon light stick.

"You know I can't tell you that."

"And ya should know, I'm only gonna ask you one more time. I swear to God. So listen hard when I say it. Who put ya up to this?"

Stevens' muscles seemed to tighten up. His forehead broke into a sweat that shined when the porch light hit his face.

"Some crazy-ass rich guy from Utah."

Tony looked back at Stevens and smiled for a long moment. "You ever seen those salt flats?"

"When I was a kid."

The smile left as quick as it came. "Why the hell ya doin' crap like this? This woman, she's a senior citizen. She gets the discounts. Maybe I should shoot ya. Wouldn't bother me none. Lois," Tony said. "Ya got a tape recorder?"

Blake's mother nodded.

"Bring it out here. Tell your daughter, Google Miranda rights on that computer of hers. This guy's gonna make a statement." Tony wiped the sweat off his face. "Ya know what, never mind. I know that Miranda speech."

"What about the bleeding?" Stevens said. Blood had soaked through his jacket.

"Hold your pants on." Tony looked him over, like he would a horse at the track before he bet on it. "What, you don't like the bandaging job?" He spoke in perfect English. "It looks good enough to me. Did you find that recorder yet, Lois?"

"I've got it, Tony," Blake's sister called out from inside the house.

"Bring it over, Lois. Set it next to this scumbag."

Tony glared at Stevens. "Listen good. I'm gonna explain somethin'. You're gonna tell us 'bout that crazy-ass rich guy from Utah, name a Kilmer. And how he paid ya to come here and scare the crap out of some old lady. Ya gonna tell how he paid ya cash to slash her tires 'cause he wanted ya to put a brake on her son's investigatin' a murder. And then, ya gonna say how, when that didn't work, Kilmer told ya to come back here, light up her car, and shoot da dog."

"But I wouldn't shoot a dog. He didn't say anything about the dog."

"I like that part. It's a nice touch. Make sure ya mention it," Tony said, smiling. "Did ya meet Kilmer in person?"

"I talked to him on the phone. I met with some guy named, Jensen, who works for Kilmer."

"That's good. I like that you're cooperatin' like a real gumba," Tony said. "Ya also gonna tell how this Jensen guy let slip the cop was supposed to been shot in a huntin' accident when he was hikin' up in the mountains. There was a hitch, ya can say Jensen said that. You headin' here was the back-up plan Jensen told ya his boss, the crazy rich guy, wanted." Tony stopped talking and let it settle in Steven's mind.

"And here's the part that's good for ya — they told ya they didn't want ya to hurt nobody, just scare em, so the detective would back off. That parts gonna make it easier on ya with the law."

"And tell me why I should confess to all this? What good is it going to do me?"

"First, I might shoot ya if you don't. And second, I'm not going to give this recordin' or that nine you were carryin' to the local sheriff when he gets here. The charges ya face are gonna be easier. Provided I get ya confession."

"You're a crazy old man. What are you going to do with the recording and my gun?"

"They'll be stashed away for safe-keepin' after I make me some copies. Ya don't need to worry about the tape, so don't go gettin' stupid and try to get it back. And don't talk to Kilmer or Jensen. We're not interested in ya, long as ya do what I'm tellin' ya."

"And I'm supposed to believe you?"

Tony aimed the gun at Steven's chest. He waived two fingers and stroked the stubble on his chin. "I'd do it now, if I was you. I'm not gonna keep talkin 'bout this." Tony turned to Blake's mother. "Turn on the tape recorder, Lois."

When Stevens finished his statement, Tony turned to

Blake's mother. "Call your neighbor. Get him up here." Then he flipped through Stevens' wallet. "Ya got over six thousand bucks in here. I'm takin' four." Tony peeled off the bills and counted them.

"You can't do that," Stevens said.

"Who you gonna tell, the Ghostbuster guys? This here's for expenses. You're gettin' off cheap." Tony rubbed his hand across his chin. "My advice to you, don't say nothin' 'bout the money when the sheriff gets here. It's not yours no more."

Blake's mother leaned over and gave Tony a kiss on the cheek.

"Put this money inside someplace," he said.

The moon was cut in half, shining above the sugar pines and the mountain ridge. They heard the sound of a three-wheeler barreling up the road, and then the headlights appeared.

"Who the hell is this?" Lois's neighbor said when he pulled up.

"Bad company . . . really bad company," Blake's mother said.

CHAPTER FIFTY-SEVEN

Blake's mood lifted when he heard Tony's voice.

"I got him. Nobody got hurt, 'sept him."

"What happened?"

"He was gonna torch ya ma's car, so I shot him."

"He's alive?"

"Took one in the shoulder. In the old days, it would have been worse for him. "

Blake pictured Tony smiling. "That's the best news I've had in a long time. Did he connect Kilmer?"

"You mean, the crazy-ass rich guy from Utah?"

"What's the perp's name?"

"Stevens. He's from Salt Lake City. I got his driver's license."

"He was working alone?"

"Nobody else," Tony said.

"Did he shoot at you?"

"Nah, I saw him comin. Once he was down, I dragged him closer to the front door before the sheriff got here, so's it would look right. It's not gonna be a problem."

"How did my mom and sister take it?"

"Your ma bandaged him up real good. She had that Walther in her hand most of the time, rock steady."

"He's the same guy who slashed their tires earlier?"

"Yeah."

"Can you overnight the tape and his driver's license?"

"No problem. Ya want the confession? I got him on tape, singin' like a bird."

"You got a confession? Make a copy of it. Send me the original. I'll have Cooper talk to the sheriff in Georgia and ask him to lose the guy in the system for a few days before word gets back to Kilmer."

"The sheriff here doesn't know nothin' 'bout the confession. Me and Stevens reached an understandin'. He's not gonna be calling Kilmer or that Jensen guy he said hired him for the job. Ya don't need to worry."

"Jensen's in a coma," Blake said. "Your guy couldn't talk to him even if he wanted to."

"Sounds like ya been busy," Tony said.

"Let me know when your flight's coming in, if Tony Junior can't pick you up."

"Ya goin' back to Utah?" Tony said.

"Oh, yeah."

"What'd ya have in mind?"

"Causing trouble, lots of trouble," Blake said. He paused, and thought for a moment. "Do you have money in the stock market, Tony?"

"Not me, that's like a big slot machine. I don't want no Wall Street guy's hands on my dough."

"I want to cost Kilmer some serious money," Blake said, "real serious."

"Most guys like him, they got an Achilles heal. Maybe it's money, maybe not. Ya need to find somethin' he wants, but can't buy. Then take it away," Tony said.

"Is that the way the mob did things in New York?"

"That was more 'bout muscle and knee caps than what we're talkin' 'bout. Ya gotta play by different rules."

"Yeah," Blake said. "Times have changed."

● ● ●

Tony's advice kept moving through Blake's mind like molten lava down a mountain. Blake pictured the notebook he scribbled in during his earlier Utah trip when he rattled his saber in Kilmer's face and talked to people who knew him. He remembered somebody saying how Kilmer just wanted the normal stuff like regular people had, how his anonymity went by the wayside once he'd become well known. The words lifted off the page like a 3-D movie — that's what Kilmer values most. All that money, like The Beatles said. It can't buy him love.

CHAPTER FIFTY-EIGHT

Cooper had the kind of bear paw grin that just made people feel better about life, and big hands, like a baseball catcher.

Blake was sitting in his office.

"Whatever you told Kathryn Winslow, looks like it worked," Cooper said. He held a wad of papers in his hand.

"Blake settled into his chair.

"These transcripts of Kathryn Winslow's conversations with her brother, the phone taps." Cooper set the papers on his desk.

"The only way Kilmer could have seen the therapist's file he talks about, is to have stolen it," Blake said. "That's a Class D Felony. He wanted to make a pre-emptive strike to protect his sister and the Kilmer family name."

"The guys he hired were probably out of that therapist's place in seconds and headed back to Kilmer's office in Utah," Cooper said. "I guarantee you those files were sitting on Kilmer's desk the next morning. His kind of money makes things happen faster than UPS or FedEx. And there's no tracking slip."

Blake smiled. "The phone transcripts, Chief. This is good stuff."

Cooper continued. "While Kilmer doesn't flat-out admit to ordering the hit on you, we know he had people watching you and his sister. Obviously, he considers you a threat. We've got a copy of the company purchase order Jensen used for the GPS he attached to your car. We've also got Jensen's call to

Kilmer four minutes after you walked out of Jensen's office, and now his henchman is lying unconscious in a hospital bed. When we add in the fact that Kilmer is now providing legal services to his sister on his company's dime. Plus what you got in Georgia from this Stevens guy. I'd say our case against him is getting tied together pretty damn tight."

"I want to put an anchor on his ankle and drag him down to the bottom of a lake," Blake said. "I've been waiting a long time for this."

"You've got copies of all the call transcripts here." Cooper stuffed the papers in an envelope and handed it to Blake. "Study them. They'll tell you a lot about who you're dealing with."

"I need copies of the audios and Stevens' Georgia confession as well," Blake said.

"What do you plan to do with them?"

"For starters, I'm going to listen to them in my car on the way to Utah so everything's fresh in my mind. Allison is staying in his house. She's going to testify against him. She's the parakeet I've got stationed in the mine."

"She's committed to doing that?"

"Yeah, but you can never be too certain about witnesses."

● ● ●

Blake called Allison on his cell an hour after he'd crossed into Salt Lake City. "Tomorrow morning is good," he said, "if that works for you. Do you have access to a car?"

"I can use my aunt's."

"There's a Starbucks across from the Holiday Inn where I'll be staying."

● ● ●

Allison looked better when she walked into the cafe. Her eyes were clear. Her skin had a healthy glow. There was almost a bounce to her step. She wasn't cupping her breasts in her hands and offering herself up to some adolescent with raging hormones or a lonely, disconnected businessman with a briefcase and pent-up frustrations.

"Maybe Salt Lake City is dull," Blake said, "but it looks like it agrees with you."

She smiled. "My father and Diego, it's like they took a bite out of me, spit it on the ground, and covered it with dirt. I hate them for it. Sometimes I hate myself, but I'm not going back to that, not ever."

"What would you like to drink?" Blake said.

"Coffee, black with some sugar."

"Tell me about life with the Kilmers?"

"Besides being married to his business, the grandchildren seem to be the part of my uncle's life he values most. There's a calendar in the kitchen with his granddaughter's ballet performance circled, and his grandson's T-ball game this Saturday. His sons don't seem to call much."

"Have you heard anything about your father's will?"

Allison grinned. "Two-hundred fifty thousand dollars for me and each of my two sisters. The same amount for my mother. Turns out, my father didn't drink up all the money. We don't know who he stole from. It's still got to go through probate."

"Congratulations. By the way, I appreciate you're telling me about the call you overheard your uncle make to your mother."

"I said I'd help. Did he really try to have you killed?"

"Twice. He made a move against my mother in Georgia as well," Blake said.

"That's insane," Allison said. "She's okay?"

"I had someone waiting to meet the guy."

"Uncle James makes his own rules. He's obsessed with having his way and controlling people. When my mother told me he'd molested her when she was a girl. It makes sense now . . . how she acted when she was around him."

"Your uncle did the same thing to your mother, your father did to you. He damaged her."

"It's disgusting, the false morality they preached to us all of us. The hypocrisy. Sometimes I catch myself wondering how many young girls my father had his way with. Who he forced himself on? How much he paid, compared to what he put in the collection plate?" Allison shook her head, paused to drink more coffee, then looked across the table at Blake. "Do you know how long he abused my mother?"

"She didn't tell me," Blake said. "Your mother was on her own when she and your dad got married. My guess is your uncle became more interested in money after she moved out."

"I feel dirty. I don't want to be a whore anymore. Who's going to want me after this?"

"That depends on who you decide to become. You made some mistakes. You can put them behind you. Life's a long road. Some people finish strong," Blake said.

"This is a real nightmare, isn't it?"

"You do it right, keep yourself clean, good things will happen. Your uncle's got to be stopped and it has to be air-tight, not just circumstantial. Do you know what an IPO is?"

"An initial public offering. You're talking about the new company he's launching, aren't you?"

"Yes. There's a meeting next week, probably at the offices of Goldman Sachs. Morgan Stanley, the other underwriter, will also be there, along with some key syndicators and hedge fund managers. I need your help."

She had a puzzled look on her face, like someone playing a complicated board game for the first time who hadn't been given a clue. "What can I do?"

"Find out exactly when the meeting is scheduled and where," Blake said. "I'll need the office suite number as well."

"Then what?" Allison said.

"Then whoever is at that meeting will get a more complete picture of who they're dealing with. Have you heard your uncle say anything about your father's death on the lake trails?"

"You mean beyond what he said in the phone conversation with my mother that I told you about?"

"Yes, that's exactly what I mean," Blake said. "This is about stepping up in a way your mother never has."

CHAPTER FIFTY-NINE

Blake had told Kathryn he needed more ammunition. She weighed the words in her head, moving them back and forth, knowing the tape of the conversation she'd have with her brother would find its way into a courtroom where her fate would also be decided. I've had it with him, she told herself. I don't need him blaming me for what he set in motion years ago.

Her brother was vindictive. James could ruin her business, bury it by funding the competition, or launching lawsuits aimed at her bottom-line. She'd seen him ruin lives and reputations when he turned against business associates and family members. He had a billion reasons to be suspicious of other people when they approached him. "He suspects everyone's motives," Kathryn told Blake, "except for his wife and his grandchildren. I've got to be careful what I say."

Blake had made a persuasive argument. Kathryn's house was paid for — she had clear title. No one else could get hold of it. She had Phillip's inheritance for the girls' futures and her own, along with his social security pension as the surviving spouse. "Your financial future is secure. You don't need to be concerned about that. Things have changed," Blake had told her.

Kathryn waited until her daughters were gone and she had the house to herself with no distractions. She dialed her brother's unlisted number, knowing her name would be displayed on his caller I.D. screen.

Kilmer picked up on the fourth ring when he heard her voice.

"James . . . It's Kathryn. I'm worried. I haven't heard from Allison since the funeral. Has she contacted you?"

"Allison called me. I gave her the money to fly out here. She's with Barbara and me." Kilmer's voice sounded calm and measured, close to monotone.

"Why didn't you let me know?"

"Why should I? That's her business."

"You didn't think I'd be worried?"

He became silent.

"I hope you've been civil with her."

"What do you want, Kathryn? I'm busy."

"I want to know how my daughter is?"

"Well, now you know. She's here. Anything else?"

Kathryn paused. "I'm relieved she's safe." She softened her tone. "Allison's so opinionated sometimes. I know you're not used to that. What've the two of you been talking about?"

"If you must know, she said she hated her father, despised everything he stood for. Which I'm sure isn't news to you."

Kathryn caught her breath.

"By the way, dear sister," Kilmer said in a sugary voice, "what about the blanket?"

"What blanket?"

"Don't play games with me, Kathryn. You know which blanket. The one with the bears on it. You know, the one in the coroner's pictures. Allison was wondering how it got to the lake. You kept it after your divorce, didn't you?"

The conversation wasn't going the way she'd planned. Kathryn took another deep breath. "Actually, James, I remember Mom giving it to you. But that's beside the point, I guess you couldn't stand the thought of Phillip taking your last name and using it to attract investors. Evidently, that was more than you could stomach."

"Phillip's death was a welcome dividend for all of us," Kilmer said. "He abused Allison."

"Abuse? That's a familiar word. How ironic you'd think of talking to me about abuse," Kathryn said.

"What's that supposed to mean?"

"I think you know exactly what I mean. Spending time in church won't guarantee your salvation."

"You better watch your mouth, Kathryn."

"Why? Are you going to tape it shut and tie my hands like you used to when I was a girl?"

"You're talking like a crazy woman, Kathryn, like Mom did."

"And how is it you think you're acting? Spying on people, shooting at detectives, threatening anyone who gets in your way. You can't run all your relationships like a prison camp commandant who demands absolute obedience. Your wife puts up with it. The rest of us don't have to anymore. It's wearing thin."

"You unforgiving, insolent little bitch. After everything I've done for you . . . the mortgage, your legal problems, this investigation into Phillip's death. You won't get a thing from me, not ever again."

"I'm your sister, James. You can't keep me locked in a closet like you used to. And like you said, I don't have Phillip to drag me down anymore, thanks to you."

"You've got some gall, Kathryn, after what you've done. Some incredible gall."

"I know how you feel about me," Kathryn said. "Just keep your hands off my daughter."

"She's innocent," Kilmer said. "She's not a slut like her mother."

The phone went dead.

Kathryn cradled the receiver in her hand.

CHAPTER SIXTY

Blake was sitting at the table next to his bed and Gideon's Bible when the phone rang. It was a picture perfect day in Salt Lake City.

"Guess what?" Cooper said, when Blake answered. "We got something good. Kilmer on the phone with Kathryn Winslow. Get yourself an orange juice out of the mini-bar while I get the tech from the surveillance room to rig this thing up so you and I can listen."

"I'm meeting Allison Winslow, for coffee in thirty minutes," Blake said.

"Relax," Cooper said. "You're gonna like this."

● ● ●

Ten minutes later, Blake was picturing Cooper smiling at the other end of the line, like a big grizzly bear at the sight of a steak left unattended. "I'll be damned," Blake said. "Clever doesn't begin to describe what she just did on the phone. She's a survivor, that woman, masterful, with a mother's instincts to boot." Blake found himself remembering what Suzanne Leeds, the woman Kate had fired along with Hamilton, warned him about earlier — don't underestimate her. Blake shook his head with a degree of disbelief and admiration, still convinced Kathryn had killed Phillip. But a jury of twelve? "She'll probably walk," he told Cooper. "She intercepted a pass with her name and her conviction written all over it, ran it back to the opposite goal line and dropped it at her brother's feet."

"I believe you're right," Cooper said, "reasonable doubt."

"Overnight an audio copy of the tape to the Holiday Inn where I'm staying," Blake told Cooper on the phone. The inadequate defense Kate had been saddled with had undergone a one-hundred and eighty degree turnaround. And if Kilmer had a prescription for the Viagra Phillip ingested at the lake, then the case against him would become that much more damaging, and Kate would appear even more innocent.

If Kate successfully threw the murder on her brother, well, that was for a jury to sort through, not Blake. Kilmer was who Blake really wanted. He'd molested Kate, hurt her, the same way Blake's younger brother had been hurt. Blake wanted to watch the money rush away from him.

● ● ●

"So you got the information for me," Blake said, when he met Allison at the convenience store near Kilmer's house.

"The presidential suite at the Marriott on the twelfth floor, on Wednesday at eleven. I'm going to be there," she said. "I talked him into letting me come. My uncle says the fire burning inside me will make me a success in business. He says he wants to be my mentor. I think he wants to control me."

She had a strange look on her face, frightened, apprehensive, but determined, Blake thought.

"Having you in the room will make it easier," Blake said.

"How's that?"

"I've put together a tape . . . your father's death, the coverup, the break-in at the therapist's office, his attempts on my life, his paying someone to torch my mother's car."

"Wow, this is good. I like it. Can I say that?" Her eyes were awake with excitement.

"When the timing is right, you're going to click on this wireless remote I'm giving you to trigger a recording that will play through the sound system in the room," Blake said. "It's small. You can put the remote in your purse or a pocket. I'm going to position some cameras in that room the night before you get there. I'll be watching everything in a room down the hall."

Allison held the remote in the palm of her hand, then slipped it inside her purse.

"Don't let anyone see it."

"This is really happening, isn't it?" Allison said.

"Yes. Everything will be in play when you and your uncle walk in the door on Wednesday. By the way, I've been wanting to ask you something."

Allison shot down a can of Red Bull.

Blake kicked some dirt around in the parking lot, with his shoe. "Your mother handled your uncle's call very skillfully. Did you talk to your mother a second time, after the funeral—before she spoke with your uncle yesterday?"

Allison looked up at Blake and almost smiled. "That's what mothers and daughters are supposed to do, isn't it? Communicate back and forth with one another?"

CHAPTER SIXTY-ONE

Allison told Blake about the butterflies in her stomach when she called him from the country road outside her uncle's house. The limousine hadn't arrived to pick them up, yet.

The video feed Blake had readied was up and already running on the TV monitor he was watching when Kilmer and Allison walked into the presidential suite. Blake was sitting in a room several doors down, his eyes fixed on the screen.

There were two pitchers of water, fresh fruit, pastries, and coffee on each end of the long mahogany table in the presidential suite. The floor to ceiling windows looked out at the Salt Lake City skyline and the Wasatch Mountains.

Kilmer was wearing an impeccably tailored Armani suit and a light blue shirt with a red power tie. He looked assured and confident. "He's invested seven years in this IPO," Blake said to the uniformed cop drinking a soda from the room's mini-bar. "Seven years for millions of dollars that he doesn't really need, and will probably never use."

"It's a whole 'nother world," the cop said. "My wife wants a new refrigerator. I can't identify with stuff like this."

Kilmer walked in first, followed by his controller, his personal CPA, his attorney, and Allison. They seated themselves to Kilmer's left and right, and made small talk.

Four middle-aged men from Goldman Sacks followed them in the door minutes later. Then two more men and three women from Morgan Stanley entered the room, accompanied by several hedge and mutual fund managers.

The stockbroker Blake had spoken to earlier at his friend
Rob's suggestion, had schooled Blake on the participants and
how the meeting would proceed.

Kilmer's security consultant, aka bodyguard, military looking and devoid of a smile, sat outside in a chair by the door
to insure there would be no interruptions.

Blake watched Kilmer on the video feed. He had an engag-
ing, low-key style. He leaned forward when he spoke and
seemed interested in everything being said. A few little jokes,
a little bit of flattery, always on-message. Kilmer controlled
the conversation. He commanded the room.

Once the introductions had been completed, Kilmer took
the floor and talked about his vision and the value of doing it
"the right way, the Kilmer way." He was in his element. "Our
edge is in the patents and the marketing plan, the strategic
alliances I've cultivated for years," he said. "I can guarantee
you accelerated growth, double digits, maybe triple, and a
healthy profit margin."

"There's always risk in a new venture like this, especially
in this economy, Mr. Kilmer. And this is technology. The
tables change quickly. Nothing is absolute," the mutual fund
manager said.

"My track record is absolute," Kilmer interjected. "They're
only a handful of people with a record like mine who can give
you the assurances I can." He tapped his fountain pen on the
legal pad in front of him and looked around the room as if he
was daring anyone else to respond. He'd projected an aura
of indisputable invincibility and succeeded in attaching it to
what he'd just said. The hedge fund managers looked at one
another, the underwriters smiled, and Kilmer kept silent. He
looked satisfied with his performance.

Blake watched Allison on the screen.

She fidgeted in her seat.

"You'll feel it," Blake had told her. "Trust me, you'll just know. It will be like the volley in a tennis match. You'll see the ball coming straight at your racket."

Blake watched as Allison's hand disappeared from the conference table. She reached below it.

Kilmer was silent at first, then visibly surprised and startled by the sound of his own voice when it filtered through the sound system Blake had gained access to the night before.

Blake watched and moved to the edge of his seat as Kilmer looked from chair to table to lamp to chair to the speakers in the corners of the ceiling.

Kilmer looked the way Blake imagined Caesar did when he saw Cassius and Brutus on the steps of the Senate as they pressed near him. Alone and shocked, Kilmer shrunk to his small measure.

The conference room fell silent. The men and women around the table began to squirm.

They have to know, Blake thought. This is criminal. The words Blake spliced together ricocheted off the walls and found their mark.

Kilmer's face turned red with rage.

"I think it's best we adjourn for now," Kilmer's attorney said.

The audio kept playing.

"We need to go forward. This isn't how it sounds," Kilmer said, his hand trembling.

"We can't, not at this point, James," the attorney said.

"A delay will cost us millions."

"That's not your biggest problem, any more. You're going to need a Plan B. The internet chat rooms will go wild with this," the hedge fund manager said. "Going forward now would be suicidal."

"He's right, James. You can't. Not from where we're seeing this at Goldman Sachs."

Kilmer shook his head back and forth as though in disbelief.

● ● ●

Blake stepped out of the room and walked down the hotel corridor with the two uniformed Utah policeman in lock-step, one on each side.

Kilmer's bodyguard stood up. He unbuttoned his sport coat.

"You do have a permit to carry that, don't you?" Blake said.

"Of course I do."

"Then sit back down and mind the store." Blake flashed his shield and nodded to the officer on his left to stay behind. He put his hand on the door and walked in to where Kilmer was seated.

"Good morning, Mr. Kilmer. Beautiful day isn't it?"

No one spoke.

"Stand up. On your feet. You're under arrest . . . for breaking and entering, for the theft of confidential records, for the attempted murder of a police officer — me, for the murder of Phillip Winslow, for arson and an attempted home invasion in the state of Georgia where peaches come from." Blake smiled. Then he read Kilmer his rights . . . "Do you need us to provide one of those government attorneys, Mr. Kilmer?"

Kilmer sneered.

"Don't say a word, James. Not a single word. I'll have someone down at the police station before you walk in the door. Is this really necessary, detective?" Kilmer's attorney said, "to do it this way?"

"Oh, it's necessary all right," Blake said, "and I'm enjoying every minute of it. Tell me, Mr. Kilmer, is this what's called a stock market crash?"

"You arrogant prick," Kilmer said.

Blake smiled. "I've got a car waiting for you downstairs. It's a Crown Victoria. You won't need the limo today."

Kilmer rose from his chair. "Have you thought for one minute about the consequences of what you're doing? Lost jobs, revenue, people's livelihoods, your future? You stupid, stupid man."

Kilmer's eyes shifted away from Blake to Allison. "And you,

Allison. You ungrateful traitor. Like mother, like daughter. I helped you. I invited you into my home. And you betrayed me . . . like Judas did, in the garden."

Allison didn't turn away from Kilmer. She stared right into his eyes. "Fuck you, Uncle James. You can take your money and hypocrisy and stick it up your ass. I don't want to follow in your footsteps. I'm perfectly capable of finding my own way without someone giving me thirty pieces of silver."

Blake cuffed Kilmer, and walked him outside the presidential suite. Two uniformed cops stood on both sides of him.

"Wait here." Blake walked down the corridor ahead of them and placed a call to the city's biggest daily and the alternative press. Then waited for several minutes, before walking with Kilmer to the elevator.

No one else had left the board room, except Allison. She trailed ten steps behind Blake, Kilmer, and the two uniformed cops.

Blake turned to Kilmer. "Just the two of us. I guess everybody else is still inside, using their cell phones before the markets close."

"You'll pay for this," Kilmer said.

The photographers were waiting downstairs at the entrance to The Marriott when Blake and Kilmer walked out of the hotel's lobby.

As the press surrounded them, jostled for position, angled for a comment, Blake turned to Kilmer. "Timing. It's critical, don't you think?" Blake turned for a quick minute, and tossed his car keys to Allison when he saw the crowd. "Follow us."

He maneuvered Kilmer into the Crown Victoria. The driver edged through the onlookers enroute to the police station in downtown Salt Lake.

• • •

Kilmer's corporate and criminal attorneys arrived within minutes. After Kilmer was fingerprinted and booked, Blake reached for his cell to call Allison. He walked out a side door, avoided the press, to meet her where she'd parked in the police lot.

"Nice car," she said and handed him the keys.

"Let's get out of here," Blake said. "You did great, Allison, really great. You should be proud of yourself."

Allison smiled. "Let's get something to eat. I'm starved."

"Pick a spot, anywhere you'd like." Blake stopped at the light and turned to Allison, intent on knowing. "Can I ask you a question?"

"Of course," she said.

"What were you thinking in there when you heard your uncle's voice on the recording? When I came in and Mirandized him? When he called you Judas?"

She looked at Blake for a moment.

The stoplight was still red. One car horn beeped.

"That was the first time he ever looked old to me."

CHAPTER SIXTY-TWO

They sat down at the restaurant.

"What's going to happen with my mother?"

"Hypothetically," Blake said, "off the record?"

"Haven't we always been off the record, Detective Blake? She fiddled with the place setting. How about if I call you, Dylan, now? She gave him her college girl, innocent smile, followed Blake's earlier advice, and waited for him to answer.

"Sure," he said.

"Off the record, Dylan," Allison said.

"Unless your uncle confesses to killing your father or Jensen testifies against him, that charge may not stick. It's up in the air. But even if it doesn't, he'll still go down as an accessory to murder. Everything else against him will stand. He'll be convicted. It's gone beyond circumstantial. He can't play God."

"And what about my mother?"

"I had a professor once in college who taught a criminology course. He was in his late seventies. He said the first law of economics is, there's no such thing as a free lunch. Someplace down the road, somebody's going to pay. Your mom felt like she had to put a stop to it, once and for all. She couldn't stand the thought of your father ever touching you again, or your sisters, or her for that matter. Your father's death was pre-meditated, but your mother is sympathetic."

Blake paused to collect his thoughts.

"Most people never have to face the fact that, given the right circumstances, they're capable of almost anything. Your mother will probably go to jail. But if it comes down to that, a really good defense attorney is going to argue for a lesser sentence, and she may just walk."

"I appreciate what you've done, Dylan." She reached across the table and squeezed his hand. "I used to worry about who'd take care of my sisters if my mother wasn't around, knowing how I was."

"I remember," Blake said.

"I was orphaned once before, a long time ago when my father molested me. Now I know, I can take care of myself, if I'm orphaned again."

CHAPTER SIXTY-THREE

Blake drove to the county jail where Kilmer was being held. He took the elevator to the interview room on the eighth floor, looked at the wall clock, and waited.

Kilmer walked in and took a seat at the table opposite Blake. He looked weary. The tension between them was palpable.

"You shouldn't have done it," Blake said.

"I like to win. I've always won," Kilmer said.

"It's over."

"You don't honestly think you're going to walk away from this just because I'm in here? There'll be consequences. I warned you."

Blake felt Kilmer's rage closing in around him. "You should have hired better help," he said. "Orange isn't your best color."

"I still can," Kilmer said. "I will."

"I expected that's where you'd want to go. I understand revenge. But you don't want to make that mistake with me."

"Come again?"

"Everything, and I mean everything . . . the incestuous relationship you had with your sister when she was growing up, the threats you made during those phone conversations with her, the attempts to kill me, what you tried to do to my mother, what Allison told me you said to her about white niggers. Even the stories about how you made all that money in the pharmaceutical business when you blocked access to low-cost drugs that wound up costing people their lives. So you could maximize profits and protect your precious patents.

All of it, has been documented and preserved. I've arranged for that documentation to be broadcast and re-broadcast, to be sent via mail and email, Facebook, LinkedIn, you name it, to each and everyone of your children, and your grandchildren, and your nieces and nephews, and the press, of course. We can't forget the press. And if anything ever happens to me or anyone close to me, those messages will go out. I've set it up that way, like an unstoppable river that'll keep charging ahead. You won't be able to stop it."

Kilmer locked his hands together on the table. The pressure turned his nails pink, and his knuckles white. He clenched his teeth. "You wouldn't dare." Kilmer pounded the table with his fist. Hate washed over him.

"I already have," Blake said. His index finger stiff against the gray table, eyebrows poised, adrenalin coursing through him. "The transmissions with their messages are ready to go. They'll bounce back and forth between servers if anyone tries to jam them, and they'll keep coming. What you've managed to accomplish. A brilliant business career, the charitable work, the legacy you've built, will circle the drain. The bleeding won't stop."

Kilmer slumped in his chair. He looked wrung out. Blake got up, pressed the button for the guard, then sat back down opposite Kilmer. "You and me, we're strong men. What breaks other people, pushes us forward." Blake stared at Kilmer. "I know you're a strong man, James."

Kilmer glared. "That goes without saying, Detective."

"I made a point of studying you . . . your autobiography, a slew of articles and postings, everything I could get my hands on. You had to have read Gandhi at some point, before you immersed yourself in spreadsheets and flow charts."

"What difference does it make. I'm no idealist."

"The weak can never forgive, Gandhi said. Forgiveness is the attribute of the strong." Blake paused and stared at Kilmer. "You'd be well served to remember that, James. Better that people see you as having made one mistake, than thinking your whole life was built on guilt and revenge."

The door to the room clanged open seconds later. Kilmer stood and stepped past Blake to where the guard was standing.

Blake turned to watch as his shoes shuffled against the floor, followed by the dull thud of a heavy metal door closing behind him. Kilmer didn't look back.

CHAPTER SIXTY-FOUR

Three days after Blake got back to California, he picked up Tony at the airport.

"Your ma and me, we're goin' on a cruise to Italy. I'm thinkin' maybe I should make her an honest woman," Tony said, with a twinkle in his eye.

"You're serious? So when did all this magic happen?"

"When your ma went for the bandages to patch up the guy I shot, and came back with duct tape, I knew I was in love," Tony gushed.

"So we could actually wind up being related?" Blake said.

Tony nodded.

"Holy smokes. You, me, and Tony Junior? You're knocking me out, Tony, you know that, don't you?"

Tony smiled. "And that's a good thing, right?"

"Helluva good thing," Blake said. "Another man in the family."

The two of them smiled all the way to Tony's house. They shook hands in the driveway. "I'll catch up with you later," Blake said. "I've got to get home and take my trusty bird dog for a walk. He's been cooped up all day. I don't want him to think I've forgotten him." Blake left Tony's place and headed home. He climbed the stairs and punched in the alarm code. Watson met him at the door, his tail moving at full throttle. Blake unfastened his shoulder holster and set his service revolver on the nightstand.

He grabbed the leash off the hook in the hallway closet.

He and Watson jogged to the park. Blake dropped the leash next to the water bowl he'd carried. Then he and Watson took off racing across the field at full speed.

• • •

Blake pulled into Julianna's driveway, and walked past the flowers he'd planted. He kissed her at the door.

"The girls are asleep," she said.

They went into the bedroom.

Everything there was to say, he could see in the lines on her face and in her eyes. Her whole life was there — discernible, mysterious, puzzling, suggestive. She was the dream he wanted. He looked at Julianna and said, "I love you."

Like the book? Tell your friends. Circulate the word on social media and via book clubs, so the book isn't lost. Post a review. I'd appreciate hearing from you. Here's how to post one on Amazon:

Go to the detail page for the item on Amazon.com.
Click "write a customer review" in the Customer Reviews section.
Rate the book and write your review. Click submit.

The author is available for select readings, including book clubs when possible. To inquire about a possible appearance, please contact **Daniel@AuthorDanielBabka.com**

ABOUT THE AUTHOR

Daniel Babka grew up in a small midwestern town. He served in VISTA, the domestic Peace Corps, attended law school and a theological seminary, managed housing in New York City's toughest neighborhoods, and ran a couple of small, start-up companies. He's an avid hiker who, like Dylan Blake, the detective he writes about, needs time in the woods.

Daniel has two grown children and lives in the Northern California foothills. He's a member of the California Writers Club and a small writer's critique group. He is presently at work on a new Dylan Blake book called *Dirt Crappis*, and several short stories.

ALSO BY DANIEL BABKA

Lightning Strikes: (available in eBook and paperback) is a coming-of-age short story set in a small, midwest American town in 1959. It's told through the eyes of a twelve-year-old boy, and centers on his grandfather, his dad, and the older black man who works for them and what happens when Angelo Cosentino drives up in his Cadillac. The story captures the moments when a boy begins to see the black, white, and gray of life more clearly.

Two States and A Thousand Miles: is a very short, slice-of-life story about two people whose lives intersect in a profound way (only available as an eBook).

Dirt Crappis: a second Dylan Blake novel, will soon be published.

LIGHTNING STRIKES REVIEWS

Jeri Chase-Ferris, author of *Noah Webster & His Words*, published by HoughtonMifflin/Harcourt, a 2012 Junior Library Guild fall selection and winner of the 2013 Golden Kite Award for children's non-fiction says: "Lightning Strikes is filled with really beautiful word pictures and wonderful descriptions of life in a small and innocent town . . . an exquisite, evocative story from a simpler, though not completely rose-colored era, captured in a young boy's eyes."

Lonon Smith, Hollywood screenwriter, director, and author of *Wise Men*, says, "I liked the story a lot. It has a wonderful feel of the heat and rain and smell of small town Midwest America, and an interesting arc that goes where I didn't expect, a plus. It's good work."

Robert Pacholik, author of *Night Flares*, a Vietnam short-story collection, *says,* "Lightning Strikes is about a child's innocence stretched to the limit by the deeds of his family, his visions of wrong, and what's right . . . highly recommended."

Lightning Strikes

Daniel Babka

LIGHTNING STRIKES

The Heights is where all the black people lived in Twinsburg, Ohio, in the late fifties. The adults I knew called it the colored settlement. My father and grandfather ran whiskey and beer up there and took me with them. It wasn't the kind of bootlegging Robert Mitchum did in the movie, *Thunder Road*, when he ran moonshine in a two-door, '51 Ford. What we did seemed ordinary. Just the same, I don't remember anybody getting arrested for anything serious before that night.

Grandpa George and I would carry the cases up the basement stairs, look sideways at the police station next door, load up the Packard, and stack the boxes on the backseat. I was twelve, but I still got to sit on top of the whiskey when he drove up the hill to where Ike lived.

My grandpa and dad both told me it wasn't just for the money. They said they took the risks because everybody had a right to drink, and no one else was willing to sell to the colored joints in The Heights that couldn't get a liquor license . . .

Made in the USA
Charleston, SC
05 April 2015